THE GLASS SHORE

THE GLASS SHORE

Short Stories by Women Writers
from the North of Ireland

Edited by
Sinéad Gleeson

NEW ISLAND

THE GLASS SHORE
First published in 2016 by
New Island Books
16 Priory Office Park
Stillorgan
Co. Dublin
Republic of Ireland.

www.newisland.ie

Editor's Introduction © Sinéad Gleeson, 2016

Introduction © Patricia Craig, 2016

Individual Stories © Respective Authors, 2016.

'The Harp that Once---!' originally appeared in *The Shan Van Vocht*, held by National Folklore Collection UCD. © Public domain. Digital content: © University College Dublin, published by UCD Library, University College Dublin <http://digital.ucd.ie/view/ucdlib:43116>

'Village Without Men' is from *David's Daughter Tamar and Other Stories* by Margaret Barrington, reprinted by permission of Peters Fraser & Dunlop (www.petersfraserdunlop.com) on behalf of the Estate of Margaret Barrington.

'The Girls' by Janet McNeill reprinted with permission of David Alexander, executor of the literary estate of Janet McNeill.

'Flags and Emblems' is from *A Belfast Woman* by Mary Beckett, © Mary Beckett 1980.

'Taft's Wife' by Caroline Blackwood. Copyright © The Estate of Caroline Blackwood 2010, used by permission of The Wylie Agency (UK) Limited.

'The Devil's Gift' is from *Women Are the Scourge of the Earth* by Frances Molloy, reprinted by permission of White Row (http:www.whiterow.net) on behalf of the estate of Frances Molloy.

The authors have asserted their moral rights.

Print ISBN: 978-1-84840-557-8
Epub ISBN: 978-1-84840-558-5
Mobi ISBN: 978-1-84840-559-2

British Library Cataloguing Data.
A CIP catalogue record for this book is available from the British Library.

Typeset by JVR Creative India
Cover Design by Martin Gleeson
Printed by ScandBook AB, Sweden

10 9 8 7 6 5 4 3 2 1

New Island is grateful to have received financial assistance from The Arts Council of Northern Ireland (1 The Sidings, Antrim Road, Lisburn, BT28 3AJ, Northern Ireland).

LOTTERY FUNDED

Contents

Editor's Introduction

Sinéad Gleeson

Books sometimes beget books. Something comes into being and, down the road, reaches out to other work. In 2011, sitting in a room crammed with books in New Island's office, I mentioned to the editor there how much I admired Evelyn Conlon's all-female short story anthology, *Cutting the Night in Two*. Originally published in 2001, another volume felt long overdue.

When I was asked to take on the project, I agreed. It was daunting, certainly, and felt like a lot of responsibility, but I was excited at the prospect of finding new writers and resurrecting older ones. It was a long process of recovery, of what a friend called 'literary archaeology'. Not just to seek out writers that had all but vanished, but to physically locate texts and work of a suitable length. The result was *The Long Gaze Back: An Anthology of Irish Women Writers,* and the response to it far exceeded any expectations myself or New Island had. The collection started many conversations about omission and exclusion, about the dominance of male voices in the Irish literary canon, and the sheer volume of writing by women that had been overlooked and marginalised. The anthology won an Irish Book Award in the same month that the Waking the

Feminists controversy began. It seemed that in 2015, we were still having conversations about women's cultural exclusion and how casually it can happen.

I chaired many discussion events for *The Long Gaze Back*, including two panels in Belfast. At both talks, many people asked questions or approached me afterwards to ask, 'Where is our book?' Lucy Caldwell contributed to both events, and also has a new story in *The Glass Shore*. She told me of growing up in Northern Ireland and hearing all aspects of life – politics, society and particularly culture – dominated by male voices. She encouraged me to take on this project and give a voice to the women writers who had been left behind. I thought of the threaded line between *Cutting the Night in Two* and *The Long Gaze Back*, and believed that a new book representing a range of Northern Irish voices needed to happen. In the weeks after Belfast, I spoke to countless writers and women who reaffirmed this absence. While not solely short stories, Ruth Carr's excellent *The Female Line: Northern Irish Women's Writers* (1985) is a diverse mix of poetry, memoir and novel extracts. It is an important book for many reasons, not least because it represented Northern Irish women writers at a time when there was little visibility.

The Long Gaze Back includes six Northern Irish writers in a collection of thirty stories spanning several centuries. *The Glass Shore* contains twenty-five stories and is structured in a similar way. There are ten deceased writers, the earliest being Rosa Mulholland (born in 1841), and six more of the writers were born in the nineteenth century. Some predate the existing border in the North, which is one of many reasons for including the nine counties of Ulster in this anthology. All anthologies are partial, for reasons of space, and I hope these stories make readers search out more work by each writer, and by other Northern writers. In these pages, there are fifteen living writers, and the youngest – Roisín O'Donnell – was born two years before *The Female Line* was published. As with *The Long Gaze Back*, I felt it was important that writers contributed new and unpublished work. The writers were given a word count, but no thematic guide. Given the geographic focus of this book, there may be an expectation of the work: that it would deal with conflict or religion. Some stories do, but many engage in a broader kind of politics: of the personal, of bodies, of borders.

These stories exist on their own terms. They talk of movement, belonging and expectation. They are set in cities, and on the coast, in Ireland, and outside it. Characters negotiate relationships, missed chances, love, social exclusion, ghosts, history and where we all come from. They look back as well as forwards. Patricia Craig, in her excellent introduction, outlines many of the stories, including their commonality and their distinctions.

In terms of women's writing all over the island of Ireland, I hope there are more anthologies, new editors and exceptional work – like the stories here – to come.

Sinéad Gleeson, Summer 2016

Introduction
Patricia Craig

Writing in 1936, Elizabeth Bowen ascribed a kind of 'heroic simplicity' to the contemporary story, along with a 'cinematic' conciseness or compression, which freed it from ponderousness. It was, she thought, in its current form, 'a child of the twentieth century'. True: but the mid-century story had roots in the past, and a strong link to the future. Sinéad Gleeson's previous anthology of Irish women writers, *The Long Gaze Back* (2015), stretched all the way to Maria Edgeworth, and came right up to the present with authors such as Anne Enright and Éilís Ní Dhuibhne. Its present-day section added up to a stunning display of twenty-first-century preoccupations and techniques, while earlier inclusions (the stylish Maeve Brennan, the judicious Mary Lavin) gave a due thumbs-up to their predecessors.

The Long Gaze Back covered the whole of Ireland; now Sinéad Gleeson has turned her attention to the North (the geographical North, that is, with Donegal and Monaghan well represented). *The Glass Shore* follows a similar format to the previous undertaking: most of the stories brought together here have been commissioned specially for the anthology, while a few older contributions (some much older) testify to a tradition of Northern women's writing which gets to grips, forthrightly or obliquely, with all kinds of topical concerns. The earliest piece in the book, 'The Mystery of Ora' by Rosa Mulholland, exploits 'sensation' to the full. Mulholland was born in Belfast in 1841, but writes about an overwrought Irish maiden on a wild mountainside in the West, a traveller, some diabolical machinations, a prisoner on an island, and so on, in a thoroughly professional manner. Two further nineteenth-century stories stand out as contributions to what was then an emerging 'New Woman' genre, as defiant feminists and Suffragettes went kicking over the traces. The name of Sarah Grand, indeed, is almost synonymous with this genre; and in 'Eugenia' she preserves a cool detachment, a hint of mockery, while pursuing a satisfactorily feminist outcome. If her story is a bit wordy, as well as worthy – well, we can put it down to the fashions of the day. Her contemporary, the wonderfully named Erminda Rentoul Esler ('An Idealist'), is likewise in the business of presenting a positive plan of action for brainy girls to follow.

Other modes were available to past Irish writers. Margaret Barrington, for example, has a stark account of female stoicism and expedience in remote Donegal in 'Village without Men', while Ethna Carbery in 'The Coming of Maire Ban' succumbs to a romanticism of the peasant-macabre. 'The Harp That Once–!' by Alice Milligan is set in Mayo during the final episode of the rebellion in 1798, and features an intrepid heroine who delays a band of Redcoats with her harp-playing, while, behind the scenes, defeated rebels make good their escape. Alice Milligan, as it happens, is not only a contributor to *The Glass Shore*, but the subject of one of its finest stories, 'No Other Place' by Martina Devlin. Here she is in old age, tending roses in the garden of her Church-of-Ireland rectory outside Omagh on the eve of the Second World War, while her past work – all her literary and nationalist activities – are deftly delineated.

'No Other Place' is beautifully judged in its effects and atmosphere, but it is not alone in this. Each of *The Glass Shore* stories embodies a unique angle of vision; the range of styles and tones is very striking. At the same time, reading through the anthology, what you're aware of is a unifying assurance and expertise. Moreover, as with all properly thought-out collections, each inclusion gains in impact from the presence of others. These are all splendid examples of the Irish short story, irrespective of gender – though it seems a balance still needs to be adjusted between male and female, which justifies the nature of the project.

You will find touches of the surreal or supernatural here, exhilarating wryness, ingenuity and depth of feeling. An impressive discovery, Janet McNeill's 'The Girls' appears here in book form for the first time, and is characteristically insightful, economical and decorous; while Caroline Blackwood ('Taft's Wife') is sharp and astringent as ever. And, because of *The Glass Shore*'s Northern orientation, the sense of sectarian imperatives is never too far away. Transgressions against a neighbourhood code of conduct are central to Mary Beckett's masterly 'Flags and Emblems', and to Rosemary Jenkinson's poignant and unsettling 'The Mural Painter'. The Troubles, too, are an inescapable fact of life, as in Linda Anderson's compelling 'The Turn' – set in a hospital ward in Cambridge at the present time, but harking back to Belfast before the ceasefires, and further back to childhood summers and 'forlorn trips to Ballyholme and Groomsport'.

Tara West's 'The Speaking and the Dead' comes replete with Belfast repartee, undercut by sadness and desperation. In Lucy Caldwell's skillful, level-headed 'Mayday', a student at Queen's University in Belfast finds herself in an age-old predicament. Perhaps the most shocking story in the book – shocking, because truthful and dispassionate – is the late Frances Molloy's 'The Devil's Gift', which recounts without recrimination the experiences of a postulant in a mid-twentieth-century Irish convent. You are left aghast at the inhumanity, not to say lunacy, evoked in this searing account. In a lighter vein, the captivating 'Settling' by Jan Carson takes a quizzical look at a moment of misgiving in its heroine's life, with the safety of the past opposing the liberating uncertainty of the future.

Painful and playful social comedy; astute documentation and comment; a destructive impulse afflicting a returned prisoner of war; a brisk account of the dangers of undue empathy; a warning about unearned confidence in a foreign situation – or indeed, about interfering in another's domestic circumstances; a strong engagement with myth and magical realism; an enigmatic approach; an out-and-out zaniness; all these you will find wonderfully represented in these pages. And more. Polly Devlin's debonair and sparkling 'The Countess and Icarus', with its discreet Northern Irish narrative voice, takes us into a realm of urbanity and insouciance (with an episode of high comedy towards the end); while in Anne Devlin's 'Cornucopia', a vividly impressionistic world comes into being, all subtle colouring and pungent connections.

The North of Ireland functions as a theme, a setting, a background, a place to own or repudiate, to wonder at or take for granted – or simply as the birthplace of the authors assembled so felicitously by Sinéad Gleeson. Home ground, broken ground, a place apart: view it as you will. Politically (six counties), it is inescapably cut off, and even in the geographical sense it has a distinct outline – and one of *The Glass Shore* stories, in particular, has a special resonance in relation to borders and borderlands, lines drawn, ironies observed and symbols upheld. It is Evelyn Conlon's idiosyncratic 'Disturbing Words', which also contains pointed reflections on death and emigration, locality and protest, all intriguingly intertwined. It rivets the attention.

But whatever your aesthetic, intellectual or imaginative requirements of the short piece of fiction, you will find much to ponder here, much to relish and applaud.

Rosa Mulholland

Rosa Mulholland was born in Belfast in 1841, and after encouragement from Charles Dickens – who admired and championed her work – became a writer. She was a prolific author of novels, novellas, dramas, and poems, including *Narcissa's Ring, Giannetta: A Girl's Story of Herself, The Wicked Woods of Toobereevil, The Wild Birds of Killeevy, The Late Miss Hollingford, Marcella Grace, A Fair Emigrant* and *The Story of Ellen*. She wrote several short story collections, including *The Walking Trees and Other Tales, The Haunted Organist of Hurly Burly and Other Stories, Marigold and Other Stories* and *Eldergowan ... and Other Tales.* Her short story, 'The Hungry Death', was included by W.B. Yeats in his collection, *Representative Irish Tales,* and is said to be the inspiration for his play *Cathleen ni Houlihan.* She died in 1921 in Dublin.

The Mystery of Ora

There is something inexplicable in the story, but I tell it exactly as it happened.

Born to the exception of wealth, certain casualties of fortune swept away my possessions at a blow. I was young enough to relish the thought of work for three years unremittingly, till my health began to feel the strain, and I resolved to take an open-air holiday. A friend who was to have accompanied me changed his mind at the last moment, and I set out alone.

I chose to visit the wildest parts of the west coast of Ireland, and was rewarded by the sight of some of the finest scenes I had ever beheld. Keeping the Atlantic on my right, losing sight of it for a time, and again finding it when some heathery ascent was gained, I walked for two or three days among lonely mountains, accepting hospitality from the poor occupants of the cabins I occasionally met with. It was fine August weather. All day the hill peaks lay round me in blue ether; every evening the sun dyed them first purple, then blood-red, while the solitary slopes and vales became transfigured with a glory of colour quite indescribable. At night the solemn splendour that hung over this wilderness kept me awake, enchanted by the spells of a more mysterious moon than I had ever known elsewhere.

One morning I began to cross a ridge of a mountain that separated me from the sea shore, and was warned by the peasant whose breakfast of potatoes I had shared that I must travel a considerable distance before I could meet with shelter or food again.

'Ye'll see no roof till you meet the glass house of ould Collum, the stargazer,' he said. 'An' ye needn't call there, for he spakes to no one, an' allows no man to darken his door. Keep always away to yer left, an' ye'll get to the village of Gurteen by nightfall.'

'Who is this Collum, who allows no man to darken his door?' I asked.

'Nobody rightly knows what he is by this time, sire; but he was wanst a dacent man, only his head was light with always lookin' up at the stars. He built himself this glass house, for all the world like a lighthouse; an' so far so good, for it did turn off a lighthouse on them Eriff rocks; that'll tear a ship to ribbons like the teeth of a shark. An' there he did be porin' into books an' pryin' up at the heavens with his lamp burnin' at night; an' drawin' what he called horry-scopes, thinkin' he could tell a man's future an' know the saycrets of the Almighty. His wife was a nice poor thing, an' very good to travellers passing the way, an' his little girl was as gay and free as any other man's child; but somehow there's no good to be got of spyin' on the Creator; an' after his wife died he got queerer an' queerer, an' fairly shut himself up from his fellow cratures; an' there he bes, an' there he remains. An' the daughter seems to have grown up as queer as himself, for she niver spakes to nobody, not these last three or four years, though she used to be so friendly.'

'Well,' I said. 'I shall keep out of old Collum's way,' and I started for my long day's walk.

I had walked a good many hours, and had crossed the steep ridge that separated me from the seaboard; had lain and rested at the full-length in the heather, and gazed in delight at the magnificent view of the Atlantic, with its fringe of white, low-lying, serrated rocks, interrupted here and there by a group of black fortress-like cliffs. I had begun to descend the face of the mountain by a winding path when I became conscious of something moving at a little distance from me. Sheltering my eyes from the sun, I saw the figure of a woman against the strong light – a figure that came towards me with such a swift, vehement movement that it seemed almost as if she had been shot from the blazing sky across my path. She put both her hands on my arm with a grasp of terror, and then stammered some incoherent words, extended one arm, and pointed wildly to the sea – that serene ocean, which a moment ago had looked to me like the very image of majestic peace, with its happy islets sparkling on its breast. What was there in that smiling storm-forgetting ocean to excite the fear of any reasonable being? My first thought was that she was some poor maniac whose all had gone down out there on some stormy night, and who had ever since haunted the scene of her shipwreck, calling for help. I could not see her features at first, so dark was she against the strong light that dazzled my eyes.

'What is the matter?' I asked. 'What can I do for you?'

As I spoke, I shifted my position so that I was in the shade while the light fell upon her; and I saw that she was no mad woman, but a very beautiful girl, with a face full of strong character and vivid intelligence. The look in her eyes was the sane appeal of one human creature to another for protection; the white fear on her lips was a rational fear. The firm, gracious lines of her young countenance suggested that no mere cowardly impulse had caused her to seize my arm with that agonised grasp.

As she stood gazing at me, with that transfixed look of terror and appeal, I saw how very beautiful she was, with the sunlight pouring round her and almost through her. Her glowing hair, which I had thought was black, had flashed into the warmest auburn, and lay in sunny masses on her shoulders; her eyes, deep grey and heavily fringed, glowed from her pale face with a splendour I had never seen in eyes before. She was poorly and singularly dressed in a faded calico gown and an old straw hat, tied down with a scarlet handkerchief; but even as she stood, nothing could be more perfect than the artistic beauty of colour and form which she presented to my astonished eyes. Almost unconsciously I noticed this, for all my mind was engaged with the expectation of what she had to tell me, with the awe of that look of the living imploring anguish, and the wonder as to what that message could be that she seemed to be bringing me from the ocean.

As she did not speak I repeated my question: 'What is the matter? Tell me, I beg, what can I do to help you?'

Her eyes slowly loosened their gaze from my face, her arm fell to her side, a slight shudder passed over her, and she turned away.

'Nothing.' She almost whispered the word, and moved a step from me.

'That is nonsense,' I said, placing myself in her path. 'Pardon me, but you are in some trouble – in some danger, and you thought I could save you from it, or at least help you. Let me try. Let me know how I can serve you.'

'I cannot tell you,' she murmured, and then raised her eyes again to mine with another wild look full of unutterable meaning. Behind her gaze there seemed to lie a lonely trouble, which peered out from its prison house and asked for human sympathy, but was crossed and driven back by a cloud of unearthly fear. I thought so weird a look had never passed from one living creature to another.

I felt puzzled. So sure was I of the reality of her forlorn anguish that I could not think of passing on and leaving her to be the victim of whatever calamity threatened her under the shadow of this lonely mountain. And I felt, by instinct, that the womanly weakness within her was clinging to me for protection in spite of the steadfast denial of her words.

'I am a stranger,' I said. 'And you are afraid to trust me; but I give you my word, I am an honourable man – I will not take advantage of anything you may tell me here.'

Her lips quivered and she glanced at me wistfully. She looked so young – so piteous! I took her passive hand firmly in mine and said again, 'Trust me.'

'I do, I could,' she faltered. 'But oh! It is not that. It must never be told. I dare not speak.'

She turned slowly round, and her eyes went fearfully out to sea, wavered towards the cliffs, and lit on a glittering point among them; then she snatched her fingers from mine with a wail of terror, and, dropping to her knees before me, hid her hands in her face and wept.

I waited till her agony had spent itself, and then I raised her up gently and tried to reason with her. But it was all in vain. No confidence would pass her lips. She became every moment firmer, colder, more controlled. All her weakness seemed to have been washed away by her tears, and yet the calm despair on her soft face, bringing out its strongest lines of character, somehow touched me more than any complaint could have done.

'I thank you deeply,' she said. 'You would have helped me if you could. Go your way now, and I will go mine.'

'I will at least bring you to your home,' I said. 'Where do you live?'

'There,' she said, pointing to the glittering point on the rocks.

I shaded my eyes and looked keenly through the sunlight, and suddenly it flashed upon me that yon glitter came from 'old Collum's glass house', and that this was his daughter.

'Is your father's name Collum?' I asked.

A sudden change passed over her – I knew not what – like an electric thrill.

'That is his name.'

'And he lives in yonder observatory?'

'It is our home,' she replied after a pause.

'Let me accompany you,' I said.

'No one comes there; he – he does not make anyone welcome. I beg, you will not mind me; I am accustomed to roam about alone.'

'I have walked a long way,' I said after a few moments' reflection, 'and I am tired and hungry. I hope you will not forbid my throwing myself on your father's hospitality for a few hours. I cannot reach the nearest village before nightfall.'

This clever appeal of mine had its effect. She no longer urged me to leave her, though a painful embarrassment hung upon her. Under other circumstances, delicacy would have forced me to relieve her from this, but I had made up my mind to leave no means untried to help her. I had a strong suspicion that old Collum was cruel to his child, and that she feared to let a stranger witness his ill-conduct. I determined to discover for myself, if I could, what sort of life he forced her to lead. We descended the mountain silently together, and, crossing a difficult passage of rocks, arrived at old Collum's house.

It was a curious, old, grey, weather-beaten building, wedged into and sheltered by the cliffs, and looking as if in some early age it might have been carved out of their grim masses. The observatory was a much newer erection – a round tower with a glass chamber at its top, resembling a lighthouse to warn mariners from these dangerous rocks. The house was of two storeys – three rooms below and three above, and we ascended a narrow spiral staircase to the higher chambers. My companion led the way to an apartment in the front – a dimly-lit, gloomy place, with two small windows set high in the wall from which nothing could be seen but two square spaces of ocean. The interiors of this room showed how very ancient the building must be. It had, in fact, been built as a hermitage by monks in an early century. The stone walls, made without mortar, had never been plastered, and the rough, dark edges of the stones had been polished and smoothed by time. Upon them hung a map of the world, one or two sea charts, a compass, a great old-fashioned watch of foreign workmanship, ticking the time loudly, and a few pieces of ancient Irish armour and ornaments dug out of a neighbouring bog. The floor was paved with stones, worn into hollows here and there, and skins of animals were strewn over it. The fireplace was a smoke-blackened alcove, and across it, sheltering its wide nakedness, the skin of a seal was hung, fixed in its place by an ancient skein, or knife of curious workmanship. On the rude hearthstone lay the red embers of a peat fire; and though an August sun was glowing in the heavens, the fire did not seem out of place in the chill of this vault-like dwelling.

As we entered, my companion cast a hurried glance into the room and seemed relieved to find it unoccupied. She threw off her hat and, opening a cupboard, began to prepare the meal which I had begged of her. All her movements were graceful and ladylike, and her beauty seemed to take a new character as she made her simple housewifely arrangements. Excitement and exaltation were gone from her manner, wildness and brilliance from her looks. No longer glorified by the sunlight, her hair had ceased to flash with gold, and had darkened to the blackness in the shadows of the room. Her downcast eyes expressed only a gentle care for my comfort and, as I watched her with increasing interest, a faint colour came and went in her face.

I took up a curious, old drinking cup of gold that she had placed on the table. On it was engraved the word 'Ora', and I asked her what it meant.

'It is my name,' she said. 'The cup was found not far from here, and my father put my name upon it.'

Now, when she said this, there was wonder in my mind, not that she bore so strange and original a name, but because the words 'my father' were pronounced in a tone of such mournful and compassionate lovingness as to startle away all my preconceived notions as to the reason of her unhappiness.

'Perhaps, if not wicked, he is mad,' I thought. 'And she is afraid of having him taken away from her.'

As I pondered this thought with my eyes fixed on the door, it opened, and a sallow, withered face appeared, set with two dull, black eyes, which fastened in blank astonishment on my face. 'Collum the madman!' was my mental exclamation on beholding this vision; but as the door opened farther, and a figure was added to the face, I saw that the intruder was a woman.

Ora turned to her, and raising her hands, talked to her on her fingers; then as the old creature began to make up the fire, said to me: 'She is deaf and dumb, but a faithful soul, and all the servant we have. She gets our messages, fetches our provisions, and does little things that I cannot do myself.'

'A strange household,' I reflected. 'An aged man, a deaf and dumb crone, and this beautiful, living, vigorous creature! Outside, the wilderness of the mountain and ocean. What a place – what company for Ora on winter nights!'

I said aloud: 'And you, and she, and your father, are really the only dwellers in this lonely spot?'

She glanced up quickly, and a shudder of agitation passed over her, such as I had seen before. She did not reply for a few seconds, and then she said in a low, pained voice:

'There are only three of us.'

A most distressing feeling came over me – a conviction that the girl was answering me with a wary reserve, veiling her meaning so that, while she did not speak absolute untruth, she resolutely kept something hidden from me. Everything about her persuaded me that this was done against her will. Her eyes expressed a candid nature; her manner trusted me, except at moments when my words jarred on the secret chord of anguish. Some terrible dread made her treat me at such moments as an enemy.

I sat at the table, and she waited upon me, serving me with an anxious care that made me feel ashamed of the pretence which had thrown me on her hospitality as a hungry man. My meal over, I felt that she would expect me to depart; and as I ate I pondered as to how I could contrive to remain in old Collum's dwelling.

I was resolved not to go without making his acquaintance – yet how was I to force myself into the old man's presence? Even as the thought passed my mind my question was answered. The door opened, and the master of this strange domicile appeared.

My first thought was that I found him much younger, keener, more vigorous and wide-awake than I had expected. Despite his long white hair, beard, and eyebrows, I saw at once that he was not a very old man; even his manner of opening the door, and the step with which he entered the room, gave one the idea of physical strength in its prime. There was no droop of the dotard about his features or figure – no dreamy, absent look of the stargazer in his fierce black eyes – no lines of abstracted thought upon his cunning brow. As he entered the room, not expecting to see me, I saw him just as he was – in all his reality; and I felt at once that had he known I was there he would have presented a different appearance. I seemed to know this by instinct, as one does sometimes divine certain things, by a flash of intelligence, in the first moment of meeting with a fellow creature.

As he stood in the doorway, looking at me with rage in his eyes, I saw his soul unveiled; the next moment – how or why I knew not – I beheld (my gaze having never been withdrawn from his face) a different being. The tension of his figure slackened; the lines of his face lengthened and weakened; the shaggy grey brows veiled the languid eyes; the forehead had assumed the look of the forehead of a visionary. He flung himself on a seat, and said feebly: 'Excuse me, sir, but I did not know that our poor dwelling was honoured by the presence of a guest. Ora, my dear, you ought to have told me.'

Ora was behind me, and so intent was I upon watching the strange being before me that I did not look to see how she had taken this address. Besides, something warned me that it would be better to notice her as little as possible in her father's presence. Striving to overcome the extreme repugnance I felt to my host, I said: 'It is I who ought to apologise for my intrusion, but' – here it seemed to me that I felt the thrill that quivered through Ora standing behind me – 'but finding myself a complete stranger in need of rest and food in this lonely region, ventured to throw myself on your daughter's hospitality. I am afraid, indeed, I forced myself upon her kindness.'

'You are welcome, sir,' he said. 'Welcome to all we have to give. We live out of the world, and have little to offer to those who are accustomed to better things.'

His civil speech seemed to clear difficulties from my path, only to put greater ones in my way. That this wily man had, as well as his daughter, a secret to guard, was an established fact in my mind. That cruelty to her was not the whole of it I felt sure. Whether his civility was proof that he feared, or did not fear, detection by me, I could not at that moment decide, but put the question away for after consideration, along with another fact that I had noted without weighing what its value might be. The man spoke with a foreign accent, and with a manner which suggested that English was not familiar to him, and had been learnt late in life. He was of foreign workmanship, as surely as was the quaint old watch that ticked so loudly over the rugged fireplace.

As I talked to my host I studied the name on my drinking cup more frequently than his countenance. Something warned me that he would not endure anything like scrutiny; at the same time, I felt that I was undergoing a searching examination from the keen, cruel eyes half hidden under their drooping eyelids.

'You are an Englishman, I suppose?' he said.

'Yes.'

'And have never been in this country before?'

'Never.'

'And in all probability what you see of it in this holiday will be enough for you. You will hardly come back.'

This was said with an affectation of carelessness which would have imposed upon me had suspicion not been aroused within me.

'Nothing is more unlikely than my return.'

As I said this, my conscience smote me, for I already felt that I could never more be entirely indifferent to the country which held Ora. The answer pleased him, however. There was a certain relief in his voice which I felt, and this encouraged me to make a bold stroke towards attaining my own purpose.

'I am going to make a request,' I said, 'which I hope you will not think impertinent. This bit of coast scenery is so beautiful that I feel great longing to explore it further. I could not do so unless you will be so very good as to allow me to return here in the evening, and give me shelter for the night. I am well aware there is no dwelling in the direction I would take, and my health is not good enough for sleeping out of doors.'

I prolonged my speech after my request was made to give him time to prepare his answer; and I forbore to raise my eyes to his so that he might have a moment to quench whatever light of ire my audacity might happen to call into them. There was a slight pause, which told me my precaution had not been an unnecessary one, but when I looked up his face was placid and bland.

'You are welcome,' he said, 'to what poor accommodation we can offer. Ora, let a room be prepared for this gentleman.'

I thanked him, and took my hat to go upon the excursion I had so newly designed. My host also rose and prepared to leave the room with me.

'The old owl must go back to his nest,' he said, with an attempt at pleasantry. 'I am a dabbler in astronomy, an observer of the stars, and my days pass in making calculations. My observatory is my home. When I entered the room some time ago I was irritated beyond measure by a problem, the solution of which still eludes me. A little society has soothed me, and I shall return to my labours refreshed.'

This speech convinced me more than ever that he was an imposter. Not only had his words of information about himself a false ring in them, but his apology for his appearance in the moment when he had stood unveiled before me revealed a depth of consciousness which was betrayed by the effort to hide it. If anything had been wanting to complete the impression made by him upon me, it would have been supplied by the evil look which he turned upon Ora as he left the room. This look he, of course, intended to be unseen by me, and I was thankful that my interception of it had been unperceived. It was a significant look of warning, and contained a threat.

He went to his observatory, and I took my way over the jagged rocks along the sea shore, thinking deeply over all I had seen and heard.

It seemed to me that I had to sum up a number of contradictory evidences. That old Collum was not the visionary nor the stargazer which public report and his own representations declared him to be, was to me past doubting. That he had some heavy stake in this lower world, and was playing a part to win it, I believed, upon the strength of my own observations. Yet what object was to be gained by a life of such entire exclusion as his? The wildest ideas occurred to my imagination as to the possibilities of leading a criminal life in this wilderness; and were rejected almost as quickly as they took shape in my mind. His well-known inhospitality forbade the supposition that he could be a waylayer of travellers; and besides, had he been a murderer, Ora would not have stayed by him. She was free to roam where she pleased, and could have easily escaped to the nearest town as she could have climbed the mountain upon which she had met me. It was more likely that he might be a forger, and an undertaker of secret journeys into the world and back again to his den. Could her knowledge of his evil life account for her conduct? I thought it might and yet, having granted this, I still felt that there was a mystery behind him which I could not unravel. One moment I felt convinced that Ora hated and feared him, and that it was from him she would have appealed to me for protection; the next I remembered the accent of love with which she dwelt on the words 'my father', uttering them in a tone that was crossed by neither shame nor terror. And another point remained in my thoughts, though I knew not what conclusion I could draw from it. The man was of a foreign nation. I believed that he was not a European. True, my informant might have overlooked this fact when giving me his slight sketch of the unloved recluse, but from his name I had concluded he was an Irishman. 'Collum' I had supposed must be a namesake of St Columb; but of course, it might as easily be a corruption of some difficult Eastern word. From an Irish mother, Ora might have inherited her wonderful grey eyes and tender bloom, together with a might and heart as beautiful as her exquisite face.

The only result my cogitations produced was a feeling of satisfaction that I was going to pass one night at least under old Collum's roof. I acknowledged to myself that there seemed very little likelihood of my being thus enabled to make any discovery; but the vague hope that during the next twenty-four hours I might find some faint clue to Ora's mystery cheered me in spite of reasonable probability. I felt no pang of conscience at the thought of playing the spy upon my host. The one fact that remained clear in my mind regarding him was that he was a criminal who ought to be detected, whose existence blighted the life of the innocent girl who had the misfortune to be his child. And then my thoughts wandered from him and rested exclusively on Ora.

As I lay upon the rocks with my hands clasped behind my head, gazing out to sea, my eyes roamed over the numerous islands that lay scattered on its bosom for miles towards the horizon. Some looked large enough to support life, others were mere clusters of rocks; yonder one was gleaming like an emerald in the sun and seeming to invite the tired traveller to a sea-girt paradise, while over there another lowered, making a spot of sinister gloom on the smiling ocean. One that bore this latter character had a particular fascination for me. Its jagged rocks were like cruel teeth; it showed no cheerful fleck of green even when the sun touched it a moment and fled away. It seemed always in a shadow, and had a fierce gloom in its aspect that made one shiver. 'All that enter here leave hope behind,' I murmured, looking at it, and fancying it might well be the home of despairing spirits.

Birds were wheeling above it, and as I watched them, now black in the shadow and now white in the sun, I fell into a sort of dream – slumbering lightly, yet never losing the consciousness of where I was. I thought I heard the birds talking loudly to each other, and they talked of Ora.

'Pluck her out of yonder dungeon,' said one, 'and carry her far over the sea!'

'I cannot,' said the other; 'she is chained to the rock. Her father has chained her, and she will not tell.'

I started out of this dream to find that the sun had set, and resolved to return at once to the observatory. When I arrived, the door of the house lay open, and I went in without seeing anyone, and ascended the winding stone stairs, which did not creak under the foot.

In the room where I had left her, Ora was sitting alone. Outside it was still daylight, but in this gloomy chamber with its small, high windows, dusk had long set in, and a small lamp burned on the table, throwing a heavier darkness into the corners around it. The young girl sat by the lamp, poring intently over a book. The lamplight fell full on her face; and on that beautiful face was such a look of horror as it froze my blood to see. So absorbed was she that she did not perceive my approach, and I paused involuntarily, pained at seeing her suffering soul thus laid bare before me once more. Surprise deprived me for some moments of the power of speech. To find Ora a student was about the last thing I should have expected. To see her buried in a study which, from the expression of her face, I could not but fancy in some way connected with the woe of her life, was a still greater cause for amazement. Could she be conning some task which had been set her; or striving

22

to forget in the pages of a book moments of terror which were only just past? But no; as she read, all her mind, all her being, were engaged with what the book conveyed to her; and as the moments passed, that fearful, indescribable look grew and grew on her face, till at last she raised her eyes and fixed them on vacancy with a gaze which seemed to threaten madness.

I could not bear it any longer.

'Ora!' I cried, touching her shoulder, 'for Heaven's sake, tell me what horrible thing you are looking at!'

She started violently, and let the book fall, put out her arm to bar my taking it up, and then sank back in her chair, exhausted by conflicting feeling. As before, I seemed to feel her passionate desire to confide in me – a desire struggling in the chains of her deadly fear. I gently put away her hand and took up the book.

'Let me look at it,' I said. 'What harm can it do? You shall not tell me anything but what you please. The book can surely betray no secrets.'

She bent her head, and I opened the book. It was old and worn, the cover worm-eaten, the pages yellow and brown with time. The type was so strange that at first sight it seemed to be written in a foreign language; but as my eye became accustomed to it I was able to read.

It was a book on necromancy, treating the power of the Evil One, and of the mighty and terrible things he enabled those to do who leagued themselves with him and played into his hands. It was written with a certain force of imagination and diction, and, apparently, a thoroughness of faith in what it set forth, which was calculated to exercise an almost fiendish influence over a sensitive and delicate mind, and of which even the strongest and most sceptical mind must for a moment feel the spell. As I turned page after page, and gradually mastered the entire drift of the book, I asked myself could it be that all the terrors of the supernatural had been brought to bear upon Ora's imagination, and that the fears which bound her were of this extraordinary nature?

'You do not believe a word of all this terrible nonsense?' I said, smiling as I closed the uncanny volume, which seemed to almost smell of brimstone.

She gazed at me with a look of amazement, in which there was for a second a gleam of something like relief.

'Ah,' she said, 'you talk like that because you are ignorant. You are not so well educated as I am. See here!'

She drew back a curtain that covered some rows of bookshelves, all filled with volumes looking like fit companions of the book on the table.

'Look over these,' said Ora, 'and you will see that my instruction has not been neglected.'

I did look through them, and found them the most extraordinary assemblage of compositions that were ever brought together for the bewilderment of human creatures. There were several long treatises on astrology, dream-like, mystical books full of fascination; then came augury, the knowledge of signs and omens; necromancy, witchcraft, and vividly detailed information regarding leagues with the person of Satan who powerfully underlays all the movements of the world.

'If these and these only have been your school books,' I reflected, 'Heaven help you, poor Ora!'

I thought of a lonely childhood and youth passed in this wilderness of rock and ocean, of winters which were probably all one long, howling storm, and asked myself how the poor girl had preserved her senses, fed upon teaching such as this.

'Are these books your father's?' I asked, hardly able to contain my indignation against the wretch who had so poisoned her mind.

'Some of them,' she answered with a quiver of the lip. 'Those on astrology.'

'And who gave you the others?'

She trembled, cast me the wild look she had given me on the mountain, and threw up her hands in a defensive attitude.

'Don't!' she said hoarsely. 'Don't ask me questions. If I answer them I shall have to hate you for evermore.'

She then turned quickly towards the wall, and leaning against it, hid her face between her hands.

The words, the movement, gave me a thrill of gladness.

'Ora,' I said. 'You must never hate me. Nay, listen to me. If you can love me instead, I will take you away out of this miserable life, with its secret dread of Heavens only knows what! As my wife you shall have every happiness that a loving heart can procure for you. And I shall ask you no questions. If ever a moment comes when you feel you can confide in me, dear, I shall trust that then you will speak.'

I drew away her hands from her face, and she looked at me with a bewildered blush of surprise.

'You?' she stammered. 'You would marry me?'

'Is that so very unreasonable?'

Her face became gradually glorified by a look of such radiant joy as showed for me an instant what happiness might make of her; but it faded quickly away: the joy went out like a light in a gust of wind, the blush was replaced by an ashen pallor.

'Oh, why has this come to me,' she murmured with quivering lips, 'only to be found impossible, only to deepen my misery?'

'Why impossible, Ora?'

'That I cannot tell you. If I were to tell you it would bring such ruin as you could not bear to hurl upon me.'

Having said this, her old, reticent calm descended upon her like armour; she withdrew herself from me, went over to the table, and taking up the book she had been reading, replaced it on the shelf with its companions, drawing the curtain across, as if to prevent any return to the discussion of the subject of her studies. Then she stood silently waiting, as if expecting me to leave her.

'You had better go to your room,' she said gently. 'He – he will be displeased if he finds you here with me.'

I obeyed her desire at once, fearing to bring down a tyrant's wrath upon that tender head.

The room assigned to me was small, but its windows were well placed, being in the gable of the house, and thus commanding both a noble view of the inland, with its mountains, and the island-strewn sea. True, it was rather out of reach, and at an inconvenient height – so that an effort must be made if one wanted to enjoy the outside world through its medium. It would seem, indeed, as if the windows of this house had been planned with a view to shutting out the perpetual sight of the ocean that was so near. Had the builder foreseen that future dwellers within the walls might find the companionship of the great ocean momentously intolerable? Whether, or not, the blindness, so to speak, of the house, and the bold and peering inquisitiveness of the observatory close by, struck me as contrasting with each other curiously.

I extinguished my light and threw myself on the bed, but felt that I was not likely to sleep. My mind flew back over all the events of the day, and I could scarcely believe that I was the same person who had parted from his peasant-entertainer in the morning, saying: 'I will take care to avoid old Collum's dwelling.' I felt as if years must have elapsed since the time when I had never seen Ora, since the moment when I saw her darting to meet me upon the mountain, as if the sun had cast her upon my path. Since I had beheld that light of love and joy in her face, I resolved that nothing would induce me to give up the hope of making her my wife – an impenetrable mystery should daunt me; no terror, natural or supernatural, should be allowed to wrench her away from me. At the same time, I must be careful not to persecute her. Ignorant as I was of the cause of her sorrow and fear, I must be content to wait patiently; if necessary, to watch over her from a distance. Time, which unveils wonders, would be certain to unravel the mystery in which Ora was entangled.

As the night advanced I became more and more fevered with tantalising thoughts and vain speculations; at last, faint indications of approaching dawn appeared, and I left my bed, and with some difficulty established myself in such a position at the window as enabled me to have a view of all the landscape beauties below. I looked down into a sheer bed of rocks, which went like jagged steps to the sea; and beyond this foreground lay the ocean, with its islands dimly discernible in the misty daybreak. One by one the darkness gave up its hidden treasures, and allowed them to creep under the mysterious grey veil of the morning.

'The sun will come,' I said to myself. 'The sun will come; and presently how beautiful this all will be!'

I was trying to persuade myself that the clouds and mysteries of Ora's life would dissolve away when a slight sound immediately below startled me, a sound no greater than the flutter of a bird's wing, but sufficient in the intense stillness to make me look to see whence it proceeded. And I did look, and beheld a sight which surprised me: Ora gliding over the rocks like a spirit, stopping to look around anxiously, as if afraid of being observed, and then hurrying on towards the sea. A shawl was around her head and shoulders, and she carried a basket on her arm. She was clearly going on a journey, and was making towards the verge of the cliffs. Was it possible her household duties could take her away to a distance at this extraordinary hour? And where could she be going by water?

I lost sight of her for a few moments as she disappeared among the rocks, but soon a little boat shot out from beyond them, and Ora was in it, rowing away from the land with all her might. Outward, still outward, I saw her darting like an impatient bird over the calm sea in the still grey dawn. The wildest thoughts came into my mind. Was she running away frantically, trying to escape from all her troubles at once: from the mystery of her home, from my love, the discoveries it might impel me to make, from every difficulty that best her? And whither? Had she any plan; or did she in her ignorance hope vaguely that she might reach by chance some goal of safety, touch with her little hunted feet some shore of peace, where, unknown and unquestioned, she might loosen the chords of misery by forgetting her own identity?

Suddenly my crazy thoughts were rebuked, and I saw that she had a simple and definite purpose in her voyage. She was making for one of the islands out yonder that was creeping one by one out of the shadows of the night. It was that particular islet of gloomy and fantastic shape and expression on which yesterday the sun had refused to shine, and over which the birds had talked and wheeled in my dream. She neared it, touched it; I saw her moor the boat and vanish among the rocks of the island shore.

After an interval of half an hour she reappeared, and presently I saw her coming, small and scarcely visible as she and her skiff were in the distance, and looking, as she plied her oars, like some dark sea bird on the wing. Landing where she embarked, she returned among the rocks with swift glances of alarm cast on all sides, and sped like a frightened dove into the shadows of the house.

I mused over this secret expedition of Ora's. Her evident fear of being seen, and the fact that she bore with her a well-filled basket, which she carried carefully, bringing back the same basket empty, forbade me to suppose that she could have gone to fetch any simple produce of the island for household purposes. Whose observation had she feared? Not mine, for she never once glanced towards my window. Had she waited till her father had left his observatory, and might be supposed to be asleep, before she stole forth on her solitary adventure? And if not, what was the purpose of her visit to the island? I felt assured that some human creature's need had drawn her to the secret expedition; she was supplying sustenance to that creature unknown to and in defiance of her father. I did not guess these facts; I divined them at once; and the knowledge gave an added pang to my mind.

Who was this person lingering in the retreat upon that gloomy island? Why did he stay there? If it were a man who had thus secured the devotion of a woman like Ora, why did he not free himself and her? Why did he not step into her boat, and escape with her into the safety of the vastness of the world? I wearied myself with asking questions, with indulging my indignation against this cowardly protégé of Ora's, who was content to lie by and let her suffer, till my reasoning powers returned, and I remembered that I knew nothing of the facts of the case.

On leaving my tiny apartment I found breakfast ready for me in the sitting-room, and Ora waited upon me as she had done the day before. She looked unnaturally pale, and there were dark circles round her eyes that told a tale of suffering. She was in her most impenetrable mood, and I scarcely ventured to speak to her. Whilst I was at breakfast old Collum came into the room, and though he kept up an appearance of civility in his manner towards me, yet I felt my hour had come, and that I must go. He had bestowed his society upon me in order that he might see me out of the house. There, in his presence, I was obliged to say goodbye to Ora, and left the place accompanied by the man, who walked with me a mile along the shore.

I arrived at Gurteen in the evening but found it impossible either to stay there or go further away from old Collum's observatory. The knowledge of Ora's lonely trouble held me like a chord, and the thought of that gloomy island, with Ora's little boat speeding towards it, haunted me wherever I turned. The overwhelming desire to know more of the mystery I had left behind me so deprived me of the power of pursuing any other idea, so ignored all difficulties in the way of discovery, that I gave up battling with it, and resolved to spend the remaining time at my disposal in hovering near the spot which I had quitted in the morning. Having rested a few hours in the village inn, I set out again in the twilight to walk back the way I had come, without having any positive purpose in so doing, and drawn only by the craving to see whether Ora's little boat would again be on the water in the still grey hours that lie between the night and the dawn.

At a certain distance from Ora's home, I found a cave in the rocks in which I could rest, with my eyes on that line across the sea from the house by the observatory to the gloomy island. A faint moonlight illuminated the track as I began my watch; but it soon vanished with its shadows, and in the pale obscurity that followed, I saw the thing I expected to see – Ora's small boat on its solitary voyage. She went and came as on the preceding night, and in the sunrise there came a vivid light across my mind. I remembered that when Ora met me on the mountain she had pointed towards the sea: she had indicated the very island which she now visited by night. I had felt that she was bringing me some message from the ocean, but afterwards I had forgotten this striking impression made by her gesture in the first moment of her appearance. Now the first and the last seemed to join and close the circle of my speculation: the beginning and end of Ora's mystery was centred in the island.

I passed the succeeding hours in making up my mind to a certain course, as a man does when he finds he must steer between two inevitable dangers. I felt that I must run the risk of incurring Ora's hate – of overwhelming her with that ruin of which she had spoken. I must dare even that in the effort to save her. And yet what ruin could overtake her innocent youth? There was no shadow of guilt on her face, and I would never allow her to involve herself in the well-deserved ruin of others. With all this reasoning I came to my conclusion, and made my arrangements with a sense of the deepest pain. I was going to win Ora, or to lose her. At all events I would set her free.

Retracing my steps to the village, I hired a boat and set out to row myself to the mysterious island. Rowing through the red sunset on my strange quest, like a man in a dream, I touched the lonely shores of my desire; and mooring my boat in a creek on the seaward side of the isle, I slowly went my way to discover what it might support or contain. Nothing did I find but rocks and heather and a sprinkling of grass. There was no sign of any human inhabitation, no evidence of life except for the occasional cries of gulls and curlews. What brought Ora here, night after night, in the silent hours? Did she come to feed the birds, or did some supernatural power compel her to a rendezvous with unquiet spirits? I smiled as this latter thought passed through my mind; but truly there was something witch-like in the shapes and expressions of the surrounding rocks as the twilight came on – something uncanny and eerie in the sough of the breeze through the heather, and the lapping and murmuring of the great, calm ocean that girdled me. All through the hours of the night I walked the island, listening, watching, straining every faculty in the intensity of my vigil; sometimes starting in pursuit of an imaginary figure, which seemed to climb the rocks before me or to dart across the streaks of the moonlight, but always finding that fancy had taken advantage of some accidental form of an inanimate thing to deceive me.

At last the moon set, and that scared wakening look came over the sea, which means the dawn; and the pale hours brought Ora. When I saw her coming my heart misgave me as to the wisdom of my adventure. I was going to spy on her, to hunt her down, to possess myself by stratagem of her secret. The fear of her hate unmanned me, but with a strong effort I thrust aside such weakness. I had come here not to injure, but to save her.

She landed close to where I lay hidden. She moored her boat and climbed the cliffs; I followed her. So safe from observation did she consider herself that she never once thought of turning her head, and I kept near her easily till I saw her suddenly stoop, and apparently vanish into the rock.

Coming to the spot where she had disappeared, I found an opening in the stone, and, stooping as she had stooped, followed her down an irregular and winding passage, which led to a subterranean cave. I had completely lost her, and groped my way in the dark; but after some minutes I heard the murmur of voices, and presently saw the glimmer of light. Approaching this light, I came into an opening in a wider cave, on the floor of which a lamp burned, throwing a dreary light on two figures who clung together in the gloom of the subterranean solitude. One of them was Ora, who had flung herself on the neck of the man, who was evidently a prisoner in this natural dungeon.

A dizziness seized me, and for some moments made me forget myself and my purpose in coming to the place. I stood as if stunned. I had no idea of listening; but across the cloud that had descended on my mind I heard the low tones of Ora's voice murmuring with infinite tenderness:

'Oh, Father! Oh, Father! Oh, poor, poor Father!'

The soft words, with their despairing, caressing monotony, flowed into my ear and into my brain like a river of light. Her father was here. The other was an imposter. Foul work had been done. I thought no more of displeasing Ora, but stepped into the cave.

At the sight of me, Ora uttered a low cry of anguish that I can never forget, and wound her arms around the old man (who looked to me like an aged, etherealised likeness of the knave in the observatory), as if she would protect him from some deadly harm. The man's eyes were turned in the direction where I stood with a look of ghastly expectancy rather than fear, while Ora's were fixed on his face with that sort of gaze we turn on the dying when the parting soul is hovering on their lips. So they remained, locked in each other's arms, waiting as if for a sword to pierce them.

'Ora,' I said. 'What does this mean? I am come to save you, not to hurt you.'

She answered not a word – she did not seem to hear me; but the old man spoke to me at last, slowly and awfully, as if from the verge of another world.

'Sir,' he said, 'you mean well; but unknown to yourself, you have brought ruin to me. This is the hour of death.'

His head sank on his breast, and again I endured a long silence, which seemed hardly broken by our breathing. I bore it as long as I could, and then I spoke again.

'Let me beg you to listen to me,' I said. 'There is no one on this island, save ourselves. I am a friend; I can help. Why do you associate me with death?'

With a long sigh the strange old man raised his head, and said: 'I know not why I am still here to answer you; but believe that I do not blame you. You are but the voice of fate. Yes, Ora; I read it a long time ago in the stars, and it was folly for me to think to escape my doom. Stranger, the blow that I expect will not fall from any human hand, but nonetheless will it fall. You are innocent of all purpose against my life, yet your discovery of me here is the signal for my death. Suffer me to pass my last moments in peace with my child.'

Hearing this speech, I made up my mind that the poor old man was mad; and resolving to humour him, I retreated to some distance and gave no sign of my existence for a considerable time. After an interval which seemed to me an age, I at last spoke again.

'Pardon me,' I said. 'But you perceive that from some cause or other the event you expect has been delayed. Will you not make use of the time thus given you to think of your daughter? The doom you speak of does not include her.'

'I have no fear for her. I have read her happy fate in the stars. Freed from me, the last of her troubles will be over. Friend, I feel a desire to tell you my story. If time be granted to me, I will do it.'

I hailed the words with joy, and prepared to listen.

'I am an astrologer. For long years I lived among the stars, and they revealed to me secrets not known to men who walk the earth looking downward. I knew early that misfortune would cloud the latter days of my life; but the nature of the misfortune was not made clear to me. When I lost my dear wife, I thought for a while that the trouble I was forewarned of had come; but my child grew up loving me, and happiness returned to my heart. I kept a close, sharp watch for the shadow that was sure to descend upon me, and yet it took me unawares.

'The winters on this coast are terrible, and on wild nights I used to place a light in my observatory as an assistance to mariners. More than once I was thanked by sailors who had seen "Collum's light" in time. Yet through this charity to others came my doom.

'One terrible night I became convinced that a ship was wrecking somewhere among these dangerous islands, and I got out my boat, and pushed my way to sea as well as I could, hoping to be the means of saving life. I heard cries, but could not reach the spot, nor discover the direction whence they came. I was driven on this island a little before dawn, and then the voices had ceased, and I felt that all was over without my having been able to afford any help.

'Pacing along the shore, my foot struck against something unusual, and by the first glimmer of daybreak I perceived that it was a chest which had obviously been washed up from the wreck. Examining it carefully, I found that it was locked and sealed. Some valuable cargo, no doubt, I thought, and wondered what I should do with it. As I bent over it I suddenly became aware that someone was near, and looking up, saw a young man standing beside me. I stared at him in amazement, for he was neither wet nor ill, nor did he bear any trace of having lately striven with death on the sea. He had a gentlemanly, thoughtful air, and returned my gaze with a half anxious, half confiding look.

'"What can I do for you?" I asked, as soon as surprise would allow me to speak.

'"Guard this," he said, pointing to what lay at our feet. "It is all I possess. Save it from my enemy. Keep it for me till I come for it."

'"Where shall I put it?" I asked, and stooped to try if I could lift it.

'When I looked up again the young man had disappeared. A second ago my eyes had been fixed upon his; now I was alone. I gazed up and down the lonely shore, and climbed the rocks and called. Nothing human met my eyes. No one replied to me. Then I remembered something strange about the young man's manner – the sudden way he had come upon me, the unsuitableness of his dress, the impossibility of his having found his way to the island without a boat; and I knew what I had seen was an apparition.

'The peculiar, anxious, confiding expression of his eyes remained upon my memory, and I vowed I would be true to his trust. I buried the chest where no man save myself can ever find it, and then I went to look for my boat.

'As I went I met with another startling object. Right across my path lay what seemed the corpse of a man, cold and blue – a drowned waif from the wreck. He bore no likeness to the young man who had so strangely appeared and disappeared, but was short and dark, with sallow skin and Egyptian features. Why did I touch him? But had I left him lying there, the stars would have been untrue in their reckoning.

'I knelt beside him, restored him to life, and brought him home. Ora and I nursed him. He was ill for some time, and I amused his sickbed with stories of my way of life, and told him many of the wonderful things that stars had revealed to me. He listened with great interest, and seemed grateful and friendly. I gave him all my confidence, and in an unlucky moment related to him the strange occurrence of my vision on the island, and of the burying of the coffer I had found. He told me he was the master of the merchant vessel that had been lost, and was concerned about all details of the wreck.

'As soon as he was able to move he asked me to accompany him to this island, that he might search for such scraps of his property as the winds and waves might cast upon its shore. He picked up several things which he claimed as his own; after he had ceased to find anything from day to day, he still kept urging me to visit this place with him. I soon perceived that he was trying to discover whereabouts I had buried the coffer.

'Finding that I would not betray myself, he at last spoke to me plainly – told me that the coffer was his, that my pretence of having seen an apparition was a trick to deprive him of his property, and that he meant to have it, whether I would or not. Now I knew that the thing I had hidden was neither his nor mine, and so I resisted him.

'We were here, in this cave, where he had beguiled me on the pretence of looking for waifs of the wreck. Suddenly he struck me on the head, and I fell senseless. When I recovered consciousness I was here as you see me, chained by the ankle in this miserable hole.

'My enemy then returned to my house, took advantage of a certain likeness to myself in his features to impersonate me, and established himself in my place. From time to time he visits me here, trying to persuade me to give up the coffer; but that I will never do till the owner comes for it.'

Here the poor creature paused, and I said quickly: 'All this I fully understand. You have been treated most foully. But why, in Heaven's name, did you not suffer your daughter to make known your state? Why do you shrink from me and talk of death in the very moment when I have come to deliver you?'

Now up to this time the old man had told his story with the air of an intelligent person; but the moment I asked the latter question a gleam of insanity seemed to dart across his brain.

'Why?' he asked excitedly. 'Because my enemy is a wizard, a magician; he is in league with the Evil One, who holds me in his claw, ready to strike death into my veins the instant my case is made known to any creature. Have I not seen Satan in the long black hours pacing up and down yonder passage, and stopping to look in and gloat over his prey? But he could not touch me so long as we – as Ora and I, kept the secret to ourselves. But I would not speak, and I would not suffer her to betray me. And so I baffled them.'

There was a ring of triumph in the poor old creature's voice as he said this, and he patted Ora's head almost gleefully, where she leaned with her face buried in his breast.

I said to myself that he was mad – driven quite mad by this solitary confinement, and his unhappy daughter had never discovered it.

'How could you believe,' I said, 'that your enemy had this supernatural power over your life?'

'How can I believe that the sun shines?' he asked gravely. 'He comes here and sits beside me, and tells me of his dealing with Satan. He has lived, and will live, hundreds of years, though Lucifer, who does his will now, is bound to get him at last. You might not have believed him, but I knew better. The secrets of the stars have taught me many things.'

'But tell me,' I said. 'If this terrible person has Satan for his servant, why does he not find him the coffer without your assistance?'

'It is a fault in the plan,' answered the old man dreamily. 'When Satan tried to see, he was baffled by an angel's wing. I cannot explain it to you, but I know it well enough myself.'

'The angel was your daughter, then. Through her I have come here. Now listen to me, old man. Why were you not brave enough to die and let your one child go free?'

He hung his head on his breast, and fondled Ora's hair.

'You are right, sir,' he said. 'I will die, and she shall go free. Let the blow fall: it is due ere this.'

'Then if you are ready, I will strike off your chain, and let Satan do his worst.'

Ora started up as I drew near and seized my arm.

'Ora,' I whispered. 'Poor child! Do you not see that affliction has crazed your father's brain? Do not you also be mad, but let me deal with him.'

I examined the chain, and found, as I expected, that it was eaten with rust. It was probably something belonging to the shipwrecked vessel that had come ashore. I laid a rusty link upon a large, sharp stone, and lifting another stone, as heavy a one as I could raise, to a considerable height, let it fall upon the iron. As I raised my arms to do this, the lamplight fell full on my face, and I glanced at the poor old maniac, who, with folded arms, awaited his imaginary doom. In that instant, as the stone dropped, a terrible cry broke from his lips, and he fell back with a groan, just as his chain split asunder.

'He is dead. We have murdered him!' moaned Ora, falling on her knees beside him.

'No, he is not dead!' I exclaimed joyfully, for I had feared that the shock of the expectation might have really deprived him of life. I poured brandy down his throat, and after a time he revived.

'The apparition,' he muttered. 'He has the face of the apparition. Ora, where is the young man who met me that morning on the shore?'

'He is wandering,' I said to Ora. 'Do not be afraid.'

'I am not wandering,' said the old man. 'What I saw I saw. Reach me the lamp.'

He raised the light to my face and looked at me with a solemn, awful look.

'It was you who met me on the shore,' he said. 'You who gave the coffer in charge to me.'

When the wretch whom I had known as 'old Collum' saw us coming in our boat from the island, he escaped on the instant, and we saw him no more. The police made efforts to track him but in vain.

I told you that there was a strange point about this story, and so, when the haze of folly and madness has been cleared away, there still remains something in it that is inexplicable. Urged by the poor old dotard whom I had rescued, I went with him to unearth the coffer that had cost him so much to guard. It proved to be my own property, and its contents restored to me the fortune I had lost.

Its loss in a ship that went down at sea had been the cause of the reverses which I mentioned in the beginning of my tale. A comparison of dates proved, if proof was necessary, that the vessel wrecked off the island was the same that had borne my heritage across the sea. The incident of the apparition I do not attempt to account for. That, on the morning of the wreck, I had spoken with him on the shore, and committed my property to his care, was firmly believed by poor old Collum up to the moment of his death – a moment not far distant from that which saw his rescue from the cave.

Wrought upon so long a knave on the one side, and visionary and madman on the other, it was long ere Ora's tender imagination recovered from the morbid state into which it had been thrown by her terrible experiences. But time and change cleared away all clouds from her mind; while the energy and devotion that characterised the wild mountain girl remained my beautiful wife.

Erminda Rentoul Esler

Erminda Rentoul Esler was a novelist and short story writer. Raised in Co. Donegal, she moved between Belfast and London after attending Queen's University. Her published work includes *The Wardlaws, The Way of Transgressors, Maid of the Manse, Youth at the Prow, The Way They Loved at Grimpat, Awakening of Helena Thorpe*, and a short-story collection, *Mid Green Pastures*. She died in 1924.

An Idealist

It was morning, and the day promised to be long and beautiful. The air was warm with the moist, misty warmth that relaxes energy, and makes the agriculturist thankful that his heaviest work is over for a season. On the whole landscape there was scarcely a human figure visible, though the shallow cup of the hills was dotted with white farmhouses, and in the distance, Grimpat lay like a jewel within their circle.

'It is a good place to rest in,' Willie Durwent said as he sunned himself on a fence with the air of a man who enjoys deserved repose. Obviously he was not a native; he was not clothed like one, he did not even lounge like one, and his eyes had not the indifference with which we contemplate the familiar, or the abstraction indicative of the absentee who finds himself suddenly amid old associations.

The fence was a boundary, dividing rich land from waste. On one side was a meadow filled with half-ripe grass that swayed softly with liquid motions, and a sheen, now silken, now silver.

On the other side was a stretch of unprofitable moor, pompous as an emperor in the purple splendour of heather and the golden glory of furze. Here a grey boulder intruded a subdued tint into the blaze of colour; there a hidden spring formed an obscure and sluggish rivulet amid which patches of rushes grew green as emeralds. Among the heather-bells bees were booming drowsily, and now and then a gay butterfly fluttered over the brilliant surface like an animated flower.

The young man sat sideways towards the moor, but his feet dangled on the side of the meadow. His position and the contrast nature afforded seemed to him allegorical, and he sighed tenderly now and then as he contemplated them. What a pity that all the solid advantages were in the meadow and all the beauty on the moor!

Jeffrey Poole lived three miles away. He was a farmer. His house stood on the top of a hill, and commanded a view of the country below, of the fields heavy with the promise of harvest, and of the roads that twined among them like ribbons.

Jeffrey's front door commanded a distant view of the wide landscape and a near view of the paved cattle-yard and the adjacent office-houses; the back door opened into an ill-kept garden where boxwood, peonies, and larkspur grew large amid more fragrant blooms. As a rule, horticulture is rather disregarded by farmers, flowers having little market value.

On this occasion, Molly Steele was weeding in the garden; there were so many weeds that her progress was obvious. Now and then she raised herself from her stooping position and looked somewhat absently into the distance. Suddenly, her expression grew alert and her gaze fixed itself sharply on a faraway point, where only country eyes, undimmed by books, could have discerned anything.

Without confiding the reason even to herself, Molly had been wont for several days to look toward that point in the landscape where the roads from the hill farm converged with the roads leading elsewhither.

Today something rewarded her scrutiny; someone had turned up the farm road, a man, a tall man, a young man obviously, as he walked so lightly. Molly stood staring, her lips slightly parted, her hands hanging limply by her sides; then she said, 'It is!' and sped indoors as if she had been shot from a bow.

Upstairs, Naomi Steele sat reading; she was Molly's sister, the elder, the plainer, the less popular. The Steeles were poorish people who had seen better days. Mrs Steele was a widow who would have been in straits but for the kindness of Jeffrey Poole, her brother, who gave her and her children a home.

Mr Steele had been a parson and something of a scholar, and traditions of such eminence cling to families in country places, and make them a little better or a little worse in the eyes of their neighbours. Jeffrey Poole was a bachelor, otherwise, perhaps, the home for the Steeles would not have been so certain.

Naomi was two years older than Molly. In her youth she had been more troublesome; as she grew up she was plainer, and both her mother and uncle observed that she was a little odd. But neither ever breathed this to the other, for, according to primitive ideas, it is destruction for a girl to differ from the orthodox pattern.

Molly was the favourite: she had all the qualities that make for general popularity; she was very pretty; she valued appreciation; was pleased when people thought well of her, said she was amiable and clever, looked after her admiringly. Naomi was indifferent to all of this; she had a world of her own; lived in the ideal; and measured everyone by a standard she had somehow formulated.

It is seldom that books are available in farmhouses, such possessions involving a waste of time and an outlay in money that does not commend itself to the agriculturist. But Mrs Steele possessed all her husband's books, having declined to part with them at a valuation; and a pedlar appeared now and then at Grimpat with volumes of the *Sixpenny Book Shelf* among his wares, *The Newgate Calendar*, *The Arabian Nights*, *The Seven Champions of Christendom* and the primers of ancient history and of science. For these Naomi bartered the odds and ends that drop off as waste products from even the most economically managed homes.

The day of the pedlar's advent was such a red-letter day in Naomi's calendar that Sarah, the hired girl, suggested that Naomi had fallen in love with the pedlar, and spoiled her pleasure of his visits for ever.

At first Naomi shared her intellectual good things with Molly, but Molly had no memory, and confused St George of Merrie England with the Deerslayer, and Romulus and Remus with Valentine and Orson. That provoked Naomi, who slapped Molly and declined confidential talks with her in the future.

At fifteen Naomi began to grow frightful; it was then she would tell Molly in a low-voiced narrative in the first person, looking straight before her, appalling things she had seen and done, extraordinary persons who had interviewed her, startling and inexplicable confidences they had made to her. Molly often stopped her ears that she might not hear these narratives, but that did not prevent her having a nightmare subsequently.

At seventeen Naomi had realised that she was different from other girls and that divergence is an unhappy thing. She felt she was unpopular, that her uncle was uncomfortable with her, her mother was a little ashamed of her, and when an invitation or a present came it was always for Molly.

No one had suggested to Naomi that she was a genius; had it been suggested she would not have understood. Who has ever discovered genius by their own fireside, or recognised at close quarters the strange, ungainly thing? When the world begins to shout hurrah! It is usually in the home of genius that the sound is heard with most astonishment. That is a genius, the child who had often been so tiresome and so useless!

But Naomi had done nothing noteworthy as of yet, perhaps never would, for she was growing shy and self-conscious, ashamed of the nonsense that used to give Molly bad dreams, and anxious for some common place, some common use, in the big, common world.

Naomi sat upstairs reading by her own room window. The window looked out on a stack of turf, but above the turf was a bit of blue, over which rags of clouds floated lazily, and that sufficed to distract her attention.

Suddenly the door burst open, and Molly entered breathlessly. 'It is Willie Durwent – coming up the road!' she gasped. 'He is coming here – to tea!'

Naomi looked around blankly. 'Oh, you know,' Molly said impatiently, as though she had replied. 'Mrs Dale's nephew – I met him last summer when I went with her to the seaside. I told you about him – or I meant to, at any rate. He is very nice, has been at the university, and is just finishing for a doctor, and – he is coming up the road.'

'Yes?' Naomi said interrogatively.

'Mother is gone to tea at Mrs Eastnor's, as you know, and Sarah is away on an errand to Grimpat. Of course I must receive and talk to him, and so I want you to get tea. You will, won't you, Naomi? A nice tea, like a good girl!'

'Certainly, certainly,' Naomi answered heartily.

'You will get things ready now, won't you? I will go out to the front door and make believe to be doing something, so that he may not knock, since there is no one to open. When he has been in some time I will ring, and then you will bring in tea, saying that Sarah is out, and we will have a cosy chat together.'

That the visitor would remain a considerable time, and that the visit was intended for her, Molly understood as well if she had been a woman of fashion.

Naomi entered on the enterprise cordially. She was very good-natured, and she felt quite an interest in the young man who had studied and seen life. She went downstairs cheerfully, stirred the fire to a blaze, and proceeded to prepare tea.

Now, the uninitiated are prone to imagine that in farmhouses dainties do abound, that there are always toothsome cakes, and rich creams, and jars of honey and preserves on the pantry shelves, and that high tea is a repast which the farmhouse can produce at a moment's notice.

In very prosperous farmhouses this may be so, but there were none such at Grimpat. Jeffrey Poole was a working farmer, who needed to exercise great care that the rent might be ready half-yearly, and Mrs Steele, who was very grateful to him for all he had done for her and her children, showed her gratitude by supplementing his economies.

On this occasion there was nothing in the house but a little tea, a little sugar, a great abundance of butter, a very ancient remnant of the baker's loaf, and some pale milk, from which the cream had already been skimmed for the evening's churning.

Now, a girl more world-wise would have understood that a repast from such ingredients was not a fit offering to place before a nice young man who had come a distance to see her sister, but in Naomi Steele there was that curious innocence in practical matters that often accompanies an exceptional development of the ideal. Even if the difficulty had occurred to her, she would not have known what to do, for Molly and Mr Durwent were already seated in the parlour, and Molly had said tea was to be brought in when she rang.

Naomi's intentions were as loyal as her heart, but when she presented herself and the black japanned tray in due time there was reason for the elongation of Molly's countenance.

'Sarah is gone to Grimpat, so I thought I should bring the tea in myself,' Naomi explained cheerfully, following instructions; then she spread a white cloth on the table and placed thereon the usual family fare and the everyday appurtenances, which

An Idealist

for a family party were rough and meagre enough, but for a
visitor, and a visitor from the town! Molly gazed at her sister,
and Naomi answered with smiles and nods intended to convey
that she had done her best.

There is nothing so sustaining as the consciousness of a
virtuous action. Naomi was so sure of having acquitted herself
well that she positively sparkled with good humour. Never had
so many clever things been heard in any farmhouse parlour as
she poured out the tea from the tin teapot. If unconsciousness
of anything needing apology is a sign of good breeding, then
Naomi was the best-bred hostess who ever presided at a
banquet. And the guest enjoyed himself thoroughly. To have
two girls all to himself and no senior present was a piece of
good luck he had not anticipated. That Molly had fallen quite
silent did not strike him, and that she considered her sister
an imbecile for her talk and everything else, did not occur to
him. He remained a whole hour and more, and when dusk was
creeping over the landscape he went away reluctantly. When he
left, the trouble began for Naomi.

'Oh, you are horrid!' Molly said, with a burst of tears.

Naomi's face fell, and all the radiance died out of her
aspect.

'Molly!' she cried, her eyes round with astonishment and
terror.

'Don't talk to me! You did it on purpose, to disgust him
and make him never come back.'

'Did what on purpose?'

'Brought in that nasty delph and the tablecloth with a hole
in it, and the lead spoons, and everything!'

Naomi looked at the table, and drooped still further.

'And nothing to eat,' Molly sobbed, 'but stale bread and
oceans of butter; the horridest, vulgarest—'

'It is what we should have had for ourselves, and I
never thought,' Naomi said in subdued tones. 'Besides,' she

brightened visibly, 'the best china was in the cupboard in this room, and I could not come to take it out before him.'

'You always have excuses; you always think you do the right thing. I shall know better than to give you a chance of shaming us again, but he will never come back, that is certain.'

And he never did. Whether Naomi's tea was too much for him, or whether family influence or personal choice decided him, Willie crossed the fence into the grassland. He was a nice young man, as there are hundreds of nice young men, more attractive in his youth than ever afterwards, not likely to achieve greatness or have greatness thrust upon him, but certain always to prove a respectable citizen. His wife's money was a great help to him at the start; he got into a nice class of medical practice, and did very well.

Years afterwards, when he heard that Naomi Steele had become famous, he remembered her tea party, and said he could quite believe it.

The impression he made on Molly was not deep or lasting, and ultimately she forgot him among other people she had known; but she took care that Naomi never prepared repasts for her friends thenceforward.

It was about a year after Willie Durwent's visit that the mail began to carry away from Grimpat and the hill farm long envelopes addressed to London, to a strange man quite unknown to the Steeles.

These were Naomi's dreams put into words – brief little sketches mostly, but so full of reality and sly humour and sweet philosophy, so redolent of the fields and the hills, that they were not declined with thanks, not one of them.

Grimpat is very proud of Naomi now, though still a little shy of her. Mothers hold her up as an example to bookish daughters, and fathers tell with awe the prices she receives for her stories, prices which the neighbourhood seldom multiplies by more than seven or eight. But when their sons say that Miss Steele has very bright eyes or a very charming smile, they hastily inform these bold juniors that Naomi is not fit for a farmhouse, and that a writing wife is a serious matter.

Sarah Grand

Sarah Grand was born in Donaghadee, Co. Down in 1854, and is the author of eight novels and short story collections. The turn of the century saw the beginning of the 'New Woman' novel, which saw a surge in literary fiction exploring greater social freedom for women. As a feminist, Sarah Grand was at the forefront of this movement. Many of her novels, particularly *The Heavenly Twins*, were criticised on publication. Her fiction includes *A Domestic Experiment, Singularly Deluded, The Modern Man and Maid,* and *The Winged Victory.* Her autobiography, *The Beth Book* sold 20,000 copies in its first week. She moved to Wiltshire during the Second World War, where she died in 1943.

Eugenia

I

I am a humble artist, studying always in the life-school of the
world, missing nothing that goes to the making or marring of
life, more especially to the marring of it, for if we would make
it lovely, we must know exactly the nature of the diseases that
disfigure it, and experiment upon them until we discover the
great specific which, when properly applied, shall remedy all
that. And it so happened that, in order to be accurate in every
detail of a work upon which I was then engaged, I required to
study human nature, as it appears behind the scenes, at the time
of night when that part of a theatre is most characteristically
crowded with the company in costume, and such visitors as are
admitted. A brother of mine made the necessary arrangements
for me, and was so good as to escort me himself, the leading
managers, to whom he had explained my difficulty, having most
courteously allowed me free access for my purpose. It happened
at the beginning of the enterprise when everything was new
and strange, but I remember that we were wedged in a crowd
of theatrical characters variously and even fantastically attired,
as if for a fancy-dress ball, and that the clatter of tongues was
bewildering. Women's voices shrilled loudly, the cockney accent
predominating. Most of the things said struck me as being
disagreeably personal and flippant, when not actually coarse and

rude. The laughter was noisy and incessant, but mirthless, and although there was plenty of excitement in the assembly, there was obviously little if any genuine pleasure, and as to happiness, I could detect no line, even on the youngest face, to indicate it. The predominant expression was one of anxiety, only relieved in the more callous by moments of sensual apathy. As a whole the scene remains impressed upon my mind as an unlovely travesty of much to which one becomes accustomed in society, but it possessed the attraction of repulsion for me, and I could have stood there studying all night.

My brother knew many of the people present, but I only saw one man with whom I was personally acquainted, and it so happened that I knew him well, for it was Brinkhampton, the eldest son of a near neighbour of ours in my childhood. The two families had always been intimate.

He was standing talking to some woman just behind me, and I recognised his voice before I saw him.

'I'm sure your waist's smaller than Kitty Green's,' he said quite earnestly.

'Aow, nao, you flatter me,' the lady responded nasally. 'Only I daown't tight laice.'

There was a little pause, then Brinkhampton asked: 'What are you looking for?'

'My fan. I laid it on the taible.'

'Here it is. Let me have the pleasure of fanning you.'

'Pleasure, indeed! Aow, I saiy! What do you want, I'd like to knaw? With those sheep's eyes! I'm on to you—' And so on all up the gamut of the cheapest inanity, silly, sillier, and silliest.

I turned to look at the lady, expecting to see something so satisfying to the eye of man that no other sense asked for anything, but she struck me as being a joyless antique, largely proportioned, well-preserved, and still able to affect a sprightliness she must have been far from feeling at that time of life. 'That was the celebrated Sylvia,' my brother told me as we came away.

'Wherein lieth the charm of her fatal fascination?' I asked.

'In *prestige*, which lasts longer than anything,' he answered.

Out of the crowd and heat and into the open air was an intoxicating transition, so great was the relief of it. I stood for some minutes on the pavement inhaling deep draughts of the freshness, feeling as if I could never rid myself of the fever and fumes of that tawdry place.

II

The next night, driving home late from some entertainment, I was forced by a block in the traffic to sit for some time at the entrance to a popular Theatre of Varieties. There was a fiendish racket going on all about me. I was busy looking out on that side, improving my knowledge of the vulgar tongue by making notes in my own mind of any peculiar expressions used, when I heard myself addressed by name through the window and at the same moment recognised Brinkhampton.

'I thought I could not be mistaken,' he was saying. 'However, much I may be surprised by your choice of a place of amusement.'

'From whence came you?' I answered tranquilly.

'From these same halls of light,' he replied, indicating the gaudy place behind him; 'and to tell you the truth,' he added, in a worn-out, weary, satiated way, 'I am sick of all that. I'm utterly used up. I think it's time for me to reform and marry. Can you recommend me to somebody who would make a nice wife? I suppose it wouldn't do for me to ask you for a seat in your carriage at this time of night?'

This was said tentatively, but I crushed the aspiration with a decided shake of my head.

'I know you are mighty particular,' he went on disconsolately, 'but I assure you I'm thoroughly in earnest this time. Let me come and tell you all about it.'

As he blocked up the whole of the window, the fact that he was reeking of tobacco and stimulants could not fail to impress me unpleasantly, and his somewhat bloated features, inflamed eyes and dissipated appearance generally rendered him still more unattractive to my fastidious mind; so, to get rid of him, I told him that I should be 'at home' the next day, and if he came early enough, he might find me alone for a few minutes. I quite expected he would have no recollection of the engagement, but to my surprise he arrived, and rather sooner too than was altogether convenient.

It was evident from the way he was dressed that the matter had cost him some thought; but no care could conceal the 'used up' look about his eyes, nor produce a deceptive tinge of health in the opaque sallow of his cheeks. The effort had not been wanting, his valet having obviously done his best, but it is only a fresh and healthy skin that really takes paint and powder well. But he was a young man still, and a good-looking one too, of the big, coarse-moustached type, a typical guardsman, broad-shouldered, and so apparently strong that a casual acquaintance would never have suspected flabby muscular tissue discounted by alcohol. With the old-fashioned sort of society-woman he was a favourite, and I confess I liked him well enough in a way myself, but then I had acquired the habit of liking him when we were children together.

'Well, and so you are inclined to marry and settle?' I said, as soon as we were seated.

'Not merely inclined,' he answered. 'I am quite determined. I've had a good time, don't you know, rather too much of a good time if anything, and now I feel it would be better for me to settle; and I want someone nice and young and fresh, with money, for a wife, so that I may repair all my errors at once; someone who has lived all her life at the back of beyond, never been anywhere nor seen anyone to speak of, and is refreshingly unsophisticated enough to mistake the first man who proposes to her for an unsullied hero of romance. And I mean to be that man, don't you see?'

'But where do I come into this delightfully delicate, original plan?' I drily inquired.

'Well, you go a good deal to country houses,' he answered, with what might have been either a dash of diffidence or a shade of anxiety in his manner. 'You must have met the kind of girl I want – good-looking, you know, with an ivory skin and – and money. Don't jeer at me. I'm in earnest.'

I composed my countenance and took time to reflect. How to decline to help him without hurting his feelings was the difficulty. There used to be a superstition in society that a man could at any time repair the errors of his youth by making a good match, and there are women still who will introduce 'used up' brothers and so on to their girlfriends as eligible husbands; but I belong to the party of progress myself, and would not under any circumstances have done such a thing. I had not the courage of my opinions, however, at that time, to the extent of saying so bluntly, and therefore I, smiling, passed the question by; but as I had not absolutely refused, he chose to take it that I would help him if I could, and thereupon he thanked me with effusion.

III

That summer saw me seated one afternoon in a shady nook on a cliff in the north, overlooking the sea. Behind me there was a lovely stretch of country, hill and dale, field and forest, with the gold of ripening grain, the scarlet glint of intrusive poppies. My meditations were not long uninterrupted that day, however, for I was aroused by the surprised enunciation of my own name, and, on looking up, I discovered Brinkhampton staring at me.

'Well!' I ejaculated. 'What are you doing here?'

'Potting rabbits,' he answered sententiously. 'I have taken to shooting.'

'You mean to be in time for it, apparently.'

'Oh, I thought I'd come and amuse myself with the rabbits. It's the fresh air I want really, you see. My nerves have all gone to pieces. I want to be out of sinner's ways for a while, and I knew fellows wouldn't come bothering much before September. I've taken the shooting with leave to live about here for six months if it suits me. In the absence of a lord, the lady of the manor lets the right, I understand.'

'Do you know her?' I asked.

'No,' he replied. 'I have not that pleasure. Do you?'

'I am staying with her now.'

Then there was a pause, during which Brinkhampton carefully examined his gun, lock, stock, and barrel. 'It's a nice place,' he remarked at last, glancing about him comprehensively. 'Is the lady as goodly as her acres?'

'Has she "an ivory skin" do you mean? You may judge for yourself, for behold her approach down yonder forest glade, hatless, gloveless, robed in white, with a purple parasol shielding the burnished brightness of her lovely tresses from the too-ardent kisses of the sun.'

Brinkhampton stared with interest.

'She's quite young!' he exclaimed.

'Twenty-one exactly,' I replied.

He was about to say something else, but Eugenia had come up to us by this time, and I hastened to present them to each other.

'It is you who have taken my shooting off my hands this year, I suppose,' Eugenia said, glancing at his gun.

'So I have just learnt,' he answered, looking into her sweet, grave face with undisguised interest and admiration.

'I hope you will find it worth your while,' she said. 'The coverts are pretty well stocked this year, I believe. Where have you put up?'

'At the village inn,' he answered with a grimace.

'Oh!' she exclaimed. 'Then you must be uncomfortable. When I heard you were coming alone, I hoped you had friends in the neighbourhood with whom you would stay.'

'It so happens that I know nobody here as yet,' he replied. 'But I really must get some more decent accommodation.'

'Why not come to the hall?' Eugenia asked easily.

'It would be a kindness to help us to occupy a little more of it. The house has suffered from having been so long shut up.'

The frank assurance of her manner seemed to surprise him. He glanced at her gloveless left hand to see if, perchance, she was married, and he confessed to me afterwards he could not quite class her when he found she wore no wedding ring, being 'puzzled to make out whether she was Americanised, unsophisticated, or not quite the right form, don't you know.' But at any rate the offer was a good one.

'I should be afraid of intruding,' he feebly deprecated.

'No fear of that,' she answered, smiling; then appealing to me, she added: 'I am sure I may say we shall both be glad to see you. We dine at half-past seven.'

We smartened ourselves up that evening, somewhat in honour of the young man, and I noticed that he and Eugenia were studying each other with a certain pleased intentness, which augured well for their future friendliness. Certainly his coming had enlivened Eugenia, as the coming of an eligible should enliven a girl, and I waited with interest to hear what she had to say about him. He had been looking his best when they met in the afternoon, the rough tweed shooting suit he wore being just of the cut and colour best adapted to conceal his defects, but his evening dress was altogether too calculated for effect, too evidently the outcome of serious attention to be manly. There was more than a suspicion of some horrid, expensive scent about him, and his cheeks had a velvety texture which was cruelly suggestive of powder – *apropos* of all of which Eugenia remarked to me afterwards in a mysterious whisper: 'I suspect stays.' But that was all she said about him, somewhat to my surprise. However, in such a case, not asking questions is no proof of an absence of interest.

IV

Eugenia and I breakfasted at half-past eight the next morning, but Brinkhampton did not appear until after ten. It was Sunday, and we were in the breakfast-room, ready dressed for church when he entered.

'What will you have?' Eugenia, as hostess, asked him, thinking of tea, coffee or chocolate.

'Aw,' he answered, looking round to the sideboard. 'Claret or hock, I really don't care which.'

Eugenia ordered both to be brought, and then we hurried away to church.

She was peculiarly situated, being one of a long line of dominant women, and the estates having descended from mother to daughter in regular succession, in accordance with a curse which had been laid upon all male heirs of the family forever – so it was said – or, at all events, until such time as an heiress should contrive to expiate the crime for which the sons of her house were doomed to suffer. Eugenia had been left an orphan at an early age, and brought up in the midst of a people who still clung fervently to all the old-world superstitions. I did not know how much of these she accepted literally, but I always attributed a certain dignity and general air as of one who is not to be trifled with, which settled upon her early, to the romantic associations of the place, and her faith in those who had gone before. They, her people, having been noble, it was proper that she also should be self-respecting and noble too – so, at least, I read her reflections when I watched her weighing the worth of those epitaphs in her own mind, Sunday after Sunday, as she grew to girlhood.

This morning, however, she was not thinking of her ancestors in the pauses of the service. When her eyes wandered at all it was to the green graves in the church yard and the old trees that sheltered them. The day was warm and bright, and through the open windows the scented summer air streamed in upon her, and also there came an incessant twittering of birds, the coo of a wood pigeon now and then, and the hoarse caws of rooks. Even Brinkhampton's starved soul expanded for the moment just enough to let him feel some joy in life.

When the service was over he walked on with me to the house, Eugenia having lingered in the porch talking to the people.

'I have found my ideal!' he exclaimed fervently, as soon as we were alone.

'Ivory skin and all?'

'Don't be malicious,' he answered. 'I'm in earnest. But I've a bone to pick with you. You seem to have forgotten your promise to me. Why did you not tell me of this lovely lady hidden away here in the hills?'

'For the reason you mention,' I answered coolly. 'I had forgotten your request.'

'How could you, when she is so exactly what I asked you to find for me too! But tell me about her. How does she come to be so situated – here, you know, like this?'

'She is in a somewhat unusual position,' I answered. 'She has no relation in the whole world but an old uncle, who was once in your regiment, by the way. All her own people died in her infancy, and she has been brought up here, principally by a very charming and excellent woman who came to be her governess, and has remained to be a mother to her. She is away just now, and I am here on duty partly, looking after Eugenia during her absence. The property's nice, is it not? It was a good deal encumbered by debts, but has been well nursed during Eugenia's long minority, and she is bent upon economy herself until it is cleared.'

'Then she really is sole heiress?' he observed, looking about him with an air of complete satisfaction, as if he already had a proprietary right to the place.

'Sole inheritress, I should say. Half the neighbourhood is hers.'

'But why should she be buried here still?' he asked, then added: 'But I am glad she has been. I should like to see her wonder when she enters the great world! Her delight when she finds what it really is to be mistress of means, with jewels and lace, a centre of attraction! She can't know what her wealth is worth until she comes into competition with other women and finds herself able to eclipse them.'

This noble thought seemed to enchant him, and I could see he was hugging himself already at the prospect of her brilliant social success, and the glory which it would reflect upon himself.

I made him no answer because I had determined to be neutral. Here were the conventional elements of most romances: youth, beauty, rank, wealth, experienced man, inexperienced girl – but not a commonplace girl either. There was no knowing exactly how she would act under the circumstances, and the uncertainty was great enough to relieve the story from insipidity. I thought it would be interesting to watch the plot unfold, and I was anxious to see for myself how this *Ouidaesque* hero would really strike a modern maiden with ideas of her own.

At our early Sunday dinner he said a good deal about diamonds, to which Eugenia listened with evident interest. She was highly intelligent, and at an age when the opposite point of view is always surprising. She was not in the habit of saying much, however. Brinkhampton was voluble, and she heard him out, then answered with a smile and in a casual tone: 'You seem to be fond of diamonds. I have a lot upstairs somewhere if you would like to see them. I used to delight in them myself for their glitter when I was a child, but now of course I only value them for the sake of any little family history that attaches to them.'

Brinkhampton stared at her, not at all perceiving that the art of being agreeable is not always effectual with some girls, and divided between the pleasing thought that Eugenia would appreciate her advantages better when she came into competition with other women, and had opportunities of testing the value of diamonds as an aid to eclipsing them.

Out in the grounds later he began to fear that there was not much to amuse her, that she must often find it very dull in this benighted country place, whereupon she made big eyes of astonishment at him, and ejaculating 'Dull?' glanced comprehensively at the surrounding wonders of sky, and sea, and shore, then added, 'Where can dullness come into a life like mine?'

The question nonplussed him for the moment. To be so unsophisticated as to not even have the slightest conception of the better life which includes shopping in London and the full swing of everything there in the season, was a little too much. 'But,' as he remarked to me afterwards, 'all this enhances the charm, don't you know; it's so fresh, and it will be fun to see how her views change as her mind is enlarged by intercourse with the world, and to hear what she thinks by-and-by of this rural retreat.'

'But do you suppose she has any mind?' I ventured.

'Oh, dear, yes,' he answered. 'Quite enough for a woman, especially if she's to be one's wife. A clever woman is apt to have "views" and that sort of thing, and lead a man a dance generally. What one wants in a wife is something nice to look at and agreeable to caress when one's in the mood, with average intelligence of course, but conventional ideas.'

'Are you going to have anybody down for the shooting?'

'Well, I don't know,' he answered. 'That was my idea at first. But my primary motive was to get away from everybody and recruit. I told you in town. I've had too good a time, and I'm quite used up. My nerve is gone, to the extent that I'm afraid to fire my own gun if I think about it. It would certainly be better for me to settle, and the more I see of the place the more I like it. The air's delicious, and I'm beginning to revive already. It would suit me down to the ground to have this quiet retreat and Eugenia to come to whenever I felt played out, as I am now.'

'Then you've abandoned the idea of making a society woman of her?'

'Oh, not at all. But I should require her to be here when I'm otherwise engaged, and can't look after her, don't you know.'

I admired his foresight, it being evident that he was preparing, with playful toleration of his own weakness, to be tempted back now and then to gloat on Sylvia's superabundant flesh, and at the same time was thinking how refreshing it would be, when that kind of thing palled upon him, to return to the rarefied atmosphere which surrounded the lily of love whom he was also anxious to secure.

V

Their acquaintance rapidly ripened into intimacy, and very soon I perceived that they had adopted that tone of light banter which enables young people to say so much to each other. The playful controversy turned for the most part on the relative merits of town and country, and the brilliancy and wit of society compared with the petty concerns which Brinkhampton held to be all there was to discuss in a neighbourhood like this.

'I am sure,' he maintained, 'you would like to hear people talk cleverly.'

'I would much rather hear them talk kindly,' she answered.

She was always ready with some such response, but he soon flattered himself that her perversity was a coquettish assumption to pique him, and would try to provoke her in return by assuring her that she would know better when she was older.

The brightness that I had noticed on the first evening of the coming of the young man into Eugenia's quiet life did not diminish, but on the contrary, increased if anything, with the ripening of their acquaintance. Her nature was naturally joyous, and under Brinkhampton's influence her manner, while losing none of its dignified simplicity, became more girlishly playful. Nothing in her attitude, however, gave me the slightest clue as to her feelings for him. I did not know in the least whether she had ever thought of him as a possible lover or not.

With him it was quite different. He talked of her incessantly, and of what he called his 'love' for her. He even got so far as to consider the settlements, and if there would be enough ready money in hand at the time of the marriage to pay off his innumerable debts, because it would be a pity to have to sell out anything, don't you know. The 'love' and the lucre longings mixed in his conversation in curiously exact proportions, but still the frank boyishness of it all was taking.

It was hot harvest weather; radiant mornings turning to turquoise and pearl-grey noons, and always exquisite amethyst seas – an ideal love-time, and it would have been strange if it had failed altogether of its effect upon two young people so thrown together. The first positive sign of serious feeling I detected in Brinkhampton was an improvement in his habits. On Sunday morning he had breakfasted between ten and eleven, on Wednesday he was up at seven o'clock. Eugenia and I were just starting for the meadows with baskets to gather mushrooms for breakfast when he appeared. He volunteered to accompany us, and wanted to carry our baskets, but Eugenia said that would only be robbing us of our occupation, and suggested that he should have one of his own.

We straggled down the road after each other. The morning was deliciously fresh, and so was Eugenia. Brinkhampton could not take his eyes off her, and, although she never glanced at him, I knew by the smile that constantly hovered about her mouth, the brightness of her eyes, the slightly heightened colour on her delicate cheeks, and the buoyancy of her step, that she was aware of his earnest gaze, and animated by his admiration. They chatted incessantly, disagreeing generally, but it was impossible to tell whether they were pulling apart or only arriving at a better understanding.

We crossed a limpid trout stream in a little wood, and, coming out into the open ground again, found ourselves on the edge of the cliff in full view of the sun-smitten sea. The many-murmurous voice of the ocean was in our ears, the vital breath of it upon our cheeks. Eugenia, standing on the brink with longing eyes, looked out first over the moving waters into the morning mist where the seabirds revelled, then turned to Brinkhampton brightly, and asked: 'Did you ever see anything like this in Bond Street?'

Brinkhampton sighed sentimentally, but wisely held his peace.

It was a high cliff upon which we were standing, and there was a narrow, precipitous, winding path, cut out of the chalk and very dangerous-looking, running down to the beach.

'Let us go back by the sands,' Eugenia exclaimed, our baskets being full by this time, and away she went, nimbly as a goat, I following without a thought. At the bottom we looked back and discovered Brinkhampton at one of the bends about halfway down, leaning against the cliff – I had almost said clinging to it.

'Anything the matter?' Eugenia cried.

'I'm stuck,' he answered.

'How thoughtless of me,' I exclaimed, and ran back to help him. He was pale, and clutched my hand eagerly when I offered it to him.

'You see, I have not exaggerated,' he said dejectedly.

'I've no nerve left for anything. I'm used up. It's high time I settled.'

My hand, however, and also perhaps the now familiar formula, helped to restore his confidence, and we got down together pretty creditably. I could see that Brinkhampton expected some sympathy for his giddiness, but Eugenia was throwing stones into the water unconcernedly when we rejoined her, and went on without a word as if nothing had happened. Near the house a tall, good-looking young man of distinguished appearance met us.

'There's Saxon,' Eugenia exclaimed when he came into sight, and greeted him familiarly, but did not introduce him to Brinkhampton.

I knew him of old, and asked him why he had not been to see me.

'We have had to make the most of this harvest weather,' he answered. 'But I shall be able to call soon now, I hope, if I may.'

'Yes, do come, Saxon,' Eugenia exclaimed. 'There are ever so many things I want to consult you about.'

'Who was that?' Brinkhampton asked afterwards.

'Saxon Wake, a friend of my youth,' Eugenia answered lightly. 'His people have been here as long as we have. They were Yeoman farmers, but now they own a part of what were our estates.'

'The yokel has passable manners,' Brinkhampton said patronisingly. 'I suppose he picks up a little veneer at race meetings and hunt breakfasts.'

'The yokel was a wrangler of his year,' Eugenia answered icily.

Brinkhampton said no more. He had not taken any degree himself.

VI

We had a private letter-bag at the hall, which was brought in for Eugenia to unlock every morning, and she usually distributed the letters herself. That day she took out one among others that instantly filled the room with some strong scent of which it was reeking. 'Ugh!' she exclaimed. 'After the open air, how coarse this is. Who can it be for? You,' to Brinkhampton. 'It savours of "Society" to me, but my rustic nose is unequal to the demands of such an assault. Please take it!'

Brinkhampton glanced at the superscription as she handed him the note, and his countenance expressed 'Faugh!' as clearly as a countenance can. He was about to put the note in his pocket, but changed his mind, and laid it beside his plate. It had occurred to him that he might draw suggestions of the mysterious 'fuller' life of a man from it with which to enhance his *prestige* with this little country girl.

'It is from Sylvia,' he observed.

'The burlesque actress?' Eugenia asked. 'I suppose you know numbers of people of that kind.'

He smiled complacently.

'You must find it very different being here with us,' she remarked.

'Of course it is a change,' he confessed.

'Yes,' she answered thoughtfully. 'But I wonder can you endure it, even for a change.'

'Oh, one would endure a good deal for the sake of some people,' he blundered.

I noticed that the shooting claimed less and less of his attention. He did not even make pretence of going out that day, and Eugenia herself had scarcely paid a visit, or had anyone at the house since his arrival. The young man, set in sunshine with an accompaniment of lovely, languid, autumn weather, had sufficed so far for an absorbing interest, but now, at last, as we loitered in the dining-room after lunch, she raised that question of 'What shall we do?' which usually implies the palling of an old pleasure and a desire for something new.

She was sitting on the sill of one of the windows with her feet on the deep-cushioned window seat, and as she spoke there was a sound of horse's feet spattering through the gravel below.

'Here's Saxon!' she exclaimed with animation. 'Saxon, I'm delighted to see you. We want something to do this afternoon. Come and consult.'

'Why not have out the coach, drive to Greenwood Sound, send the saddle-horses by the shortcut across the fields to wait for you there, and race the tide home round Towindard Head,' Saxon rejoined from below. 'The tide will be just right for the ride if you get off in half an hour.'

'Excellent!' Eugenia exclaimed. 'But you must come with us, Saxon. One gentleman is not enough for two ladies, and Lord Brinkhampton does not know the coast. Do ride round to the stables and order the coach and despatch Gould with the horses. Come, boot and spur, my Lord,' she called to Brinkhampton as she dragged me from the room.

'He doesn't look very gracious about it,' she said, as we ran upstairs, 'and I expect he'll take an hour to adorn himself. I suppose I shall be obliged to let him drive. Saxon won't, I know. But I do wonder what kind of a whip he is. If he can't drive, however, he shan't pretend to, for I don't believe true womanliness consists in letting a man do badly what a woman can do well. But let us hope he has forgotten to provide himself with the last thing in driving gloves. He would never use anything already out of date by a season.'

This last little sarcasm, although playfully uttered, sounded significant, but if Brinkhampton had gone down in her estimation for any reason, he rose again when it came to offering him the reins, by the frank way in which he acknowledged he was no whip, and had never been able to handle a team in his life.

Contrary to our expectation, he was waiting for us in the porch when we went down, and was amicably discussing the points of the horses with Saxon.

VII

Brinkhampton sat beside Eugenia on the front seat, Saxon and I were behind them, and at the back was Baldwin, the old family coachman, and a groom with the coach-horn. The horses, dark, glossy bays with black points, were mettlesome beasts. They danced down the drive as if unaware of the coach and its load behind them. It was a wonderful thing to see Eugenia, a slender girl, almost standing against her high seat with her feet planted firmly in front of her, controlling the four, great, prancing creatures without apparent effort. One could not help calculating what the nerve-power must be behind such ease, and the strength of the sinews that were masked by her 'ivory skin'. She never looked better than on that occasion. Her riding habit, clinging close, showed the perfection of her figure. The sun was still hot, and she wore, slightly tilted back, a low-crowned white sailor hat, the roundness of which set off the delicate oval of her cheeks. Her eyes danced in liquid light; one could trace the course of the blue veins beneath the transparent skin, and the fresh air and exertion had brought a brilliant colour to her cheeks. But for those with the inner eyes that see beneath the surface, there was more about her to attract than mere good looks and the ineffable charm of youth. There shone in her face the happy spirit that makes much of the smallest joy in life, and sees in the most obvious admiration of her friends only an evidence of their own good dispositions. There is more beauty than character as a rule in the delicate curves and lineless smoothness of a young girl's face; but still, in studying Eugenia, one felt that, for all her soft voice and gentle, courteous bearing, she was not a person to be trifled with. There are natures which may be taught but must not be dictated to, and hers was one of those.

She was essentially a modern maiden, richly endowed with all womanly attributes, whose value is further enhanced by the strength that comes of the liberty to think, and of the education out of which is made the material for thought. With such women for the mothers of men, the English-speaking races should rule the world.

As he watched her, Brinkhampton's petty disdain of Saxon the yeoman sank into the background of his consciousness. One could see his countenance expand until he looked superlatively happy as his delight in her loveliness gained upon him.

And Saxon, sitting beside me with his arms folded, thoughtfully watched her too, but there was a somewhat sad expression on his handsome face. They had been playfellows, but still he saw in Brinkhampton only what was appropriate to her station in the way of a suitor, and there was no bitterness in him. It was what he had all along prepared himself to be resigned to eventually. Brinkhampton himself was not so proudly conscious of the difference of position as Saxon was; but Brinkhampton was accustomed to consider only his own interests in regard to women, and naturally assumed that Saxon was equally inferior.

It was ten miles from Towindard Hall to Greenwood Sound, but the horses seemed to have covered the ground in no time, for it was still early in the afternoon when we halted in a shady lane between the river on our left, and a high bank on our right, dotted with clumps of fern, and crowned with trees, beneath which sheep were quietly browsing. No one would have suspected that we were near the treacherous ocean and dangerous shore. The horses, apparently only refreshed by their ten miles' scamper, pawed the ground impatiently, tossed their heads till the harness jingled, and recognising their stable companions who were already awaiting us under the trees with their saddles on, saluted them with loud neighs joyously.

'We must make tea here, there is plenty of time,' said Saxon as he clambered down.

'Oh, how delightful!' Eugenia exclaimed. 'I forgot all about tea. You always remember everything, Saxon.'

She threw down the reins.

'Come,' she said to Brinkhampton, 'come and collect sticks.'

Brinkhampton went of necessity, but he was not one of those men who readily adapts themselves to any position, and as he picked up the sticks his whole attitude was awkwardly condescending, and he evidently did not agree when Eugenia contended that it was half the fun on these expeditions to do all that kind of thing for one's self. I saw that she observed how he picked up the sticks by their driest ends, and held them away from him daintily; but her countenance remained unruffled. Stooping made Brinkhampton red in the face, and giddy, and he had to stop frequently to recover himself, and always when he did so, he looked about him haughtily, as if he were asking nature to be so good as to observe that a Peer of the Realm was picking up sticks.

We soon had a big fire blazing in the shade, and while we were waiting for the kettle to boil, we lolled about on cushions and by degrees were gained upon by the enchanting day.

'Is this Greenwood Sound?' Brinkhampton said suddenly.

'Yes,' Eugenia answered. 'And when I am here I am always overpowered with a strange feeling of remoteness. It is as if my kindred claimed me – not as if they came to me here, but as if they took me to themselves – to their own times. This is a spot which has been specially sanctified by the sins of my ancestors.'

Brinkhampton asked her if she were superstitious. 'I don't know,' she answered, in a surprised tone. 'I never thought about it.' Then she reflected a little. 'But certainly,' she added, 'no son of the house has ever succeeded.'

'Are these church lands then?' Brinkhampton asked.

'No, the tradition is older than that,' she said. 'By the way, isn't it evident they worshipped the Evil One of old? Their cursings were so effectual, while their blessings were of such small avail. But, Saxon, tell the tale. You know it best.'

'The country folks hereabouts preserve it in ballads,' he answered unaffectedly. 'They give the vague date of hundreds of years ago, when Towindard Hall was a castle owned by a miserly old earl. He was a direct ancestor of yours, as you know, and he had an only daughter whom he meant to barter for gold to the highest bidder when she was old enough to marry. She was a girl of magnificent physique, with a spirit as fine as her form and features, and moreover she was dowered, says the legend, with caution, and the gift of silence, so that when at last her father ordered her to prepare to marry a man she had hardly seen, and was not prepossessed by, she held her peace instead of raising useless objections, and waited until she should know more of him. It does not say that she ever really disliked him, but at that time a man had to have as much physical courage as he has nowadays. Have moral courage to recommend him to a girl—'

'A man must have both,' Eugenia put in decidedly.

'Well, at any rate,' Saxon pursued, 'from what your ancestress saw of Lord Willoughby, her suitor, before they were married, she shrewdly suspected that he was a coward, "Unmeet with me to wed", as the ballad says; but there was no getting out of the match, she being her father's chattel and entirely at his disposal. She determined, however, that before she settled down for life with the man, she would test his courage to see who should be master. So, she stipulated that on their wedding day he should let her drive him from Greenwood Sound (where we are now), to Willoughby Chase (his place), by Towindard Head. He refused her nothing, the ballad says:

The day broke cloudy, the wind was high,
The storm clouds fought in a murky sky,
The wild waves whitened the sands with scud,

The sunset brightened the sky with blood.
O wild! O wild! Ah, well-a-day!
Does the bridegroom note that the bride is gay!
The chariot stood at the castle door,
The hinds were holding the horses four,
The storm wind tosses the horses' manes,
The bride has gathered the fluttering reins.
O wild! O wild! Ah, well-a-day!
Does the bridegroom note that the bride is gay!
From Greenwood Sound to Willoughby Chase,
By Towindard Head in a chariot race,
Four horses racing the rising tide,
A white-faced bridegroom, a desp'rate bride.
O wild! O wild! Ah, well-a-day!
For the gale blows fierce in Towindard Bay.
"Now, good, my lord, though art pledged to race,
From Greenwood Sound to Willoughby Chase,
To race the tide round Towindard Head,
But methinks thou art frighted, my lord," she said.
O wild! O wild! Ah, well-a-day!
"Crouch down on your knees at my feet and pray."
At Willoughby Chase there was dole that night,
The bride has arrived all scared and white,
And the four black steeds have reached the shore,
But the bridegroom cometh again no more.
O wild! O wild! Ah, well-a-day!
Lord Willoughby sleeps in Towindard Bay.'

'She had drowned him then,' Brinkhampton exclaimed.

'So it was eventually supposed,' Eugenia answered easily. 'She was not suspected of having done so at first, however,' she pursued. 'It was believed to have been an accident, and so it may have been, for my greatest great-grandmother was evidently one of those people of strongly marked character and independent habits, around whose name all kinds of stories collect by degrees, until at last there are so many that they must have done something notable on every day of their lives in order to accomplish such an amount. By Lord Willoughby's death she became mistress of Willoughby Chase, and as she inherited Towindard also, she was in a powerful position for the times. She married again and became my ancestress, but of her second husband, my ancestor, nothing is known except that there was such a person. He was apparently one of those people who don't count.'

'And is that all?' said Brinkhampton.

'No,' Eugenia answered. 'The most important part is yet to come. According to the story, everything succeeded with my remarkable ancestress during her life, but on her deathbed she was seen to be in sore distress of mind, and at last she sent for a priest, but exactly what she confessed to him was never revealed, only it was observed that, when he left her, his eyes were wild and his cheeks were pale. And it is known that he had laid a curse on one daughter of the family in every generation. A celibate priest naturally did not understand women; he thought property and power would be a bane to us, so he condemned one of us to inherit the estates always, until such time as we should discover how to remove the curse!'

'And you have not done so yet?' Brinkhampton said.

'Nobody has ever tried that I know of,' Eugenia answered naïvely. 'It's rather hard on the boys, but if it had not been for the curse, there probably would not have been any property by this time.'

'Churchman's justice is peculiar,' I interjected. 'I can't see upon what principle the unoffending innocents were condemned to death.'

'But there was some sense in the penance that the priest prescribed for your ancestress,' Saxon pursued. 'He condemned her to drive her wild black horses against the rising tide with her cowering bridegroom crouching at her feet forever, or until such time as her troubled spirit should be released by one of her descendants:

> And so for evermore
> Along the shore
> She hears the swift, wild surges roar,
> For evermore she urges
> Hot, headstrong steeds to brave the roaring surges.
> With tightened traces
> Full speed she races—
> And those who ride
> Shall hear their thund'ring rush against the rising tide.'

'But has anyone ever heard them?' Brinkhampton objected.

'We all have,' I answered, whereupon he looked mystified, because he did not consider me superstitious – nor was he.

This broke the spell. The tea was ready, and brought us back incontinently to the most skeptical mood of our own day.

'But what exactly are we going to do?' Brinkhampton asked.

'Oh, just race the tide round Towindard Head,' Eugenia answered casually. 'If we are there first we shall get round easily and find ourselves near home, but if the sea is before us, it complicates matters. What about the weather, Baldwin? Here in the hollow it seems to be perfectly stagnant.'

The old man looked up at the sky, and then out over the river through the gap in the greenery, which formed a frame for the shining, sluggish water.

'There'll be no sea on today, Missie,' he answered deliberately.

'You're coming with us?' said Eugenia.

'Ah'm certainly comin' wi' you, Missie,' he answered decidedly.

The servants had had their tea by this time, and were preparing to take back the coach. We mounted our horses.

'I suppose you can calculate the state of the tide pretty accurately,' Brinkhampton remarked as he settled Eugenia in her saddle. I might have been mistaken, but I thought I detected a shade of anxiety in his voice.

'No, that is the difficulty,' Eugenia replied. 'The weather affects it. Sometimes it is a rushing racehorse, white-crested and impetuous, and sometimes it is a crawling snake, equally swift, you know, but insidious. You are caught before you suspect there is danger.'

'I suppose you love the sea,' he rejoined, in a tone which affected to be as casual as her own.

'Yes,' she answered. 'And I also loathe it. I look upon it as a treacherous enemy to be outwitted, and dote upon its changeful beauty all the same.'

We were off now, down the winding lane. The green bank was behind us, grey sand dunes were on either side, ahead was the desolate wide waste of shore, and far out, under a low and leaden sky, little, bright, sapphire wavelets, scarcely flecked with foam. Some suggestions of boundless space are more elevating than the mountains. Away to our right, the flat shore shot up suddenly into precipitous cliffs, and these, curving out with a fine sweep seawards, resulted abruptly in the towering promontory that was our object to ride round. But between us and it were miles of desolation.

Our horses were now being tried by the ruts of the heavy cart track which formed the only road across the sand dunes.

'This is slow going,' said Eugenia. 'But I warn you, they will pull like mad the moment we are on firm sand, so sit tight.'

The warning was not unnecessary. A few more struggles, then suddenly their feet were free of the heaviness, and feeling the resistance of the firm sand, they plunged about excitedly, and then set off in a frantic gallop – the hoofs beat rhythmically.

We were well away now, with the sea on our left, the land on our right, and on in front, looming gigantic through the haze, Towindard Head.

'Onward and northward fierce and fleet,
As if life and death were in it!
Tis a glorious race, a race against time,
A thousand to one we win it.'

The sea-sweet air was wildly exhilarating. Even the horses seemed seized upon by the gladness there was in rapid motion and in windswept spaces. Every face was eager now. I felt I should shout aloud upon the slightest provocation.

Our gallop was checked by a sudden wild commotion. I was aware of old Baldwin shouting something, of Saxon spurring on ahead of me, of Brinkhampton's horse floundering, of a scared look on his face, of Eugenia catching his reins, giving her own horse its head, and swinging her heavy whip with sounding slashes. The horses responded gallantly, plunging and straining. I don't know if we all shouted encouragement, but it seemed only an instant till the incident was over, and we were off again, tearing along in a body, having swerved inland considerably.

When the pace relaxed, Brinkhampton wiped his forehead. 'What was it?' he asked.

'The outer edge of the quicksand,' Eugenia answered. 'It shifts. The last time it was here, where we are now, and I thought we were giving it a wide berth today. Forgive me for touching your reins. There was such a racket, I despaired of making you hear, and you were pulling right into it. Look at the horses, poor brutes, how terrified they are. It would be humane to pull them up for a breathing space—' she looked on ahead, then added significantly, '*if there were time.*'

We had been keeping a middle course between the sea and shore, but now we began to bear down towards the water. The horses glanced suspiciously this way and that, ready to shy or swerve at the least occasion. They kept their ears pricked too, or laid them back in a nervous way, and were foaming at their mouths; every now and then they broke out of the steady canter at which we were endeavouring to keep them in order to save them for a big spurt, if necessary, towards the end of the race. But in the midst of these efforts, and without the slightest warning, my horse made an awkward stumble, which sent me gracefully circling from my saddle to a safer seat on the sand. Old Baldwin, seeing what was coming, had roared 'Look out!' but not in time to save me.

Brinkhampton, being on in front, did not see what had happened, and his shattered nerves, shaken already by horror of the quicksand, betrayed him. The moment he heard the shout, without waiting to see what was wrong, he let his horse go, and galloped on some distance, leaving us to our fate.

''Is Ludship 'e doan't like yer wickstands an' yer ghosteses,' old Baldwin chuckled as he picked me up.

But Brinkhampton had discovered his mistake by this time, and was cantering back to us with a deprecating look on his face, like that of a diffident schoolboy who finds he has done the wrong thing and is covered with confusion. The expression suited him, and, being a splendid horseman, he looked so handsome as he approached Eugenia that I thought with a qualm: 'She will pity him.'

'My horse is very nervous,' he said apologetically.

She glanced down at the horse's feet, and then looked straight before her without a word, her air of calm indifference being exactly the same as she had worn when Brinkhampton and I joined her after he had been stuck on the cliff and found her watching the stones she was throwing make ducks and drakes on the water. On this occasion her demeanour so disconcerted Brinkhampton that he lost his head, and contradicted himself as soon as he had spoken.

'I thought it was a signal to double,' he said to me.

'No, it was not a signal,' I answered, 'but a stone, which my horse apparently mistook for a bit of seaweed.' We had moved on again, and were close to the water's edge by this time. The monstrous sea, oily and waveless, crawled up in great, irregular curves over the shining sand. The horses kept their eyes fixed on the incoming stream in frightened anticipation, and leaned away from it, as if ready to swerve if the horrid thing should touch them. Now and then, so insidious and imperceptible was its oncoming, we found ourselves surrounded, and our startled steeds strained away for the shore, prancing and splashing till they churned the flint-coloured shallows white with foam. A few more minutes would bring us abreast of the great overhanging cliffs, and the space between the sea and shore was narrowing always, so that presently we should be forced up under them. A certain gravity had settled upon us, there was a look of expectation on our faces, and we pulled up abreast of each other involuntarily, Baldwin and all.

'I confess I always feel awed,' I said, with an uneasy little cough, but Eugenia did not appear to hear me. She was sitting straight, with her head held high, and her eyes wide open, listening intently.

'Why awed?' Brinkhampton asked.

'The ghosts, my Lud,' old Baldwin ejaculated.

Brinkhampton looked about him with a superior smile, and certainly anything more unlike a suitable setting as a preparation for ghosts than this slumberous autumn afternoon could not have been arranged, but the inappropriate is often as astounding as the unexpected.

And now, suddenly, in the distance, coming apparently from under the cliffs, there arose a dull, muffled, thudding sound. The horses noticed it as soon as we did, and pricked their ears enquiringly. They had been going at an easy canter, but in order to gratify their curiosity they relaxed their pace, and instantly the sound ceased. The sudden silence startled them as a noise might have done, and with one accord they bounded forward, Brinkhampton being nearly unseated by the unexpected move, and instantly the thudding recommenced, drew nearer, and swelled into the unmistakable throb of galloping hoofs on sand. The horses broke into a frantic gallop, and Brinkhampton, rising to it, turned his head and looked back with straining eyes, first over one shoulder and then over the other; but there was nothing to be seen even when the sound was just upon us, deafening us. It came with a rush, touching us as it were, and that instant it was over. The horses stared right and left, at the same time slackening their pace, and we realised a strange blank, as of an empty space in that region of consciousness upon which the thundering hoofs had sounded.

Brinkhampton was the first to speak after gazing up at the tall cliffs critically: 'I suppose it is an echo,' he said, looking hard at us each in turn, as if he expected us to deny it. 'And the legend was probably invented to account for the echo,' he added.

'But the echo does not account for the failure of male heirs in my family,' Eugenia objected drily.

From this point on, however, there was no time for talk.

'If we're to get round Towindard 'ead we mun ride, Missie,' old Baldwin decided.

'And if we don't get round?' Brinkhampton asked.

'We must climb the cliff or take our chance with the horses,' Eugenia answered quietly. 'Baldwin, we lead,' she said, and the old man rode on with her on the offside, beaming. Eugenia on the alert, with flushed cheeks and sparkling eyes, her excitement well-contained beneath a steady, calm exterior, was lovely to behold in her youth and strength as she passed on in front and set the pace. It was racing speed now, going against the tide full-tilt. We could measure the rate at which we were going by the lumbering look of the seabird's flight above us.

"Tis a glorious race, a race against time. A thousand to one we win it!'

The keen salt air through which we were rushing, meeting us full in the face, had freshened us at first, but now, all at once, I became aware of a change in it, from dry to damp. I was behind Eugenia, but could see by her attitude that she was peering into the distance intently, and she raised her heavy whip and held it suspended over her horse's flank.

Baldwin was standing up in his stirrups and keeping his sharp old eyes about him. 'Stick to the sea, Missie,' he commanded in his hoarse voice. 'Stick to the sea for your life.'

We met the mist and plunged into it. There was no fancy work about the horses' paces now. They had buckled to in sober earnest, with ears laid back and heads stretched out, and anxious eyes that no longer glanced askance at the treacherous water, but strained on into the mist. It was the snake-sea today, swift but deceptive. The fog had gained on the headland by this time; the nearer we approached the less we saw of it.

'For your life, Missie, for your life,' old Baldwin kept muttering mechanically, and the hoarse growl mingled with the mighty murmur of the ocean appropriately.

We were well-mounted, but some of it was heavy going, and now the horses began to flag perceptibly. Eugenia swung her whip round her head and brought it down relentlessly. The horse responded with a bound, and the others, animated by the effort, followed his example.

'Surely that is the head?' Eugenia cried. We looked up simultaneously. Something certainly loomed black above us.

'Stick to the sea, Missie, stick to the sea side for your life,' old Baldwin roared. There were ridges of rock all about here under the cliffs that would have cost us many precious minutes had we come upon them.

Eugenia went boldly on, but we were late. Splash – helter-skelter – the horses were scattering the shallow water now and inclined to baulk; but down came that relentless whip again, right and left, we following the example, and once more the mettlesome brutes responded gallantly. And now there was less helter-skelter and less splash. The leaders were up to their knees. Were we silent? Were we shouting? That last wave washed up to our girths. That last wave was a seventh wave. Count six more slowly. Supposing they are taken off their feet by the next, could they swim with us? Brinkhampton's horse staggered on the slippery bottom, which was stony here, mine slipped too – what a sickening sensation! Now he went down, and the water came up cold about me.

Silence had settled upon us – the panting silence of suspense. It was touch and go whether the horses would be washed away or not. All at once, however, I noticed a change in the tenseness of Eugenia's attitude. Surely she is bearing away to the right – she is out of the water – we are following – we are splashing through shallows again – are ceasing to splash. The horses found firm footing and started away of their own accord for a final spurt of relief. We were out of the fog, and there was the coach waiting for us. Eugenia pulled up, threw her reins on her horse's neck, dismounted, and stood, smiling and satisfied, but wet through.

'We shall catch our death of cold if we have far to go in these clothes,' Brinkhampton exclaimed, impatient of this discomfort.

'Pooh! Salt water will do you no harm,' Eugenia rejoined.

'That was a near un, Missie,' old Baldwin observed. 'Ah thowt it were all oop wi' us twicest.'

'It was one of our best, I think,' Eugenia answered. 'And I was agreeably surprised, for I was afraid it was going to be tame.' She was all animation, and when we had taken our seats on the coach in the same order as before, she addressed

Brinkhampton in the bantering tone they used to each other as a rule: 'Now tell me,' she said. 'After this, do you still pretend to offer me in exchange the vitiated air of your great, wicked city, and the modest pleasure of a ride in the Bow, or of being driven on a coach by way of squalid Hammersmith and pretentious Chiswick to eat without appetite at a tawdry hotel in Richmond?'

VIII

The next morning, I was writing in my room upstairs with the windows wide open when I suddenly became aware of an altercation between Eugenia and Brinkhampton on the lawn below.

They went off together, however, with every evidence of cordial agreement between them; so much so, indeed, that I sat on the windowsill long after they had crossed the lawn and disappeared among the trees, once more weighing the probabilities, and wondering if she would accept him.

When they returned together to lunch, I could see that something had happened, but as they were both flushed and both looked discomfited, I fancied there had only been a rather more serious dispute than usual.

Directly when lunch was over, however, Brinkhampton announced that he was going to order his man to pack.

'Are you off then?' I asked.

'Yes, I'm off,' he answered doggedly.

'Now why should you go?' Eugenia exclaimed.

'I can only stay here on one condition,' he said with severity.

'Well, that is the only condition on which I can't ask you to stay,' she answered instantly. 'But I do think you are stupid to give up your shooting on that account.'

'You don't appreciate my feelings,' he said with a hurt air.

'I hope I do,' she answered. She rose from the table as she spoke, brushed a crumb from the front of her dress and quietly left the room.

Then Brinkhampton looked hard and inquiringly at me. 'I can't think you have prejudiced her against me,' he said.

'I should hope not,' was my dry response.

'But have you said anything about me to her?'

'As much as I have said about her to you?'

'Next to nothing, that is – then how does she know?'

'If she does know anything about you, she must have arrived at it by some process of induction,' I answered, not able to imagine what she could know.

'Well, I think you might have warned me,' he exclaimed, and began to pace the room with agitated steps.

'I am afraid I have been to blame,' I retorted ironically. 'It would doubtless have pleased you better if I had told you all I know about her opinions and character while carefully concealing from her all that I know about yours.'

'A girl has no business to have opinions of any kind, she should adopt her husband's when she marries,' Brinkhampton ejaculated. 'Nothing but mischief comes of women thinking for themselves. She would have accepted me but for her opinions.' He reflected a little upon this, frowning portentously, and then broke out again: 'I've been regularly taken in! I gave her the credit of being a nice, little, English, country girl, quite uninformed, and here I find her old in ideas already, and, worst of all, advanced. She didn't tell me coarsely in so many words to my face that I'm not good enough for her, but, by Jove! That is what she meant. She says she always thinks of me as a sort of man out of a novel by Ouida. What on earth have you all been doing to let her read such books?'

'It was an old uncle of hers, an ex-guardsman of your own corps, by the way,' I rejoined, 'who first introduced her to that kind of literature. He used to give Eugenia Ouida's books as they came out, with the emphatic comment, 'She shows 'em up! She shows 'em up!' and Eugenia, after careful study of them, has drawn her own conclusions.'

He pondered upon this also for a little, and then resumed: 'By Jove! I was astounded! What do you think she said to me, right out? "I have no taste for nursing," she said. "And you are so delicate." "Delicate!" I exclaimed in astonishment. "Well, you require to begin your day on wine, you know," she said. "I don't require it, I take it because I like it," I said. "Oh, then you are self-indulgent," she rejoined, as quick as thought. "And if you are so much so now, the weakness will grow upon you to a quite dangerous extent by-and-by, and gout and bad temper will be the order of the day." She said it lightly, but by Jove! She meant it.'

'Then she has rejected you?'

'Emphatically! Yet she doesn't see why I shouldn't stay and finish the shooting!'

'And why not, if it amuses her to have you here?'

He looked at me in tragic disgust. 'Would you have me stay here simply for her amusement?' he thundered.

'Certainly,' I said. 'It is merely a turning of the tables. You came here simply for your own benefit, and in return the least you can do is to stay if it pleases her to ask you.'

'You have a nice consideration, both of you, for my feelings!' he exclaimed.

'Your what, Brinkhampton?' I asked, laughing.

He stood before me a moment, trying to annihilate me with a look, and then stalked straight out of the room.

IX

'So you have rejected him,' I said when next I saw Eugenia.

She was taken aback at first.

'So he has told you,' she ejaculated. 'Well, I wonder if he thought I should be mean enough to betray him! I asked him to stay on simply because I didn't want you to suspect that I had had to humiliate him by refusing him. It is hateful to hurt people's feelings. Besides, as a guest, I like him, and further, it is good for that kind of man to be with ladies.'

'Then you are by way of elevating his tastes if possible?'

'Oh, by all means. My principle is to do anything honourable for that kind of man except marry him.'

I was silent, and she reflected for a little: 'He said I did not appreciate his feelings, but indeed I think I do – debts, difficulties, debilitated nerves, and everything else that went to make up his motive for marrying me. Why, when I engage a servant, he has to have a character.'

'Nevertheless, I think he cares for you in his own way. He told me he had found his ideal in you.'

'Very likely,' she answered. 'But before one can feel flattered by such an assertion, it is necessary to know what his ideal is – a nice, quiet, little thing, I fancy, with lots of money, and no inconvenient intellectual capacity.'

I could not help smiling; she had gauged him so exactly.

'But he is not my ideal at all,' she pursued. 'I want Sir Galahad, and society provides me with Gawain, or Lancelot at the best, when all my longing is for "the blameless king".'

'I wonder where you will find your ideal?'

'In Saxon Wake,' she answered instantly. 'Bit by bit his family have been developing every quality in which my own was deficient. For hundreds of years the two have been living here side by side, ours slowly deteriorating, losing by degrees much of what they possessed; his, by their virtues, gradually acquiring what we lost. Compare Saxon's father with Uncle Paul, for instance! And Saxon's career with Lord Brinkhampton's! Not to mention their respective abilities. Give me him for a husband!'

'Whom?' said Saxon himself, coming round the corner.

'You,' she blurted out, turning crimson. 'Why don't you care for me, Saxon?' she went on desperately – on the in-for-a-penny-in-for-a-pound principle, I suppose. 'Why won't you ask me to marry you? But I know. You will leave me lonely and miserable for all my life just because I am richer than you are.' She wrung her hands as she spoke, and the young man, who had stopped short, flushed and turned pale, looking from her to me in confusion.

'I hope he has more sense,' I cried, flinging the words at him as I fled.

X

When I returned to the house, there was a carriage at the door, and I found Brinkhampton ready to depart.

'I suppose there is really no chance for me?' he said, in the dubious tone of one who is still venturing to hope.

'No, none,' I answered. 'Eugenia has just proposed to Saxon Wake, and I left her trying to persuade him to accept her. It seems that he has some scruples on account of the difference of wealth and position.'

'Good Lord!' Brinkhampton ejaculated, quite forgetting himself. 'If this is your modern maiden, then give me a good, old-fashioned, womanly woman who knows nothing and cares less so long as you put her in a good position and let her have lots of money. But,' he looked hard at me, 'you are joking, surely.'

'No, I am not,' I said.

'And you approve. I can see you do.'

'Yes, I do,' I answered. 'Under the circumstances.'

Brinkhampton could conceive of nothing more eligible for a husband than a man of good manners with a fine position. He stood for some seconds looking down at his boots after I had spoken, as if considering, but nothing came of it except another withering glance, the last token with which he favoured me – poor fellow, as Eugenia said.

We were standing beside a table in the hall on which his covert coat lay, and now he picked it up, put on his hat, took one last look round, as if bidding farewell to the comfortable possessions he had been so confident of making his own, then walked straight out, got into the carriage without another word, and was driven away.

And now I hear he says the most unpleasant things about myself and Mrs Saxon Wake, but happily Eugenia's maternal duties are too all-engrossing to allow her to trouble herself over idle gossip from that section of society, which, as her Uncle Paul maintains, 'Ouida shows up.'

Knowing the curious fatality which had befallen the sons of her family ever since that legendary curse was pronounced upon them, I had a horrid qualm one day as I sat watching her playing with her baby boy.

'He looks strong enough,' slipped from me inadvertently.

Eugenia smiled.

'You are thinking about the curse,' she said. 'I have thought a great deal about it myself since this young gentleman arrived, and I believe I see the mistake we women have all made in the choice of our husbands. It is a universal mistake. We admire mere animal courage in a man, which is only one form of courage, instead of requiring moral courage, which includes every other kind – until I came. But I chose my husband for his moral qualities.'

'Then perhaps you have.'

'I am sure I have,' she concluded. 'I have removed the curse unawares.'

Alice Milligan

Alice Milligan was born in Co. Tyrone in 1865 and attended school at the Methodist College in Belfast, intent on becoming a teacher. In 1888 she and her father wrote *Glimpses of Erin*, a political travelogue of the North of Ireland. This was the beginning of her lifelong career as a writer of poetry, plays, journalism, and the novel *A Royal Democrat*. As a passionate nationalist, she founded and edited two nationalist publications with her friend, Ethna Carbery: *The Northern Patriot* and *The Shan Van Vocht*, and first published the early political writing of James Connolly. Milligan died in Omagh in 1953.

The Harp that Once—!
A Story of Connaught after Humbert

Her Ladyship the Dowager said they were loyal and gallant gentlemen who had served their king, and that they must be entertained in noble fashion and have the best that the kitchen and cellar could afford. Her pretty granddaughter, Mabel, when she heard this news from Mrs Kelly, her old nurse, stamped her foot and said she would not sit to dinner with a party of *butchers*. So she called the officers of a company of Hussars who had come to the castle gate, and, asking leave to water the horses, had been bid to stay and dine – the men in the courtyard, the officers with her Dowager Ladyship, and Mabel.

'What do you say, Farmer?' said the captain to the lieutenant next in command when the invitation was conveyed to him. 'Our duty is urgent in the town. There is no time to be lost. And yet – and yet – we must dine somewhere. The men and horses must feed somewhere – as well in the castle here as in some wretched village hostelry where the people will look as if they would like to poison us.'

'We will lose no time by going up to the castle, no more than the time occupied in riding up the avenue,' said Lieutenant Farmer, who read from his captain's face that he desired to stay. Her Ladyship's invitation was accepted. Therefore, the troopers had dismounted in the courtyard, attended to their horses and then to their own requirements. The captain and two lieutenants clinked their spurs in the drawing-room, talking courteously to the Dowager, but keeping all the time their eyes on the door, for rumour had noised abroad that her Ladyship's granddaughter was the belle of the county.

The said belle, meantime, as you have heard, stamped her pretty foot and vowed she would not dine with them.

'Oh, Miss Mabel,' said Mrs Kelly, bursting into tears. 'Oh, darling, dear; is it down to the village beyant the red-coated scoundrels are goin'?'

Mabel nodded. Mrs Kelly threw up her arms and screamed, 'He's lost then for certain! He's lost, Alannah!'

'Who is lost, Nursey dear?' And the young girl put her arms round the sobbing woman's neck. Softly, the latter whispered, 'Denis. My one boy. Him that was your little foster brother, but me own child.'

'But Denis is in America,' said Mabel in bewilderment.

'He came back, dear; he came back – he's in the village now.'

'But then, Nursey, you should be glad.'

'Glad! Oh, Alannah, can't ye see what I'm manin'? He came back *with the French*.'

'With the French?' said Mabel. 'Oh, I see, I see. He has been fighting all these weeks. That's why you've been so down-looking and me not to know! Nursey, you might have told me.'

'And now,' said the poor woman. 'The soldiers are going down to make a search. There will be some that know him, for he was seen in Killala the very day he landed. His name's on a list, and there's those who will swear to him. Oh, my fine boy, my one boy, that he should be lost from me!'

'Send him word,' whispered Mabel. 'Go yourself, Nursey.'

'There is no time. The captain has given the men word to be ready and mounted on the stroke of eight. The cook has the dinner ordered for seven on the stroke. There's but an hour, and it's two hours' walkin' for my slow feet. There's no other I can trust.'

'I would go – I could ride – but there's no one to saddle my horse. The courtyard is full of troopers or I would do it myself.' Mabel puckered her brows.

'My own bird, as if I would let you! Oh, not even to have his life.'

'Then, Nursey,' she said, almost laughing, 'see if I don't keep them from starting at the stroke of eight! Get ready and slip off. Walk as fast as your poor, dear, old feet can carry you. Trust to God and trust to me.'

So, after all, her Ladyship's lovely granddaughter did dine with the 'party of butchers', and made herself particularly agreeable to one and all of them, but perhaps most particularly to the captain. Let me explain that the reason why Mabel had not been inclined to honour them with her presence was that her heart had gone with the people in the great struggle that was now dying down in her native Connaught. She had been frightened, it is true, when she heard the French were coming and the British flying before them, but frightened and all as she was, she wanted them to win. By her mother's side she came from an old, Gaelic, noble house that had fought for Ireland at Athlone, Limerick, and Aughrim. There was rebel blood in her veins, and it had been warmed to flame in this year '98 by the stories she heard of the people's sufferings. Her old nurse had poured such tales into sympathetic ears. Then, once in Dublin, she had seen Lord Edward and his lovely little French wife. She treasured the memory and wept hot tears when she heard of his death and poor Pamela's sorrows.

It was with a feeling of ill-conceived antipathy that she first greeted the captain. He was quite a distinguished person – had done *good service* against the rebels. Mabel knew what *that* meant; knew, too, what errand he was bound on that very night, and made up her mind to foil him by a woman's wit.

Ere they passed from the drawing-room to the dinner, she smiled very archly and asked if he cared for music. 'Tis but poor entertainment we can offer to a gentleman who has been in London and heard all the opera singers, but if you are not too hurried, I would be pleased to have your judgement on some of our old Connaught airs.'

What could a mortal man say in answer to this? What especially could a man say who had but his soldier's pay to live on, and who knew that the lovely girl who thus graciously addressed him was heiress, in default of a male heir, to broad lands in Connaught, to a castle, to family portraits, heirlooms, silver, jewels – jewels that were now flashing on a round white neck and snowy arms. Could he deny himself the pleasure of seeing those white arms stray along the harp strings, those lovely lips chanting exquisite music? Captain Warren was but a mortal man, and in spite of his thirst for military glory, could deny himself none of those things. Dinner concluded promptly before eight. 'We have some minutes to spare, your Ladyship,' said he to the Dowager. 'Quite ten minutes, I see, and since your charming granddaughter has deigned to promise us some music, I will just send orders to the men, and for ten minutes we can indulge ourselves.' He said this for the benefit of the lieutenant, to whom he would not for the world have shown himself a lax disciplinarian, but when he talked of ten minutes he had not reckoned on the time a harp takes in tuning. Mabel seemed a long time about it, and he dared not look at his watch. Perhaps he was delaying her, for he kept quite close to the instrument, feigning great curiosity to see how it was done, and Mabel graciously chatted a good deal to him during the process. At last she swept her fingers over the chords, pronounced all ready and threw back her head, showing a lovely profile and dazzling white neck, with bewildering brown curls dancing around her ears and forehead. The white arms swept from the strings a weird, sweet melody. The lieutenant stood spellbound. The captain was enchanted. He had lost all thought of fleeting time before six bars had been played, and then, suddenly, cr-r-r-ack went something.

The captain jumped as he never had when bullets whizzed past him.

'A string gone! How provoking!' said Mabel. And yet she smiled. There was a roguish dimple in either rosy cheek. She had screwed that string so tight. 'You are not in such a hurry, Captain Warren. You must let me mend it.'

The fixing of a string was an even more tedious process than the tuning. The captain had vowed a little while before that he thought the harp the most delightful instrument in creation. He did not think so now. It was nearly ten minutes before Mabel had all ready, and then 'The Coolin' was only beginning. It seemed that it would never end. Mabel played and played and played, and all the time she smiled to herself triumphantly. The captain threw discretion to the winds and tried to enjoy himself. All the while he had an uneasy feeling that it was not a very wise thing to ride within a few miles of a place that you wanted to make a sudden raid on and stop at that distance, leaving time for the news of your coming to be there before you.

At last the strains died away. Mabel rose; the captain too. Rapturously, he thanked her. The strains of that enchanting melody would haunt his ears till death. He had to tear himself away. Duty must be done.

Mabel curtsied, but did not give him her hand as he had presumed to hope she would. There was mockery in her smile. Bowing low to her and kissing the Dowager's hand, he passed from the room.

'I'll be hanged,' said one of the officers to the other, 'if that little lady was not tricking the captain. There was mischief in her eye. If she were not the granddaughter of her very royal Ladyship, I would say she had delayed us on purpose. It will be a bad thing if any of those fellows get off.'

93

The troop rode into the night. They rode quickly. Halfway to the turn a woman stood into the ditch to let them pass. The captain called halt. No loyally disposed person should be out at that hour of night. He shouted at her to come down to his side, then, bending from his horse, peered into her face. 'Who are you? What's your business?'

'I am from the castle, sir. Your men saw me in the hall this evening when they arrived.'

A trooper here was called forward and verified her statement.

'Name,' said the captain curtly. 'And your business!'

'Business for Miss Mabel, sir! I am her Ladyship's nurse, Nancy Kelly.'

'Hmm,' said the captain. 'Ride on, men.' And to the lieutenant he added, 'I fear the pass is sold.'

In the village that night they found not one of the rebels whose hiding places informers had told them of. None of the arms they expected. No documents. Nothing! Nancy Kelly knew why. So did Mabel.

Whilst the Hussars raged through the village, up in the castle Nursey sat with her arm around her darling young lady. 'I saw my Denis,' she said. 'He is gone in safety. Please God he will get to Galway, then out to America. How did you work it, my dove?'

Mabel laughed. 'I tuned my harp; I tuned it *very* slowly. I broke a string; I strung a new one. Then I played 'The Coolin'. I played it over and over again. He can never forget it while he lives – that horrid captain. And oh, Nursey, he will never forget me either. I was never so sweet to anyone in my life.'

Rising, she surveyed herself in the mirror.

'I think I looked well tonight, and what with my dimples and my diamonds I made an impression. I actually played the coquette. It was very, very naughty, but then, Nursey dear, it was to save your Denis!'

Ethna Carbery

Ethna Carbery was born in 1866 in Co. Antrim as Anna Johnston, and was an actress, journalist, poet, and author. She co-founded two Nationalist magazines – *The Northern Patriot* and *The Shan Van Vocht* – with Alice Milligan. Her works include *The Four Winds of Eirinn, In the Celtic Past* and a short story collection, *The Passionate Hearts*.

The Coming of Maire Ban

(All Souls' Night)

Dermot Lally swept up the hearth after dusk had fallen and set his dead wife's chair in its cold place by the fire. 'She will be glad to see it there when she comes,' he thought. 'She always liked that warm corner, poor Maire.' He sighed heavily as he looked round the lonely kitchen, and his eyes fell upon a wicker cradle perched on top of a high chest that almost touched the rafters, where it rocked gently backwards and forwards when the quick, sharp gusts of wind ruffled the thatch.

'The child too – God help us – it never had breath – it cannot come with her. I hardly saw its little face that day, for how could I look at it with my Maire drifting from me, and my arms that are strong enough for other work,' he threw them out in a stress of bitter impotence, 'too weak to hold her back? My darling, 'tis the black world surely since you went away and left me here behind in sorrow.'

He bent to pile more turf on the fire, stopping once or twice to listen to the clamour of the storm outside. Then he crossed himself affrightedly and crouched down on the hearth, a desolate figure, with his back leaning against the whitewashed wall and his feet gathered under him. The light fell full on his face, whose strong youth gleamed strangely through the intensity of its agony. And, as he cowered there, keeping watch on All Souls' Night for his year-dead wife, Dermot Lally seemed to see the shine of her eyes in the leaping flames, and his heart forgot its pain for a moment while it went wandering back to the joy-time of the past, before he learned in his hour of trial that even Love itself cannot prevail against Death.

How curiously clear those days rose out of the depths of memory – days when Maire, his little playmate, was his all in all; his companion when he went forth to heard the sheep upon the hillside; his patient follower down the rugged lanes when blackberry picking was at its height and her small, swift feet went after him in his track over the thorns and jagged stones, sometimes bleeding too – though that was borne uncomplainingly in her contentedness at being his chosen comrade. How they had huddled together from the rain, wrapped in her plaid shawl, under the thick thorn hedge, safe and warm, cheek to cheek, as happy as a pair of vagrants that the summer shower could kiss; and when the sun shone out again in glory, what a burst of melody trilled right above their heads from the wet branches, and underneath from the stone ditch as wren and thrush and blackbird flew forth, singing. He was so pert, that gay blackbird, with his twinkling, round, sharp eyes, whistling loudly and triumphantly to drown the love song of the speckled thrush, who was never aggressive, nor jealous, but always and only sweet, sweet, sweet. And the tiny wren, Maire used to call it the nan-bird, sat preening its glossy feathers demurely at the edge of its little hole, giving a dainty chirrup now and then, like a faint soprano in the choir of songsters.

Ah! Dear God, how short is happiness! He remembered when the neighbours said that Connor Moran had won her heart. Connor, his friend, his boyhood friend. But it was false, for Connor had gone across the seas to push his fortune, suddenly, no doubt, and then pale Maire Ban gave her word to Dermot. She *was* happy, she said, when he questioned her wistfully, as the months went round and the smiles lit her face but seldom – perfectly happy; how could she be otherwise with such a good, kind fellow to take care of her, and soon, perhaps, when the baby came, she would grow quite strong again. But, alas! Mother and son went out of life together, and slept under the bleak November sky in Kilbride churchyard.

He had but one consolation during the lonely year that followed – the hope that her spirit might be allowed to revisit her home on All Souls' Night. For this he prayed unceasingly, and now that the moment was at hand, the fear that grips one's heart at the thought of things unearthly, even though the spirit should be that of one beloved and passionately mourned, came over him until he cried aloud in utter dread. Hush! Was that a footstep on the cassey outside? He rose to his feet unsteadily and turned his startled eyes towards the window. Saints above! Was that a white face pressed against the pane? The latch rattled, and a quick, impatient knock sounded on the door. Here was no ghostly visitant, surely. He sprang forward to unbolt it, and a gust of storm and rain swept in behind the man who entered. Dermot started back.

'Connor! Good God!'

'Aye. Connor, true enough,' said the newcomer. 'Connor, as rich on the day we parted, come back to the old place. Have you no welcome for me, Dermot?'

'Welcome? O, lad, yes, from my very heart. 'Tis gladder than I can say to have you home again. But where are you coming from this wild night? Have you been to see the old people yet?'

'No, not yet. I'd fancy to look in on you first, so I peeped through the window. I didn't mean to disturb you, only just to take one look, but you caught me. Are you alone?' His voice faltered strangely, and his eyes turned towards the door that led into the sleeping room beyond.

'Alone? Yes,' said Dermot quietly. 'Alone since this night twelve months.'

'Maire, your wife—' Connor breathed as if he had been running hard.

'Is under the sod in Kilbride.'

The two men looked into each other's eyes for a silent space. Then Connor staggered, and would have fallen but that Dermot's strong arm went around him and led him to a chair.

'I'm weak with the travel,' he murmured apologetically. 'That and the wet. And it's a tough climb over the hill from Gortawarla. Let me rest for a while and I'll soon be better.'

He bowed his head in his hands and sat there, gently rocking to and fro. Once Dermot thought he heard a sob, but it might have been the cry of the tempest instead. Why should Connor cry? he wondered numbly. Only those who had cause for grief should grieve. Then he went over and touched his friend on the shoulder.

'Will you watch with me, boy, tonight?'

Connor lifted his handsome, young face and stared at him pitifully. His thick, black hair fell in damp, tossed locks upon his brow, but his eyes were dry.

'Watch with you? What watch, and why?'

'Watch with me for Maire Ban. She may come tonight when the souls are travelling. I prayed all year for this, and now I am afraid – Christ, pity me – afraid of my own darling.'

The other sprang to his feet with a glad shout. 'Afraid, are you, man? *I'm* not afraid – no, not if she came in all the ghastly horrors of the grave, with all the loathsome changes of death about her. I'd never be afraid, for I loved her. I speak it out at last. I loved her – her blue, blue eyes, her warm, red lips, every curl of her golden hair, her soul – her beautiful, white soul that may come tonight. Oh yes, I'll stay with you, Dermot, to give her welcome – you cannot grudge me that. I never wronged you in any word or deed, but I loved her, and I went away.'

Dermot's hand reached out and clasped his closely.

'Was that why you went away, Connor, *a stóir*, to the wandering and the strangers? Well, I can't blame you for loving her – no man could help it; half the boys in the valley were hers if she had looked at them. But *I* loved her always, you know, and we were bespoken since we were children together.'

'Yes; she told me that, and I tried to hate you, Dermot, so it was best for me to go. But now, thank God, I may see her again, once again.' He ran his hands through his hair in a distracted fashion. 'Tell me how she died, friend.'

They drew their chairs nearer the flickering fire, and neither looked at the other. Dermot Lally told Connor Moran the story of Maire's one brief year of wedded life, and of how she died.

Connor said never a word, but sat staring into the burning turf, and when the tale was ended both men lapsed into silence. Sometimes a low sigh would break from the dead woman's husband, a sigh that made Bran, the dog lying under the table, turn uneasily in her sleep. Outside, the storm had quieted, the rain struck lightly now against the window, and the cradle up in the rafters had ceased its rocking.

The hours had drifted on towards midnight, and the watchers still kept their unnatural, strained calm, with heads bent forward, listening. But the ears of Love were dull that night, for it was the dog who heard her coming first. With a sudden, joyous bark it bounded up and fawned as if at the feet of someone, while Dermot rose, trembling, from his seat, and stretched out his arms into the shadows. He was half-conscious that Connor had risen also, and was it his fancy, or did he hear his friend's voice repeat in a persistent, fretful monotone: 'I cannot see her – I cannot see her. Oh, dear saints, I cannot see her.'

There the spirit of Maire Ban, the beloved, stood on the floor to which Dermot Lally had brought her as his bride. He saw the glint of her bright hair as it hung straight down the folds of the grave-clothes; he saw the pale lips unclose in a sweet and happy smile. But her eyes did not seek those of her husband, they looked past him instead, and into them a light had leaped – her dead eyes, hidden under the coffin-lid for twelve sad months, burned now with a brilliancy he had never seen them hold for him on earth. It was as if an unexpected, welcome sight had struck upon them, and had drawn all the gladness of her soul into those radiant blue orbs. She was looking at Connor, who seemed to feel the gaze, for he stood rubbing his eyes in a dazed way, and watching the dog still crouched upon the floor. Dermot had dropped to his knees with hands uplifted and his voice rose in prayer. He called her name in a wild entreaty: 'Maire, Maire, my Maire Ban, my wife, won't you turn to me, *colleen* óg? Won't you turn to the heart that has been breaking for you this weary year – for you and the child? Here is your chair, love, come to it and rest. Surely God will leave you with me for a little while. I have waited so long for this hour.'

Maire Ban still stood smiling at the man who leaned in terror against the wall, in terror because he could not see her spirit nor hear aught save the pleading of Dermot and the whining of the dog. Then she came towards him with her ghostly hands held out for his greeting, came close to him until her cheeks almost touched his, and her eyes met the sad, dark ones that were filled full of tears and trouble. She laid one hand on his shoulder. He seemed to feel it, for he shivered, but his arms hung down by his side, inert, while he wondered at the heart-broken horror slowly growing on Dermot Lally's face. Then Maire Ban shrank back, disappointed, her shadowy smile fading, her shadowy fingers interlocked as if in pain, and her eyes pallid with anguish. Faint and fainter yet became her image, until the outline only was dimly visible; then it faded away in a thin, barely perceptible wreath of mist. With a sudden cry that rang long after in his listener's ears, Dermot Lally fell face downwards on the floor.

When the day dawned – the chilly November day – the two men gazed at each other's haggard countenances across the dead fire; Connor stupidly wondering what he had heard the old folks say concerning the fate of those who talked with ghosts, and Dermot realising at last why his friend had wandered afar over the seas, and why Maire Ban had died.

Margaret Barrington

Margaret Barrington was born in Co. Donegal in 1896 and studied at Trinity College, Dublin. In 1939, she wrote her critically acclaimed first novel, *My Cousin Justin*, which drew on her marriage to the writer Liam O'Flaherty. After the war, she moved to West Cork and wrote criticism and short stories for *The Bell*. Her highly regarded anthology of short stories, *David's Daughter, Tamar*, was published after her death in 1982.

Village without Men...

Weary and distraught, the women listened to the storm as it raged around the houses. The wind screamed and howled. It drove suddenly against the doors with heavy lurchings. It tore at the straw ropes that anchored the thatched roofs to the ground. It rattled and shook the small windows. It sent the rain in narrow streams under the door, through the piled-up sacks, to form large puddles on the hard, stamped, earthen floors.

At times, when the wind dropped for a moment to a low, whistling whisper, and nothing could be heard but the hammering of the sea against the face of Cahir Roe, the sudden release would be intolerable. Then one or another would raise her head and break into a prayer, stumbling words of supplication without continuity or meaning. Just for a moment, a voice would be heard. Then the screaming wind would rise again in fury, roaring in the chimney and straining the roof-ropes; the voice would sink to a murmur and then to nothing as the women crouched again over the smoldering sods, never believing for a moment in the miracle they prayed for.

Dawn broke, and the wind dropped for a while. The women wrapped their shawls tightly round them, knotted the ends behind them and tightened their head cloths. They slipped out through cautiously opened doors. The wind whipped their wide skirts so tightly to their bodies that it was hard to move.

They muttered to themselves as they clambered over the rocks or waded through the pools down to the foaming sea.

To the right, Cahir Roe sloped upward, smothered in storm clouds, protecting the village from the outer sea. The ears of the women rang with the thunder of the ocean against its giant face. Salt foam flecked their faces, their clothes as they struggled along in knots of three or four, their heads turned from the wind as they searched the shore and looked out over the rolling water. But in all that grey-green expanse of churning sea, nothing. Not even an oar. All day long they wandered.

It was not until the turn of the tide on the second day that the bodies began to roll in, one now, another again, over and over in the water like dark, heavy logs. Now a face showed, now an outstretched hand rose clear of the water. John Boyle's face had been smashed on the rocks, yet his wife knew him as an incoming wave lifted his tall, lean body to hurl it to shore.

For two days the women wandered until the ocean, now grown oily but still sullen with anger, gave up no more. Niel Boylan, Charley Friel and Dan Gallagher were never found.

The women rowed across the bay to the little town of Clonmullen for the priest. After the heavy rain, the road across the bog was dangerous, and the village was cut off by land. The young curate, Father Twomey, came across. When he looked at the grey, haggard faces of these women, all words of comfort deserted the young priest. His throat went dry, and his eyes stung as if the salt sea had caught them. What comfort could words bring to women in their plight? He could with greater ease pray for the souls of the drowned than encourage the living to bear their sorrows in patience.

The women had opened the shallow graves in the sandy graveyard. They lowered the bodies and shoveled back the sand. Then for headstones, to mark the place where each man was laid before the restless sand should blot out every sign, they drove an oar which he had handled into each man's grave and dropped a stone there for every prayer they said. The wind blew the sand into the priest's vestments, into his shoes, into his well-oiled hair, and into his book. It whirled the sand around the little heaps of stones.

As the women rowed him home across the bay, the priest looked back at the village. The oars in the graves stood out against the stormy winter sky like the masts of ships in harbour.

The midwife was the first to leave the village.

As they brought each dead man up from the sea, she stripped him and washed his body. For most of them she had done this first service. From early youth, first with her mother, then alone, she had plied her trade on this desolate spit of land. These same bodies, once warm, soft, tender and full of life, had struggled between her strong hands, and now lay cold and rigid beneath them. She washed the cold seawater from these limbs, from which she had once washed the birth-slime. Silently she accomplished her task and retired to her cottage. Of what use was a midwife in a village without men?

She wrote to her married daughter in Letterkenny, who replied that there was work in plenty for her there. Then, two weeks later, when the hard frosts held the bog road, she loaded her goods onto a cart and set out for Clonmullen, from where she could get the train to Letterkenny. She took with her young Laurence Boyle, John Boyle's fourteen-year-old son, to bring back the donkey and cart.

The women watched her go. A few called God-speed but the others, thin-lipped, uttered no word. Silently they went back to their houses and their daily tasks. From now on their bodies would be barren as fields in winter.

All winter the village lay dumb and still. The stores of potatoes and salt fish were eaten sparingly. The fish might run in the bay now, followed by the screaming seagulls, but there were no men to put out the boats or draw in the gleaming nets. The children gathered mussels to feed the hens.

Then, in the early spring days, the women rose from their hearths and tightly knotted their head cloths and shawls. They took down the wicker creels from the lofts, the men's knives from the mantleshelves, and went down to the rocks below Cahir Roe to cut the sea wrack for the fields. The children spread it on the earth. Then, with fork and spade, the women turned the light, sandy soil, and planted their potatoes, oats and barley. The work was heavy and back-breaking, but it had to be done. If they did not work now with all their strength, their children would be crying for food in the coming winter.

Driven, bone-tired, sick at heart, they rose early and worked all day, stopping at midday as their husbands had stopped, to rest in the shelter of a stone wall, to drink some milk or cold tea, and to eat some oatbread their children brought to them in the fields. At night they dragged their bodies to bed. There was no joy, no relief to be got there now. Nothing but sleep; the easing of weary muscles.

Their work in the house was neglected. The hearths went untended, their clothes unwashed. They no longer white-washed the walls of the cottages or tended the geraniums they grew in pots. They did not notice when the flowers died.

The next to leave the village was Sally Boyle. She was to have married young Dan Gallagher after the next Lent. There at the end of the straggling village was the half-built ruin of the house he had been getting ready with the help of the other men in the village. All winter she moped over the fire, only rousing herself when her mother's voice rose sharp and angry. Now in the spring she began to wander about restlessly. She would leave her work and climb the great headland of Cahir Roe, there to look out to where Tory rose like a fortress from the sea – out there across the sea in which Dan Gallagher had been drowned, the sea which had refused to surrender what should have been hers. At night in bed she could not control the wildness of her body. She pitched from side to side, moaning and muttering. Her whole mind was darkened by the memory of soft kisses on warm autumn nights, of strong hands fondling her. She felt bereft, denied.

She slipped away one day and joined the lads and lasses in Clonmullen who were off to the hiring fair at Strabane. Later her mother got a letter and a postal order for five shillings. Sally was now a hired girl on a farm down in the Lagan.

Then, in ones and twos, the young girls began to leave. With the coming of spring their eyes brightened, their steps grew lighter. They would stop and look over their shoulders hurriedly, as if someone were behind. They would rush violently to work and then leave their tasks unfinished to stand and look out over the landscape, or out to sea from under a sheltering hand. They became irritable, quarrelsome and penitent by turns. Somewhere out there across the bog, across the sea, lay a world where men waited; men who could marry them, love them perhaps, give them homes and children.

The women objected to their going and pleaded with them. Every hand was needed now. The turf must be cut in the bog, turned and stacked for the coming winter. Surely they could go when the crops were gathered in? But tears and pleading were in vain. Nature fought against kindness in their young bodies. Here no men were left to promise these girls life, even the hazardous life of this country. They gathered their few garments together and departed, promising to send back what money they could. But their mothers knew that it was not to get money they left. It was the blood in their veins that drove them forth. And though the women lamented, they understood.

No use now to give a dance for the departing girls. There were no men with whom they could dance. No use to gather the neighbours into the house to sing. The voices of women are thin and shrill without men's voices to balance them.

Larry Boyle found himself the only lad in the village. The other boys were many years younger, and those who were older had been lost with their fathers in the storm. The winter gloom, the silence of the women, and his loneliness drove him to day-dreaming, to the creation of a fantasy world. He saw himself, in coming years, stronger and taller than any man, towering over humanity as Cahir Roe towered over the sea; impregnable, aloof. Boats, fields, cattle, houses; everything in the village would belong to him. For as yet the outside world meant nothing to him, and women had no power over his dreams. They existed but to serve him.

At first the women paid no more attention to him than they did to the other children. He ate what food was set before him: some potatoes, a piece of dried salt fish, a bowl of buttermilk. He performed such tasks as were set him, helping with the few cows, carrying the sea wrack, heeling the turf. Indeed, he was despised rather than otherwise, for the girls of his age were more nimble and less absent-minded than he. But slowly, as if in answer to his dreams, his position changed. In every house he entered he was welcomed and given the seat by the fire. He was never allowed to depart without food and drink. The older women baked and cooked for him, kept the best for him, gave him small presents from their hoard: a husband's knife, a son's trousers. They began to compliment him at every turn on his strength and growth. No one asked him to work.

Now he allowed his hair to grow like a man's. The stubby quiff vanished and a crop of thick, fair curls crowned his forehead, giving him the obstinate look of a fierce young ram. He became particular about the cleanliness of his shirt, refused to wear old patched trousers and coats. Gradually he dominated the whole village. Even the dogs owned him sole master, and snarled savagely at one another when he called them to heel. The younger boys were his slaves, to fetch and carry for him. He scarcely noticed the girls of his own age, never called them by name, never spoke directly to them. Unlike them, he had no wish to leave the village.

A day came when Larry Boyle went from house to house and collected the fishing lines, hooks and spinners that had belonged to the drowned men. They were granted him as if by right. He took them to the rock behind the village where formerly the fish had been dried and where the men had then met in the summer evenings to talk, away from their women folk. It was a day of shifting sun and shadow, and the wind from the west was broken by the headland.

He sang as he carefully tested, cut and spliced each line. He rubbed the hooks and spinners clean of rust with wet sand from the stream. He made a long line, tested each length and wound it in a coil between hand and elbow. He fastened the hooks and the lead weight. Then, satisfied, he went down to the shore to dig bait.

He swung his can of bait over his shoulder and picked up his line made for Cahir Roe. He was going to fish for rockfish.

A deep shelf ran round part of the headland, and from this the men had fished in the drowsy heat of summer days when they could spare time from the fields. He clambered along the shelf and stood on the edge. The sea heaved and foamed beneath him. Far out, Tory rose, a castle against the white line of the horizon.

He fixed his bait carefully and placed the loose end of the line beneath his heel. Then, clear of the beetling rock behind, he swung the coil of line above his head and threw it far out. His body, balanced over the edge, seemed to follow it as his eye watched the untwisting of the cord, the drop of the lead towards the sea. He bent down and gathered up the end.

He could feel the movement as the length of the line ran through the sea, and the weight sank slowly through the heavy water. His hand knew what was happening down there beneath the surface. He felt the lead strike the bottom. His fingers, born to a new delicacy, held the line firmly so that the bait should float free. He could feel the gentle nibbling of the fish at the bait, nibbling cautiously, daintily, as sheep nibble grass. Twice he drew in his line to re-bait the hook. Then one struck.

Excited, breathing heavily, his eyes distended; he drew in the line slowly, letting it fall in careful coils at his feet. Then the fish left the water and the full weight hung on the line. It plunged about madly in the air, twisting and flapping. The cord rubbed against the edge of the shelf as it passed from hand to hand, dislodging small stones and dirt from the crumbling surface. He had to lean out to jerk the fish over the edge, at that moment unaware of everything but the twisting, flapping fish. He threw it well behind him so that it could not leap back into the water. It lay there, twisting and turning, its brilliant orange and green colouring coming and going, its belly heaving, its panting gills shining red. Then it lay still, and from its open mouth the brick-red blood flowed over the stones. Another leap, another twitch. It was dead.

Larry passed the back of his hand across his forehead to wipe away the sweat. Before he stooped to disengage the hook from the jaws of the fish, he looked around him, at Tory on the far horizon, at the towering cliff above, the heaving sea beneath. For a moment his head reeled as he felt the turning of the world.

The women liked the new schoolmistress. They liked her modesty and reserve. Though young, she knew how to keep the children in order, teach them their lessons and their manners.

They looked after her with approval when they saw her walk precisely from the school to the cottage where she lived, her hands stiffly by her sides, her eyes lowered. They admired her round, rosy face, her light hair, her neat figure. She appeared so young and lovely to these women whose bodies were lean and tired from hard work and poor food.

She never stopped at the half-door for a chat, nor delayed for a moment to pass the time of day with a neighbour on the road. She never played with the younger children. She walked around encased in herself.

Every Saturday while the road held, she would mount her clean, well-oiled bicycle and cycle to Clonmullen. On the way she did not speak to anyone nor answer a greeting. With gaze fixed on the road before her, she pedaled furiously. In Clonmullen she would make one or two purchases, post her letters, and cycle back home. All attempts at conversation were firmly repulsed. She did not even stop to have tea at the hotel.

She lived alone in a small cottage built on the rise of ground just beyond the village. For an hour at a time she would kneel in the shelter of the fuchsia hedge and gaze hungrily at the houses she did not wish to enter, at the women to whom she did not care to speak. She knew all their comings and goings, all the details of their daily life. She watched them at their work, in their conversation. She watched the children at play. She watched Larry Boyle as he wandered along the shore towards Cahir Roe to fish, or passed her cottage on his way to set rabbit snares in the burrows.

The July heat beat down on the earth, and the blue-grey sea moved sleepily under a mist. He was returning home when he saw her, standing in the shelter of the bushes that grew over the gateway. She was looking at him with fierce intentness. He stood still and gazed back, his eyes wide and startled. The fear of unknown lands, of uncharted seas, took hold of him. His mouth dropped open, his skin twitched. His throat hurt and there was a hammering in his ears like the heavy pounding of the surf on Cahir Roe. He could not move hand nor foot. With a sudden movement her hand darted out and caught his wrist. She drew him towards her, in the shelter of the thick fuchsia hedge. Frightened by her intent stare, her pale face, her quick, uneven breathing, when she put out her other hand to fondle him, he pulled away and burst through the bushes. Quietly, with lowered eyes, she listened as his boots clattered over the rocky road. She sighed and turned back into her house.

But he came back. Furtively. He would steal into her kitchen when she was at school and leave some offering: a freshly caught fish, a rabbit, and some rock pigeon's eggs. He had so little to give. She did not seem to notice. She did not stop him to thank him when they met. She passed without even a greeting, once again encased in her rigid calm. Then one evening, as darkness fell, he lifted the latch of her door. She was seated on her hearthrug, gazing at the glowing turf fire. He approached in silent desperation, and with the same wild desperation, she answered.

Such happenings do not remain hidden in a small world. Without a word spoken, the women came to know. Primitive anger seized hold of them. They said nothing to Larry. Their belief in man's place in life, and the fact that they had denied him nothing shut their mouths. All their rage turned against the young teacher whom they had thought so modest and gentle. They became as fierce as hawks at the theft of their darling.

They ceased work. They came together in groups, muttering. They buzzed like angry bees. Their lips spoke words to which their ears were long unaccustomed as they worked themselves into an ancient battle-fury. They smoothed their hair back from their foreheads with damp and trembling hands. They drew their small shawls tightly round their shoulders.

From behind the fuchsia hedge the girl saw them coming like a flock of angry crows. Their wide, dark skirts, caught by the light summer breeze, bellowed out behind them. Their long, thin arms waved over their heads like sticks in the air. Their voices raised in some primitive battle cry, they surged up the road towards her.

Terrified of this living tidal wave, she rushed out. The uneven road caught her feet. It seemed to her that she made no headway as she ran, that the surging mass of women came ever nearer. Stones rattled at her heels. She ran on in blind panic, unaware of where she was going. Her chest began to ache, her throat to burn. A stone caught her shoulder, but she scarcely felt the blow. Then another hit her on the back and she stumbled. Still she ran on, not daring to look back. A stone struck her head. She reeled and fell over the edge of the narrow bog road, down the bank towards the deep, watery ditch. Briars caught her clothes. Her hands grasped wildly at the tufts of rough grass. There she lay, half-in, half-out of the water, too frightened to move or struggle.

When they saw her fall, the women stopped and stood there in the road, muttering. Then they turned back. They burst into her neat little cottage. They threw the furniture about, broke the delph, hurled the pots out of the door, and tore the pretty clothes to ribbons. Then they left, still muttering threats, like the sea after a storm.

Later, shivering, aching, sick, the girl dragged herself back onto the road. There was no one there now. The flock of crows had gone. She stood alone on the empty road. There was no sound but the lonely call of a moor bird overhead.

The next day, Larry, too, left the village.

The war when it came meant little to these women. The explosions of mines on the rocks could not harm them now that there were no men to risk their lives on the water. The aeroplanes, which from time to time circled over the coast, seemed to them no more than strange birds, at first matter for wonder and then taken for granted. Sometimes the sea washed up an empty ship's boat, some timbers or empty wooden cases. One morning scores of oranges came dancing in on the waves. The children screamed with delight and, not knowing what they were, played ball with them. But since the oranges did not bounce they soon tired of them and left them along the shore to rot. The women only realised that the war could touch them when the supplies of Indian meal ran out.

All that winter storms lashed the coast. Snow whirled around the houses, blotting out the sight of the fierce sea that growled savagely against the headland of Cahir Roe day and night. Not once during the bitter months did the snow melt on the mountains beyond Clonmullen. The wind tore at the ropes that tethered the thatched roofs, rotting and grass-grown from neglect. The north-east wind drove under the doors, roared in the chimneys; it hardened the earth until it was like a stone.

Yet now it seemed that the silence was broken, that terrible silence they had kept in mourning for their dead. Now in the evenings they gathered round one another's firesides. They told stories, old Rabelaisian tales heard when they were children from the old men of the village. Such tales as lie deep in the minds of people and are its true history. Tales of old wars, of great slaughter of men, of the survival of the women and children, of tricks to preserve the race. They told of the Danes and their love of the dark-haired Irish women. They laughed quietly and spoke in whispers of the great power of the Norsemen's bodies, of the fertility of their loins.

Over and over again they told the story of the women of Monastir, who, when widowed and alone, lured with false lights a ship to their shore. What matter that their victims were dark-skinned Turks. Their need was great.

The eyes of the women grew large and full of light as they repeated these tales over the dying embers of their fires. A new ferocity appeared in their faces. Their bodies took on a

116

new grace, grew lithe and supple, as the body of the wild goat becomes sleek and lovely in the autumn.

Spring came suddenly. After the weeks of fierce winds and wild seas followed days of mild breezes and scampering sunshine. The women threw open their doors and stepped out with light hearts. As they cut the sea wrack for their fields, they called to one another and sang snatches of old songs. Sometimes one or another would stop in her work and look out over the water at the sea-swallows dipping and skimming over the surface of the water, at the black shags as they swam and dived, at old Leathering standing in his corner in wait. The older children laughed and shouted as they helped to spread out the wrack on the fields. They younger ones screamed as they ran along the shore and searched under the rocks for crabs. They called and clapped their hands at the sea-pies as they bobbed up and down on the waves.

On and on the children ran, their toes pink in the sea water. They clattered together like spies over each fresh discovery. They travelled along the shore until they found themselves out on the point of land beside Cahir Roe, facing the open sea. There they stood and looked out to sea from under sheltering hands.

For some minutes they stood and stared. Then in a body they turned and ran towards the women, shouting all together that out there, coming in closer every minute, was a strange boat.

The women straightened their backs and listened. Even before they understood what the children were shouting, they let down their petticoats and started for the point. There they stood in a group and stared, amazed that a boat should put in on this inhospitable shore. Close in now, with flapping sail, the boat came.

They could make out only one man and their eyes, used to long searching over water, could see that he was lying across the tiller. Was he alive or dead? Could he not see where he was going? If he did not change his course now he would fetch up on the reef below Cahir Roe. They rushed forward to the water's edge and shouted. The man bent over the tiller did not move. They continued to shout. They waded into the sea until the water surged against their bodies and threatened to overbalance them. Their dark skirts swirled round them in the heavy sea as they shouted and waved their arms.

Then the man at the tiller slowly raised his head. He looked around him, at the sea, at the screaming women, at the great, red, granite face of Cahir Roe. With great effort he pulled his body upright and swung the tiller over. Then he fell forward again. Even before the keel had grounded on the gravel, the women had seized the boat and dragged it up onto the beach.

Six men lay huddled in the bottom of the boat. Great, strong men, now helpless. The women turned to the helmsman. He looked at them with dull, sunken eyes. He moved. He tried to speak. His grey face was stiff, his lips cracked.

'Scotland?' he asked, and his voice was hoarse.

The women shook their heads. Then the man slowly lifted one hand, pointed to the men at his feet, and then to himself.

'Danes. Torpedoed. Ten days.'

The women cried aloud as they lifted the heavy bodies of the men. Their voices sang out in wild exultation.

The Danes. The Danes were come again.

Janet McNeill

Janet McNeill was a prolific author and playwright of over thirty works of fiction for adults and children. Born in 1907, she was raised in both Ireland and England, but finally settled in Co. Down, where she worked for the *Belfast Telegraph*. She explored life in Northern Ireland in works such as *The Maiden Dinosaur, Search Party, As Strangers Here, The Child in the House*, and several short story collections for children. She worked on the BBC advisory council and was elected as the chairman of the Belfast Centre of Irish P.E.N. later in life. After 1966, she began to concentrate on writing children's novels and won an Honorary Book Award in 1968 at the Book World Children's Spring Festival.

The Girls

His neighbour on the right stirred her coffee and laid the spoon in the saucer. 'All summer,' she continued, 'postcard after postcard with pictures of Norwegian fjords and glaciers, incredibly blue and impersonal, like blind men's eyes, if you know what I mean. They're camping, of course. Modern youngsters are marvellous, don't you think, Mr Armitage?'

He said, 'They certainly make the headlines.' Her eyesight must be better than his; he hadn't been able to see across the knives and forks to decipher her place-card. In any case, her married name would have meant as little to him as his surname evidently did to her.

'You can't help remembering them when they were small and took hold of your hand as soon as you went through the gate,' she said. 'I mean, it doesn't make any difference, but you can't help remembering.' She lowered her green-caked eyelids. 'Of course they mature so much earlier nowadays,' she said, and in case she had admitted any hint of sourness, added gaily, 'Bless them!'

'My wife and I have no family,' he said, and she looked at him in the way that women always looked when he said this. Accusation? Curiosity? Pity? He wasn't sure. Was this Joan he wondered, or Phyllis, Beatrice or Judith? More than likely she was one of the hockey team whose flat virgin faces looked out from the photograph that Alice had hung on the bedroom wall the day they came home from their honeymoon. 'Do we have to have them there?' And Alice said, 'The girls? Oh, John, of course!'

The sight of her cross-stitched nightdress-case lying on the bed startled and pleased him, and he didn't argue. She had embroidered it, she told him, in the Upper Fifth. Miss Finch had been wild because she hadn't matched the colours properly.

Whichever of the girls the lady on his right was, she now turned her attention to her other neighbour, presenting him with an oblique view of her chin and solid bosom. He was in disgrace. Since the soup, he had accompanied her through a detailed history of her children, almost from their conception, as if since he was attending the Reunion Luncheon as a husband, it followed that he must also be a father. Now she knew her confidences had been misplaced; he should have told her earlier that he and his wife were childless. She had been deceived.

The lady on his left, one of the senior Old Girls and certainly not in the photograph of Alice's hockey team, had been working through an agenda with her other neighbour since they took their places, and was still fiercely engaged. Alice was seated across the table from him, two places to the right. In spite of her attachment to the photograph, this was the first of these functions she had attended – his work, she protested, the journey to Ireland, the Dahlia Show: in any case, what would be the point? It wasn't as if she had kept up with any of them since she sent to each the first matinee coat. Even Christmas cards had long since dwindled.

Unexpectedly, she had decided this year to come, shrugging his surprise and the Dahlia Show aside. It would be amusing; they would make an autumn holiday of it, would stay a night or two at the hotel where the lunch was to be held, in the town that had been their home. It was arranged.

He looked at her now with the double eye of critic and husband, hoping she wasn't sorry she had come, making a private appraisal of her public face. She looked different from her companions and younger than she did in London. This was probably because she was wearing on her head that wisp of black lace and velvet, whereas the other women were formally and magnificently hatted. Below the netted threads her hair blazed, the colour unaltered since it had lain in plaits on the shoulders of her gym tunic. She wasn't joining in the conversation, but sipped her coffee as if she was wholly absorbed in making a judgment on it. Then she put her cup down briskly and began to talk.

He turned his ear to listen. Alice was never much of a talker, not in public, nor would he have thought of her as a name-dropper. Names fell from her now like leaves in Vallombrosa. It was blatant, but she was doing well. Even those names her listeners might not recognise were made to sound significant. Names of his colleagues in the television world occurred frequently.

'So I said to Leonard – Leonard Styles, you know – how do you grow those quite amazing roses?' That was as much as she had found to say to Leonard Styles when confronted with him for a few seconds at a sherry party – 'Your roses are lovely' – before someone else had snapped him up. Now she made it sound like a stroll through a scented garden, blue fingers of evening lying on the grass.

'Estelle Leyland – we bump into each other sometimes when I go to have my hair done.' She thought she had heard Estelle's voice once in the cubicle next to hers, but though she hung about afterwards, she wasn't able to positively identify Estelle.

Alice looked up and saw him. She knew from the surprise on his face that he had been listening. Instead of the shy look she usually gave him when their eyes met in public, she threw him now a cocky challenge – 'Doing all right, don't you think?' and in a voice loud enough for him to hear without effort, she spoke of the Head of Programmes as if he had been a favourite uncle.

It hit him then why she was doing it. Pops and Protests, O Levels, and Menstrual Sluggishness: these were the topics she was offered. She chose her own. That thing on her head was a flag of freedom flown to celebrate her escape from provincial convention, to point out her difference before anyone else pointed it out.

Her small spurt of display ended abruptly, as it had begun, and had earned her no response. As soon as she had finished her neighbours returned to their discussion of Streaming in Schools, Teenage Sex and What Was the Church Doing Anyway? Her lower lip had thickened, her face forbade him to look at her and offer any kind of comfort.

Someone at the top table was tapping for attention. He disciplined himself to listen to the speeches.

'The speeches weren't up to much, were they?' she said later in their bedroom in the hotel. She was sitting at the dressing table in conference with three reflections of herself. He stood at the bay window feeling the coolness of the glass against his hands. Outside, the pale curve of the beach was deserted, the tide was low, pools already threw back light to the sky.

'That militant woman who spoke first—' he said.

'Mabel? You know she was terrible. She used to be Head Prefect. She was always terrible. I've told you how terrible she used to be.'

'She was the best of the bunch.'

'Which wasn't saying much.'

'How was Phyllis?' He picked a name at random, hoping to steer her into some nostalgic schoolgirl chatter.

'Phyllis? Well, you tell me how she was!'

'What do you mean?'

'You were sitting next to her.'

'Was I? Was that Phyllis?'

'Surely you knew! On your right.'

'Look, I only met Phyllis once, and that was all of fifteen years ago, for five seconds, milling about in a conducted party at a stately home – anyway, she hadn't a clue who I was.'

Alice frowned. 'She should have had.'

'Oh come off it,' he said, though he agreed with her. 'Hardly over here.'

'Phyllis never could remember names – she cheated like mad in exams. Anyway, why be so interested?'

He pointed out, 'She was your friend – you're the one to be interested.'

'Tell me then – how was she?'

'Busy?'

'Good works? She thirsted after good works.'

'No,' he said. 'Children.'

He could have dodged it but he was angry with her for being so sour about the girls, her friends. What had they come for? He had been ready to smile at sentimental reunions; now he felt he was on the inside of the photograph, making a claim for affection.

She said, 'Ring down to the desk, will you, and ask them to send up some China tea with lemon.' When he had done this, she said, 'I'm glad we're in one of these big front rooms, anyway. We never really thought we'd be staying here, did we? Years ago, I mean. Do you remember looking in through the revolving doors when we were on our way to the half-crown dances at the pier?'

He said, 'I remember. I kept a cardboard calendar in my locker and speared the days out with my penknife from half-term.'

She wriggled her feet free of her shoes. 'This carpet, it must have cost a packet. When people say, 'Of course young folk mature so much earlier these days', it makes me want to laugh.'

He remembered Alice on her bicycle, hair like a flag, turning the corner of the lane from her parents' house, then lighting down beside him, all movement suddenly arrested, and the passionate innocence of the first moments, only their breath meeting across their passive hands. 'You're late.'

'I couldn't get away any sooner, John. She made me swear to God I would do my piano practice. How English you've got – more English than ever.'

'I have not.'

'You have so.'

And gradually Alice became Alice.

Now he heard rain on the window and turned. Large single drops studded the glass. The sparse necklace of lights was already lit along the promenade, though it was only mid-afternoon. The dying season was making the most of itself.

'Phyllis should have known,' she said. Usually Alice wore his success modestly, the way she wore her fur stole; now she seemed inclined to brandish it like a banner.

He said, 'I'll take a walk. Why don't you go down to the lounge and meet up with some of them and get all the craic?'

'Listening to the returning native!' she mocked. 'You wouldn't have said "craic" in London.'

'Why don't you, anyway?'

'Maybe I will when I've had my tea.'

With the arrival of the tray he made his escape. The rain had lifted. He enjoyed walking across the beach, steering a course through the tracks the seagulls had made, treading so that each imprint was sharp. All the nostalgia he had expected to experience vicariously through Alice he now exploited in himself. He went quickly and was ready for the bank of shingle at the far end, remembering how his feet would slide in it.

The man was unfastening the chains on the swings; he had put up the notice beside the roundabout. No one would come, not on an afternoon like this at the thin end of the summer. The horses and ostriches on their barley-sugar poles leapt bravely, but they would have no riders today. From the shelter a few rug-wrapped regulars turned their heads to watch the stranger.

He reached the road and started to climb, pausing only for a moment when he came to the gate. They had cut the shrubbery and made a lawn for clock gold; no vestige remained of that aromatic, unmapped jungle. A lettered board hung on chains above the door: 'Sea Crest Guest House'. Sauce bottles showed through the window; an unhurried gnome fished.

The church was unchanged, the churchyard tidier than he remembered it, smelling of lawn mowings. It would have suited his mood to find the grave deep in drenched and seeded grasses, but it looked tame and seemly, an upright stone, a rectangle of granite chippings surrounded by the flat marble plinth where the words 'TO THE GLORY OF GOD' were carved. The rain had filled the letters, making each 'O' into a small rock pool. Four O's, four pools.

He took the marbles out of his pocket and polished them against his sleeve, then crouched and took aim. Flicked from his thumb, they fell accurately into place one after another, rattled for a moment and lay still while the rock pools spouted. The coloured cores in the glass embellished the letters. Satisfied, he gouged the marbles out and put them in his pocket, then came down the hill again. He could hear the thin bouncing tune from the roundabout. So there had been riders for the horses after all.

Three riders – two shrimps of boys and Alice. The children leaned forward on their horses' necks, intent on a winning post. Alice had chosen an ostrich and sat upright. The velvet bow on her head fluttered; she rose and fell smoothly. There was a half-smile on her face; her knees, exposed below the tightened skirt, shone large and pale. Four times she passed by him. The fourth time she passed, she saw him and waved.

When the ride was over she dismounted, smoothed her skirt and came to him. 'Oh, John – years and years since I've had such fun!' She laid her cheek on his; he fancied she smelt of toffee and ink. 'Come on,' she urged. 'Try it – why not?'

He paid the man, helped Alice to mount and chose an adjacent ostrich for himself.

'Good thing no one saw us,' she said when it was over. 'I suppose we were silly.' They walked back across the sand, hands clasped and swinging like children. The tide was coming in again, all the runnels widening. Ahead of them the hotel was dark and enormous, decorated with lighted windows. 'What have you been doing with yourself?' she asked. 'Go on – tell!'

He told her then about the gravestone and the marbles, the day long ago when he stood there fidgeting about in his pockets, sick with the misery and nuisance of dying while his father discussed with the clergyman the arrangements for his grandmother's funeral. Then his father's shadow fell across the stone. 'What's that you have there, John?' He held out his open palm. 'Only marbles, Dad.' 'Show us here.' His father took the marbles and sent them flying into their sockets with satisfying precision. There had been late slanting sunlight, the colours in the glass shone.

'I always kept those marbles,' he said to Alice.

'They were in the box with your cufflinks.'

Without any need to explain the rite, they had arrived at a new kind of intimacy.

'What did you do after I went out?' he asked her.

'I went down to the lounge like you said. Everyone was there, talking. Everyone, John! It was splendid, just like old times, such fun! I expect I talked too much,' she added, waiting for him to contradict her.

'And did you?'

'You are miserable,' she laughed. 'Anyway, they know now who you are.'

He dismissed a pang that they should have had to be told and said, 'They do, do they?'

'Several of them said they'd wondered if it could be and had decided it couldn't. They're longing to meet you. Before dinner, I said – drinks. I'll wear the yellow.'

Her gaiety was infectious. Why pretend he wasn't looking forward to the evening? With Alice in this mood it could be fun. Life incognito hadn't been as amusing as he'd expected.

As they approached the hotel a car that had been waiting at the entrance drove past them, gathering speed.

Alice cried, 'Look! It's Phyllis!'

'Is it? Are you sure?'

'It is! It is! Wave, John!' She prodded him. They waved. The woman in the car was seeing nothing and made no acknowledgement. 'How odd! Phyllis was crazy to be introduced. I didn't think she was leaving till tomorrow.'

As soon as they went into the lounge his practised ear detected the tragic key. People were standing about in little knots, talk was guarded. Alice didn't notice. 'There's someone over there I simply must talk to!' she declared, heading across the room.

He heard the news at the bar. There had been a telephone message from Norway. Crazy youngsters, what made them do it? As if they needed to prove something. The mother of the boy had left immediately. These things happened, they could happen to anyone.

Not quite anyone. As he came through the lounge again, looking for Alice, they said, 'I think your wife went upstairs, Mr Armitage,' not really seeing him.

Alice was in the bedroom when he reached it. She was sitting at the dressing table but hadn't turned on the light.

'I don't think I'll go down to dinner after all, John.'

'Oh surely—'

'You know it wouldn't be any good,' she cried irritably, because her evening had been spoiled. She snapped on the light. 'We should never have come,' she said. 'Even before this happened it wasn't really the same.'

He felt sick with envy at the people in the lounge who were exposed to this kind of grief.

'We could have something sent up if you'd rather. Or there's a late plane if you'd like that.'

At once she turned, smiling again. 'Oh, John, could we?'

'We'd just have time to make it.'

'We'd never get the seats.'

'I think I could manage it.'

'Of course, *you* could!' Already she was unfastening the clasps of her suitcase. She was on her way back to the girls. Tonight she would sleep with the faces of Phyllis and Beatrice, Judith and Joan, blessing the bed that she lay on.

Mary Beckett

Mary Beckett was born in Belfast in 1926. In her twenties, she began writing radio plays for the BBC. She published one novel, *Give Them Stones*, two short story collections – including *A Belfast Woman* and *A Literary Woman* – as well as several children's books. She was awarded The Sunday Tribune Arts Award for Literature in 1987, and died in Dublin in 2013.

Flags and Emblems

In a hollow in the sand dunes on the far side of the town the girl lay, dreaming. Her pink linen dress was crumpled, and her warm cheeks were brown with the sun. Hazy with heat, the waves of sound could have been strong breakers on the shingle or cheers in the breeze from the town, or only the beat of blood in her ears. Then she heard shots; she was sure she heard shots, and her eyes were alarmed as she listened, her head tall on her neck. She parted the whins and ploughed through the dry sand towards the sea, bare-legged, her sandals in her hand. On the broad stretch of the inlet only a trickle of water remained. On the edge, remnant of the backwash of a boat, a bubble of froth formed and drifted uncertainly out towards the current, for the sea. Another followed, and another, each single, untouched, bumped now and then by a ripple, a feeble, unending procession. Her sudden energy sucked back into the whirling impatience within her; she stood watching while her briar-scratched feet sank down where the weak waves receded. Then she sighed, pushed her limp hair back from her cheeks, and turned in towards the town.

The flags were all hanging still, their colours softened beside rose brick and flaming glass, reflecting a bar of red below a cloud at the mountain. Down at the railway station where the guarded parade had gone, white puffs strayed across the sky that was a cheap, chocolate-box blue. Knots of women

133

gossiped to prolong sensation in the littered street. All day, deafened with drums beaten loudly in greeting to sleek, royal cars, crushed and dazzled with the brightness of silk and gold braid, they had flapped little triangles of bunting, or ranted at home against them. They brushed against the girl, not noticing her, and through the flitters of their excitement she could see her own emptiness.

Her father's shop was shuttered: the house was closed tight, door bolted, the snib on the window. She rapped and was drawn into the dark hall by her aunt, plucking off burdensome glasses. They disturbed the usual arrangement of her hair over her ears so she tucked and patted it.

'Was there shooting? I thought I heard shots,' the girl said, but her aunt hushed her to talk in whispers. 'It was maybe an echo. Your father's in bad form. Don't cross him now. I don't know what we're to do.' Her defenseless face wobbled.

'Because father's in a temper!' the girl exclaimed, and the cold weight that had all day been heavy in her breast made her voice mocking.

'You'll maybe agree I have cause this time,' her father shouted, his lower lip protruding in bitterness.

'Somebody tramped on your toes, I suppose,' she scoffed, and he glared at her with the hatred that lodged often under his drooped lids because the world didn't please him.

'What's the matter?' she asked more gently, and he muttered, 'It's Fergus,' and put his head down on his hand.

'What about him?' she asked, quiet in fear. 'Did they give him the sack when he wouldn't line up at the works to cheer?'

'I wish to God they had,' her father said. 'I could be proud of that – a man standing up for his principles. Then maybe that wife of his would take herself back to the Unionist brood that she came from.'

'Poor Rachel,' her aunt intervened. 'Would you separate husband and wife?' She rattled the ashes in the grate so that the

134

whole sunset was obscured by spinning dust, and then wiped ineffectually at her glasses.

'I would separate Fergus from anyone that made a disgrace of him, and count myself justified too.' He thumped his fist on his knee.

'Nobody could make a disgrace of Fergus,' the girl flared. 'What are you creating a scene about? Some footling thing that matters to no one!'

'How would you like to see your brother out walking the streets this day with a flag – a Union Jack – in honour of our royal guests?' His sarcasm was thick on his tongue, but the girl's quick laughter choked him. 'What are you laughing at, you fool?' he raged at his daughter. Not even his surliness could suppress her spurt of merriment. 'Oh, Father, don't be silly,' she said. 'Fergus waving flags! That's what I'm laughing at. You would do it yourself before he would. Don't ever let him hear that you believed such a thing.'

His face was a twist of anger when she began, but the old lines fell back into place before she had finished, and he said with slow deliberation, as if each word would not leave his lips: 'Out for a walk with the young lad he was, and a wee flag in the child's hand, and the wife looking after them from the door.'

'Oh…' the girl said, realising that only in this way could the news be true. 'Who told you?'

'Half the town,' he answered. Then he added, 'Owen Devlin met them head-on just past his gate, and he didn't even tell the child to put the flag in his pocket then.'

'No, he wouldn't,' the girl said, shaking her head, and her father said, 'Ach!' hard in irritation. 'Why wouldn't he, and not have Devlin sneering at him: "We'll hardly see you at the club tonight. Who'll we get for secretary now?"'

The girl suffered for a second the slight on her brother's self-esteem: the father writhed at the blow to his own. The aunt tried to divert them: 'But it wasn't his fault. It was Rachel's.

Blame Rachel. Her people were Loyalist, always. She had given Michael the flag to carry and Fergus wouldn't wish to go against her.'

'And why wouldn't he?' the father blazed. 'Lord God, before I'd disgrace my name and my people I'd have him rip the flag from the child's hand and hurl it in her face, and if she didn't like it she could leave him. A man's got to live up to his ideals.'

The girl looked sad. 'Is that the way an idealist should act?' she considered. 'Perhaps it's because his ideals dignify his mind that Fergus is gentle, unlike most men around here. Dead words and empty venom are all I can hear in what passes for idealism nowadays. You now,' she said coldly, 'is there not in your rage an envy of those shops that made money on ribbons and flags while you couldn't, and will you lose custom perhaps if people fall out with Fergus?' She hated herself for taunting so cheaply.

'Look out, would you, talking to your father like that!' the aunt waved her hands in alarm and then relapsed into self-pity. 'The pair of you were out all day and did I once have my foot past the door? No, I've been cooped up in here watching the crowds pushing until I pulled the blind, only that made the thud of their backs on the windows sound worse with the way they were pressed off the street to let pass the big motor cars and policemen. And then home you two come and I've to listen to bickering and fighting all night. Well, I'll not stay. I'll go to my bed.' She rose and began bundling her knitting into its white cloth wrapping.

'Ah, sit your ground,' he ordered, and she did so meekly. 'Damnation take these Unionists,' he said out of a few moments' silence, 'with their visitors over from England and their flags and their lunches and processions. What right have they to wreck us? And why couldn't he keep to his own sort instead of marrying one of theirs in such a big hurry?'

'Well, he loved her,' the girl said.

'Oh ho, listen to that now!' her father mocked. 'And she loved him too, did she? And so they lived happy ever after. Is that it? Why does she do this to him then? Shame him? Make a renegade of him!'

'He's not shamed,' the girl insisted hotly. 'A wife has feelings to be considered, principles haven't. You don't seem to see what courage it took.'

'Courage! What use is courage like that?' he said.

'No use indeed.'

The aunt shook her head. 'Poor Rachel. Fergus will never forgive her. He'd save her face outside, but you couldn't expect him to take kindly to her again. It's well she has the child. Poor Fergus that was so busy every night with the Hibernian Hall and the Casement Commemoration Committee and all the rest of them! He'll have nothing now that his evenings with the men are taken away from him. But there's nothing we can do. We may go to our beds; it's a dark night.'

'It's not time. We'll go no earlier than usual. We'll see this day out if it has ruined us,' the father ordered.

'This day, every day. What difference?' the girl said bleakly. She left them and went upstairs to her room and opened her window. The distant, lipping whisper on the sand and the sucking puffs of little breezes from the hills taunted her with their lack of violence. She closed her eyes, and across the darkness came the staid line of wobbling foam rings that would never reach the open sea. 'The shots,' she said to herself, remembering. 'The shots were only an echo. The fuss of the visit has happened before and will happen again, and it is so arranged that nothing happens at all. The only real thing today is between Fergus and Rachel.'

In his house in a new street at the edge of the town where the builder's gear was not yet cleared away, her brother sat withdrawn, his mouth set thin. Rachel's hands were clenched together in her lap while her mind scurried from the fear that this blankness between them would continue. Some neighbouring child had dropped the flag in the hall and, picking it up, a moment's blind anger against the affairs that kept Fergus from her made her push it into her son's hand and look back in defiance at her husband's shock. It was when she saw Owen Devlin meet them that all her resentment died in sorrow at what she'd done. She realised that she had impaled him, not for one afternoon, because in a small town hoarding memories, it would be for the length of his life. He would suffer for his weakness and she would suffer with him, and the knowledge that she shared his expiation would intensify it. She searched his face for some sign of forgiveness, unable to bear it that he should leave her now, more alone than ever.

'I'm sorry, Fergus,' she said, the ache in her breast and her throat making her voice tremble.

He half-shrugged, and without lifting his head from the paper, said, 'There's nothing to be sorry about'. Helpless, she would have offered twenty more years of her starvation to have undone the moment's revolt and left him undisturbed, occupied to his own satisfaction. She got up and laid her cheek against his arm, against the ridge under his coat where his shirt sleeve was rolled up in spite of her early insistence that he wear his cuffs neatly linked at the wrist. His body stiffened but she said humbly: 'I wish I had not done it.'

He drew her to him, and she pressed her head against his chest so that the badges in his lapel tangled in her hair, and the pen and pencils in his pocket dug hard against her forehead. 'I'm very sorry, dear love,' she repeated, and he said gently, 'It doesn't matter'. He stroked her head as it leaned there, and swiftly the wealth that had almost disintegrated in despair through his neglect came to warm, stirring life in his arms. They strengthened round Rachel and she lifted her face. 'It doesn't matter at all, love,' he murmured, and she watched his lips, neither aware what words had been spoken, only glad that their tone had been tender. A gust of strong wind round their house rattled their windows, unnoticed by them. Their love grew and engrossed them till they rested together in deep peace.

Caroline Blackwood

Caroline Blackwood was born into an aristocratic Ulster family, the first child of the Marquess of Dufferin and Maureen Guinness. She began her writing career in the 1960s as a contributor to various magazines and newspapers, including *Encounter* and *The Sunday Times*. Her first book, *For All That I Found There*, combined sections of fiction and memoir and was published in 1973, followed by a debut novel, *Great Granny Webster*. Her books include *On the Perimeter, The Stepdaughter, The Fate of Mary Rose, Corrigan, Darling, You Shouldn't Have Gone to So Much Trouble* and *The Last of the Duchess*. She published a short story collection, *Goodnight Sweet Ladies* (1983) and her collected stories, *Never Breathe a Word*.

Taft's Wife

Mrs Arthur Ripstone finally told Taft, the social worker, that she would agree to see her son, Anthony, if he was brought to have lunch with her in one of the big, West-End, London hotels. First she suggested The Ritz, then she decided she would prefer Claridge's.

'You understand, Mr Taft, that if I agree to this meeting I will have to insist on the utmost secrecy.'

'Absolutely.' Taft already disliked this unknown woman just from hearing the affected rasp of her voice over the telephone. She had an unpleasantly over-ladylike accent that masked some coarser, underlying accent with unmelodious results.

'I must also ask you, Mr Taft, never again to try to contact me at my home.'

'You can trust me, Mrs Ripstone. I would like to apologise for having written to you at your house. We were extremely anxious to reach you and we could think of no other way.' Taft's deep voice was soothing, studiedly avuncular. Through the years he had learned to cultivate an ultra-comforting manner – so much of his professional life was spent trying to reassure and cajole.

As he went on speaking to Mrs Ripstone he imagined himself speaking to an obese and arrogant lady in her early fifties. In his mind he endowed her with an ugly, high-bridged nose that accentuated the weakness of her chin, which receded in crêpe-like wattles into a corpulent, rose-pink neck encircled with expensive pearls.

He noticed that when he invented a picture of Mrs Ripstone he made her much older than he knew for a fact she was. Only that morning Taft had looked up her age in the orphanage files. Taft deliberately imagined her as old and hideous. Mrs Ripstone's appearance might come as a shock to her son, but Taft, as the adult who was going to be present at this painful hotel meeting, wanted to be immune to any nasty surprises. He therefore prepared himself for the worst in advance.

'You appreciate, Mr Taft, that at this moment I am not speaking to you from my own house. I am talking from a call box in my local village. I only tell you this to stress how violently I feel the need for your discretion in this whole business.'

'You can rely on my discretion, Mrs Ripstone.'

'Do I sense something sarcastic in your attitude, Mr Taft? Maybe you feel I am making an unnecessary fuss about the need for secrecy!' The lady-like voice was hissing with defensive anger.

Taft realised he would have to be more careful. The telephone was a dangerous instrument. It magnified the tiniest nuance of tone. Mrs Ripstone had not been deceived by his treacle-sweet courtesy. Her paranoia obviously had given her more sensitivity than he wished to credit her with. Unconsciously, he must have conveyed to this unknown woman some small particle of the hostility he felt for her. Unless he was more convincingly sympathetic towards her, he feared she might do the thing he dreaded – she might refuse to come to lunch.

'No doubt you see me as some kind of loose woman, Mr Taft!' Mrs Ripstone gave a hectic trill of a laugh. 'I promise you – nothing could be farther from the truth. I am happily married. I have a lovely, happy home down here in Surrey. We have a swimming pool. We have a tennis court. I have two adorable children. They are beautifully brought up ...'

Taft pressed the telephone receiver so hard against his ear that it hurt him. He rolled his eyes to the ceiling, and his face contorted in an expression of agonised embarrassment.

'I have a *very* good marriage, Mr Taft... My husband is older than me. He is a popular and respected man in the community. He is a wonderful human being. He is a retired judge...'

'Yes ... yes ...' Taft knew this response must sound inadequate, but he could think of nothing better to say.

'Have you quite understood, Mr Taft, that my husband is totally unaware of the boy's existence?'

'I rather assumed that, Mrs Ripstone.'

'And I intend for things to stay that way.' The affected voice hissed with such aggression that it reminded Taft of the sound of a steaming kettle. 'My husband – in his thinking – is an old-fashioned man, Mr Taft. He is deeply religious. The whole thing would come as a great shock to him. His heart is not strong. The past is the past. I see no reason why it should be allowed ruin the present.'

'I assure you, Mrs Ripstone, I have not the slightest desire to create any trouble in your private life.'

'You sound as if you are blaming me, Mr Taft! But I not only have to think of my husband – I have to think of my children.'

'Of course you do, Mrs Ripstone.'

'As long as you understand that... Anyway, we will all meet next Sunday, Mr Taft. I think Claridge's would be as good a place to meet as any. I used to like The Ritz, but lately I have found it gloomy. I think The Ritz has rather a dead feeling about it.'

'Exactly,' Taft said.

'Claridge's is so much gayer. After all, we want the meeting to be a pleasant one. Claridge's serves very nice desserts. When

I bring my children up to London to visit the dentist they always try to force me to take them to Claridge's. They *so* adore the desserts.'

'Claridge's it shall be,' Taft said.

'There's one thing I must warn you, Mr Taft; you have put a lot of emotional pressure on me in order to make me agree to come to this lunch. I therefore feel you have certain responsibilities towards Anthony.'

'Responsibilities, Mrs Ripstone?'

'Responsibilities, Mr Taft. I feel it is your duty to warn the boy that he mustn't get ideas. He mustn't be allowed to think these meetings can ever become a habit.'

'I don't think Anthony expects very much from this lunch, Mrs Ripstone.' Taft was lying. He wanted to save the boy's pride. He remembered the thrilled, half-tearful expression on Anthony's face when he had been told his lost mother had been traced. Taft knew that Anthony was secretly hoping that once his unknown mother met him she would want to remove him from the institution and take him to live with her.

'Well, goodbye, Mr Taft. I am looking forward to seeing you at Claridge's on Sunday. I've a feeling we are going to like each other!' Taft noticed for the first time all belligerence had vanished from Mrs Ripstone's voice. It suddenly sounded both coy and flirtatious. Hearing this new note, Taft shook the receiver with a violence. It was if he was trying to shake Mrs Ripstone off the wire.

'You have a very nice voice, Mr Taft. I don't know if anyone's ever told you that!' Mrs Ripstone gave a tinkling, seductive laugh. 'See you on Sunday, Mr Taft!'

'Bitch!' Taft said aloud when she had rung off. 'Bloody fucking bitch!' He rarely swore. He went to his desk to write out a report on battered wives in order to try to forget Mrs Ripstone and the unpromising lunch that he and her abandoned son were soon to have with her.

When Mrs Ripstone told Taft she liked his deep voice, it was by no means the first time a woman had said that to him. The compliment was so familiar that it antagonised rather than flattered him. He reacted with much the same irritability and embarrassment when women told him that he looked like John Wayne.

Taft had always disliked John Wayne as a celluloid hero, and he was bored by his films. John Wayne's swaggering and sharp-shooting myth was repugnant to him. Taft identified with losers, and although his strong, broad build and his rugged, craggy face resembled that of the actor, he always felt ill at ease and demeaned when anyone told him he looked like the tough cowboy hero.

As a social worker, Taft was dedicated and assured. In his dealings with the people he met through his work, he was unselfish and straightforward. He became genuinely concerned with the 'cases' under his care. He identified with their problems, and they found him practical, reliable, and kind.

In his private life, Taft was much less assured, and he was often unreliable and devious. He knew he was attractive to women, and he had become adept at warding them off. In his sexual relationships he was mistrustful and ungiving. By nature he was solitary. He had a horror of human intimacy. Any girl who tried to get close to him aroused his terror and dislike, for he saw his emotional self-sufficiency as his strength, and he felt she was trying to cripple and ensnare him. Taft was prepared to do his best to meet the varying needs of the 'cases' that were assigned to him. But he was in no way prepared to meet the needs and demands of any woman in the bruising hugger-mugger of domesticity. He had chosen to be known only as Taft – he liked the formality. He hated it if anyone called him by his first name, for he resented the familiarity.

Taft lived alone in a neat one-room flat near Paddington Station. In his kitchen there was one mug, one plate, and one knife and fork. The deliberately sparse utensils in Taft's kitchen made a defiant display of his stand.

At night Taft often went to the pubs alone, and he drank quite heavily, for he liked to try and blunt the feeling of hopelessness and despair that came over him at the end of the day when his work had exposed him to a seemingly bottomless ocean of human pain, poverty, squalor and humiliation.

Drinking in pubs, Taft was often picked up by women, and if he found them attractive he allowed them to seduce him, but he was careful to see that his love affairs had no sequel. As a lover he merely obliged. He was never the hunter. He was promiscuous, not out of excessive lust, but out of excessive passivity.

Taft slept with girls on the sofas of other peoples' houses – in other peoples' double beds. In the night he got up and left them to go take a bath in his monastic flat. By morning it was as if the sexual experience of the night had been wiped off the slate of his consciousness like an unimportant chalk-mark.

Taft had a horror of female scenes and recriminations. The women he slept with were often encouraged and challenged by his elusiveness. Their pride was piqued by the indifference of this handsome, rugged man who treated them with avuncular protectiveness and then became without explanation suddenly so busy and unavailable they could hardly believe he was spitting them out of his life as if they were cherry stones.

Through the years, Taft had learnt to devise a technique that helped spare him from the unwelcome consequences, the frantic telephone calls, the tantrums, the insults and the suicide threats to which he had often been subjected to in the past as a result of his fickleness and promiscuity.

Taft had invented a wife. Every time Taft started a new sexual relationship, he warned his partner that it could never become serious on his part, for he still loved only his wife. Taft's imaginary wife had been killed in a car crash just a few weeks after he married her. She had helped to disentangle him from so many relationships, which he saw as a threat to the astringently lonely existence he had chosen for himself, that in a sense it was true, he did love her.

Taft had told so many different women about his wife that he now talked about this mythical and ill-fated figure with enormous natural dignity. She had become so necessary to Taft as a protection that often she seemed more important and real to him than the girls to whom he described her, and he could therefore often forget he was lying when he claimed he was incapable of recovering from her loss. Shielded from the repercussions of his promiscuity by the excuse of his fabricated bereavement, Taft felt that the dishonesty with which he treated his mistresses was justified because it helped to prevent him squandering emotional energy which he felt was better spent on his 'cases'.

The Sunday morning following his conversation with Mrs Ripstone, Taft arrived at St Michael's to pick up Anthony in order to take him to meet his unknown mother at Claridge's. He then travelled with the boy on the Underground to Oxford Street.

Sitting on the train, Taft examined Anthony's face without making it obvious he was doing so. The boy looked so pale and strained and corpse-like that it was as if the ordeal of meeting his mother had interfered with the natural flow of blood in his body. One of the nuns at St Michael's had whispered to Taft that Anthony had hardly eaten or slept in the last week.

Usually Anthony looked so scruffy that his appearance suggested he got some kind of defiant satisfaction from looking memorably wild and unkempt. Today he had made a self-conscious attempt to look neat. His shaggy, over-long hair was slicked down with some kind of cheap hair-oil. It looked flat and unnatural, as if an oily wig that had been pasted on his head with glue.

Taft saw the boy had put on his best suit – the one he wore for Church on Sundays. It was second-hand, shiny, and ill-fitting. Its trousers were too big for him, and they hung in baggy folds round his legs. He was wearing a shirt and a tie, and this too made Taft feel uneasy. Rarely before had he seen the boy wearing anything except grubby, torn T-shirts and ragged jeans. Anthony kept fidgeting with his shirt collar as if he was trying to unfasten a noose that was choking him.

As he surreptitiously examined Anthony, Taft found himself trying to guess what impression the boy would make on his mother. Anthony was surely quite a nice-looking boy… But his eyes had a dazed, unfocused expression that made people feel uncomfortable. Anthony was tall and well-built for a boy of fourteen, but he moved awkwardly with a deliberate stoop that betrayed his lack of confidence.

'Are you nervous, Anthony?'

'A bit, Mr Taft.'

'You shouldn't be.' Taft spoke in his usual deep, reassuring tones, and he felt a disgust at the hypocrisy of his own comforting paternal manner. Why shouldn't Anthony feel nervous? Taft himself was feeling extremely agitated, though he was much too well-trained and controlled to show it. He felt that this lunch at Claridge's was going to be a catastrophe, and he blamed himself for having brought it about.

Looking at Anthony's chalk-white, tormented face, Taft wondered if the whole orphanage policy in regard to the missing mother was wrong. The staff committee at St Michael's had decided that if any of the 'unwanted' children in the orphanage expressed any wish to get to know their unknown mother, every effort should be made to find her and organise a meeting. The mothers were often hard to trace. They had married – changed their names and their lifestyles. Frequently they had moved to different parts of the country. It had taken Taft a lot of time and dedicated sleuth-work to track down Mrs Ripstone.

Now having found Mrs Ripstone living in her Surrey house with her swimming-pool and her retired judge with his 'old-fashioned thinking', Taft wondered if it might not be better for Anthony if she had never been found.

But Taft couldn't be certain. Almost all the 'unwanted' children that he had worked with through the years seemed to have a longing to know what their mothers looked like. This longing was tied up with their need to establish some form of identity. Physically they were all bruised, and they suffered from a painful feeling of confusion as to what they were and how they had come into an existence that condemned them to live in a beggar situation at the mercy of a sparse charity of an institution. Feeling themselves to be outcasts, they were plagued by self-blame and hatred, and it was hard to convince them they were not intrinsically undesirable.

Taft had tried to stop the term 'unwanted' from being used at St Michael's to describe the abandoned children. He felt the word had a pejorative brutality that was likely to reinforce their belief that there was something essentially wrong with them. Taft would have preferred them to be known simply as orphans. But children like Anthony, technically, were not orphans, and so the term 'unwanted' was still applied to him.

Taft remembered the unpleasantness of Mrs Ripstone's affected voice on the telephone. Would one meeting with the owner of that distasteful voice help cure Anthony's insecurity? Were these meetings between abandoned children and abandoning mothers destructive events – rather than the valuable ones that the staff at St Michael's believed them to be? Taft felt an immense psychological fatigue. He simply didn't know.

'What do you think she will be like?' Anthony asked him.

'I'm afraid I can't tell you, Anthony. I only talked to her on the telephone.'

'Maybe I won't be like she hoped.'

'Maybe she won't be like you hoped.' Taft wondered if he should warn Anthony that he had got an unsympathetic impression of his mother. He decided there was no point.

Taft had originally hoped Anthony would choose to meet his mother alone. But as the idea of lunching with her without a third party to act as a buffer clearly terrified the boy, Taft had felt it would be cruel to refuse to go.

Taft and Anthony went through the swing doors of Claridge's. The lobby was crowded with well-dressed people who were either arriving or leaving with a lot of expensive-looking luggage. Two Arabs with tired and decadent faces were making air-travel reservations at the desk. Taft glanced sideways at Anthony, and he saw the boy was shaking.

She seemed to appear from nowhere. Suddenly, Mrs Ripstone was shaking hands.

'You must be Mr Taft! And you must be Anthony!' She gave them such a welcoming coquettish smile, Taft suspected it concealed a certain hysteria.

Mrs Ripstone was in her mid-thirties. She was so over-dressed for this lunch that Taft thought she looked as if she had been gift-wrapped. She was wearing a fur stole over a sleek dress that emphasised the curves of a neat little figure. Her face was small and pert and pretty and she had put such brilliant patches of rouge on her cheeks that they appeared to be inflamed. Her neck and her wrists were gleaming with flashy jewellery, and on her head there was a provocative little hat with a waving feather.

Mrs Ripstone was wearing long, black, spiky, false eyelashes which quivered and struggled when she moved her lids, like the legs of an overturned beetle.

'I'm so delighted to meet you, Mr Taft. Why don't we go into the restaurant? I'm sure we must all be starving. I've reserved us a table.'

Mrs Ripstone led the way into the restaurant. Taft noticed that she minced when she walked and she had very pretty ankles.

'Wait*a*! Wait*a*! I have a table reserved for three.' Frantically she waved a fawn-gloved hand at various indifferent-looking waiters. The more she tried to show that she was at ease and in control in this expensive international hotel, the more she seemed to have the dangerous lack of control of a driverless car that slips its brakes and goes skidding down a hill. None of the waiters seemed to want to find Mrs Ripstone's reserved table. Her grand manner and her over-stylised gestures of command had no effect on them at all.

After what seemed to Taft like an intolerable amount of commotion, complaint, and hand-waving, and after she had made everyone in the restaurant stare at her, Mrs Ripstone was escorted to her table by the head waiter.

'Now what is everybody going to have!' She picked up the enormous and elaborate menu. 'They have very nice desserts here,' she said, turning to Anthony. 'Do you like desserts? My children always make pigs of themselves when I bring them up to London and we all have lunch here after the dentist.'

Did she plan to say that? Taft wondered. Or in her state of confusion did it just slip out?

'Personally, I'm just going to start with a very strong Martini. I've been rushing around London all day shopping and I'm exhausted. Won't you have a Martini, Mr Taft? Surely the grown-ups are entitled to a few little rewards as the price for growing old!'

Taft agreed that he needed a Martini. Looking round the restaurant with its crowded tables of cheerful, chattering people who seemed to give off a smell of opulence that mingled with smells of over-rich food, Taft wondered if there could have been any more unsuitable place to have this humanly gruelling lunch.

'I recommend the *hors d'œuvres*. Would you like that Anthony? I also recommend the vol-au-vent,' Mrs Ripstone said.

Anthony looked blank. Mrs Ripstone realised he didn't know what either of these dishes were, and she explained in a patronising way.

'Don't you do any French at your school?' she asked.

Anthony nodded and blushed. Taft had never seen the boy look so stupid. His second-hand suit looked particularly shabby in contrast to the elegant clothes of the other people in the restaurant. Anthony's unhappy, unfocused eyes stared at his mother's face as if he was trying to memorise it.

'Anyway … Mr Taft says you are doing very well at school, Anthony. And I'm very pleased to hear it.' Mrs Ripstone was lying in order to be pleasant. Taft had never told her Anthony was doing well at school. Anthony was a very poor student and he found it hard to concentrate.

Taft said he would like *hors d'œuvres* and a vol-au-vent. It seemed easiest. He had rarely felt less hungry. Mrs Ripstone started to show off again. She ordered herself some turbot and gave a bored-looking waiter elaborate instructions as to how she wanted it prepared.

The woman is under immense strain, Taft thought. The situation must be a difficult one for her. Shallow as she appears to be, she probably feels more guilt towards Anthony than she chooses to show, and her guilt is useless, for there is no way she can make reparation to him. After this lunch she will go back to her Surrey home and try and forget him. Anthony is an unwelcome ghost from her past that she would like exorcised. She can hardly feel that his exorcism has been successful while she sees him sitting in Claridge's staring at her with his damaged-looking eyes. Feeling the boy's unvoiced accusations, she can only wrap herself even more tightly in the cocoon of her own snobbish values in order to defend herself. Taft wondered briefly if he ought to feel sorry for this silly, overdressed woman. He longed for the lunch to be over.

Once the *hors d'œuvres* arrived Mrs Ripstone once again turned to Anthony and made another self-conscious attempt to charm him. 'You seem very grown-up for your age, Anthony, I didn't expect you to be so tall and handsome!' Mrs Ripstone gave her son an awkward and seductive look.

'Have you got a girlfriend yet, Anthony?' She let out a high and suggestive giggle, and she lowered her eyelids so that the black spikes of her eyelashes fluttered.

Anthony blushed and shook his head. He looked desperate.

'I don't believe you!' Mrs Ripstone gave her son a playful little poke. 'I bet all the girls are after you!'

'It's horrible,' Taft thought. 'She doesn't know how to relate to the boy. She feels so ill at ease that all she can do is flirt.'

'The vol-au-vent is delicious,' Taft said. He found it disgusting, but he was hoping to draw the fire of her attention to himself so she would stop tormenting her son with her unnatural badinage.

Mrs Ripstone turned to Taft with relief. She examined his handsome, craggy face with approval. It was as if she had felt too agitated to notice him until that moment.

'I'm *so* glad you like it, Mr Taft.' Her eyelashes lowered in a girlish flutter. She suddenly seemed tipsy. As this difficult lunch progressed she had been ordering herself more and more Martinis.

'It's such a pleasure to meet you, Mr Taft. You are a lucky boy, Anthony, to have such a charming, intelligent man as Mr Taft taking an interest in you!'

She ordered Taft and herself two more Martinis and said it was time to have dessert. She suggested that Anthony should have the chocolate mousse and Taft should have the lemon soufflé. Both of them nodded feebly, and Taft felt he was behaving as if he was as stunned as the boy.

Mrs Ripstone said that she couldn't resist an éclair. She ran her hands voluptuously down her body in order to draw attention to the trimness of her pretty little figure.

'I'm going to be naughty for once,' she said. 'This is rather a special occasion!'

She turned to Taft and said she felt he must have a very interesting life. She then ordered him another Martini without asking him if he wanted it. For the first time, he looked her directly in the eyes, and he noticed that she was examining him in an extremely predatory way through the spiky veil of her lashes.

Anthony sat there, unhappily picking at his chocolate mousse. He seemed to have ceased to exist for his mother. She behaved as if she and Taft were alone.

'I had the feeling we were going to get on, Mr Taft. I liked the sound of your voice on the telephone. It's a funny thing about voices ... they tell you so much about a person.'

The double Martinis were throbbing in Taft's brain. He had a feeling of nausea and unreality.

Mrs Ripstone placed her hand on his in a proprietary and intimate way. 'I hope you are going to keep in contact with me, Mr Taft.' Her voice had become husky with sexual insinuation. He noticed her hat was a little askew. Her eyes looked bright and greedy and they never left his face. He wondered if she was a nymphomaniac.

He felt her hand tightening its grip on his hand. 'Now we have met at last, we must really keep in contact. You will be hearing from me,' she gave a coy little laugh. 'I want to have news of Anthony.'

Taft felt the tremor of Mrs Ripstone's touch sending something rippling through his body like a sharp current of electricity.

'I want to ask you something, Mr Taft! Has anyone ever told you that you look like John Wayne?'

She was bound to say it. The dreaded compliment hardly irritated him. He couldn't feel it mattered. Neither did he feel it mattered that she had started slyly kicking his ankle under the table – or that he was obediently kicking her back.

Pressing Mrs Ripstone's foot with his foot and looking as confident and rugged as John Wayne, Taft had rarely felt so defeated and depressed. He felt he had failed Anthony at this lunch, but even that hardly seemed to matter, for he could see no way in which anyone could have made this meeting have a more successful emotional outcome for the boy.

Taft could see by the distraught expression in Anthony's eyes that it had been a shock to realise that his mother and himself could only be forever strangers.

The boy had hoped that there would be some kind of automatic human bond between them – but it simply didn't exist. Taft could see that Anthony was disturbed by the fact that he could feel so little for this chattering woman with the over-rouged cheeks – and that Mrs Ripstone obviously felt nothing for him. If they could have felt a mutual antipathy, Taft had the idea it might have been better. It was the absence of any relationship at all between mother and son that made this lunch so tense and embarrassing.

Since his birth Anthony had been 'unwanted', whether Taft winced at the harshness of the term or learnt to tolerate it. All his life Anthony would remain 'unwanted', and Taft couldn't see there was anything anyone could do about it.

Taft continued to press Mrs Ripstone's foot under the table, though he felt not the slightest desire for her. It was as if physically he wanted to make some kind of contact with this woman because he hated to see the way that her son found it so emotionally impossible.

Taft saw the boy's future as incurably bleak. When Anthony left the comparatively kindly haven of the orphanage he would be unemployed and homeless. Without friends or relatives, with only social workers to encourage him, he would start to feel desperate in his isolation. Like so many of the 'unwanted' children that Taft had worked with in the past, he would probably knock about the streets and eventually turn to petty crime. Taft had visited too many children who had been put in St Michael's and years later, with much the same friendly and cheery manner, he had visited them after they had been put in prison. He found it horrifying that they seemed condemned to spend their lives in some form of institution.

Taft pressed Mrs Ripstone's foot even harder – there was aggression in his gesture. But she didn't notice. He saw her look of triumph. She was delighted to think she had made a conquest.

She is probably an unhappy and frustrated woman, Taft thought. It's very probable that she leads a dismal life with her retired judged, who may well be too old and doddery to satisfy her. The illegitimate birth of Anthony was all too likely a tragedy. She is profoundly conventional, and she cares only for appearances. Presumably she saw her pregnancy as a catastrophic disgrace, and now her whole life seems to be dedicated to regaining the respectable image she feels she lost through it.

Taft suspected that Mrs Ripstone was only making such an overt sexual play for him because he knew about the event in her past which she most hoped to hide. Knowing he could never be impressed by the act of ultra-pure respectability she put on to deceive the old judge and her Surrey neighbours, she felt she had nothing to lose if she showed him the side of her nature her life now was spent trying to repress.

Mrs Ripstone raised her glass to Taft and gave him a toast, 'Let's drink to the most interesting man I've met in a long time!' She gave him a meaningful smile. Taft wondered if Anthony had noticed how amorously she was behaving.

If Anthony noticed he gave no sign. He just sat there looking depressed. Anthony's general predicament was so unenviable that Taft couldn't believe the boy would feel that things were made much worse for him by the fact that his mother and his social worker had chosen to carry on a pointless flirtation.

Taft assumed this lunch must have been a harrowing occasion for the boy in the sense that it finally must have smashed any hopes that, late in life, his mother could start to provide him with the affection of which he had always been deprived. But if this lunch, for Anthony, had been a tragic event, it had lacked the dignity that Taft felt should be associated with the moments of human tragedy. It had been a meal of unleavened triviality – it had been nothing more than a sticky stew of flirtatious chit-chat, chocolate mousse and double Martinis.

And now, pressing his foot against Mrs Ripstone's sandal, Taft knew he was debasing this ignoble lunch even further by his surreptitious shows of sexuality. He found this vulgar little woman extremely unattractive. He responded to her advances only out of some kind of apathetic anger that could find no other outlet. He longed for this insufferable meal to be over. By making passes at Mrs Ripstone, he felt he maintained some control over her. He also wanted to have something to do to help kill the time until the bill was paid.

'I have your telephone number, Mr Taft. I think it's best if I ring you. There might be complications if you were to ring me at my house!' He hated the slyness in her laugh. 'I think you can guess why!'

My God! She means it! Taft thought. Because he had been play-acting when he flirted with this woman he had assumed she was doing the same thing. Now he saw she was serious. She intended to see him again. He stared at her with such horror that she noticed.

'Is there something the matter, Mr Taft?'

'Yes ... I mean, no... ' Like someone hallucinating, Taft had started to have a horrendous vision of the future. He saw the devious Mrs Ripstone slipping quietly from her Surrey house while Judge Ripstone was taking a nap. Taft saw himself passively receiving the call she would make him from her local call box. Her voice would be breathless with intrigue. A secret meeting in London would be arranged, and soon he would be standing on a station platform looking just as stalwart and confident as John Wayne as he stepped forward like a robot, devoid of will-power, to greet Mrs Ripstone as she alighted, mincing and overdressed, from her train.

After that, Taft saw the lunch. The lunch would be at Claridge's, and they would both drink many double Martinis before they went up in the hotel lift to the double-room that Mrs Ripstone had taken for the night...

'You look so peculiar, Mr Taft! Is anything the matter?'

Taft was staring at Mrs Ripstone in such a weird, unseeing way that she was frightened. He was having a vision of Mrs Ripstone and himself grappling in the hotel bed. Their love-making was brief and perfunctory. Once it was over Taft saw himself lying naked beside her. He was starting to warn her that she must never expect their relationship to become deep or permanent for he would never be able to love any woman as he still loved his dead wife.

'Are you feeling unwell, Mr Taft?'

'I'm not feeling too well, Mrs Ripstone.' Taft suddenly felt sickened by the idea that many human choices – choices that were to have disastrous and long-lasting consequences – were made in a haphazard and frivolous fashion. Important decisions could be taken in much the same idle and capricious way that Taft saw the people at the neighbouring tables ordering their courses from the menu of Claridge's. First they thought they wanted steak, then on a whim they felt they preferred to have the chicken, then at the last moment they changed again and decided to have fish.

Taft turned his head away from Mrs Ripstone. He couldn't bear to look at her. He found it too easy to see himself with her in that imaginary hotel bedroom. He was with her as a feeble victim of his own pattern of compliance rather than as a prisoner of passion. He suspected Mrs Ripstone was much stronger willed than he was, although his square jaw looked as if it jutted with resolution.

Taft's ugly fantasy of himself in that shared bedroom was so vivid that he found himself carrying it further. As a result of that brief loveless liaison, Mrs Ripstone would become pregnant. Once again she would conceive in exactly the same unlucky, careless way that she had once conceived Anthony …

'I'm so sorry you don't feel well, Mr Taft. Is there anything I can do for you?'

'No, there's nothing you can do, Mrs Ripstone,' Taft said. There was nothing she could do. He felt that was the trouble with this dreary little sex-hungry woman with the feather in her hat. She couldn't even stop him carrying through his distasteful fantasy.

Taft saw the impregnated Mrs Ripstone confessing everything to her silver-haired husband. The ancient Judge Ripstone would think of his own good name and be extremely anxious to avoid the scandal of a divorce. He would promise to forgive her if she hid abroad for nine months and agreed to place the infant at birth with some adoption service …

Taft had withdrawn his foot. Under the table, Mrs Ripstone's sandal groped wildly as she tried to find it. Taft had tucked his legs away so they were out of reach under his chair.

In Taft's hallucination he was no longer lunching with Mrs Ripstone and Anthony. He was in Claridge's alone, and it was fourteen years later. Across the restaurant he could see Mrs Ripstone, but she couldn't see him. She looked much older. Her face was raddled but her curls were still the colour of a marigold and the patches of rouge were just as brilliant on her cheeks.

Mrs Ripstone was lunching with a social worker who was many years younger than Taft. Also sitting at her table was a teenage boy. He was ashen-pale and she had a psychotic expression. Mrs Ripstone was ordering him a chocolate mousse …

Taft got to his feet in such a masterful way that he felt he must be acting like John Wayne. He had stopped hallucinating. He was back with Mrs Ripstone in reality.

'Will you excuse me?' he said to her. 'I'm afraid I'm really going to have to leave. I'm feeling extremely unwell. I will take Anthony back to St Michael's and then I'm going home to lie down.'

'But this is terrible ...' Mrs Ripstone was stuttering, 'I hadn't realised you felt so bad.'

'I'm feeling very bad, Mrs Ripstone.' Taft's deep melodious voice had acquired the piously remorseful tone that always crept into it when his indolent sexual compliance ceased and he became ruthlessly determined to terminate a relationship that he found insufferable.

'I'm afraid I'm not myself,' Taft said. 'I'm suffering from shock. I had a tragedy last week. My wife was killed in a car crash ... '

Polly Devlin

Polly Devlin is a writer, broadcaster, filmmaker, art critic and conservationist. She was born in a remote area in Co. Tyrone in Ireland in the 1940s. Her perspective on life was informed by this atavistic childhood. She comes from an extended family; her brother Barry Devlin, now a writer and filmmaker, was the founder member of the Irish rock group Horslips, and her sister Marie Heaney has written *Over Nine Waves*, a version of Irish myths. Her first jobs (when she was twenty-one) were as features editor on *Vogue*, and as a columnist for the *New Statesman*; she had her own page in the *Evening Standard* a year later. She went to live in Manhattan as a features editor and writer for Diana Vreeland on American *Vogue*. She attended the National Film School in England on a director's course and made the documentary *The Daisy Chain*, now in the archives of the Irish Film Institute. She is the author of six books and her first, *All of Us There*, is now a Virago Modern Classic, and stories from *The Far Side of the Lough* are frequently broadcast and dramatised on the BBC. Her last novel, *Dora*, was read on BBC's Woman's Hour. In 1993 she received an OBE for services to literature. She is also a regular contributor to BBC's Round Britain Quiz representing Northern Ireland. She lives in London and is a professor at Barnard College, Columbia University in New York.

The Countess & Icarus

He came spooling out of nowhere, hit the water hard, broke both his legs and most of his ribs. It was thought he would not walk again. Martine told Dora all this with a certain relish. Martine had had it in for Victor for a long time. Who could blame her? She had been married to him for a long time.

Some time before the plummeting from the sky, Simon had watched Victor pick up a girl in a restaurant and had told Dora with an almost weary interest of how he had set about it. The girl was not, Simon said, exactly pretty, but she was young and with an air, and Victor had eyes for her as soon as he saw her, as indeed had many of the men in the restaurant.

'Had you?' Dora enquired.

'Of course,' Simon said. 'But Victor set about getting the thing with real determination.'

'How?' Dora asked. 'I can't think where he gets the energy. And to think of calling it "the thing".'

'Simple enough, thingy,' Simon said. 'He sent a drink over and when she looked across he made extravagant gestures of adulation.'

'He never did.' Dora said. 'And she bought into the deal?'

'She bought into the deal,' Simon said. 'She laughed and Victor shot across, got her telephone number, and that was that.'

'Was she a tart?' Dora asked.

'Not at all,' Simon said. 'A very nice girl. Elise, out for an evening with her friends.'

'And what happened?' Dora said.

'How do you mean?' Simon said.

'Did he make it? Did he get his onions, did he hit base, did he score, did he hook up? I don't know what the term is any more,' she said, cross as anything. 'Where does he get the energy? And why?'

The very idea of the amount of time and energy needed to start an affair with anyone, let alone someone twenty years younger, filled her with resentful rage.

Simon said, 'She's keen on Victor, she's now his girlfriend, and when it comes to sex, Victor is a young man.'

'Do you think Martine realises?' Dora asked. She thought she knew the answer, but she liked to amass information about Simon's reactions to infidelity in case she ever needed the information.

'Not the details,' Simon said. 'But she'd be pretty foolish not to guess after all these years. I expect that's why she's so often cross.'

Martine was small, dark, closed, competent. Dora had met her when, for the first and last time, Victor had taken her on one of his business jaunts to London.

'Why this time?' she asked.

'Because a so-called friend has told her of the food halls in Harrod's.'

'They're not a patch on any good shop in Paris,' Dora said, surprised.

'It is more for her to have seen it,' he said.

Afterwards, Dora walked around the food halls with Martine, who took many photographs of the fish arrangements.

She invited Dora and Simon to stay with them in Brittany, in a large, gloomy, half-timbered house that made Dora think of Madame Bovary. She was a cook with a nose and an eye for food, like that of a collector. She roamed the woods, the markets, visited fishermen and came back with mushrooms, herbs, trout, and then cooked food as Dora had never known it. Delectable feasts, food that often had a carapace; mussels, *boeuf en croute*, casseroles with a crust, *brûlée* – things that burst and oozed nicely when cracked open. Martine's crust now remained intact as far as Dora knew, but presumably had, once upon a time, yielded and oozed nicely for Victor.

Dora surmised that Martine's closed coldness, which Simon said amounted to shrewishness, came from living in a condition of misery; she treated the world with a modest reticence that made Dora admire her. Just once, the reticence vanished; she asked, as it were in passing, 'Did Victor know Simon first or you?'

'Simon,' Dora lied. Martine looked at her and said nothing.

He had thought himself Daedalus. At least that was how Martine presented it as she told Dora about his accident, how he had fallen from the sky, his little, helpless engine strapped to his back. Dora didn't say that as far as she remembered Daedalus had kept going, had landed safely in Sicily, that it was Icarus who was the pillock. Whatever. Victor took a long time to fall. Martine said that he had hit the water with a terrible thump. As he fell, did he think he was going to die? Dora desperately wanted to know. She'd read that time elongated at such moments. She wanted to know, too, whether such untoward tumbles change a man and make him appreciate any bit of life he's got left. But there seemed no way to wheedle such real revelation, such proper news, from another world out of Victor without asking him herself, which she could not, would not do. A matter of time, geography, sensibility, and Simon refused to pose such questions to Victor. 'Perhaps it's to do with nationality,' Dora said. 'Your lack of curiosity. That's a very English thing. The Irish are curious.' She noted again how, when talking to an Englishman, any Englishman

– even her husband – she managed to put a good gloss on any characteristic, however unpleasant, that she attributed to the Irish, and thus, of course, to herself.

When Dora was young, she had regarded men as creatures from another planet altogether, and this had prevented her from taking men seriously. The longer she lived, the less the manifest difference between men and women mattered. But the fact that a man could fall for an appreciable length of time through the ether and into the Mediterranean from an unclouded sky, and one of his closest male friends would not question his reactions during that plunge, made her feel the gap again. Or else her manners were at fault. You never quite knew with Simon.

Victor had always seemed older than his age to Dora, and quintessentially French. Any foreign man seemed older to her, as though being born in a foreign land automatically added on years, and part of the Frenchness was that as long as she had known him, he had always had a mistress. Even when Dora was his lover she knew that his mistress lived in Paris and his wife Martine lived in Brittany, where he joined her and his children at weekends. As a young woman Dora had harboured an image of the archetypal Frenchman, gleaned from her reading of Arthur Mee's *Children's Encyclopaedia*. This Gallic type wore a *casquette* jammed on his head, a Verdun-style moustache attached to his upper lip, and a cigarette to the lower. He gesticulated a lot and trundled about in a Deux-Chevaux. Victor somehow seemed to answer to this image, even though he drove a large Mercedes very fast, wore an English trilby that he fancied himself in, and smoked cigarillos. The way he walked, the set of his shoulders, how he entered a room, his bulk and compacted power, made him irresistible to her for a time.

Then, in Paris, nearly twenty years after Dora had first met him, and soon after he had taken up with Elise, the *jolie-laide* of the bar, Victor introduced Simon to a woman who he said had finally called him to account. She took him for her lover rather than becoming his mistress, and for the first time, he said to Simon, he felt jealousy. He rather liked the new sensation but wanted the cause of it to stop and did not know how.

'A certain age,' Simon reported later to Dora. 'Extremely well preserved, beautifully turned out, vivacious almost to a fault and absolutely exhausting. Victor likes the demands she makes, jumps up and down like a little dog. Well, a big dog actually. And what tickles Victor most of all is that she is a Countess. He gets a real charge out of that.'

'I didn't know Victor was a snob.' Dora said.

'I don't think he is,' Simon said. 'It's not her title so much, as that he relishes her insistence on it, her entitlement as it were. She's insolent and he's always been the insolent one.'

Dora was surprised by this perception. She had never thought of Victor as insolent but, after all, what he had done to her was insolent. That had been part of his charm. He had charmed her, in the old-fashioned sense, cast a spell on her. And now, long-married to Simon, her affair with Victor far in the past, she was still charmed by him. Dora had introduced Simon to Victor years before. From that first meeting in the *Closerie des Lilas*, when they had both ordered sweetbreads and Simon had grinned with pleasure at Victor's choice of wine, they had liked each other, and from liking had grown admiration. Each felt that the other embodied the most admirable of their national characteristics.

Over the years Victor told Simon of his affairs; the pursuits, the conquests, the dramas, the denouements, the tragedies, the renouncements and the endings. Dora refused to wonder about reciprocity. She did not even countenance the idea. As Victor grew older and matured in looks, he seemed to be even more attractive to women. He was not one of those aging philanderers who only seek solace in between the narrow thighs of post adolescents. His mistresses were any age he fancied.

Dora still occasionally had lunch with him in London, and waiting for him in a restaurant, she could see how the force of his entrance caused even the most hardened customers of the restaurant to raise their collective heads. Women in particular became alert. He looked theriomorphic, one of those broad-faced bull creatures with a curling fringe, turned into an animal by a large, angry goddess, but who retained enough human characteristics to hark back to their original form. He, though, was the obverse version – as though the goddess had touched an animal for her own amusement and turned it into a human. She knew that he knew the effect he created; it was his way of making a fiefdom.

In the restaurant he kissed her, expanded himself into the little slatted seat and parodied himself, bunching fingers to his lips to fling kisses to show her how glorious she was to him, to all the world.

She beamed. 'And why are you in such good looks?' she asked. 'Love again?'

'It is to me to ask you the same question except that you are always in good looks. And yes. Love again and again.'

He said this with such a leer of satisfaction that Dora burst out laughing.

'You are incorrigible, Victor,' she said. 'The way you keep at it.'

'Not *again* like that,' he said, smiling. 'Though that also. Again and again. Twice.' He repeated the word triumphantly. 'Twice.'

'Again and again', Dora said. 'I look at you with respect. I can't remember what once feels like, never mind over and over.' She felt a twinge of disloyalty.

'Ah, Dora,' he said. 'What a waste – but it needn't be so.' But she could see his heart wasn't in it.

'Twice women. And what is more I adore both.'

'But you've always had twice,' Dora said, genuinely bewildered by his air of revelation. 'Martine and whoever. Me, for example.'

'Ah,' he said. 'Then three women, if you are counting my wife. But Martine does not enter into this equation.'

'Do they all know about each other?'

He looked at her as if she was crazy. 'Are you mad? No, no, no. No one knows nothing... And they are different as the cheese and chalk. They arrive... different backgrounds, different ages, different habits. It is most enjoyable.'

'I've heard,' Dora said. 'But say no more till we order some food.' My, she thought, my priorities *have* changed.

Dora had first met Victor when she was still a girl, half wordly-wise, half a fool. He had picked her up on a flight from London to Paris. Her first journey to Paris, in fact. A film company had paid her fare; she was travelling first class and enjoying it. The big, glamorous Frenchman in the seat beside her charmed her against her will, ordered champagne, put his hand lightly on her knee and offered to drop her off at her hotel. 'It's absolutely on my way,' he said, but somehow her hotel became the destination, where after a magical lunch she went to bed with him. Her childhood dispensation had infected her with the disease of gratitude as well as the inability to say no, and a ride from the airport in such a big car, lashings of champagne, and an expensive lunch induced a fat, sleepy gratitude. Victor changed her ideas and outlook on men and sex. She had no idea that a man could be so pleased and interested by the very fact of womanhood. That wonder had made her lapse into a pleasure mixed with rage at her promiscuous collapse, the sinfulness of what was happening, the sheer, swooning badness of it.

For a time Victor came to London a lot and they met in the expensive hotels where he stayed. Once after making love, Victor still caressing her, she remembered a conversation she had had with her mother when she was, what, ten or eleven, and had just finished reading a novel called *Sorrel and Son*, in which Sorrel had had a talk to his son about what he called 'The business of sex'. He had not, search as the young Dora might through the pages, ever got down to the business of telling exactly what this business was, so Dora, summoning up courage from she knew not where, asked her mother: 'What is the business of sex?' 'My mother informed me,' Dora told Victor, 'that it meant the gender choice when you are filling in forms; and come to think of it – not half it doesn't, as the bishop said to the actress.' She had a merry time explaining all this to Victor, who was indeed paying careful attention to filling her form.

Now in the restaurant, they talked as old friends, of the pursuit of Elise, who, it appeared, adored him, and of the Countess who had captivated him at a garden party given by the local mayor in Brittany.

'She was capering about and I asked the Mayor who is that marvellous woman.'

'Is the Mayor a friend?' Dora enquired. 'Is she beautiful? I love capering. Where did you learn such a good word?'

'My friend Jean Claude is now the mayor,' Victor said. Dora had met Jean Claude, who was Victor's compatriot and hero. He was mayor of the village, as his father had been until the fall of France in the war. He had starved to death in a concentration camp for his part in the Resistance, and was commemorated by a statue in the village. 'She was not exactly beautiful, but she had a message. Capering, you gave me. It means moving vivaciously.'

Dora nodded, smiling, remembering Simon's description of the Countess – vivacious to a fault. 'And she was charming. She charmed me.'

'And what did Jean Claude say?'

'He said, "Ah, you like Françoise? La Comtesse de Gescancourt. *Elle couche. Mais pas avec tout le monde.*" '

'He didn't.' Dora was shocked.

'I was *bouleversé*,' he said. 'And I am not *tout le monde*. This woman, Dora, you must understand, is fun. Tough, you know, and very demanding. Also, there's no question, but I send flowers after every time. I never heard of such a thing.'

'Every time? Dora said, her eyes widening theatrically. 'You mean you pop out between times?'

Victor gave a scowl of pleasure. 'Every meeting. Which is often.'

After lunch they walked down Sloane Street, and he went into a smart flower shop and bought her a strange, green-striped orchid. 'Extravagance, Victor,' Dora said, grinning. 'Or habit now, after training by La Comtesse'.

He looked melodramatically wounded. 'You will never be a habit,' he said. 'You will always be like the orchid, a beautiful caprice.'

'An orchid is a parasite as I remember,' Dora said, smiling; the assistant had a neat, little, reptilian head. 'Silly old bats.' Dora could imagine her saying to herself as she took their money.

Then, as the months went by, the fragile scenario started to fall badly apart. Simon brought back increasingly desperate-sounding snippets of gossip about Victor. The Countess was becoming more elusive, and his affair had developed into an obsession, so Elise had been banished. Martine in her fastness in Brittany had stopped cooking and had become restless and angry in a way she had never been before.

Victor began to plot. 'I don't wish to marry her,' he told Simon. 'I am a practical man. But I would like to make her permanent in my life. She has a certain look now, a look I know on the face of women I've made love to; but this look is already there when I visit her. I am very jealous. I am torn.'

'*And* he's frightened of Martine,' Dora said. 'She'd screw him for everything he's got. And quite right, too.'

'Quite,' Simon said.

There were other things that disturbed Victor. When he visited her apartment he saw lilies, which he hadn't sent. He plied her with caviar, bagatelles, even jewellery, and as Victor, though rich, had been a somewhat careful man with money, it was irrefutable proof to Dora that he was in over his head. Then he found out the enemy. The Countess had taken up with a full-blown, no-holds-barred general.

'Has she indeed?' Dora said admiringly when Simon told her. She didn't envy her; she was appalled at the idea of having to try to satisfy that old itch, but as she had once admired Victor's energy, she now admired even more that of the mysterious Countess who could so insouciantly leave one demanding lover for another.

'He's famous, or perhaps infamous, in France for having led Algerian troops into Germany in 1945; troops who then went totally out of control and did atrocious and terrible things. Dreadful things. A famous black spot in the war.'

'Why haven't I heard of it?' Dora asked.

'Oh, there were atrocities on both sides,' Simon said. 'But black spots fade when set against real darkness.'

'Is Victor jealous of the General?'

'Dreadfully.' Simon said. 'And even more, hates him for what he did to France. He was appalled to think that she might marry the General, who, it transpires, is very fit and *sportif.*'

Victor began to take exercise, to be preoccupied with '*la ligne*', to have his hair tinted and styled, to pay more attention to his clothes.

Since Martine had stopped cooking he had lost weight, or perhaps he had fretted it away. He determined to win the Countess back by becoming a hero. He took up micro-light flying.

'Sounds like he's trying to rise above everything,' Dora said, and imagined him, a bulky Phaeton strapped into one of those little rickety machines that always looked as though they were constructed from old bicycle wheels and wire when they chugged across Dora's sky in England. They irritated her, their snitchy sound above her disturbing the air. Victor chugged across the sky and out across the Mediterranean until the machine suddenly stopped working, the wires slackened and he fell a long, long way into the sea.

Martine telephoned Dora and Simon to tell them the news. It was the first call Dora had ever had from her. 'He has broken both his legs, most of his ribs, and they don't think he'll ever walk again.'

Simon visited him in hospital in Nice as often as he could. Against the odds Victor began to recover, day-by-day and limb-by-limb, until eventually he could shuffle a little further around his bed each day, urged on by a strong physiotherapist who brooked no nonsense. He was always glad to get back into bed. 'Ahhh, bed…' he said to Simon. 'When we are very young we're in it all the time for one reason; when we are grown men we want to be in it for another; and now I think I will never again get out of it.' At these words the physiotherapist yanked him out of the bed and Simon said goodbye as patient and carer began their linked shuffle around the hospital room.

'Victor has fallen further than he knows,' Simon said to Dora.

When he was sent home, Martine entered into her kingdom. The gloomy house became a fortressed hospital. She nursed him with the same brisk competency she brought to whatever she did.

When Simon went to visit him in Brittany he found Victor fatter and more determined on revenge. 'He wants to visit the

Countess and he wants to do it when I'm next in Paris. He says he needs my support'.

'Moral or physical?' Dora asked.

'Both, I should think,' Simon said. 'I suspect it's a final meeting with the Countess. And I think he would quite like to do in the General.'

'Final?' Dora interrupted, horrified at the idea of Victor dying.

'No, not final in that sense,' he said. 'But it's over, the affair is over. It already was before the accident, though Victor refused to admit it. In any case, he seems a different person, and the Countess isn't one to stand around waiting for a convalescent to recover his energies or restart old engines.'

'I should think he's had quite enough of engines,' Dora said.

'And she's probably had enough of waiting.' Simon said. 'For a start, time isn't on her side. I believe she's much older than Victor has let on or admits. She's moved to an apartment on the rue Lille. He thinks the General bought it for her'.

'Will Martine let him go to Paris?' Dora said. 'I should think she has her ways of keeping him inside Maison Bovary.'

'We'll see.'

'Well,' he said when he returned from Paris. 'Victor picked me up at the Gare du Nord. He'd hired a smart car and driver – no question of taxis. He looked much better and very dapper. He was lugging an enormous bunch of lilies and when we got to the rue Lille – to an imposing apartment block – the driver helped him out of the car, arranged the lilies about Victor's person, and rang the bell. It was apparent when the Countess answered that she was not expecting anyone, never mind Victor, who I suppose she thought was safely incarcerated in Brittany.'

'But hadn't he arranged it?' Dora asked, astonished. 'Surely he didn't just show up? The French never do that. Could she have forgotten?'

'I don't think it was so much that she'd forgotten as that she hadn't really taken it on board. He'd telephoned from Brittany quite a bit beforehand, and perhaps she thought he was indulging in a spot of wishful thinking. In any case, it was obvious that we weren't expected. I could hear her little squeaky voice on the intercom: "Oh, my dear Victor, we're just going out. Any other evening…" She pleaded desolation, inconsolation, the lot. But he wasn't letting go. He must have known when she said *we* that the General was with her, but he had his mouth stuck to the intercom like a humming bird at honey. He just dug in his heels and said he must see her, he was going to camp there if needs be, so finally she pressed the buzzer. We struggled upstairs with the lilies and it was apparent that in the interval between us ringing and climbing to her apartment door there had been terrific activity.'

'What? Putting on their clothes?'

'No … I don't think … I think they were comfortably settled for the evening, perhaps a bit unbuttoned, and the old General didn't much like being disturbed.'

'Especially by a rival,' Dora said.

'I should think he minded terribly. And when she opened the door to Victor, peering out from between a huge bunch of lilies like a mad ferret, she was all of a flurry and directly opposite, in another doorway, stood the General, moustachioed and red-faced and fierce. Just in front was a tiny table with bottles and glasses and drinks and little plates of nuts and things. They'd obviously put it all out while we were climbing the stairs. Just then someone came in through the courtyard door below and a whirlwind of a draught, a real gust, came whistling up the stairs and caught the little table, which see-sawed for what seemed like ages; just before it fell the General rescued the wine, and then the table quite slowly toppled over, drinks, plates, glasses, nuts and all, with the most tremendous crash.

175

'I bent down sharpish, if only to hide my face, and began to pick up the nuts and crisps and bits of glass. The sight of Victor caught up in the lilies with a deal of yellow pollen over his face and clothes, thrusting them at the Countess, who was scrunching over nuts and glass, and the General who was cursing and swearing, was more than I could take. I got the table upright again and put what I'd rescued back on it and as I rose, I saw the General put the wine bottle back on it rather hard – and very slowly the whole thing toppled over again, exactly as before, except this time in trying to stop the table falling Madame dropped the lilies. I couldn't control the laughter this time. Victor has a good turn of phrase when roused, and the old General was swearing even more fluently, and Madame began to hyperventilate and clutch at herself. All I could do was get down on all fours and crawl about among the shards, crying too, but crying with laughter.

'The General went off to get another bottle of wine, and the Countess disappeared with the rescued lilies and the General came back, muttering furiously with a dustpan and brush, and finally all was mopped and brushed and we more or less settled down. No one spoke to me after the introductions; I was beyond the Pale – a lunatic, laughing Englishman. And then Victor did what I suddenly realised he had come to do. He launched into an attack and a lament about the village in Germany where the atrocities had been committed by the Algerian troops under the General's command. The General couldn't believe his ears. I don't suppose the affair had been mentioned to him to have it said so plainly – and by a rival lover of his mistress was more than he could stand.

'I thought he might have a heart attack, but he charged towards Victor, who showed a fair turn of speed and got up and threw his wine over him. The General knocked Victor down and then turned and rushed out the room. I thought he'd gone to get a sword or a gun or claw hammer to finish Victor off, who was still lying on the floor looking somewhat surprised.

'The Countess rushed out after the General, and I helped Victor to his feet, and there was a lot of screaming from the kitchen, and then the Countess rushed back in in tears, her mascara everywhere, lipstick smeared, and told Victor that he had ruined her, her life, her dreams, her illusions. Then she rushed out again.

'Victor was shaky on his pins and kept dabbing at his bruised face. We started for the door and when the old girl came back in, I must say my admiration for her shot up. She was in perfect control. It was as if she had rewound and wiped the whole scene so that it had never happened. She was very dignified and said that we must leave. So we bowed and backed towards the door, but I had to ask to use the loo – you can imagine – and I passed by the open door of the kitchen. A little supper for two was laid up on the kitchen table, and the General was sitting at it, staring straight ahead, looking a very grey colour indeed. I'm not sure he wasn't dead. He certainly didn't move when I came out again. On the way home Victor perked up. He seemed to think he'd scored a famous victory.'

'I have my honour,' he wrote to Simon. 'I loved her, and I detested to see her with this man. I am a patriot, that is how I am, how I was born. Jean Claude's father died for France, and a pig like this lives. He is not an honourable man by any means. I have my honour, but my wings have been clipped. I have taken up archaeology, and walk the fields picking up flints and writing in a journal. Tell Dora I fill the forms.'

Dora thought of him falling, falling, falling, and thought too of their first meeting in the sky on the way to Paris, and her afternoon in the hotel where he had shown her what it was like to leave the ground. She began a letter: 'My incorrigible Icarus,' she wrote. 'I am glad you landed safely', and left it at that.

Frances Molloy

Frances Molloy was born in 1947 in Dungiven, Co. Derry. Her 1985 autobiographical novel, *No Mate for the Magpie*, discussed her experiences growing up during the early years of the Northern Troubles. Her short story collection, *Women are the Scourge of the Earth,* was published in 1998. She died in 1991.

The Devil's Gift

Harry Ryan sat sullenly in a big wooden chair at the top of the table.

Mary, his wife, an ample woman of forty, was dishing out food. John, their son, tried to lend an air of good humour to the whole procedure, while his sister, Clair, helped serve up. Harry didn't keep them in suspense for very long.

'Well, Holy Christ!' he started, addressing no one in particular, 'I thought I'd heard it all, but a nun, our fine lady, a nun!'

John pulled his chair closer to the table and clenched his teeth.

Harry repeated the taunt, 'A nun, a nun, our fine lady, a nun!'

Mary threw a listless look at him across the table. 'I thought I asked you to leave her alone,' she said. 'Haven't you been at her long enough?'

'Long enough. Long enough,' he mimicked. 'Don't long enough me, woman. Heading off to become a bloody nun, just when she's old enough to earn a bit of money.'

His wife only argued with a sigh, absently changing the baby from one breast to the other.

'Listen to yourself,' John shouted, pushing his chair away from the table in disgust. 'If you'd ever learned to keep your trap

179

shut, Clair might not be running off to throw her life away. She thinks all men are like you, and could you blame her?'

The younger children made a quick retreat under the table when their father rose to his feet. He drove his knife into the table.

'You see the kind of a rearing you have there, woman?' Harry roared at his wife. But amazingly, there were no fireworks. Harry just grabbed his coat from the back of his chair and stormed out, banging the door behind him.

At nine o'clock next morning when she'd closed the door on the last straggler off to school, Mary sighed.

'Thank God,' she said to Clair, 'Now we can have a cup of tea to ourselves before we start cleaning.' The room was its usual early morning mess: shoes and dirty clothes strewn about the floor, bulging cupboards hanging open exposing every imaginable kind of junk.

Clair wet the tea and made space for two cups on a corner of the table. Mary continued talking.

'It'll take them the best part of four hours to drive from Athgar. Just as well, too, with the work we have to do. And don't forget, as soon as we have the house cleaned, you need to wash and change into your new frock. You look like a scarecrow.'

'Well,' Clair said, laughing as she started to pour the tea, 'Look who's talking!' As she spoke she nearly dropped the tea pot. Two nuns were opening the gate, their habits flapping vigorously in the wind.

'Mammy, they're here, the nuns,' she gasped.

Mary jerked to her feet. 'Holy Mother of God, what are we going to do?' she asked. 'We can't bring them into a house like this, and we can't leave them standing on the doorstep.'

Mary dashed towards the back bedroom. 'I can't see them. Tell them I'm sick,' she said.

'Mammy, please don't,' Clair pleaded. 'If they think you're ill, they won't take me.'

They made a frantic effort to tidy the place, opening the bedroom door and pitching armfuls of clothes and shoes out of sight. The knocking grew persistent.

'We'll have to let them in now,' Mary whispered. 'You go, Clair.'

'No, Mammy, please, you go.'

In the end they went to the door together, one looking as flustered and embarrassed as the other. On the doorstep stood two women, dressed in the habit of Francis of Assisi.

The oldest of the pair, a frail woman of fifty, spoke first. 'Mrs Ryan? I'm Reverend Mother Virtue, and this is Sister Veronica, our directress of vocations.'

'I'm pleased to meet yous both. This is Clair.'

Clair opened her mouth to speak, but when no sound came she closed it again and lowered her head.

'Oh dear, I've forgotten my manners, won't yous come in?' said Mary. A picture of Jesus, his heart exposed and bleeding, watched impassively from a vantage point high up on the wall above a votive light, flanked by jam jars packed with wild flowers and evergreens from the hedgerows thereabout.

'Yous'll excuse the state of the house I hope, the wains have just gone to school,' Mary continued, clearing armfuls of soiled clothes from two chairs. Both nuns continued to stand.

'Would you like a cup of tea, Reverend Mother?'

'No, thank you, Mrs Ryan.'

'How about you, Sister?'

'Thank you, Mrs Ryan, you are most kind,' she answered with a half smile.

'How many children do you have, Mrs Ryan?' the Reverend Mother enquired as she examined her surroundings.

'Ten.'

'Is Clair the eldest?'

Clair felt her heart leap; this was the first time her presence had been acknowledged.

'No, Reverend Mother, she's not. I have a boy, John, one year older.'

The nuns sat down.

'So you think you have a vocation in the religious life, Clair?'

'Yes, Reverend Mother.' She faltered, then added almost inaudibly, 'Well, I think so, Reverend Mother.'

'Do you think you will be able to study, Clair?' Sister Veronica asked. 'I understand from your letter that you have little schooling.'

'I didn't get a lot of schooling, Sister,' she blurted out, 'but I've always wanted to learn more.'

'Good, very good,' Sister Veronica smiled. 'God expects us all to try our hardest, Clair.'

'What kind of work does your husband do, Mrs Ryan?' the Reverend Mother enquired.

'Well, you see,' Mary began, stalling, 'there has never been a lot of work around here for Catholic men. Mind you, he takes anything that comes up. He's a good worker and never likes to be idle. For the past few weeks,' she added, her confidence growing, 'he's been working on my father's farm.'

'Your father is a farmer, Mrs Ryan?' the Reverend Mother said.

'Indeed he is,' Mary bragged. 'All the land to the road belongs to my father.'

Clair, smarting with mortification, began sweeping the range.

'You see that machinery in the big field up there?' Mary said, pointing, 'and them cows, they all belong to my father.'

The nuns exchanged knowing looks.

'Are you depending at all on Clair's future earnings?' the Reverend Mother asked.

'There's no need to be worrying about the like of that, Reverend Mother,' Mary assured her serenely.

'Very well,' the Reverend Mother said slowly, casting a slightly deprecatory glance around the room.

'We receive postulants twice a year,' she said. 'On 2 February and 15 August. Which date is most convenient?'

'February,' Clair replied, heart in her mouth.

'Should you not ask your mother's permission first?' Mother Virtue asked with a smile.

'No, no, it's up to Clair to decide,' Mary broke in, tears choking her voice with the realisation of what had been decided.

'Very well, I'll expect you on 2 February, my child. Now we must be off,' she said, rising. Mary began to rummage through her purse.

'Here's a wee something to help you with the petrol.'

Clair looked on in astonishment as the Reverend Mother slipped the five pounds into a slit at the side of her habit.

'I'll see that Clair gets something nice with this when she comes to us,' she said.

When the nuns had gone, Clair made fresh tea for the two of them and pored over the documents left behind by the Reverend Mother.

'Are you of legitimate parentage?' Clair shrugged, determined to borrow a dictionary, and read aloud the next question. 'Is there any public stain on the family?'

'Was Daddy being in jail a public stain on our family?' Clair asked.

'Clair Ryan,' Mary exploded. 'Your father never appeared in a court in his life. He was dragged out of bed in the middle of the night by B men and thrown in Crumlin Road Jail. I didn't know whether he was alive or dead. Public stain, indeed. Stormont is a public stain. In truth, I'll have something to say to these nuns if they try to public stain me.'

'Sorry, Ma,' Clair said, gently easing the paper from her grasp. 'Sure wasn't Francis himself locked away?'

'That wouldn't surprise me in the least,' Mary fumed. 'Nothing would be low enough for them B men.'

The nun's documents became a focal point of the family's attention over the next few days. Neighbours called in to scrutinise them. The list of personal belongings that Clair was supposed to take with her created the greatest sensation, with everybody clamouring to find out what a nun wore under her habit. Great surprise was expressed that she should need twelve pairs of black stockings. What for, nobody could be sure, except John, who said they'd make a great rope ladder if she wanted to escape. An old lady took Clair aside and put her right. Twelve, she explained, was understood to be the total number of undergarments required. The nuns could not write such words as knickers, brassieres and suspenders, for reasons of refinement and decorum.

As the leaving day approached, a heaviness descended on the family. No voice was raised in anger or in mirth, and every precaution was taken never to allude to the coming event. Outside the house, all was friendliness. Everyone wanted to talk to Clair, to shake her hand, to seek her opinion.

Some mothers brought their errant teenage girls along to her, with requests that she put them back on the right path. Why their daughters could not be more like Clair, these mothers could not understand. Mere acquaintances showered her with gifts, with money, and with requests for prayers. Elderly ladies drew her aside and confided their secrets to her. Clair was everybody's favourite. The toast of the town. When 2 February came round, she had amassed what she considered a huge fortune: seven hundred and eighteen pounds, two shillings and sixpence, to take with her as a dowry.

The journey to the convent was strained, almost silent, and took the best part of four hours. In late afternoon they reached their destination, two miles outside Athgar. The convent, an imposing, gothic, country house, stood gaunt and rambling at the end of a tree-lined avenue. Away to the left, half-hidden by trees, Lough Nellen appeared dead and lifeless, reflecting the heavy February sky.

Her father braked the car abruptly at the first unexpected sight of the house. He leant his head down over the steering wheel for several seconds before speaking. Mary sat beside him mutely, and Clair, watching from the back seat, felt a stab of guilt dart into her. Her parents looked old and defeated.

'Listen, pet,' her father faltered, an unfamiliar shake in his voice. 'I've been thinking. Me and your ma, has been thinking,' he corrected himself, looking towards Mary for support, 'and John,' he added hurriedly. 'We've all been thinking, that maybe what you need is a wee holiday. Look, I have the money,' he produced his wallet. 'I got a loan from the Credit Union. How would you like a week in Dublin? We'll see that you get a grand time, and I'll see the people that gave you presents, and give them back myself. I'll explain that we talked you out of going till you were older. What do you say?'

Clair couldn't speak straight away. Her answer never came. They were interrupted by a tapping on the windscreen. A nun, who introduced herself as Sister Mary Patrick, urged them on to the house for fear they should catch their deaths in the cold. That was that.

Mother Virtue greeted them. Clair was sent away down a long corridor with a young nun. She followed, matching her pace to that of the silent figure who walked her through the building, then up a wide staircase. No sound penetrated the thickness of the walls. As they neared the top of a second flight of stairs, Clair was gripped by panic. 'I didn't say goodbye to my parents,' she said in alarm. 'Have they gone?'

The young nun placed an index finger over her lips before turning silently to mount another flight of stairs. Clair followed quietly, tears brimming.

On the second floor the nun beckoned Clair into an open doorway. 'I couldn't answer your question on the stairs, Sister,' she whispered. 'It is a breach of the Holy Rule to speak in any part of the house except the novitiate, and then only during the hour of recreation. In special circumstances it is permitted to speak like this in an open doorway. But not in a corridor or on the stairs. And yes, Sister, you will see your parents before they go home. They are in the parlour having tea, but first you must change and go to the refectory for tea.'

They entered a large room. 'This is the postulants' dormitory,' she said. 'Our bed is the one with the curtain drawn around it. On our bed you will find our postulants' garb. Change as quickly as possible. I'll wait for you here.'

'Our bed?' she repeated in astonishment.

'Yes, Sister,' the nun replied. 'In the convent we do not have personal possessions. Everything we use, we refer to as ours.'

Her parents left for home an hour later, following a brief reunion. Clair was then introduced to her new companions in a large room on the first floor, directly beneath the dormitory. The novitiate was where novices and postulants spent most of their time. Three long tables, positioned edge-to-edge lengthwise, occupied the centre of the floor. A row of bare wooden chairs stood on either side. Facing each other at the opposite ends were two high-backed chairs. These belonged to the novice mistress, Mother Peter, and Sister Mary Helen, her assistant.

Mother Peter, a small, plump woman with warm brown eyes and a ready smile, had been novice mistress in the house for nearly twenty years, and was affectionately referred to as 'Our Mother'. Sister Mary Helen was large, clumsy and surly, and was affectionately referred to by no-one.

'Being the youngest and most junior sister in the house, you must sit beside me, Clair, so that I can keep an eye on you,' the novice mistress told her when the introductions were over.

Seconds later, the door opened and Mother Virtue entered.

Everyone in the room bowed reverently, saying, as if with only one voice, 'Good evening, Reverend Mother.'

'Continue, please continue, Sisters,' she said. 'Let the party commence.'

It was customary in the community to give a welcoming party for new entrants. Clair, as guest, was invited to be seated in the company of Mother Virtue, Mother Peter, and Sister Mary Helen. The entertainment began at once, with a choir singing a verse to the tune of Dan O'Hara:

'Now it's here you are today
In this convent by the lake,
Even though you may be feeling broken-hearted.
But we soon will chase your gloom
With our antics round the room,
And we'll help you to forget
From whom you've parted.'

Then four novices danced a lively hornpipe to music from a record player. Two girls from the Bogside, sisters in real life, sang 'Greensleeves', a plump young woman with protruding teeth banged out the 'Blue Danube' on a piano. Every one of the forty novices and postulants took their turn. Some sang, some danced, others played instruments, and last of all, a novice called Sister Mary Thelma recited, in a strong Cork accent, Joseph Mary Plunkett's poem, 'I See His Blood Upon The Rose'.

When the frolics finally ended, Clair, very moved by this treat, rose to her feet to thank them and applaud. Clair stopped clapping and sat down quickly. The Reverend Mother spoke to her directly. 'It's your turn now, Clair.'

'But Mother, I couldn't.'

'Remember why you are here,' said Mother Virtue. 'It is your turn.'

Overcoming her embarrassment, she recited 'The Ballad of Peter Gilligan', by W.B. Yeats.

It is well-known that the more devout and holy a soul, the more prone it is to temptation from the devil; in a moment of idleness, the evil one can take possession of an unsuspecting soul and turn even the most fervent around in her tracks, making a complete debauch of her in the twinkling of an eye. So never a moment is spent in idleness in a religious house. So it was in the Franciscan convent of the Holy Angels, Bloomchamp, Athgar.

The day began at half-past four in the morning with the ringing of the awakening bell. Each sister, rising from her bed, would say, in answer to the bell, which to her represented the voice of God, *deo gratias*. She would then kiss the floor, an exercise in humility, before washing, dressing, making her bed and hurrying to the chapel for the first prayers of the day. These prayers and the mass lasted three hours, and ended with the Reverend Mother leading the community in single file out of the chapel and to the refectory for breakfast, chanting psalms all the while. Fifteen minutes later, breakfast finished, dishes washed, the same procession would snake its way back to the chapel to give thanks for the gift of food.

The hour between half past eight and nine-thirty was set aside for household chores. It was considered desirable that one should work alone, but where this was not possible, and two or more sisters had to work together, ejaculations were recited aloud and carefully counted so that each nun could later calculate the number of indulgences gained. To the uninitiated, this practice could appear confusing. 'JESUS, one, JESUS, two, JESUS, three, JESUS, four, JESUS, five, JESUS, six, JESUS, seven, JESUS, eight,' the sisters would chant in unison as they descended upon a sackful of carrots. Inevitably, as they scraped away, the emphasis would naturally shift to the count, 'ONE THOUSAND THREE HUNDRED AND EIGHTY FIVE, Jesus, ONE THOUSAND THREE HUNDRED AND EIGHTY SIX, Jesus, ONE THOUSAND THREE HUNDRED AND EIGHTY SEVEN, Jesus.'

Between nine-thirty and noon, Monday to Friday, novices and postulants studied. The Angelus Bell at mid-day would call the community to prayers before lunch. Twenty minutes were set aside for this, the main meal of the day. Hefty helpings from the lives of the saints, depicting scourgings and stonings and every conceivable torture ever inflicted on saintly bishops or holy virgins, would be served with each course to counteract any adverse effects on the spiritual wellbeing of the sisters, derived from too much enjoyment of food.

Thanksgiving prayers in the chapel followed. Then an hour's preparation for the next day's lessons. A brisk walk in the grounds, then a lesson in deportment.

Choir practice, meditation, Stations of the Cross and reading from the Holy Office filled the hours to supper. During this meal, penance for infringements of the Holy Rule were performed publicly in the refectory. An hour's recreation followed. During this hour, sisters were permitted to speak, but only about edifying things. Then private prayers were said in the chapel before all retired for the night at nine-fifteen.

On her first morning, Clair was taken aside by Mother Peter and instructed in the rules and customs of the house. Seating herself behind a desk, the novice mistress ordered Clair to kneel. 'Today,' she intoned gravely when the girl was settled, 'is the first day of a new life for you, Clair. A life dedicated to God. In order to serve God, my dear child, you must practise humility, like our Holy Father, St Francis. You are now a postulant. Postulant means "begging to be admitted". You are begging to be admitted to the holy order of St Francis. In six months' time, if God wills it, you will be received into the order and given a copy of the Holy Rule by which you will live the rest of your life. As a lay person, you may not read the Holy Rule, but I may quote it to you.'

And she read: '"A sister must, at all times, keep proper custody of the eyes." This means that you must at all times keep your eyes downcast. Do not allow them to wander about in the way they did at breakfast this morning. "A sister must, at all times, keep proper custody of the lips." We have a rule of silence, Clair, a strict rule of silence. A sister is never permitted to speak to a companion while alone. She must never discuss her past, her family, or her previous occupation with another.

'"The hours between night prayers and the awakening bell are called the Great Silence. It is absolutely forbidden, except in cases of serious illness, to leave one's bed or to make any sound during the period of the Great Silence.

A sister must, at all times, keep proper custody of the hands."

'You must at all times keep your hands under our cape. You must never touch another sister. You must never have a particular friendship. Treat all your sisters in the same way. If you should break a rule, it is your duty to confess it to a superior. If you observe a companion in breach of a rule, it is your duty to report her. You are here to serve God, my child, and to do penance for your sins and the sins of the world.'

The long journey of the previous day followed by a sleepless night had left Clair feeling weak. To add to her discomfort, her period had started unexpectedly early and she had no sanitary towels. She sagged into a more comfortable position, leaning her bottom on the backs of her heels. Mother Peter's voice rose.

'Is that a proper way for a lady to kneel, Clair?' she squeaked. 'You must learn to be a lady before you can be a nun.'

Clair knelt up.

'In this community,' Mother Peter continued, 'sisters live by the vows of poverty, chastity, and obedience. With the vow of poverty, sisters give up all rights to personal possessions. Any item brought by you from home must be placed in the storeroom.

'With the vow of chastity, sisters give up all rights to personal friendships. You must remove yourself from all human affections, dear child, in order that you may belong entirely to God.

'With the vow of obedience, sisters give up all rights to personal opinions. From today on, for the rest of your life, you must submit your will, in all humility, to that of your superiors who have been invested with authority from God. Now, Clair, I am giving you a copy of *The Imitation of Christ*. You shall keep *Imitation* with you at all times and read from it at every opportunity. *The Imitation of Christ* is the bible of the true religious. Only the Christ-fettered are free. You may kiss the floor and go.'

Clair kissed the floor and rose, relieved to find an opening to speak.

'Please, Mother, can you tell me where to find sanitary towels?'

'Can it wait until after prayers?'

'No, Mother, I need them now.'

'Then remain here, Sister,' Mother Peter said, and went out.

Above her desk was a picture showing Francis of Assisi helping Christ down off the cross. She had recently read in a life of St Francis that he was born in the twelfth century. 'That's strange,' she thought.

Mother Peter returned minutes later.

'Here is what you require, Sister,' she said, handing a bundle of rags to the girl. 'Take them to our locker now, then go straight to the chapel.'

'What are these?' Clair asked, bewildered.

'These are our sanitary towels, Sister.'

'But, but Mother ...' Clair stuttered.

'They are towelling squares,' Mother Peter explained.

'Wash them after each use in our washing bowl. The one on our locker in the dormitory.'

'The one for washing myself in?'

'Yes, Sister. We must keep before our minds the fall of our first mother, Eve. All women who came after her, with the exception of the blessed Virgin Mary, have been tainted by her stain. That stain is God's way of reminding women how corrupt their flesh is, and of warning them never to sin again.'

That evening, when the community assembled for supper, Clair lay face down on the centre of the refectory floor with her arms outstretched in cruciform and said aloud in a trembling voice, 'I accuse myself of having spoken disrespectfully to a superior.' Then she got to her knees and crawled from place to place along the line of dining tables, begging a portion of supper from each sister in turn.

Over the next few weeks, Clair grew accustomed to her new way of life. She tried to keep the rules, yet every evening found herself in the centre of the refectory doing public penance. She found an explanation for all her misfortune in Thomas à Kempis' *Imitation*:

> *It is good for us to encounter troubles and adversities from time to time, for trouble often compels a man to search his own heart. It reminds him that he is an exile here, and that he can put trust in nothing in this world. It is good, too, that we sometimes suffer opposition, and that men think ill of us and misjudge us, even when we do and mean well. Such things are an aid to humility, and preserve us from pride and vainglory. For we more readily*

turn to God as our witness, when men despise us and think no good of us.

Clair committed the passage to memory and redoubled her efforts to improve. When her superiors misjudged her after that, she knew it was the will of God.

After six months in the convent her turn came to ring the bell. This was a major event in her life as a postulant, the bell's peal representing, as it did, the voice of God. Each postulant took it in weekly turns to ring every bell of the day, from the awakening bell in the morning to the final bell at bedtime.

The most crucial test of any new bell-ringer's skill came on a Friday night when the *De Profundis* bell was sounded five hundred times for the souls of the dead. This bell was wrung fifteen minutes after the community retired, in a dark, eerie corridor on the ground floor, said to be haunted by the ghost of a mad nun who drowned herself.

Twenty minutes after the rest of the nuns went to bed, while she was ringing the *De Profundis* bell, a sudden apparition on the stairs so terrified Clair that she nearly dropped the bell. She only just managed to muffle a scream before realising that it was Sister Mary Thomas, a first-year novice, sliding down the bannister in a long white nightdress.

After lunch the following day, Clair was summoned to Mother Virtue's office.

'Do you really want to be a nun, Clair?' she asked, seating herself with a display of grandeur before the kneeling girl.

'Yes, Reverend Mother,' Clair answered with a heavy heart. She had failed to report the incident of the previous night.

'This morning, one of your companions, with contrite humility, admitted to a serious breach of the Holy Rule.'

Clair felt weighted to the floor.

'I have prayed, I have prayed, I have waited, I have waited, I have hoped, hoped, hoped, Clair, that you would come to me and humbly confess. But no, you are too proud. Too lacking in humility. Do you think the Holy Rule does not apply to you, Sister?'

'No, Mother,' Clair replied.

'Did you observe a sister in breach of the Holy Rule?'

After a moment's silence, Clair said feebly, 'Yes, Mother.'

'Have you read the chapter of the Holy Rule which states the duty of a sister who finds one of her companions in breach of a rule?'

'No, Mother,' Clair answered.

'And why not, Sister?'

'Because,' Clair answered, with a confidence that surprised herself then, 'as a lay person, I am not permitted to read the Holy Rule.'

That was the wrong answer. The worst possible answer. Mother Virtue rose.

'Your parents are very proud to have a daughter in a convent, are they not?' she asked, standing over the girl.

'Yes, they are.'

'Yes, indeed,' the superior repeated, turning with a grand, sweeping movement towards her desk. 'A letter arrived from your father last week.'

The desk contained a large pile of letters. She picked up the wrong letter first. Discovering her mistake, she returned it to her desk. She picked up another letter. 'Yes,' she said, shaking it in Clair's direction. 'This is your father's letter. I shall read part of it to you now.'

My dear Clair,
It was great to hear from you as usual and great to hear that you were doing well in the convent we got a letter from John he is doing well for himself in england he is

*working on a building site making good money he sends
ten pounds home every week to his ma he is staying with
an irish woman and she looks after him well he is always
asking after you all the wains is doing well they are always
asking after you as well I didn't tell you before but when
you went away our wee Bernadette took it wile bad we
had to get the priest to her thank God she is alright now
father Doherty was great he come up to talk to her every
day now she wants to be a nun too maybe ill be lucky and
have two daughters nuns God knows that would be great
youll never know how proud your ma and me is of you
pray for your brother in england and pray for us all we are
all looking forward to seeing you on your big day august
the fifteenth father Doherty tells us it is a wile big do with
the bishop and all your ma has bought herself a new hat
and sent my suit to the cleaners …*

She folded the letter, returned it to the desk and stood again
before the kneeling girl.

'How, Clair,' she said solemnly, 'would your parents feel if
you were dismissed as unsuitable?'

Clair was aghast.

'Humility,' Mother Virtue intoned, 'is the virtue most
pleasing to God. Practise humility and God will reward you.
God turns his back on no one. Even your father. Yes, Clair, we
know all about the years he spent in prison. From your own
priest, Father Curry. But even your father is now a reformed
character. Your father has turned to God and the Lord has
rewarded him with a righteous and contrite heart. You must
do likewise. Now go to the chapel and pray to God for this
great gift. May God bless you, child, and always keep you in
his sight.'

Clair kissed the floor, and before rising, as was customary,
asked Mother Virtue for a blessing. When the woman placed

her hands on her shoulders, Clair felt a shudder run all the way along her spine. On her way to the chapel, her thoughts turned tenderly towards her home and her family. With a sting of pain she tried to imagine her father sitting at a cluttered corner of the table, with the din of the younger children ringing in his ears, clutching an unfamiliar pen in his clumsy hand. Her heart grew sick as she thought of him, struggling for words to write to her, unaware that she would never read them.

A novice could normally expect to end her stay in the novitiate after seven years. Ten days before reception or profession, a sister was expected to withdraw from normal activities and move to one of the isolated cells in the most secluded part of the house, known as the hermitage, to prepare herself, through solitary prayer and meditation, for the important step she was about to take.

Six senior novices were due to make final vows on the same day as Clair's reception, and to move on to work in the schools and hospitals in Latin America. On the evening before the retreat commenced, Mother Virtue announced that only five of the six would be leaving to take up missionary duties. Sister Mary Philomena, a novice some ten years older than the others, was told that she must remain behind to take up the duties of assistant cook in the convent kitchen.

Mother Virtue left the house on the day after the suicide. Some said she had been called to the mother house in Rome to give an account of the tragedy to the Mother General. Others, that she had gone into hiding following threats from the dead nun's brothers. Some were even sure she had had a nervous breakdown. Rumour followed rumour for a number of months until the day she arrived back, from where nobody knew.

At first, she did not visit the novitiate, but spent hours kneeling motionlessly in the chapel, like some spectre from another world. Then, with the approach of Christmas, she threw off her cloak of silence, and returning to the novitiate, plunged into the festivities with unexpected enthusiasm.

On Christmas Eve she gathered the novices and postulants together in the novitiate, and announced that she had an important message to communicate. 'If we are to live in a modern world, sisters, we must learn to move with the times,' she began in elevated tones. 'We must throw open a window to the world and allow the fresh winds of progress to blow away the cobwebs from our minds. Sisters, I give you the news that from now on you will all be permitted to use disposable sanitary towels. Isn't that wonderful, sisters?'

There was a general murmur of approval and some suppressed laughter disguised behind faked coughs and shuffling feet. Only Clair regarded her with angry silence. 'We must throw open a window on the world.' How could she choose those words after what happened to poor Sister Philomena?

'I can see we are not all agreed, Sister Mary Joseph,' the superior addressed Clair as a novice for the first time. 'Do you not think this news is wonderful?'

'No, Mother. Not wonderful,' Clair answered. 'If violence, cruelty, greed, hunger and disease were wiped from the face of the earth, then Mother, I would describe that as wonderful,' Clair said.

Clair expected no normal reprimand or penance for this outspoken act of defiance. She expected to be sent home, but when Christmas and New Year passed without the expected summons to the office, she started to suppose that Mother Virtue had really changed and had decided to forgive her. The superior visited the novitiate every day and behaved as if the incident had never happened. It was noticed, too, that since her return, she had not handed down a single penance.

During the first week of February, when Clair's turn came to ring the bell, Mother Virtue paid an unexpectedly early visit to the novitiate. She was not her animated, exuberant self. 'Sisters,' she said gravely. 'I would like you all to follow me.' She led them from the room, down the stairs, along a corridor, and out through a seldom-used door at the back of the building.

The baffled novices walked behind her in single file until she halted them at the far corner of a garden. There they found Sister Mary Helen in a pair of waders, her habit hitched up around her waist, standing knee-deep in an open sewer, shovelling shit, sanitary towels and boxes of chocolates out onto the ground.

Explanations for Mary Helen's insanity circulated in whispers among the novices and postulants all morning. One of the two sisters from the Bogside said her insanity must have been hereditary because, looking at Mary Helen, you could tell right away that she wasn't all there. Others, that Mother Virtue had driven her mad. Sister Mary Hilda, a novice from Dublin, believed to have had a university education, explained how a doctor named Freud could show that sexual perversion was directing Mary Helen when she dug all the shit out of the sewer and mixed it up with chocolates and sanitary towels.

At four o'clock that afternoon, Sister Mary Helen walked into the novitiate looking neat and clean in a fresh habit. Every eye in the room followed her. She walked up to Clair and ordered her to go to the office. Clair was perplexed. Was Mary Helen better? Should she go? After a moment's indecision, Clair decided to obey and walked down the corridor with Mary Helen on her heels.

When she got to the office she was met by Mother Virtue, Mother Peter, and Sister Veronica.

'What time did you get out of bed this morning, Sister Mary Joseph?' the Reverend Mother asked as the girls were sinking to their knees.

'At the usual time,' Clair answered, then remembering, corrected herself. 'No, I got up when the clock alarmed, and this morning, for some reason, it went off fifteen minutes early.'

'Did you set it to alarm early?' Mother Virtue asked.

'I am not permitted to set the alarm. That job is Sister Mary Helen's.'

'Did you set the clock to alarm at the usual time?' the superior asked, turning to Sister Mary Helen, who was sitting with her head bowed awkwardly to hide a face crimson with embarrassment.

'Yes, Mother,' Mary Helen muttered without raising her head.

'You have heard Sister Mary Helen's reply. What have you got to say for yourself?' the Reverend Mother demanded.

'I can only repeat what I said before,' Clair answered, confused.

'If the alarm woke you too early, why did you not stay in bed?'

'Because I did not realise that it was too early. I put my hand out to stop it automatically. I probably did not open my eyes. It was four in the morning. When I became fully awake, I followed the rules precisely. I got out of bed, kissed the floor, made a morning offering, washed, dressed, stripped our bed, and checked the time.'

'Very well, Sister, but would you mind telling us what you did then?' Mother Virtue asked and forced a smile.

'When I realised I had extra time, I went down to the novitiate.'

Mother Virtue clapped her hands and turned to the others triumphantly. 'She admits it, Sisters,' she said. 'We have found our thief.'

'Admits what?' Clair asked, half rising. 'Did you call me a thief?'

'Yes, Sister. You went to the novitiate this morning while the rest of the community was asleep, and stole boxes of chocolates from the cupboard.'

'I did not. I went to the novitiate to our drawer to get a peppermint to freshen our breath because I had not toothpaste. Sister Mary Helen can tell you that I asked her for permission to go to our suitcase yesterday to get a fresh tube as the one I had went missing…'

'Did this novice seek your permission to get toothpaste from our suitcase yesterday?'

'No, Mother,' Mary Helen muttered.

Mother Virtue turned to Clair again. 'Are you accusing Sister Mary Helen of lying?' she demanded.

'No, Mother,' Clair said. 'She may have forgotten.'

'Are you a forgetful person, Sister Mary Helen?' Mother Virtue enquired playfully.

Mary Helen, continuing to blush, replied, 'No.'

'Sister Mary Helen has not forgotten. What do you have to say now?'

'I went to the novitiate to get one of our peppermints.'

'If that is the case, why did you remain there for two or three minutes? It wouldn't take that time to take a peppermint from our drawer,' Mother Virtue continued.

'I had to stay there long enough to eat the peppermint because it is forbidden for a sister to eat in any part of the house, save the refectory or the novitiate.'

'Well, well,' Mother Virtue addressed the other nuns. 'Now she claims to be concerned with keeping the Holy Rule.'

'I am telling the truth, Mother,' Clair exploded. 'And since entering this house, I have always done my best to keep the Holy Rule.'

'Do you hear that?' Mother Virtue shook her head. 'Now she is mocking God.'

Clair spoke in a quiet, firm voice. 'The Holy Rule says that a sister is absolutely forbidden to leave her bed during the Great Silence. I was the *only* sister with permission to be out of bed before the awakening bell this morning. The Holy Rule was breached by the person who watched me go to the novitiate. If she had been less anxious to cover up her own fault, she would naturally have followed me into the room to find out what I was doing there. Who was that, Reverend Mother? Was it you?'

A bell, a bell that Clair should have been ringing, sounded in the corridor below. Everyone rose to go.

'Stay right where you are, Sister Mary Joseph,' the superior snapped as Clair bent down to kiss the floor. The other three women bowed and left.

When they were alone, Mother Virtue did not speak at first but paced slowly around the room, apparently deep in thought. When she broke the silence at last, Clair was almost disarmed by her friendliness. 'My dear Sister,' she began, coming to a halt before Clair and placing a hand on each of her shoulders, 'you are here to serve God. Isn't that so?'

'Yes, Mother,' Clair answered cautiously.

'And the best way to serve God is to obey your superiors. Isn't that so?'

'Yes, Mother,' Clair answered again.

'Now, Sister, you must listen while I read to you a passage from *The Imitation of Christ*. A passage on obedience.'

She went to the desk and picked up her copy.

Everyone gladly does whatever he most likes; but if God is to dwell among us, we must sometimes yield our own opinions for the sake of peace.

She stopped to look at the kneeling girl before continuing:

If your opinion is sound, and you forgo it for the love of God and follow that of another, you will win great merit. *It may even come about that each of two opinions is good; but to refuse to come to agreement with others when reason or occasion demand it,* is a sign of pride and obstinacy.

'Did you understand all that I read to you, my child?' she asked.

'Yes, Mother,' Clair answered.

'You have already agreed that the best way to serve God is to obey your superiors in all things, isn't that so, child?' she continued in the same friendly manner.

'It is, Mother,' Clair agreed again.

'Then, Sister, I'm sure you would like to be chosen to do something very special for God. Something that would bring blessings not only on you, but also on your parents, brothers and sisters.'

'Yes, Mother, I would,' Clair answered.

'Good,' the superior smiled warmly. 'You are learning true humility. At last you are coming to realise that only the Christ-fettered are free.'

She placed an affectionate arm round the girl's shoulder. 'Here is what I want you to do, Sister,' she said, looking earnestly into Clair's eyes. 'When the bell rings for supper this evening, I want you to go to the centre of the refectory, and bearing in mind the words of Thomas à Kempis, I want you to confess to the community that you took boxes of chocolates from the novitiate this morning, and that you later panicked and flushed them down the toilet. In this way, dear Sister, you will gain great merit.'

Clair was stunned almost to the point of paralysis. When she could speak again, her voice appeared to be coming from a place far outside herself. 'I cannot do that. You are asking me to bear false witness.'

'I have not been mistaken,' Mother Virtue snapped. 'You have not yet learned humility. Kneel down at once. You are vain and full of self.'

Weary, confused and on the verge of tears, Clair knelt down. Again Mother Virtue paced the room. Again she returned to stand over Clair. 'I will give you one last chance,' she said. 'If you obey, the whole matter will be forgotten. If you do not, tomorrow I will call in a friend of mine, a senior detective. You will be arrested and charged with theft. Your name will be in all the papers. Your family will be in disgrace.'

'So be it,' Clair answered, a cold anger taking possession of her. 'I have nothing to fear. I will get a fair hearing in a court. I have nothing to fear from newspapers either. They'd love to hear all about you. Call whoever you like, I will not be bullied, I will not lie.'

'You will not serve God. That is quite clear,' the Reverend Mother shrieked. 'The devil is the one you serve.'

'I serve God,' Clair corrected. 'The God whose greatest gift is free will. But I will not serve your God.'

'You are possessed by the devil. Satan has given you the gift of tongues,' the superior spat.

Clair could not stop herself. 'Look what you have done to Sister Mary Helen. Your lying has driven her mad.'

'Get out of here, you devil. Get out at once,' Mother Virtue screamed, hurling herself at Clair and kicking her several times before she managed to struggle to her feet.

Clair stumbled out of the office in tears. She had no idea what to do or who to turn to. It was already dark outside and Athgar was two miles away. She was not even sure in which direction. She decided to walk to the nearest farmhouse and ask to use a telephone. Ring Father Doherty. He would tell her what to do. She looked with uncertainty at her habit. She was not sure whether she should wear it or not. She decided she would. It would only make matters worse for her if she went to the storeroom to change without permission.

She made her way quickly to the ground floor and along the corridor leading to the outside door. It was securely locked and bolted. Hearing footsteps approach, she turned around and saw Mother Peter hurrying towards her. The novice mistress embraced her and offered her the kiss of peace. Clair broke down and sobbed loudly. 'What is going on, Mother? Why did Mother Virtue try so hard to make me lie?'

Mother Peter led Clair into a doorway before replying. 'Please do not think of the events of today again, Sister,' she said softly. 'As you know, the Lord acts in strange and mysterious ways. It is not for us to question his ways, but to accept them. We must all carry the cross he has laid down for us. If your cross is a heavy one, Sister, that is merely a reflection of how deeply he loves you. He is testing your vocation. Let us go to the chapel and pray for a moment in silence. Then I will take you to the refectory and find you some supper.'

Clair did not sleep that night or for several nights after. Regardless of how hard she tried to quell them, questions kept churning around in her mind. Questions that she could at first find no reasonable answers for. Was it possible that Sister Mary Helen was mad, after all? And if so, could she have cooked the whole thing up and managed to convince Mother Virtue? It was possible. She was certainly responsible for the clock. But that did not account for Mother Virtue's behaviour. Mother Virtue was not mad. Mother Virtue was something entirely different. That woman had, for some reason, tried to set her up and had not quite succeeded. If that was the case, would she try again? And what was Mother Peter's role in all this?

But as the days that followed passed quietly and stretched into weeks without further incident, Clair's mind began to settle and her sleep returned. It was then, for the first time, that she thought of Mother Peter's words of comfort that night in the corridor: 'The Lord acts in strange and mysterious ways.'

She wondered why she had not thought of them earlier. It was so simple. Everything became clear to her. God was testing her vocation. In the light of this new understanding, Mother Virtue's behaviour became explicable. During the interrogation she had been acting the part of devil's advocate. Other novices were probably put through similar tests. Maybe even the same one.

Following this revelation, Clair felt guilty for having misjudged the Reverend Mother and, satisfied that the matter was finally closed, she dismissed it from her mind and settled back into her normal routine.

One Tuesday evening eight weeks later when the novices were at choir practice, Sister Mary Helen came to Clair again and whispered, 'Follow me, Sister.' Clair obeyed and was led down a strange corridor to a part of the house she had never been to before. She was ushered into a room that was unfurnished, save for a table. On top of it sat Clair's suitcase. A door opposite the one she entered opened off the room on to a pathway that led to the drive.

Mother Virtue entered.

'Take off your habit and put on your secular clothes,' she ordered. 'Then leave by that door. Your father is waiting.'

Clair obeyed. She didn't resist. She didn't want to. It was over. She changed back into her clothes. They no longer fitted. When she started to fold her habit, the thin voice addressed her once more. 'Take your hands off the holy habit, you have defiled it for the last time.'

Looking into Mother Virtue's eyes, Clair was violently confronted for the first time with her own folly and innocence. Burning with anguish and anger, she turned to walk away.

'Just one moment,' called the Reverend Mother, drawing an envelope from the slit at the side of her habit and holding it out to her.

'Your money is in this envelope. Check it before you leave.'

Clair took the envelope and opened it. Inside she found a crumpled five pound note, the rent money her mother had given the nuns more than two years before. She clutched it to her and walked out into the light.

Una Woods

Una Woods grew up in Belfast in the 1950s and 60s. After spending some years in the south of England and Dublin, she returned to her home town where she raised her two children and where she continues to live. Her first published poems and short stories appeared in the late 1970s/early 80s in the New Writing Page, edited by David Marcus, in *The Irish Press*. *The Dark Hole Days*, a novella and short story collection, was published by Blackstaff Press in 1984. She subsequently contributed poems and stories to anthologies in Ireland, the UK and the USA. Her play, *Grace Before Meals*, was staged by Cello Productions Theatre Company at various venues in Ireland, including Dublin Theatre Fringe Fest and Earagail Arts. A novella, *Mr and Mrs McKeown: the Accidental Maze*, was published by Ashtrees in 2010. She has published three collections of poetry with Ashtrees: *Afternoons, An Icicle for an Eye and Splintered Vision*.

The Diary
An Everyday Fable

One day he went about his house as usual.

The next day, sitting at his table, he opened a small notebook and looked at the first empty page. He held his pen ready for a time, then found himself staring out into the yard. An old iron thing sat on the flagstones.

Then, like an overflow of light, the sun came out. A tiny piece of dirt dangled on the wall. Caught in a spark of cobweb, it trembled tight.

Later, in the scullery, rinsing out his teapot, he thought, I need to find a starting-point for this diary. Water splashed into the cold stone sink. Out in the entry, someone pushed something that squeaked. The roofs of the street behind sat slated in the midday sun.

Back at the kitchen table he wrote, I never managed to make a go of it. No one ever explained to me what it was, or what I should do with it.

It's directly in my line of vision, if it wasn't right in the middle of the yard, he thought, looking through the window. But what's the point in speculating, I can't move it. And it's too private to ask someone off the street. Then he looked at his watch. I've an hour and a half at the diary, he thought, before lunch and the

207

news, the way I've calculated. Except I've just noticed something, I'm cold. It's time to light the fire.

As he was shovelling out the ashes he glanced up at the clock.

Damn, he thought, that doesn't give me much time. Still, that's a tidy fire. In the scullery, he gave his hands a good soapy wash, a thorough rinse. Now, he said, going back into the kitchen, all is in order.

Staring at the page, he thought, I've used up the energy I should have kept for inspiration.

For a moment I mistook myself for someone who had something worthwhile to say, he wrote, but my life has been a contradiction of worth. I am a fire someone has forgotten to light, an empty ship too heavy to float.

Then he considered, what's the point if my diary only reflects my emptiness. Is there no imagination? Inner world?

In the afternoon, on his stroll through the town centre, he found himself staring through a shop window at shelves of brightly covered books with interesting titles. It's a world away from the diary, he thought.

*

Meanwhile, in the kitchen, the iron thing sat up at the table in front of the open notebook. After a moment it scraped:

when we were together a blue high day as we sat on the height of field one August one afternoon our voices said the height of life is sky or words dissimilar in the warm summer sun stopped on a day preserved as a monument to possibility moments that passed for sudden there it is as we sat by chance or choice a bit of both as the grass stretched to where our knowledge faded as green feinted into blue and then it was the sky again or was it voices that said in other words if we never do another thing there is this day this afternoon this perfection of place we hope we will do another thing but who knows so let's not forget let's make a pact here we are as the sun slips down the sky and we silent witnesses or talking amongst ourselves our murmur dulled by miles of air as we suspected more as we stood on a mound and kept to ourselves hey this day will save us

Then it considered a moment how what seemed like a revelation had come about and already vanished.

*

When he opened the door it was as though some light had been turned on, which gave him a moment's unutterable joy. He went over to the table and looked down at his last words in the diary. An empty ship, he sighed.

A while later he was standing in the scullery waiting for the kettle to boil. When I look out, it's always the first thing I see, he thought. If it has any purpose it's a mystery. Have I not had it long enough to know what it is? He had a plain biscuit with his tea.

Two days later a coincidence happened.

A young man in grubby clothes and with black marks on his face stood on the step.

Have you any old iron, or that kind of thing?

Soon the two of them were standing in the yard looking down at the iron thing. Eventually the young man said, I'll take it, and lifting it in both hands, he carried it out the door.

The day after, pushing his breakfast dishes aside, he stared out at the pale patch where the iron thing had sat.

Somewhere along the way something was lost, he wrote in the diary, something that gives life. Or it is still there, and

I am prevented from using it? What is it? Is it within me or without me?

Then he sat back and re-read the last few lines.

*

A few streets away, in a kind of workshop-cum-scrapyard, the iron thing sat wedged between a corroded water tank and a very old car engine. When it strained, it could see the changes in light through the open door, which seemed to make a difference. It found a piece of paper lying nearby and, when things were quiet, when the workers were out and there were only distant sounds of traffic and a slant of sunlight on the houses opposite it scraped:

throw a stone hop jump there is a landing on the ground a shiver on the skyline ripples the road with gold someone slips out by the gate no need to stop the game no need to do anything but land on a slab of pavement a curtain flutters nearby a stone goes crack land and off a volcano of evening rays that send a dust of frailgrey down upon the city save where the chalk glints its private confrontation all eyes on it in the dimming light tremble on one foot close to that powdered white lift a stone

Then it re-read what it had written and could see no change it could make. Noticing an old chest of drawers nearby, it reached out and put the page into the bottom drawer. The water tank turned and said, 'It's not as if we're going to read it.' The iron thing answered, 'It's my case for the defence.' It felt the stares of the water tank and the car engine.

That night, the big door of the workshop was closed. There was one window high up and through this, the yellow fuzz of a street lamp cast an eerie glow. The iron thing remembered this light. Suddenly and forever. It also felt a great urge to be back in the small yard from where it might have him in sight, moving about in the kitchen, or at the scullery sink, staring out at it.

'I supplied a whole family,' the tank said out of the blue. 'For years, emptying and filling, always that sound of water. The odd overflow. I remember the trap door opening and the gleam of light from the landing. On occasions, children would climb up into the attic and look into me, for a long time just staring in, their faces waving slightly through the water.'

The tank sat doleful in the faint yellow glimmer.

'I was in a jaguar, you know,' the engine said brightly. 'Out on the open road that smells of grass, the breeze along the hedgerows. I haven't given up on that.'

The iron thing had no idea whether it had hope or not, and if it had, what kind of hope it was. As for its past, there seemed to be something blocking it from such straightforward memories, so that it was terrified of being asked ordinary questions like, what did you do? Or, where did you come from?

Feeling forced to explain itself, it blurted out, 'The images I have seem to shine at the same moment they disappear. So what's revealed is at once concealed.'

The tank and the engine stared blankly then the engine began,

'Well of course coming originally from a Jaguar—'

The iron thing interrupted, though losing heart with every further word, 'Sometimes I think I'm just a thought banished to the tip of an iceberg, do you know what I mean?'

'Mm, occasionally the water that came in was a brownie colour,' the tank murmured. 'It took ages to clear.'

'That would have been road-works,' the engine said. 'I circumnavigated them many's a time.'

'Oh really?' the tank said, as if irritated by this piece of late information, as if it detracted from the memory, or questioned its authenticity.

*

Good, a distraction, he thought, walking down the hall.

It was the man from the workshop.

There's been some interest shown in that old iron thing, his voice droned against the traffic.

What kind of interest?

Well let's just say as to what it was, he said, winking confidentially.

I don't know what it was, its previous owner said.

What if I said there could be some money in it for you, the man said hesitantly. After a moment's silence he added, I'll give you a couple of days to think about it. Then he was gone.

*

The next day the iron thing felt a strange, familiar premonition as a man and woman walked around it, whispered amongst themselves, stood back, frowned, came close, nodded. Then they left, still talking.

'What do you make of that?' the tank said.

'I don't know,' the iron thing said, trying to work out its conflicting reactions to the incident.

'Probably just a storm in a carburettor,' the engine dismissed. 'Sure I've had people in looking at me and they never came back.'

'So much for optimism,' the tank said.

'I'm only saying you have to fit the requirements exactly, otherwise it will be worse for everybody in the end. Being from a Jaguar, I've been involved in some disputes, so I know what I'm talking about.'

'I've led a largely unremarkable life,' the tank said.

Then the young man came and lifted the iron thing up carefully. He took it to a small room off the main area where he set it down on a heavy wooden unit and left, closing the door behind him. There was a small window high up in this room, out of which the iron thing could see the sunlight sparking off clouds. Am I closer? it thought. Am I going backwards? Or forwards? It had no idea except a strange sensation of suspense. And lightness.

*

He found himself unable to rise from the table. The routine that had kept him afloat through the years suddenly seemed insufficient to move him. He had made some progress with the diary, though he could not be sure it would last. Certainly it was not a breakthrough.

I have lived an imaginary life up until this point, he had written. I have lied to everyone I met just to keep myself going. There is not an aspect of my life that I have not invented. What I did not invent was not worth inventing. I can't even remember it. Even this could be another invention.

At that minute, there was a knock at the door. When he opened it the ironmonger spoke quickly.

You wouldn't have the rest of that iron thing anywhere? In a shed in the yard, say?

I have no shed in the yard, only a coalhouse and there wouldn't be room for anything else in there.

You don't remember what it was used for?

I don't remember anybody using it.

Where did you get it from, well?

It was always in the yard, as long as I can remember.

How long's that?

Since I was a boy, I suppose.

And why did you keep it, if it was no use?

It never occurred to me I could move it. Most of the time I didn't even notice it. Until recently for some reason.

Right then, if anything occurs to you let me know.

He lifted his hand by way of departure, turned his back and went down the path.

The next day a clean sun lay on the flagstones.

I feel cheerful, he thought as he sat down at the table, wiped of crumbs. He lifted the diary out from the drawer of the table and opened it. Well yes, he muttered, but today I'm in a different mood. He sat looking above the yard wall awhile, then he wrote, The light is flitting about as though about to touch down.

*

Back in the scrapyard office, the iron thing had been on its own all afternoon. It did not know how, when the door opened, its fate might change. In order not to panic, it had to create for itself an oasis, believing that it could stay there forever. Even though it might not want to. It stared up through the small, square window at the light in the sky, until it felt detached, or attached a moment. To something out there. Or to a previous state – or a future one. The blue of the sky was now touched by a distant sweep of grey. There was a sudden laugh somewhere out on the road. Utterly familiar followed by a damp ringing echo. The door opened sharply and the scrap man came in with another. Between them they carried a strange iron object. If they think they're going to connect me to that, the iron thing thought. The two men put the iron object carefully on the floor and then they came towards the iron thing. The other man said, 'I think it might be it,' and the ironmonger said, 'Let's hope so.'

*

In a strange way grey excites me, he wrote in the diary after looking out to the yard, which had dulled. I no longer have high expectations, he continued. If I could have done anything else with my life why would I not have? The thing that prevented me will probably never be known. But maybe I have a way of settling for that.

A pigeon landed on the back wall.

A pigeon's feathers ruffle, causing the grey light to shimmer, he wrote.

He glanced at the top of the wall where the pigeon had been joined by another. The clock on the mantelpiece chimed. Damn, he thought, I hate that sound. But, he considered, I'm starting to control this, am I not?

*

The iron thing reflected on how it had almost tasted its former state. It would have been a moment of great rejoicing, it thought, had I fitted, although surely I would have recognised that object had I ever been a part of it. Strangely elated, it flicked over a scrap of paper and scraped:

quick as a swallow swerved by the window like a featherdart the day was bluemisted voices over the orchard little cracked laughs and summerdulled sounds of play the hazeflickered distance hung low didn't move the hungflickered blue sat low on hills sounds made no difference either sounds made no sound but dappled silence with another version of itself so it shunned interruption and lightcapped infinity as if by disassociation a trace of everywhere or home full circle to the danksweet hay

Then the distinct smell of warm, enclosed hay. The iron thing sat perfectly still on the wooden unit and felt vindicated. Instantly it knew where it was and where it had been.

Later that day, who should arrive in the office but the previous owner. The conversation went back and forward – I can give you it back – at a price – but it wouldn't be still here if it was worth – until the previous owner took one more look at the iron thing and left.

And so it sat there, two possibilities having come and gone.

Well, I suppose, it thought, at least it's a distraction. Then the door knocked and the previous owner stuck his head in. The ironmonger looked up from the desk where he was standing, flicking through papers.

I've just noticed an old water tank back there, I might take it off your hands.

I don't know if it would hold water.

Och no, I was thinking of growing plants in it.

Oh?

*

The iron thing tried to imagine the water tank sitting out in the backyard filled with soil and flowers peeking up over its top. When in fact if it doesn't hold water it's no longer a water tank, it thought. But then, it considered, to keep the illusion going and without the burden of water. Not to have to be a water tank any more but to be something completely different. Could that not be considered a type of freedom?

*

He left the workshop and walked up the street.

Amazing, he thought, when I look out the window there will be a burst of colour. It will take a lot of soil, though. And I have to be sure to choose the right flowers for the conditions. He rushed towards the corner, the traffic passing by, and bumped into a woman coming the other way. Jesus Christ, she muttered, has somebody died or what? He paused, looked back at her. No, no, on the contrary, he said.

He was flicking through the diary when the entry door knocked.

*

The iron thing meandered through the sleeping objects to where the water tank and car engine sat. A silver slant of moonlight cast an eerie ray, which seemed to abandon everything it lit. Like the moon on headstones. But the iron thing had other news. It shuffled up to the side of the water tank and nudged it.

'Looks like my arrival was fortuitous,' the iron thing whispered.

'What do you mean?' the tank mumbled.

'Well,' the iron thing said, 'there is a chance,' it paused, 'that you might be rescued.' 'How can I put it,' it continued carefully. 'How would you react if someone were to tell you you could have a new life?'

'You mean I'm going to be used again?' the tank's voice was almost shrill.

The car engine woke up. 'What's going on?' it grumbled.

'Sshh!' the iron thing said sharply, at pains to calm the situation down. Then it whispered into the tank's side, 'Not as a water tank as such.'

The tank was silent a moment. The engine, which was now all pistons, said impatiently, 'What's this about? Go on, hurry-up!'

There was no turning back now, so the iron thing said in a straightforward way, 'What about a flower bed?'

The tank repeated slowly, 'Me, a flower bed?'

The engine looked it up and down and then croaked with laughter, 'I can't see it.'

As though it was now its duty to encourage the water tank into a completely new way of thinking, while at the same time minimising the change, the iron thing offered, 'Is there that much difference between a flower bed and a water tank, between soil and water? If anything, is soil not slightly superior, given what it can grow?'

'I've always been a water tank,' the tank said in a dull, fatalistic tone.

'Yes,' the engine hooted, 'and is water not equally important for growth?'

The iron thing had to think on its end, which it was not used to doing. At the same time, it was beginning to enjoy what was turning out to be an exchange of ideas. 'Not stale water from a water tank,' it said.

'I was the container,' the tank stated. 'It wasn't up to me what kind the water was. My function was to do the things a water tank does. I can't imagine anything else.'

'But you don't do the things a water tank does any more,' the iron thing said. 'Imagine lovely flowers on a summer afternoon sticking up out of you, imagine knowing you had nurtured them. And then, looking up to see the sky above you instead of attic rafters—'

'It would be the soil,' the engine interrupted, 'that would be doing the nurturing, and the sun, and the rain. Not water tank.' Then aside it said, 'Sorry to be frank, tank, but I'm on your side.'

'It's true,' the tank agreed. 'I would still be a water tank without water. Except for the rain.'

The iron thing insisted, 'You would soon realise what it was to be free of the burden of water, it might even be what you've always wanted and who knows, after a while, with ivies and other trailing plants covering your sides, no one might recognise the fact that you were ever a water tank.'

Then, worried that it was getting carried away, and not having had time to consider how much of what it was saying it actually believed, the iron thing fell silent.

'Well, it's all speculation anyway,' the engine said. Then, turning to the iron thing, it asked, 'What are your prospects?'

'Well,' the iron thing said, already starting to shuffle away. 'I have moments of general anticipation.'

'If you hear of any old cars – it doesn't have to be a Jaguar…' the engine's voice tailed off.

*

The first thing he seemed to notice was how white the entry cement was in a dazzle of light, which was not present anywhere else. Then he was looking at an old rusty water tank.

He and the ironmonger carried it into the yard.

About here, he said, pointing to a spot near, but not touching the outline where the iron thing had been.

I know a man who can deliver the soil, the dealer said. Sure we'll go inside and complete the business.

We can maybe come to an arrangement about that iron thing, the dealer said, putting the money for the tank in his pocket. When he left, banging the entry door behind him, it was as if sound stopped everywhere.

*

There was a commotion at the back of the workshop, and it emerged that the engine was inconsolable. The iron thing felt compelled to offer sympathy, but it was lost for words. It had not developed a language for these circumstances; it knew things instinctively or not at all. It had forgotten already the arguments it had used to prepare the water tank for the impending move. I know I spoke positively but what did I say? In the end it mumbled words about time and healing, then hating itself, it swivelled round and shuffled away.

Once up on the wooden unit, it tried to justify its failure. I only know things at a certain point, it told itself. The point at which I know them is the point at which I was broken off. If I was reconnected to my original part I would know everything. I would be able to console car engine, water tank, and all the other objects. The way I remember is of no help to anyone, because it's sudden, it cannot describe the memory, but only its reality. For example, I have a sense of joy at this moment; I am connected to it in every way. At this point, I am neither my broken-off self nor my reconnected self, but a kind of glimmer of neither happening. This is where I am, so how can I tell car engine or water tank that there is hope for them?

So the iron thing sat on, staring up at the square of imperceptibly changing light in the sky, now and then scraping on a piece of paper. At other times jumping up from nowhere, the dazzling images of an elusive, familiar way of life.

*

The soil was fresh, brown and springy. It took several large bags to fill the water tank. Then many buckets of water from the scullery tap to dampen it down. He flopped into his chair at the table.

Later that afternoon, he carried in a big tray filled with small plants and bulbs, ready for setting. Some were already in bloom. There was a small, shiny, green trowel, which he viewed the way a child would a new toy. In fact he could hardly wait to get over to the kitchen table to sort through everything.

He pushed the diary aside.

Thus it was that, late in the evening, just before dark, when he looked through the kitchen or scullery window, he saw an array of colour where before there had been grey flagstones.

The last entry he put in his diary that evening after supper was, My little garden speaks for itself.

Going up the stairs he found himself thinking of how he would look after his plants and watch them grow.

Before he pulled his bedroom blind down he looked out across the rooftops of the city; he stood transfixed by a straight light gleaming up from a few streets away. Then he lost it as it merged with the strange, moonless glimmer of the night sky.

Sheila Llewellyn

Sheila Llewellyn is a writer from Northern Ireland. In 2011, she won the P J O'Connor RTÉ Radio One Drama Award, followed by the Silver Award for the Best Broadcast Radio Drama in the New York International Radio Drama Festival in 2012. She has been shortlisted for the Bridport Short Story Prize, the Seán Ó Faoláin Short Story Prize, and shortlisted twice for the Costa Short Story Award. Her short stories have been published in *The Bridport Prize Anthology*, 2014; *Surge, New Writing From Ireland,* 2015; and *The Hilary Mantel International Short Story Prize Anthology*, 2015. She has just finished a PhD at the Seamus Heaney Centre for Poetry, Queen's University, Belfast and has also completed her first novel: *The Thousand Yard Memory*.

Capering Penguins

I drag the book out from the bottom of the kitbag, leaving the back cover stuck to the canvas. On the flyleaf, mottled with mildew, is George's careful copperplate: *For the voyage home, 1946.* I remember it arriving the day we boarded the troop ship in Bombay. I'd skimmed the first page, riffled through the rest, then stuffed it down the side of the bag, knowing I'd never read it.

His paperbacks had kept me going during the war. They'd fetch up like weary homing pigeons wherever we happened to be. I devoured them all, sheltering in Burmese bashas, monsoon rain rattling the bamboo walls, or hunched in silt trenches under tarpaulins – anywhere they told us to hole up and wait for orders. For a few peaceful hours, I was back to being a schoolboy again, working in George's bookshop for pocket money, hidden between the rows of shelves and reading the books rather than sorting them.

Then, finally, it was over – the Americans dropped the bomb, the Japanese surrendered, we thought we could all go home. But they kept us out there another year, the rumours that we'd be off to fight someone else slowly wearing us down. Our nerves were shot. I swung from high anxiety to deep melancholy and stopped reading altogether.

Captain Evans understood. 'Comics are just about my limit,' he said. We were in hospital together, getting over a bout of malaria. We'd pass the time on the veranda, sharing abandoned copies of *Superman*. He struck a mock romantic poet pose, fingertips on forehead, reciting:

> '*Books; what a jolly company they are…*
> Christ! How does it go? I've forgotten …
> de-dah-de-dah-de-bloody-dah –
> *Which will you read? Come on;*
> *O do read something; they're so wise …*
> *all the wisdom of the world is waiting for you*
> *on those shelves…*'

His face was uncharacteristically sad. 'I never realised the full irony of Sassoon's words before.' He shook his head. 'I'm supposed to be going back to Cambridge after this lot. Quite fancied myself as a warrior poet. But I can't imagine ever opening a wretched book again.'

His words come back to me now as I chuck the book, water-stained and musty, into the waste paper basket. Then, remembering George and his past kindnesses, a tug of guilt prompts me to fish it out and drop it on top of the other paperbacks scattered across my desk under the bedroom window. It lies there among their oranges and reds and blues, dishevelling their little pool of brightly coloured vitality like a small brown trout. These books are also courtesy of George.

'He brought them round ages ago, thought you'd enjoy a decent read when you got back,' my mother said. 'Why not go into town to thank him? It would do you good to get out.'

I don't particularly want to see him. He never spoke of his time in the Great War, but now he might think there's an understanding we can share. The last thing I want to talk about is his war, or the misery of mine. I don't want to talk about anything to anyone. The plan was to rest up for a few days. The few days have stretched to a month, and what had felt like plain tiredness has drifted into heavy-limbed lethargy. But my mother's right, I need to get out. George's shop, tucked away behind the art gallery in the city centre, would be somewhere definite to aim for.

The two, old, wingback chairs are where they've always been, cramped in a tiny alcove off the kitchen. We sit facing each other; a low table between us piled high with paperbacks. I shift my weight a little, taking in the way his eyelids slide down and up in a slow blink, more owlish than ever. Old. He's grown old. He tamps down the tobacco and goes through the ritual of lighting and puffing and pausing and puffing again. The first release of sweet smoke mingles with a definite hint of mouse from the overstuffed upholstery.

'So what did you think of *The Odyssey*?' he says. He reaches across the table and takes the top book off the pile, placing it in front of me. 'The very first of the Penguin Classics, out January this year. Very timely.'

An image flashes into mind of my copy at home, lying among all the others, abandoned and unread on the desk.

'I liked the idea of you reading it as you made your way home,' he says. 'A bit corny, I know, but still.'

My thoughts are racing as I try to invent plausible details of a struggle to read the book against the odds. 'It was awkward to read on the go,' I say. 'We travelled in trucks, trains, ships – the ship was the worst – it's hard to keep your eyes on the page when you're swinging in a hammock, trying to read by torchlight, and the man below you is being sick in a bucket and the man above is either farting or snoring or both.' I hope I've made it sound amusing.

He nods. 'Maybe you need to read it after you've got to where you're going.'

'Maybe.' I feel myself drifting away. *Books; what a jolly company they are … Christ, I've forgotten how it goes …*

de-dah-de-dah-de-bloody-dah... I know he wants to get into literary conversations, like the old times, but I can't concentrate. I'd once believed what he'd told me, that books were a civilising force. That they led us to some sort of truth. *A world of wisdom.*

A wave of loss washes over me.

He waits patiently, like a kindly teacher trying to encourage a shy student.

I have a vague memory of the first page. 'It's a straightforward translation, sounds like everyday English, not too highbrow,' I say, making an effort to drag myself back.

He puffs on his pipe again, three little pops of pleasure. 'He's good, old Professor Rieu. Sound choice for the job, I think. Penguin wanted someone erudite, which he is, of course, but also someone who'd make Homer come alive for ordinary folk.'

I can sense him getting ready to give a lecture, the sort of thing he'd give to his Worker's Education Association students on how Penguin are planning to bring the Classics to the masses.

I stare past his head at the two shelves of paperbacks, blue and orange and green and pink, the little penguin logo standing plump and firm on the spines of books published in the '30s, a much skinnier version dancing a jig by 1945.

The penguins begin to caper round in my head.

His voice floats in from far away. 'Did you notice the illustration on the front?'

'Sorry?' I look at him, taking a moment to sort out where I am. 'The what?'

'The illustration.' He taps *The Odyssey* cover with the stem of his pipe. 'Look.'

He points out the roundel, about the size of a penny piece, centred under the title block. Inside it is a sketch of an ancient Greek ship in choppy waters, gusting along against the backdrop of a busy-looking cloud.

I've not really studied the cover before, beyond noticing its dullness. Now I see that the colours aren't drab at all, but done in subtle hues, the soft sea-green of the ship washing across the acorn brown of the cover, the elegant Greek border of wave scrolls giving it the look of a classical pamphlet.

'It's beautiful,' I nod at him, thinking this is what he wants to hear.

'It certainly is finely done, like the detail on an Attic vase.' The puffs on his pipe are almost toots now. 'But look at these.' His finger follows the single row of oars ready to pull forwards, slanted back along the side of the ship.

My finger traces after his, down the fine lines depicting each oar. 'They look like perfectly ordinary oars to me.' I'm beginning to find this game childish.

'The boat's under full sail. You never have your oars out under full sail. You certainly don't see that in Greek art; well not to my knowledge, anyway. Looks very odd.'

I look again, taking in more of the detail. The boat *was* under full sail. The oars *were* out. So? I want to say. So?

'The artist, whoever he was, got it wrong.' He puffs, then smiles, then puffs again. It's just the sort of thing he'd spend hours deliberating over. 'There's been quite a fuss about it.'

'I see what you mean.' I'm beginning to drift again.

'It's so important to get these details right, don't you think?'

'Very,' I say, sighing. 'The most important thing in the world.' The sarcasm hangs in the air.

His face falls a little. He does his slow blink, then puts his pipe down on an old copper ashtray and heaves himself out of the chair. 'Best tidy the old place up a bit.' He gathers up all the paperbacks, leaving Homer on the table, and turns to put the rest away.

I find myself getting more and more irritated watching him sorting them out. Lining them up in colour order, rearranging them by author, then re-sorting them, probably by publication date. Fat penguins, thin penguins, shuffling across the bookshelf.

I go back to staring at the Greek ship in the roundel, feeling as though I've just failed some little test, but not quite sure what it was.

Finally, he seems satisfied with what he's done, and turns towards me.

'I'd better be off,' I say, not giving him time to sit down.

He pats me on the back as I go out into the street. 'Call and see me next time you come into town.'

Such decency, after my pettiness. I can't look him in the face. I can't bring myself to apologise either. All I feel as I walk away is a rising resentment, as if it's his fault I've behaved so badly.

I make my way back towards the bus stop. The rain has turned to sleet. As I turn the corner leading round to the art gallery, a sudden shower of icy pinpricks needles my cheeks and I'm almost lifted off my feet by a gust of freezing wind at my back.

A woman's face wavers into focus. She stares down at me, pencil poised, eyebrows raised, professional smile. The warm fug of a café. The quiet hum of conversation around me.

A fist of anxiety flexes in my chest. I have no idea how I got here.

The waitress repeats the question loudly, as though I'm deaf. 'Would you like to order, sir?'

Panic threatens to cut off my voice. I clear my throat. 'Could you tell me where I am?'

She senses my agitation, stiffens a little, and then takes a step back. 'Where you are, sir?'

I realise I've unnerved her, so I try to recover, smiling and settling my face into what I hope is an 'aren't I a duffer?' expression. I wonder if she gets many loonies in here. 'Sorry – I mean the street we're on. I'm new to the city. I seem to have lost my bearings.'

Her body relaxes. 'You're in Queen Square, sir.' She sweeps the pencil round over the tables, most of them occupied by women in smart hats. 'And this is the Kardomah. The best café in town.' She raises the pencil to her pad again. 'Now, what would you like to order?'

I mumble that tea would be good. I look around, slowly recognising the familiar décor, faded now and wartime shabby. The cosy Kardomah, my mother used to call it. She'd bring me here for Welsh rarebit after our visits to the art gallery when I was young. The sensation of melted cheese and hot toast suddenly fills my mouth, and the sharpness of mustard prickles my nose.

The waitress comes with tea and dubious rock cakes.

I stare at her as she weaves her way back through the tables towards the kitchen. I'm still struggling to get my head right. The last thing I remember is passing the art gallery and feeling the sleet on my face and the wind at my back. The Kardomah is in the opposite direction to where I was heading. I check my watch. It's a quarter past three. At least five minutes of the fifteen since leaving the bookshop are a blank.

It's as if there's been a slippage in my head. Like a film breaking down at the pictures, whirring black, then clicking on again, and you're back in the story.

Five minutes. Whatever I've done in that time is on the edge of my remembering and I can't reach it. A rush of nerves skitters up the back of my neck into my scalp. I think I'm going to keel over but it passes, leaving my whole body weak.

I signal to the waitress to bring the bill. She looks at the uneaten cakes and purses her lips.

I walk out into Queen Square, the sharp cold after the warmth of the café taking my breath away. I need George. Need to talk to him. Need to ask him about slippages. Maybe he'll know what's happening to me. The bookshop is only ten minutes away. I hurry back, but when I draw near, the sign says 'Closed' and everything is in darkness. A flush of rage takes over. I need you, George, I really need you, and you're not here.

The sleet shows no sign of slackening off. I decide to let myself into the shop, make a cup of tea, warm up before I go home. I go round the back to the shed where he keeps odds and ends.

A few broken shelves. A paraffin heater. His old bike with the basket. Before the war, he'd ride round the city, the basket full of books, bringing great literature to the workers. A regular Mr Chips.

The spare key is where it's always been, under the tiny plant pot on the shed windowsill.

I don't bother with tea. I stride straight through to the shop. Up and down between the rows, pulling out leather volumes, part of this or that set, first editions, tipping them over, enjoying the flap and the splat and the thunk as they hit the floor. The shelves are soon looking like rows of bombed-out terraces, the odd old volume left leaning at the end, or wobbling defiantly in the gaps.

His paperbacks are next. I think of him fussing about, placing them in order, then shuffling them again. I grab armfuls and take them outside near the shed, and heap them up, orange and blue and green and pink, Homer clothed in his acorn brown on top. I soak them with paraffin from the heater. Set them alight – *a jolly bonfire of jolly books, de-dah, de-dah, de-bloody-dah.* They're capering now, alright, his precious Penguins, flippers semaphoring like crazy as the flames tickle their flat little feet. Pages curling up nicely, burning a treat, and all their bloody wisdom with them.

I check the bike. Its tyres are pumped up. I take it and ride it home, the wind at my back again, funnelling straight down between the buildings. The wind, gusting me along like an ancient Greek ship in full sail, battling through sea-green choppy waters, a line of oars out where there really shouldn't have been any.

The back door slams shut and I lean against it, groaning a little, my shirt soaked with sweat. The house is silent; my mother must be in the village on some late errand. I go over to the sink, get a drink of water, hold it to my cheek, feel the ice-cold glass burn through my flesh then numb the skin. The sweat cools on my back and I begin to shake. I sit at the kitchen table, sipping the water, soothing myself. As I set the glass down, I notice all the extra marks on the deal surface. Five years of life I know nothing about, mapped out in food stains and knife cuts and cup rings.

My mother will be back soon. I need to be in my bedroom, alone, safe.

She's been in the room to make the bed. Tidied up the books. Sorted them by colour and arranged them in a neat row at the back of the desk. Except for one. She must have decided it's in too much of a state to be with the others.

It lies there, in the middle of the faded green blotter on the desk, waiting for me.

Linda Anderson

Linda Anderson was born and educated in Belfast. She is an award-winning novelist (*To Stay Alive* and *Cuckoo*, both published by The Bodley Head) and writer of short stories, performance pieces and critical reviews. Her short fiction has been published in magazines and anthologies including *H.U.*, *The Big Issue*, *Wildish Things*, and *The Hurt World: Short Stories of the Troubles*. She taught at Lancaster University, becoming Head of Creative Writing from 1995–2002. In 2006, she launched creative writing at the Open University, chairing the largest writing course in the UK until 2014. She is editor and co-author of *Creative Writing: A Workbook with Readings* and co-author of *Writing Fiction*. She lives in Cambridgeshire in England, writing fiction and non-fiction, as well as working as an editor.

The Turn

There were just four beds. A lot of space lay between them, making the ward look like a stage set. Paintings decked the walls at regular intervals: ethereal women, swooning hollyhocks, a thatched cottage; nothing out of the ordinary. Supper plates were being cleared away, and Anna noticed smells etched on the air: fish and melted cheese with an undertow of disinfectant and commodes. The hospital had its own climate, hot and stuffy, unconnected to the early May evening visible through the windows, with its pale coral sky and fluttering treetops. It's only one night, she told herself.

She looked at the other three patients, wondering what predicaments had landed them in the acute assessment unit. Opposite her, a large woman with a mane of golden blonde hair was breathing with the help of a gurgling nebuliser. Lung disease, maybe. It was impossible to guess her age. Her affliction could have heaped years on her. She was perched on the bed with one leg tucked beneath her and one foot dangling over the edge, like a plump Lorelei.

To her left was an elderly woman, very tall. Even in bed, her height was imposing, despite her slumped posture. Her hair looked parched and greasy – thatchy crown and slick ends – as if she had been in hospital a long time. She wore big, ill-fitting spectacles. She was muttering to herself and Anna began to make it out. 'I can't climb up … I can't talk on the phone … I can't write to them … I can't tell anybody … I can't do the buttons … I can't find the purse … I can't count the change … I can't explain … I can't say what is a dream… I can't get past.' A litany of incapacity. Noticing Anna's gaze, she suddenly addressed her: 'Please, will you help me?' Anna started to walk towards her, stopped in her tracks by Lorelei, who removed her breathing mask to shout a warning: 'You have to ignore her. She does that all the time.'

Anna stood still, torn between her impulses to respond to the imploring woman and to placate the imperious one. Obviously Lorelei was the finger-wagger of the girls' dorm.

'She forgets that she's been to the toilet. She forgets that she's already had her coffee. She asks a thousand times.'

'Sorry,' Anna said to the elderly woman. 'I'll ask a nurse to help you.'

The woman groaned and gave an incredulous pout, keeping her bright eyes fixed on Anna. In the grip of dementia, Anna realised. Or more like a loosening. The free fall of dementia. Get a nurse, she thought, looking round for the alarm button. She changed her mind. Someone was bound to come soon. *Oh God, a moral and social dilemma and you've only just got here.*

The woman to her right was even older than the amnesiac. Her mouth was crumpled and caved in, as if she had missing teeth. Her eyes were haunted and staring. Drape a shawl over her hair and she would resemble a refugee in flight from Syria or Afghanistan.

A cheery male orderly brought round a trolley and dispensed hot drinks. The amnesiac opened a yogurt to have with her drink, but then did not proceed to eat it. Meanwhile, a meal arrived for Anna. It was not what she had imagined when she asked for macaroni cheese with raspberry yogurt for afters, wanting pasta clogged with golden crumbly cheese, not this tomato-saturated mess and this bubble-gum pink gloop devoid of actual fruit. But she ate dutifully, remembering that she had to be 'nil by mouth' from midnight. Also, she deserved something. She deserved a feast. It had been a hard day since that moment, standing in the kitchen, when it felt as if a slipknot had loosened in her womb and a gush of hot blood shot down her thighs. She had been bleeding for weeks, but just a slow, pinkish trickle that had led to a round of investigations of her kidneys, bladder, and finally womb. Despite the sudden haemorrhage, she managed to call an ambulance, which arrived in a few minutes, zipping through the Cambridge traffic. She didn't care about a couple of gawking neighbours who saw her carted off. Once in A&E, there were repeated questions and painful 'intimate' examinations. Like herself, the gynaecologist was a woman originally from Belfast, and for once, Anna found the accent comforting. There was an offhand charm to it, a lack of concealment. The doctor kept her in for observation overnight and to undergo diagnostic tests the next day 'to see if it's anything we need to worry about.'

'I've got cancer, haven't I?'

'I don't know. But there is a lot of blood and there is a mass. You must brace yourself.'

Anna could not help staring as Lorelei unwound herself from her bed and glided over to the amnesiac. Wordlessly, and with no eye contact, she moved a spoon to within the other woman's reach so that she could tuck in to her yogurt. It was like righting a crooked picture on a wall. So, she's not heartless, after all? Anna thought. It was a self-sparing kindness, that's for sure. But she was right, really. She didn't have the lung power to engage in a futile conversation.

I'm exhausted too, Anna realised. Doctors had reassured her that most post-menopausal bleeding did not mean malignancy. But she was haunted by memories of a novel she had read as a student, Thomas Mann's *The Black Swan*. Rosalie, a widow aged fifty, falls for her son's tutor. She starts to bleed from the womb and sees it as rejuvenation. No dignified matron status for her, oh no. She is experiencing an 'Easter of her womanhood'. In fact, her newly fertile womb is breeding a voracious cancer. At the time, Anna thought the story cruel and implausible, ridiculing a vain woman's inability to give up on her youth and her romantic chances. No one could possibly be such a fool as to believe that falling in love could reverse the menopause. As she grew older, she realised that people will believe anything, deny anything, to make life tolerable. Even her own sister, Isabelle, had insisted that the menopause was entirely avoidable (although through drugs, not dalliances). Only an old-fashioned idiot (like the clueless Anna) would allow herself to go through it. After fourteen years on HRT, Isabelle had been forced to endure nocturnal sweats and hot flushes, an unleashing of banked up menopausal symptoms, along with chemotherapy for an unstoppable cancer.

'Well, you dodged the HRT, but it's your turn now for the rest!' There it was: Isabelle's trilling, triumphalist voice sounding in her head. Her sister's death six years ago had made little difference to their relationship, which had been marked by prolonged estrangements, but continued with a kind of shadow-boxing fuelled by spiteful comments and 'news' transmitted by other family members. It was an everlasting argument that required no physical presence.

The woman on her right had a visitor, a small man with sandy hair and beard. He looked like a foreman in a factory, glum and authoritative. Anna could see no likeness between them, but guessed he was her elderly son. They sat in a strained silence, with only occasional utterances. Suddenly he launched into a tirade, making Anna jump. He lowered his voice but continued in a raw, aggrieved tone. She could hardly make out his words, but he was haranguing the woman about not speaking up for herself, not asking for things, not explaining her problems. The woman looked anguished but passive, saying nothing. He was on to her hearing aids now. 'If they're not right, tell someone.'

Anna squirmed, clamouring with defences on her behalf. *She's told you, hasn't she?*

The one-sided quarrel ended and the man got up to go. No affectionate goodbye or renewal of peace. He stalked out, face thunderous, but something sheepish in the set of his shoulders.

A few minutes after he left, the woman got out of bed and grabbed her walking frame. She steered herself round to the other side of the bed, turned her back on the ward, and leaned heavily on the frame. She muttered to herself – no, to him. It was to him. Answering back in not much more than a whisper. Anna knew from her body language and her hurt, defensive tone. She was holding her head up defiantly, responding to the charge list.

You'll never know, Mister, how much you stung her, or what she has to say for herself.

A couple of nurses came round to carry out blood pressure checks. Anna got the one who was bristling with fussiness, even in her uniform: a dazzling white dress with navy blue epaulettes and a breast pocket lined with pens.

'I'm concerned about that woman,' Anna said, inclining her head to indicate the bully's mother. 'She's so desolate.'

'No, no, she's fine.'

'She doesn't look fine.'

'Focus on yourself, okay?'

Anna shrugged. There was nothing to be done about it. Who knew what was wrong, or how many decades of wrongness there might be behind it all? She felt like a useless bystander, passing the time with a bit of voyeurism. Distracting herself from the fact. *The fact that I am bleeding incessantly. The fact that I don't know what to do. Why do I have to be surrounded by babbling old women anyway?* It was going to be a long night. No phone, no visitors, no whodunit to lead her to some improbable, neat ending.

'At least I had fourteen extra years of looking good.' Isabelle was sounding in her head again.

'No, you didn't. You looked frozen in time, a small-town Bette Davis.'

'Oh, I looked like a Hollywood star? How tragic.'

'Same hairstyle for forty years, same scarlet lipstick. Crash dieting was the only fashion you followed.'

'Jealous! You always tried to compensate with your *a-ca-dem-ic* achievements. Dry as dust. No wonder your husband dumped you.'

What does it matter now, how good we looked? Look at the four of us here, like some demoted harem, captives of Old Father Time, the bloodiest of Bluebeards. Live long enough and the body turns against you. Your brain can be erased before you are.

Would she cling to the wreckage, though? Eke out every possible hour, no matter what the conditions? She remembered her father's body, so big and strong at first, but it had always made her cower. The dense materiality of it, the way his presence darkened everything, quelled all merriment or enthusiasm. Once, when she was seven years old, he crashed down in the porch as he left for work. It was like a great tree keeling over. She couldn't believe at first that something was wrong. He must be resting his face against the mosaic tiles for the sake of their coolness. She sat in awe with her little brother while her mother sought help. It was impossible that the giant was lying collapsed and unable to move. It was thrilling. She thought of all his snapped orders, his jibes, his bread-winnerly rectitude. 'Think I'm made of money?' 'It's time when I say it's time.' And then the doctor came, levered him to his feet, almost toppling himself. He caught the reek of his breath. 'Yes, whiskey. That's not a breakfast beverage, you know. Keep off the booze if you want to keep your job. And this lovely woman.'

It was the first time she had witnessed her father scorned, cringing at a rebuke.

He went on turning his body into a millstone. It was his life's work: drink, a sixty-a-day habit, jam sandwiches and Jaffa cakes. He got worse after joining the Police Reserve part-time, 'doing his bit to protect the community'. She had fled to London as soon as she could, heart soaring as the plane left the ground and climbed up, up and away. Once, on a fraught visit home, she could hardly believe the schism in her life: one night enjoying torrential talk with friends in a Covent Garden wine bar; next night watching her almost wordless father dismantle and clean his gun at the kitchen table. She remembered a couple of forlorn trips to Ballyholme and Groomsport, where she and her mother roamed the beach while he stayed immured in the car. The scenery was enough for him, he said. Northern Ireland was the 'best wee country in the world'. *Yeah, great place, Dad.* A fragment of a country, a blood-soaked tatter of a place with its 'peace walls' still standing, more than fifteen years after the ceasefires. No wonder she liked living in the east of England with its flat, undramatic terrain, its population from all over the world and its mostly manageable crimes.

She reached over to open the drawers of her bedside cabinet: nothing, nothing, and then a wine-coloured Gideon Bible. *Get at me in here, why don't you.* She flicked through some pages, reciting her own articles of unfaith. No Original Sin, no Fall, no Heaven, no Hell, no Easter Rising of my womanhood, no Resurrection.

It had taken her years to realise how fearful her father was, how servile. He was no churchgoer, but he bought into all the rules: the superstition without the solace. Three score years and ten was the allotted life span. He made it to seventy-one, playing truant for an extra year. Belief in Resurrection gave him a terror of cremation. Come the Last Day, God would surely need at least a bag of bones to work with to reconstitute his fleshly self.

'Oh, I've never seen anyone read that Bible before!' It was the nurse she liked, clad all in blue and with no trace of brisk bossiness.

'I'm not really reading it. I'm just desperate.'

'I can get the chaplain to have a word with you in the morning, if that would help?'

'No, I mean ... desperate for something to read.'

'*Take a Break* works for me.' They both laughed. 'Time can drag in here. Would you like something to help you sleep?'

'I guess we're not talking Horlicks?'

'You could have that too.'

'Great. I'll have both.'

The sludgy drink came first, then the tiny white pill. It made her feel drunk and then heavy, pinned down in the bed. Night began to fall, finally turning the darkness beyond the window as black as the bottom of a well. The blue light from the nurse's station was the same as the underwater blue of swimming pools. Anna drifted in and out of sleep, feeling as if she had the bends each time she surfaced. A sob came once from Lorelei's direction, but the space between them was like a moat, unsurpassable. The painting on the wall above Lorelei's bed caught her eye. It had its own lustrous light, moving in from the side like the advent of morning. The painting was somehow separate from this night. She was able to make out more of its shapes, some kind of country churchyard. She recognised it then, and stirred with a protest she was too tired to sustain. It was Stanley Spencer's *Resurrection*, the one at Cookham. How wrong to hang such a gloomy, grave-stuffed picture in a ward. She would complain, yes, tomorrow. Maybe there would be a form to fill in, something in triplicate. The painting grew and she was inside it, hemmed in by vicious stumps of headstones. Villagers were clambering out of their graves in their Sunday best. Their faces were soft and genial. Wives brushed the soil off their husbands' jackets and mingled with neighbours for an overdue natter. Anna recognised others: newcomers, infiltrators. There was Rosalie, the amorous widow, with her black swan on a leash. Or was it a noose? Her own dead were there. Isabelle, fifteen years old, wearing a white sundress with spaghetti straps. A wasp buzzed round her head. And then an older Isabelle, in her frothy wedding gown, her eyes mascara-streaked. Anna's grandparents appeared, a genial man not looking at his wife's disapproving countenance, and there was her mother's dreamy face, half-hidden behind a tree. In silence she led Anna to a body swathed in a blanket behind a tomb. Anna understood it was someone who needed to be found. A young man with a gouged torso. Unburied, unstirring. His face was smooth, hair like a hank of flax. She could hardly count the number of his wounds.

'You remember him?' She jolted awake. It was her father's raspy voice, but outside her head, in the room. She looked up at the red twinkling light of the smoke alarm. She was in hospital, a place far too impersonal to harbour ghosts. And yet it was a place of passing over, of last breaths.

She tried to keep her eyes open but a hot, heavy daze kept engulfing her. *Yes, I remember.* He was a student, twenty years old. She saw him out on the road somewhere near Newry, thumbing a lift. He gets in a car; it's the wrong car. Did he hesitate, seeing the other passengers? *Hop in – the more the merrier.* They would have been affable at first – and then the questions. Not many. Name? Where did you grow up? What school did you go to? And then what, a pre-arranged signal, an exchanged look in the mirror? The driver veers off track, not headed for Belfast, not yet.

The voice broke in again, softer, urgent. 'The grass was moving but the air seemed dead still. He was dumped in a ditch, face down. He looked like a slumbering child. I ran ahead and hunkered down, tried to turn him over. The others were yelling at me. But I forgot everything I had been taught.

Don't touch the body. Could be booby-trapped. I pounded his heart, trying to make him come back. And then we all lifted him, one limb each, and ran like madmen, desperate to get him away from that foul, ditchy place. Back at the station, we couldn't look at each other. As if we were the guilty ones.'

'I remember you stumbling through the door. I had never seen you cry before. I had never heard you say that life is all that matters, that hatred is stupid. That you loved me and wanted me to be safe always.'

'You couldn't stand it. Slapped my hand away.'

'I couldn't trust it. You turned back into yourself soon enough.'

'Or what if that was the real me?'

'Dad? Dad.'

He was gone. None of it could be helped or fixed. The murdered man; her lonely, stricken father; herself stuck in a habit of rejection. She cried until her throat ached. Just before she sank back into sleep, there was a touch, the lightest caress of her brow.

When she woke, the ward was filled with a clean, watery light. The other women were eating breakfast. All three looked serene, the despairs of the night neatened and folded away. The painting over Lorelei's bed had reverted to a nautical scene, some sailing boats on a choppy sea. Anna went to the window. *Dark gives way to light, light to dark, no matter what.* She saw trees, sky, flickering blades of grass, a burst of hawthorn blossom, and a workman in a canary yellow safety helmet, a taxi driver standing by his car with a gigantic carton of coffee. She was ready for the day, the tests, the facts.

I have risen.

Anne Devlin

Anne Devlin was born in Belfast in 1951. She worked as a teacher in both Bushmills and Bristol before publishing short stories in the early eighties. Her most translated story is *Naming The Names,* self-adapted for screen, which was written for Faber Introduction 8. Prior to the opening of her stage play, *Ourselves Alone*, she was made Writer in Residence at the Royal Court Theatre in 1985/86, becoming Tutor in Playwriting at Birmingham University until 1989. She co-authored the Birmingham Community Play *Heartlanders*, followed by a Residency at the University of Lund, Sweden, until May 1990. When she returned to Birmingham she began working for Paramount Pictures and then the Royal Shakespeare Company. Since returning to Belfast in 2007 with her husband and son, she has been writing and publishing short stories for a new collection.

Cornucopia

Sometime in the middle of the 1950s, the goddesses arrived. There were two of them. They were a gift to my grandmother Frances from her younger brother James, recently returned from Rome. One had a curved, shell-like horn at her feet, out of which tumbled fruit and flowers. The tail of the horn curved upwards, towards the flung hand of the woman who was leaning with her other elbow on a half plinth, next to a basket of wheat. Her twin, the other woman, was plainer in her adornments. While she also leaned on a half plinth, she held a scroll in her outstretched arm. They seemed to me, in their pale, unvarnished state, to represent a challenge to the gaudy saints of my grandmother's baroque Catholicism. The household had its share of statues: there was a Virgin crushing the head of a snake with bare toes on the 'tall boy' in her bedroom. When we had overnight guests, usually other relatives, I slept there on a small divan at the foot of her bed. Once, I turned over to discover the snake's jewelled eyes glinting at me in the dark. Higher up in the house, on another landing, stood the Child of Prague, like a small Velasquez infanta with wide crimson and gold skirts. I remember my mother and father standing on a Drogheda street once, on holiday, trying to work out if they had enough money left to pay for it. It became my grandmother's favourite. On New Year's Eve she ran in and out of the front door with it in her arms, for luck. I never noticed much difference in our luck after the New Year; if anything, since Grandfather's death, things got a little worse. Until the year the Roman women arrived.

The goddesses had bodies with curves rather than just fat draperies. They were placed in the parlour at first, and then quietly put away. Until exploring my aunt's out-of-bounds bedroom, I spotted them sitting in the unlit hearth, the grate banked high with empty Gallagher's Blues packets. Skating boots clacked amidst blue and yellow net petticoats against the door. Auntie Kathleen was lying in late, after the Saturday Plaza. Emboldened, I asked her from the hearth: 'What is this thing at her feet? This horn?'

She spoke from the depth of her bed, rackety cough following: 'It's a cornucopia.'

'What's a cornucopia?'

'A Horn of Plenty.'

'Uh-huh. And the scroll?'

'It's a book. Books were a different shape then.'

'When?'

'In ancient times,' she said, and added grumpily: 'Now go away and let me sleep.'

My father and aunt had a disputatious relationship. I liked drama, so I always carried the things she said to me back to him, to see how they stood up.

'What kind of book is she holding?'

'That's not a book, that's the Rule of Law. One goddess represents the Law. And the other is Agriculture. Don't forget the wheat.'

The word 'cornucopia', once you've heard it, is hard to resist. It casts a bigger spell than Agriculture. He wanted me to study Law because he was a baker and went to night classes. What I didn't know then was that he'd been a prisoner, and he wanted me to know my rights. But it was my grandmother in one of her more lucid moments who named the goddess with the horn.

'This is Fortuna. She's from Ostia.'

'How do you know that?'

'She's in the Vatican Museum. She has the power to give but also to take away. I don't like her much. Watch out for her.'

About the scroll woman, I was still in the dark. Until Grandmother suggested: 'It's a diploma. It represents Learning.'

'Aye, but in Law,' my father said.

My aunt's voice contradicted him: 'Law as a goddess would have scales, and a sword.'

'That's not Law, that's Justice.'

In an attempt to resolve the dispute between them, the goddess remained unnamed. During this time one of the arms holding the scroll was damaged. Somebody must have broken it, maybe it was me. Someone repaired the limb, I don't remember who. Afterwards, an amber line marked the place of attachment to the elbow.

All lofty aspirations about my future were lost sight of when my mother's eldest brother came back from Canada on a visit: 'This house is too big for Frances at her time of life,' he said, glancing at me. So the pair moved into a small apartment. It was the beginning of the sixties. They proved hard to integrate either in terms of place or function. Grandmother shared her bedroom with the Virgin and the Child of Prague, while Kathleen kept the goddesses on the stainless-steel draining board in the kitchen. I returned to my parents' flat above the bakery, which promptly moved them up the housing list. My mother complained I was spoiled. I didn't like sharing a room with the younger children, and I was out of the orbit of the goddesses. They came to me after Kathleen died. The scroll she held was very much reduced; the long curved edge was shortened and sanded to a stump in her tight grip. Her sister Fortuna remained as blooming and intact as ever. A Rastafarian carpenter made a special niche for them from some bookcases he was recycling. He placed them in the centre of the wall in a house in Shepherd's Bush. Here they were revealed to have a purpose no one had discerned before, as book ends.

She remembers them. They wore blue overalls in her dream. They looked like porters, or mental health workers from the hospital; the ones the institution used to restrain people. It was a nightmare she was glad to wake up from. She had this dream a few months before they were to move. Then, one morning, glancing over the stairwell, she saw real men in blue overalls make their way upstairs towards her. The threat they posed in the dream had become reality; the dream had prepared her for an invasion of her life by forces over which she had no control. The twins had gone away to university; an action that seemed to prompt her partner's midlife crisis. She went down two floors to pack up her own room. She was unable to finish a book. He was already in there, the boss, his job to organise the others. But here he was standing in her room with the goddess holding the cornucopia, laid flat on a small rug ready to be placed in a box. The woman, when you turned her over, had a braided crown of hair around her head and a luxurious coiled rope down her back. For the rest of her life she will remember that image, not of the goddess lying unwittingly on the blanket, but of the man's careful examination of what he held. When she opened the box later, the cornucopia was crushed. All that remained of the female body was the braided head, which she threw away at once with the rest into the trash. The broken one alone remained. When her partner left, the house was sold to two brothers from the city. The youngest one said: 'Take the bookcases, we don't want them.' Her partner had taken out three mortgages to pay their credit card bills. The debt belonged to both of them. He had simply kept the extent of it from her. She didn't have a house to put the bookcases into.

The winter I left, the snow on the Antrim plateau was deep, having fallen for three days. In Germany, the street signs are written in a gothic script, which was familiar from my first Irish grammar lessons, the umlauts and circles with tails being my speciality. I find my way to the student settlement very quickly. It's on the edge of a frozen lake. We are driving between high banks of snow on roads that seem to be centrally heated.

The mathematician who is showing us the apartment is from Ohio.

'A *putzfrau* will come in the morning with towels, sheets and keys,' he explains. 'She also cleans the kitchen and the bathroom we all share.'

A tiny Vietnamese woman is shifting a heavy pot that is belching steam to the kitchen window. 'Visiting professor,' he tells me. 'Our neighbour.' The Ohio student returns to his guests, and I open the door on a functional room, which seems like an office with a corner alcove where my bed is tucked, in this house of exiles.

The next day I find the institute, in a different part of town. It's a fine old house with turrets. Celia is a New Zealander who speaks German with an antipodean intonation, which to my ear makes it infinitely easier to understand. Then there's Johann who only speaks Hochdeutsch, which I have no ear for at all. Because it's my first day, they take me to a Weinstube for lunch; normally they would eat at the Messa. The waitress refuses to serve Johann; she'll accept halting German from foreigners, but no upper-class nonsense from him. 'His parents were diplomats,' Celia explains. 'Professor, Doctor, Frau, Eva Müller is the boss and she's married to a non-academic lawyer, so she's rich,' Celia tells me airily. 'She owns a large house with four floors, three of them are let; in fact, she's my landlord,' Celia adds. 'She fucks all the young men in the department and you have to give her all her titles, Professor, Doctor, Frau, in that order.' In my head I rename her Frauprof.

Later I meet Netta and Josh, a married couple. Netta is Polish, and tried to live in Israel but gave up because it's the desert and she prefers Europe. Josh is Austrian with very sad eyes and a voice like a cello. 'You're very ballsy to come here on your own,' she says, 'especially with such poor German.' She offers to teach me; we meet for tea and German conversation on a weekly basis. They live, the newlyweds, in the gothic part of town near the institute where little trams hum quietly up and down the street. The coffee shops have ovens of porcelain with pastoral scenes on the tiles. The Japanese at the institute are like me and have chosen a modern apartment; but it is modern expensive, in contrast to modern functional. Yoshi is visiting from Kyoto with his wife Akiko, a baby and his mother-in-law; he has also brought his ancestors. He keeps them in an urn by the door shrine. It reminds me of my grandmother's votive altars, lit candles in front of the Virgin on the tallboy and the Child of Prague.

It's a comparative and international department, which would explain the presence of so many foreigners, but I am really wondering if I'm ever going to meet any Germans apart from Johann, when I meet Elsa Berg, a fiftyish blonde with gold-rimmed glasses and shoulder-length hair. She explains that all those donnish young Englishmen who hover around Eva Müller are actually young Germans whose English was finished at Oxford. Elsa is from the north, and her presence in the department is a corrective to Eva Müller, who is from the south. Like revenants of both sides in the 30 Years' War, they jointly run the department. The two women are not friends. But I also don't expect women who have reached their positions of power to be helpful or friendly to younger females. Then

Elsa surprises me by being entirely supportive even when I feel I've screwed up my first seminar. 'My energy ran out halfway through and I let three things pass,' I tell her.

'That's teaching,' she says.

On Saturday, at the end of the first month, I meet my Ohio researcher from the first night. He has a German friend, Sabina, another student. We go to a Chinese restaurant, an elaborate pavilion. I am given chopsticks.

Ohio says: 'Try to speak German.'

Sabina asks: 'Why are you here?'

'Okay. I will try chopsticks or German, but not both at the same time.'

We lapse into English. Ohio keeps stroking Sabina's arm and saying: 'Peachfuzz.'

He draws our attention to the honey gauze halo that sits on her limbs, until I have to look away.

The student settlement, like all student organisations, is a place in transition. By contrast the institute is formal and hierarchical, and in two parts: one part is science, and the other law. The lawyers seem to be ascendant. So when a group of lawyers who appear to run the institute invite me on a ski trip to the Jungfrau and Engelberg, I accept.

I have been living on a Council of Europe Fellowship. I have it for five months during which I'm expected to finish my PhD. The teaching allows me to subsidise my income, which means I can extend my stay.

Celia, who is not coming with us because she's not one of the skiers, explains: 'This is Eva Müller's trip, Elsa Berg doesn't ski. So if you join it, you need to make sure you have Elsa's blessing. How did you learn to ski anyway? It's all very green and wet where you come from.'

'Every weekend I go up to the nursery slopes of the Black Forest. I joined a class.'

'Where did you get the gear – the skis, the boots?'

'I bought them in a sale in London on the way.'

Celia is wide-eyed: 'You are one seriously ambitious woman.'

I have let Celia's machine-gun-delivery floor me. I have begun to do this in class as well – letting things pass. Another voice somewhere deep inside, like a child in another room, is protesting, but is too far away to be heard.

I go back to Sabina's unanswered question in the Chinese pavilion: what are you doing in this country?

Ohio tells us the subject of his thesis: something about temperance movements in Germany in the nineteenth century.

'That's not why you are here,' she says.

'No, I came here to avoid the draft. Vietnam.'

'The war is over,' she says.

'But my thesis is not.'

'I'm avoiding a war too,' I add.

'What happened to the man who drove you here?' Ohio asks.

'He has a life in another country.' He has a wife in another country.

'You aren't a scientist and you're not a lawyer; how did you get into the institute?' she asks.

'My thesis is scientific: what constitutes a literary text?' This is usually a conversation stopper, but not with these two.

'Is that wise?' Ohio asks. 'Don't you want a bit of mystery?'

Sabina gives him a warning look and changes the subject.

March. The toughest term in my teaching is now behind me.

'How do you think you performed?' Elsa Berg asks me on the eve of my trip to the mountains.

'I did half of what I'd set out.'

'That's about right for a first time round,' she says. 'It's much easier for the rest of us; we're supported by the principle of seriality, makes it less exhausting.'

I'm wondering if I'll get a second time, or if I've made a mistake in joining the ski faction, when a horrific cable car crash in the Italian Alps that winter compounds my anxiety. I have deliberately folded away pages of *Stern* with all the photographs of crushed bodies in the snow. Netta has been using *Stern* to set me translations. Usually there are lots of stories about British Royals. They mostly involve love affairs with people in the theatre: a duke with an actress, a princess with a playwright. This time all the magazine text reveals is German prejudice about the Italians' lack of care with their ski machinery.

'The operator wasn't properly trained,' Johann explains. I allow myself to be re-assured. 'And the snow conditions are perfect,' he adds. He is regarded as the leader of the snow party.

In the hotel lobby on our first day of skiing, I find Eva Müller staring at me as if I have suddenly become visible. The usual haughty smirk has given way to a cloudier, less confident face.

'I wish I'd thought to get a new ski suit, this old thing is twenty years old,' she says.

Everyone looks at me. It's true they are tall, lean and athletic, Müller most of all, but they are all in black. They look like a bunch of deep sea divers. My mother made costumes for a living, so she taught me something very simple: look the part and you can go anywhere. Walking towards them clad in sapphire blue, a body-hugging jacket and pants, everything matching, including my hat, I'm wondering if I've overdone it. I've compensated for my lack of skill by blinding them with style. But even I know from the creature that eats my insides when I'm afraid that my advantage will not last.

Netta, with her fragile candyfloss hair, is standing at the entrance to the funicular railway in sunglasses and snow boots. She's not a skier; she's come to take in the views. She hands me a tube of cream.

'Don't get burnt at the top.'

At dinner the previous evening, while the Swiss waiters were being given a blasting by Eva Müller for handing out menus to the women with prices withheld, I asked Netta why lawyers were so important at a scientific institute.

'They are patent lawyers. They have to determine what part of an idea or discovery is owned by the scientist and what by the corporation.'

'Are you a patent lawyer?'

'No, I'm an art historian.'

I'm halfway up the slope before I think to question this further. I recall that she doesn't have to share an office. She's going to the sun terrace at the first station to sit in a deckchair with a blanket.

The skiers pair off to the lifts that will take them to the top of the glacier. It is when we reach the third and final station, travelling up the face of the Jungfrau, that Johann, who is accompanying Eva, suddenly looks over and says, 'What level are you? This is a black route only.'

My moment of truth has arrived. The tight panels of my suit are holding me in at the sides. 'I'm a beginner.'

'You should have got off at the last station.'

'I'll get a cable car down and meet you at station two.'

'There is no cable car down,' he says. 'We shouldn't have let you come up so high.'

Outside on the glacier, Johann begins to allocate places. The safest place on the whole route is next to the leader. 'You will have to ski in my tracks,' he says. Then he turns to Eva, who is a very experienced black route skier. 'Will you go third? Then if she gets into trouble you can lead the line.'

Yoshi follows Eva, who is followed by a trio of young lawyers who are her constant companions at work.

Out on the frozen concrete of the mountain, an American woman is swearing and slamming her skis together. Finally she hurls them and screams at them. 'Mud Fucker.' We make our first traverse past her. I am deep in Johann's tracks and skiing across the face of the glacier. The first relentless traverses are fine, and the skis bite into the mountain. Then we hit the ice field and it's like skiing on marbles. Everyone loses control, but I make it because I have locked on Johann's ski path. Eva takes a very bad roll across down the field and we lose sight of her. Later, when we have all skied around an overhanging boulder, which takes us to the very edge of the glacier, Eva crashes above our heads onto Johann's shoulders.

We reach the second station with relief and, unobserved, I steady the tremor in my limbs. I am not the only one having to struggle with the body's rebellion. It took enormous concentration and skill to lead us out of the ice field.

The designated routes have become icy with congested traffic, so we ski off-piste into the deep powder snow of the woods. And in this way we travel for an hour, through the darkling afternoon, flitting in cushioning silence towards Engelberg.

That evening we went to an inn that specialised in fondue. Netta is puzzled by the mood of the ski party. We raised our glasses through entwined arms.

'You may say "du!" to me,' Eva says to Johann.

'You may say "du" to me,' Johann says to me.

'Do to me,' I echo.

'You do something to me,' Josh sings to Netta.

Johann's conquest of our hearts was evident as I watch Eva tilt her head back and stretch her neck towards him.

'And this,' he says, holding up the heated cheese on a fork, 'is called the nun, and this is the best bit.'

'I recover stolen paintings,' Netta volunteers. 'They are hidden as fakes. You could help me. You have great eyes.'

'I couldn't. My eye and my brain don't know each other.'

I do know that I will not finish my PhD. That Elsa Berg will not extend my stay. And neither will Eva Müller. And I have risked all this to have sex with Johann.

When I return from the mountains, Ohio has already moved to Sweden. Sabina must have gone too. A group of strangers is living in the student settlement.

I get up from the table to find the loo. The wine is having an effect.

'Who took my cup?' I ask when I come back.

The faces at the table smile and resume their conversation. I am speaking a foreign language. My friends have gone. My insides plunge like a lift losing power and falling to the basement. My ears are full of noise. I am petrified by the volume of the crash when it comes, and it comes. I am gone for twenty years.

The lawyers lived their lives in such conformity; they knew all the rules, so they were always on the alert for places without any, like off-piste skiing. It wasn't simply dangerous thrill-seeking; they were looking for the uncharted, something off the map. It wasn't an escape. It was a confrontation. What they wanted was to test their courage for liberty. I wanted to escape. It was peace I was seeking, though it looked like liberty at the time. This would put me on a road that would bring me to that moment in a room in Shepherd's Bush when the carelessly held cornucopia lay in a blanket, unwittingly waiting to be dropped. That man with his little bullet head and his close-cropped hair bent over her. After the house is sold, she wakes with a throat of fire, in her temporary rooms; something has fallen during the night. Silver flakes have skied across the carpet. A mirror propped against the fireplace has fallen over into the hearth, tumbling the surviving goddess, whose limb has become detached again. Up close, it looked as if she was holding the phallus in her tight grip. It was an earlier version of the virgin crushing the snake's head with her toes. I broke my arm twice; I had forgotten. Once I fell down on a road when I went back to live with them. My father took me on the night bus to the hospital to have it set; all summer I wore it in a sling.

I fell again under an ambush of stones, on the road during a civil rights march, on the same arm – detached again by the fall. The limb carried the weight of our projections. Isolated on the desk it looks, for all the world, like a reminder to give someone a hand job. Somebody once said that you have to be ruined twice. The mirror in which I look is very unforgiving. I had not escaped the pattern after all.

In the few weeks before I leave London I am invited to a screening. An actor I once had a crush on is across the room. He told me he left Wales because he used to open doors to rooms where he found his aunts weeping behind the debris of objects that piled up and kept them from leaving. I have him down as another liberty seeker. I have a great desire to cross the room to speak to him. But the self is so receded and the distance to the world so vast that the effort defeats me. I glance away, over my shoulder. That's when I see them, sitting on the window ledge, looking in: the goddesses. Ten times the size. We are five floors up in Piccadilly. I get out of the chair in which I have been sitting and move across the room.

To celebrate my fiftieth birthday, the Italian baker in our neighbourhood made the cake; it was iced with a cornucopia. He placed sprays of real berries among the marzipan fruit and flower-heads. Two days before the baker delivered this cake, the first plane went into the Twin Towers. I went ahead with the party.

On the day, everyone came, solemnly ate the cake, and left early and all at once by the basement door. A bell clanging in the distance from Milton's church, never audible before, called time in the house; stacked cake plates clacked in response. A small blue and yellow mayfly made of plastic glass and wire, a township souvenir, tumbles from the London window onto an Ardoyne sill, through the Alpine light of the darkling year.

Evelyn Conlon

Evelyn Conlon, born and reared in Rockcorry, Co. Monaghan, is a novelist, short story writer and occasional essayist. Her books include *Telling*, *Selected Stories*, published first by Blackstaff Press, re-published this year by Books Upstairs, and *Not The Same Sky*, based on the lives of Famine orphan girls shipped to Australia. She was editor of *Later On*, an anthology compiled in response to the Monaghan bombing and subject of a set of Italian conference papers on the language of war. She was co-editor, with Hans Christian Oeser, of *Cutting the Night in Two*, a predecessor to *The Long Gaze Back*. Her work has been widely anthologised and translated into many languages, including Tamil and Chinese. The title story of her second collection, *Taking Scarlet as a Real Colour*, was performed at Edinburgh Theatre Festival. Her story, '*Dear You*', about the Irish woman who attempted to assassinate Mussolini, has been published recently in Italy. She lives in Dublin.

Disturbing Words

I know you're wondering what I'm doing up here, not just up here, but here at all. The last you'd heard I was away out foreign someplace. So foreign that you don't even know the name of it, and that's a hard enough thing to achieve these days, when there is always some lurker beside you with infinite information on his telephone, as well as his entire life. Infinite does mean that there's no end to it, which is never a good thing. You mention a place, the strangeness of it lovingly on your tongue, its faraway mysteries tucked into the silence that you're trying to leave around it, and your man has whipped out his gadget: 'How do you spell that?' he bellows. Perhaps not bellows, but it feels like it, the roaring cult of the amateur know-all. Your youth was gloriously lived with the photographs kept in an album and only taken out if there was a reason to do so, something to check, or an emigrant visiting, something to do with them when the talk of their grown children and their new fridge had run out of steam.

Actually, in all honesty, it's so long since you heard the last of me I could have been dead. And you're right, I have been away in a peculiar place, almost desert really, a place with red earth, spindly bits of mangy grass and heat that is laughable. And a neighbour whose job is building underground car parks in mosques.

But I had come home for my parents' funeral, naturally. And I say *home* when I'm here because it's easier. Demanding that anyone call my air-conditioned desert pad home would be a bit much. My parents had died within a day of each other and luckily enough the first funeral hadn't taken place, so the two wakes were held together. In the passing around of the word it got mixed up which of them had gone first but it didn't really matter. Not to outsiders anyway. It did to me. But over the few days, the more I accepted condolences, even I got confused as to which of them had died of the broken heart. But I could have worked it out by trying to remember who was named when my phone went in Abu Dhabi. Because I was on my way home after hearing about the first when they rang me to tell me about the second. I had thought that they were just checking to see how my flights were going so far, no delays, that sort of thing.

On the first evening after the coffins were got and all the other essentials seen to, the neighbours came in with their manners and their good thoughts and after some sadness they proceeded to garden the memories so that there could be a shape put on the next few days. And a discrete map made for themselves, one to move on with next week. Before the day was up, between us we'd have looked at a lot of things about the lives of my parents, how they had met, and although we wouldn't say it, how love had changed them.

'They're pulling from our pen now,' my father's oldest friend, John Moloney, said.

He had meant it to be heard only over in the corner, where the slagging men had gathered. But there had been a bit of quiet and it travelled further into the room. Brian Gallagher bristled. He wasn't too well himself at the minute. Mrs Clancy jumped in with sandwiches and the talk took up again.

For as long as they could remember, my father was a pernickety sort of man, particularly around language, and my mother seemed to follow suit. Although some of the women weren't sure if the following suit was a sleight of hand, they thought that it might have been her who started it. She was known as a reader. Serious reading hid in her very nerves. She got terribly annoyed about the man who had come walking here and lied in a book about things she had told him. When she brought it up with the women, they could see that it mattered more to her than it did to them. 'Imagine pretending to have been places that you weren't,' she said indignantly. 'As if we wouldn't find out, as if we didn't read on the border.'

They nodded their heads towards her. She spoke the truth.

And now they were gathered, talking their way through the shock of them both gone. 'Remember the time he dressed you down for saying UK?' someone called to Gerry Moore.

And Gerry, who was a perfect mimic, brought my father's voice straight into the room.

'Let's not get lazy, it's England, or Britain if you want. United Kingdom of Great Britain and Northern Ireland? Not around here. And as for an Ulster Scot, that's a Monaghan woman in Edinburgh. Scotch Irish, that's how it goes. If we mind our language the rest will follow.'

And we all stayed quiet in honour of the man who had thought that language mattered and the woman who liked the sound of the truth.

My father had been hurt young by the border; the line ran on the top of their ditch. His mother had mourned the loss of her friends, from both sides of the house.

'That's making them from a different country. How could that be?'

She stopped to think about it some more.

'So if you were born in the six counties before now, where will they say you were from? You can't have been from somewhere that never was.'

She looked some more out over the imaginary divide, as people have always done, that is, people who have lived on borders, who have heard the river running from one place to the other, not hesitating as it crosses the line.

'But you haven't lost them,' my grandfather said. 'You'll just have to go through a checkpoint to see them.'

'You'd soon get tired of that,' she said, looking out to the field, third from the window, that would now be in a different country.

Now that it had been mentioned, I remembered the day that Gerry had got dressed down. They were moving cattle from the field that had all the grass eaten. This always caused a problem because they had to manoeuvre the cows over territory that had been disputed. In other places moving cattle caused problems because of cars coming around a bend too fast and landing on top of you, or a cow throwing back her head with the freedom of the road and making a run for it. They had all had a great weekend over at the Forkhill Singers' weekend. The pub had been lit up with sound. Singers had come from all over the country as well as England and Scotland. Funny enough, there were none from Wales. The songs had happened, tied in with each other, ebbing and flowing all night. It could have been thought to be a funny thing, grown men and women hanging on to the words of songs. But if you were there you could see the sense of it. It would appear that at some stage Gerry had gone outside and found a soldier with his ear up to the back wall, lost in an air from his own place. Those of us who know that can never forget it.

After the cattle had been successfully got into the new field and had disappeared in a cloud of joy to its far corners of shining abundant grass, the conversation slid into border things. It must have been the songs that did it, or Gerry seeing the soldier and feeling sad for him, because they were usually careful to leave that sort of talk for behind their own closed doors. And somehow or another things got out of hand and descended into a shouting match and the evening became known as that time of the big row, a singular description, out on its own, the big row. Some of it carried across the fields, so we know about bits of it, but other things were said that passers-by couldn't hear. My father came home quiet.

That shouting had been the end of something or the beginning of something else. My father left the modern world, stopped listening to the news. Funny enough, my mother didn't, but then women can be like that, just in case there's the equivalent of a washing machine being developed, and they'd need to know. And in her case, something being written that might make sense of things. In time, though, she too said that there wasn't much of use going on and she retreated from the radio, back to her books. She did get a mobile phone, but she didn't charge it up that often. They ate their dinner quietly, making happy little remarks about the taste of things.

And I began to know that I would go away.

Around here they were all good at going away. The town down the road was so dead it didn't even know it. Gerry said that even Country and Western singers wouldn't darken the door of what passed for the pub, although mind you, things were cheerful enough in the one on the actual border, the one where the singing had been. They had lots to laugh at there: the Traynor boys being caught smuggling a load of drink in an ambulance that they'd bought and converted; the Murtagh boys having their load taken off them by Customs men who turned out not to be Customs men at all, but maybe the Traynor boys dressed up. They concentrated on those bits, not serious things, only matters of money.

Yes, I had gone away. First to Dublin, where they couldn't stop hearing the headlines in my accent, and then to further away, where it didn't matter. And as soon as the next plate of sandwiches was handed around, maybe I'd go away again, slip out the door and up the lane. Or at least start packing my bag to the murmur of them in the kitchen.

Before I left for the faraway place, my mother had said, always live away from the border.

On the second morning of the wakes, I took a breath and opened the desk in the back bedroom; I would take a very quick look. I had no notion of going through things. All that could wait. But the tidy bundle, strung together with a loose hessian bow, on the very top of all else, was clearly meant to be looked at. I was so glad that my brother hadn't come yet, not until this afternoon. My mother would have hated his suburban wife going through her things, not understanding what they meant, trying to put a value on them.

I undid the twine and spread out the papers. There were pages and pages of meticulous notes on all things border. All things to do with partition. Who had mentioned it first. How it had come about that it was six and not four. And which six. There were notes on the Border Commission and chapters of books photocopied. There was a fortnights' reading in it, even for the first skim. One page had a large printing of the word 'Gerrymander'. It was my mother's handwriting below it. It stated that 'Gerrymander' was first used in the nineteenth century in the *Boston Weekly Messenger*, referring to the new voting district, which Governor Elbridge Gerry had carved out to favour his own party, the map of which resembled a salamander. Behind that was a picture of my parents at the filling in of the cratered roads, those blown up by the British Army. You could see them happening in the look they were giving each other. A split second of light between the trees, their futures hovering together. This was now where they wanted to be. They'd met, apparently, on the third day of the filling in. My grandmother must have loved that. At least something good would come out of it. As they worked, some of the photographers caught shadows of soldiers passing along the hedges. They didn't hate them yet, but they would if needs be. And in time, they learned how to look out the car window, straight ahead, silent, as the camouflaged men with blackened faces examined their driving licenses.

And then there was my first letter to them from the desert. On the back of the envelope was a tiny map, which I couldn't make out, the writing was so small, but there was our barn door, and all sorts of lines drawn down from it. It took me some time to find the larger version, which turned out to be a perfectly precise architectural flourish. My father and mother had drawn a plan to build a basement that would cross the border and thus they would live in two places. I wanted to believe that telling them about the underground car park in the mosque had helped. I really wanted to believe it. But in the meantime there was the tree. There was a picture of it, pinned to pages and more pages of horticultural notes. Clearly they had cultivated the tree to make sure that its roots, and now its branches, would spread across the line. I was struck still by the amusement of it all, who would ever have thought of it.

I heard movements begin as the morning started and I was needed downstairs, but first I had to check the barn. I would slip out before the serious day began. I pushed open the door, multi-coloured in layers of new paints gone old. I fumbled my way to the far corner and there it was, a velvet curtain hanging as if on front of a stage, covering a large opening. Just for one second I heard a tapping sound, a small noise as the job was begun, and then a bigger one as the larger pick was used. I stared down into the darkness and wanted to see how far they'd got, but heard my name being called, again. Later would do.

During the actual funeral, the parts that are said to remind us of the end, I thought of their beginning together and could dimly hear their laughs in chorus, as they drew to their hearts' content. So that's what they'd done when they left the news behind.

We were saying goodbye to some of the mourners when we saw the big yellow machine negotiate its way in the gap of the field on the other side, over the bog, up the hill. We watched as it stationed itself, belching out bad fumes. A cutting device unfolded and edged towards the tree. I don't quite know what got into me, but I ran for it and made up through the branches as if I did this sort of thing every day. There was no thinking about how to get up a tree, no thinking about why, and what after. I had never known that I had such speed, nor that I could climb so high. The men roared at the machine and soon the driver saw me, perched up on the top, and he withdrew the blades. So here I am. With no plan.

I have plenty of time to think, although you'd be surprised how much there is to do. I have to organise the food and other things that they send up to me on a pulley that Gerry made in jig time. Eating takes a bit of work; it's not like I'm sitting in a kitchen. It's amazing what you can see from up here, how the people organise their days, how they move about, where they hide their scraps, how people sometimes break into dance in their kitchens. Although in the first few days, it would be hard to know if perhaps they didn't change their routine, open their curtains earlier than normal. But that could have been to look at me. I'm also sure that George Wiggins never put out a flag every day before this.

Between myself and the people below, we've decided that if I can manage to stay long enough the point will be made and they'll leave the tree alone. That's the general idea.

The big question now is, what is long enough, when do I come down? I do have a life waiting for me, with friends in it, and I will eventually need to be in a place where I am not known as the person who went up the tree that went over the border.

Epilogue

I did come down. And went back to the desert where we had a party and discussed borders we had crossed. And Famagusta, the sound of the name, and the ghosts whistling through the deserted city. Cancer, the Equator, Capricorn. One of us had stood with women shouting to their relatives across in Jordan. The remark was made that the proximity of the border had a serious effect on Anselm Kiefer. What about Alsace Lorraine, back and forth, back and forth? Korea, we said. Another of us, a tent maker, had more truck than most with borders. He had seen a lot of people looking over lines. He told us that while the rest of us forget, get distracted by newer tragedies, the people forced to move often take excursions to look back. When the sun dropped down and the barbecue was over no one could remember how the conversation had got started. I get occasional cards from home, and apparently the tree has not been touched, and Gerry spends a lot of time in our barn.

Mary O'Donnell

Mary O'Donnell is a short story writer, poet and novelist who has been publishing since 1990. Her most recent novel is *Where They Lie*. Other novels include the best-selling *The Light-Makers, Virgin and the Boy,* and *The Elysium Testament.* Her short story collections are *Strong Pagans* and *Storm over Belfast,* the latter long-listed for the Frank O'Connor International Short Story Award in 2008. She has also published seven collections of poetry, most recently *Those April Fevers.* She has won several prestigious prizes, including the Fish International Short Story Award, and the Listowel Writers' Week Short Fiction Award. Her short fiction has been published in *Fiddlehead Review, Scéalta, The London Magazine, Stand, Irish Short Stories, Splitting the Night in Two, Phoenix Irish Short Stories,* and also *The Mail on Sunday* and *The Irish Times.* Awards include the James Joyce Ireland-Australia Award, as well as a residency at the Irish College in Paris. She teaches Poetry on Galway University's MA course and is a member of Aosdána. www.maryodonnell.com

The Path to Heaven

It had been a beautiful autumn. She was glad not to live in Poland, where her housekeeper Kalina reported that snow had fallen. There were other reasons not to want to be in Poland, of course. She sometimes strolled and kicked her way around the garden and through the fallen leaves, encircled by a wall of tree-fire. Trees she and her husband had planted years ago that were now mature. Their ground was hidden in a hollow far below the distant motorway from which morning commuter traffic droned. A gravel path led to the bottom end, and to a break in the ancient wall that enclosed a forest.

Kalina came on Tuesdays. Sometimes her face was bright and happy. She looked like a girl and not a mother of young daughters. She would chatter about the weather. *Very nice day!* or *In Poland now minus ten degrees ...*

With her movement and smile, she carried a fragrant energy into the house. But sometimes, with hair pulled sharply into a thin, high ponytail, she could look severe and sharp. There were grey circles beneath her eyes, and a worried pucker nicked the smooth skin between her eyebrows. Dressed in a worn, pilled fleece and tight jeans, she looked careworn. Lauren sometimes wanted to console her instead of having her clean the house. But it was part of the unspoken contract: the Irish woman employed, the Polish woman worked.

Sometimes she would listen from her study to the sound of the vacuum-cleaner on the stairway. They often talked together, usually while Kalina vacuumed.

She felt a certain guilt at having another woman do work she herself was not willing to do. She also felt guilt as a writer, because people, including Kalina, thought writers were wealthy, and sat at home and gazed at their navels during the day before heading out to quaff wine at some merry evening book launch.

Each week, before Kalina's arrival, Lauren had already sorted the laundry herself, folded and smoothed it. She removed all underwear except her husband's vests. The only items Kalina had to iron were his vests and shirts, then the sheets and pillow-cases. He changed his shirt every day, and was a size fifty-two, so these were large garments.

Kalina never took a break for tea, never accepted a biscuit. She would laugh and say she had to watch calories after having two babies. *Children such work! And I still breast-feeding.* At this, she would make a sucking gesture with her mouth, and smile shyly.

Even so, suspicion found its way into Lauren's thoughts. She could even isolate quite precisely its portal of entry. Three times during her first encounter with Kalina's partner, he informed her that in Poland he was once a Physics lecturer, but that now, he had no work. He loomed in their doorway with a parchment face and thick hair threaded with grey. He was serious and unsmiling, but, feeling at a loss, she offered sympathy and the hope that his chances would improve. From what Kalina told her in the ensuing months, he seemed selective about the work he would do. He would certainly not clean houses and offices as Kalina did. Instead, he stayed home every day seeking work on the online job sites that offered opportunity after opportunity, yet none for him. He also minded their two infant girls. He disliked this. It was not a man's work.

Once, she asked Kalina if he prepared some lunch for her when she arrived home. But he was too busy reading and researching, then minding the children as well. Kalina laughed incredulously at Lauren. Her partner often reminded her that she was a cleaner, but that he was a man of science.

Lauren was as old as Kalina's mother in Sobibór, Poland, but according to Kalina, she was more glamorous and much younger-looking than her mother. Sobibór lay close to where the borders of Belarus and Ukraine nudged against Poland. It was also the name of one of the more secret extermination camps during Nazi occupation. Lauren had never heard of it. The familiar list of Auschwitz-Birkenau, Treblinka, Belsen, Dachau, Mauthausen and Buchenwald sprang immediately to mind, but Sobibór?

Kalina's family remembered the time of the camp, but nobody talked about it anymore. Her grandmother would like to, Kalina confessed, but her parents were modern Polish people. They avoided such talk.

From week to week the women discussed different topics: men, education and children, cultural differences between Ireland and Poland, the fashion for tattoos and body art, and whether or not Kalina should have herself sterilised. Lauren already understood that this last subject was out of the question for Kalina's partner, and it intrigued her that some couples still played Russian Roulette in the bedroom.

He is a good man, Kalina would insist, as if to defend him. *Sometimes, I think he depressed.*

One night, Lauren had a monochrome dream, devoid of people. It unfolded like a grainy movie, with cloud shadows, muffled sound, unclear forms and tilting, unstable buildings.

Everything was indistinct, but she was in the scene, walking through fog along a narrow, rubbled street, watching in fear as the tops of the buildings curved and tilted, waiting to be crushed beneath the falling bricks. She felt terrified, and woke with a jolt. Her dream was recomposing what she already knew about terrible histories, projecting it into the space left open by Kalina's comments about Sobibór a few weeks before. She tossed and turned, imagining the place that Kalina's parents didn't want to discuss. Her husband ground his teeth in his sleep beside her, then turned, pulling the bedclothes with him. She lay still, but her eyes remained wide open in the dark as she recalled the horrific elements of the dream.

The following morning, she opened up her laptop. Her grey eyes darted rapidly down the screen. Sobibór: built in 1942, dismantled after a prisoner revolt in late 1943. Almost a quarter of a million people died there. Jews themselves prepared other Jews for the gas chambers, collected shoes, advised them to tie the laces together so that the pairs would not get lost; Jews also removed the bodies afterwards. These helper Jews accompanied the people about to be gassed as they walked along a path in the forest, later referred to as 'The Path to Heaven'. Even though the path was bordered by barbed wire, the tube-like, and bucolic final walk gave hope to the unwitting people – they believed that they were going to have a shower after their arduous train journey.

Lauren paused to look out the window, allowing her gaze to fall on an almost leafless birch. Birds were still singing, though it was late in the year. She imagined the birdsong of Sobibór, the verdant, fertile summer of that year, the faint glisten of hope in people's minds as they trekked along, thinking this camp was not going to be so bad after all. They had been welcomed on the station platform. And now, they could shower. The soldiers had seemed quite civilised, considering the things one heard. Everything would be all right.

She tried not to dwell on the next part. It was the same in all the camps of death, and just over seven decades ago, Kalina's very young grandparents would have sensed all what was happening. They would have inhaled the infamous, sickening smell; it would have been part of their everyday breathing. They would have known. Everybody must have known that the second railway track, which forked away from the main station track and into the camp, was not a picnic site after a sight-seeing trip.

Autumn deepened into early winter. It was the end of November. The first Sunday in Advent had passed and Lauren resumed an annual ritual of lighting a candle on the breakfast table. She wasn't religious, but anticipation gripped her as days darkened, as twilights became cobalt with cloud and bare branches and stems conversed with frail light. Kalina was due at ten.

Over breakfast, Lauren and her husband discussed Christmas arrangements. Their son and daughter would fly home from London. There would be bedrooms to have made up, a tree to bring in and gifts to buy. She felt the sheer privilege of all their lives. Her books were selling, and her husband was starting to think about retiring from his legal firm. There were still good years ahead.

That morning, her husband sat beside her in his slightly too-tight shirt (there would be a diet after Christmas, she knew), and the prospect of seeing their children for a week of news and mischievous modern cynicism filled them both with happiness. She poured herself another coffee as he cleared up the breakfast dishes and put them in the dishwasher.

By mid-morning, although Kalina was already in the house, she hadn't popped her head around the study door as she usually did. Lauren sighed critically at what she'd just written. It was going to be a day in which she'd have to force herself to stay put, to somehow drive sentence to follow sentence, when she'd rather catch a bus to the city to chat with friends in some bookshop cafe, an espresso and a glass of water to hand. She sloped down the long hallway – tracksuit bottoms and loose sweater – past yellow walls on which vivid blue plates hung above a bookcase, and pushed the door open.

Kalina didn't look up. She was mopping the floor and stared downwards, as if absorbed by the tiles. No, she didn't want a cup of tea, thank you very much. No, she was not hungry either.

She leaned on the mop and turned to Lauren. *Very tired today. Children awake all night.* She shook her head hopelessly and continued to mop the floor.

Lauren moved towards her, reaching to put a hand on her shoulder. As she did so, Kalina released the mop handle, which fell to the ground with an ear-splittingly sharp crack. Tears sprang to her eyes, and she hastily withdrew a tissue from her jeans pocket. *You must not tell anybody! I – embarrassed – you must not tell anyone!*

There had been an argument about money and about who did the most work.

He get angry with me all the time … then he say that I friends with other mens – and last night… Here she paused and shook her head. Her voice dropped again. *Something bad … he do something very bad to me. Children do not see, but he hit me. And then … hit me again in our bedroom …*

Lauren sounded calm as she asked where he had struck her.

On my back. Only on back. Three times. I have mark today. Red mark. I tell him I never looks at other mens. Never! I would not do that. But he say he don't believe me. And after, he not say sorry either.

Lauren, while wanting to jump into the car and rip his head off, could still hear his voice intoning the words *I am Physics Lecturer.* Brutus addressing the crowds from the steps of the Roman Senate building. It was laughable that occasionally she had pitied him because she knew how eggshell-brittle egos could be, including her own.

She tried to form a plan. What could Kalina do, with two children, no money, limited English? Something must now happen because something had happened then, the night before.

Lauren's sense of consequence rose to a spike of insight. Feeling suddenly inspired, she gripped the girl by both shoulders and looked her in the eye.

'Would you like to go home to Poland for a few weeks? Stay with your mother? You could bring the children.'

She'd pay for the flights and make something happen. It was hard to know what Kalina thought of the idea. She hesitated, then spoke.

Thank you, Lauren. I think about it. Nobody else help me – you are good friend when I have trouble, she whispered.

She drove Kalina home. The girl waved goodbye before disappearing through the front door of the semi-detached rental. Lauren glimpsed Kalina's husband through the big front window, bent over a computer. He kept his head down as if he hadn't heard Kalina coming into the house.

A week passed.

I think – I want go home. I take children and return to Poland.

The atmosphere in Kalina's house hovered on a scale of frost to permafrost, and the only voices that spoke were those of the children.

'If you're sure, give me dates and I'll book the flights.'

Later that day, she told her husband that Kalina needed their help.

'Are you fucking crazy?'

His glasses slid down his nose. He had just come in from work and was opening envelopes, glancing at the contents and dropping them quickly on the kitchen table. His expression was quizzical, and his unclipped auburn eyebrows danced as he reacted to Lauren's news.

'What's wrong with the idea?' she pressed. 'I want to help her.'

'Everything. You're going to make things far harder for her. Mark my words, they'll kiss and make up and then they'll both see you as a relationship destroyer. I have only one word, Lauren. *Don't.*'

Now he was bending down over the kitchen bins, lifting and tying the plastic sacks.

'I've told her I'll help her.'

'Well un-tell her. Tell her I won't allow it. She'll understand the caveman approach. She probably hasn't grasped that Irish women aren't under the thumb of the lord and master anymore, so tell her I've said no.'

He disappeared out the back door, rubbish sacks in hand. A knifing wind blew in as he left.

'It's assault and battery,' she said as he came in the door again, wiping his hands on his jeans.

'There's the police and free legal aid if she wants to take it further.'

'Fuck it, but that's the kind of attitude that allowed six million Jews to be gassed during the last war.'

He stood stock-still and regarded her. 'What in God's name has that got to do with anything? We're talking about a man who gave his wife a clip on the back,' he paused and turned to the wine-rack, 'and you're talking Holocaust? Are you fucking joking?'

She fell silent. A clip on the back? How annoying he could be, how thick. How could he not understand her reference to the Holocaust?

He eyeballed her. She stared back. Was that a shiver of amusement she detected in his eyes?

'I can help her.'

The words slithered out as her throat began to constrict with tears of frustration. She left the kitchen. A moment longer, and she might have walloped him, in itself a turn of events she was not entirely at ease with. She stood glaring at books on the hall shelf, without actually seeing any titles. From within the kitchen came the sound of a bottle of wine being uncorked, the thin clink of a glass. She slammed the door to her study.

Kalina had mentioned a date on which to travel: Thursday of the following week, when she knew that her partner would be in the day clinic. He was having his annual colonoscopy, she said. Immediately, Lauren began to scan online for flights to Warsaw, and hence to Sobibór. One way or return, she wondered. She could hardly take a decision like that without first consulting Kalina, so she decided to wait until the following Tuesday, two days before the flight.

She would book Kalina and her daughters onto a morning flight the following week. She could choose to do this, and there was no better motive than to remove a younger woman from danger, whose children were also at risk.

That night, she removed herself from the bedroom and slept in her daughter's room. Her husband could be glib and trivial about the situation, it was all in a day's work to him, an argument on paper, but he had to realise that there was something at stake, a principle of assistance to others which she was about to uphold.

When Kalina arrived on Tuesday, she pulled the kitchen door behind her, shrugged off her jacket. Lauren, smiling, wanted to talk about the flights. To her surprise, Kalina hesitated. Lauren peered closely at her. The girl looked, if anything, radiant.

Everything much better, Lauren. I talk to him. He talk to me.

Her eyes were bright, and Lauren could see that a new joy flowed through Kalina, as if a healing river had overflowed its banks and saturated her soul. She said nothing for a moment. Her thoughts, which had been smooth and definite, were now choppy with judgement.

'So, you're going to stay?'

She knew the answer even as she asked the question.

Yes, she was going to stay. *We have big talk*, she said in a voice that was almost joyful, *and I think that Adam depressed. He very depressed,* she went on. *I tell him I not his enemy, that I his friend. True friend.*

'And did that help?' Lauren asked.

He make promise he never hit me again. He say sorry.

Despite this latest promising turn of events, she felt disappointed by Kalina. It was just as well she hadn't booked the flights. So what had she expected? A decisive air-strike against the enemy? She hoped Kalina understood the significance of what she had been about to do for her. She felt slightly acidic about it all, about the 'big talk'. Did a man who beats his partner once ever really gain the self-control not to have the urge to do it again?

'I'm glad you've made it up. And I'd miss you if you went away,' she said, which was the truth. Then, an afterthought. 'He will see a doctor? It sounds as if he might need an antidepressant.'

At this, Kalina shook her head firmly. *No antidepressant. Bad for health. He a strong man. He feeling better already, now that we happy again.*

So they'd sorted it out. And her partner's body was such a temple that it could not be polluted by a chemical that might make him feel a little better. Oh, something had happened all right, but not in the way she'd imagined.

'So you're okay now?' she asked.

Oh yes, yes, we definitely okay, thank you, Lauren. I love him. He a good man, and I know that.

Later, Lauren told her husband what had happened.

'Didn't I tell you?' he said mildly. 'These things have a way of sorting themselves out.'

'I still think we should get involved when something is wrong,' she said. 'But yes. You were so right.'

She considered how much better the alternative outcome she had open-handedly offered Kalina, if only she had travelled. But now, there would be no dramatic rescue and dash to Dublin Airport and on to Poland for Kalina and her children. Her partner wouldn't be left to regret his unkindness and violence. There would be no grand-style justice and retribution. This time, he got to kiss and make up.

That night, she removed herself once again from the bedroom, and slipped into her daughter's bed. In some way, her husband had offended her, but she could not quite explain how, even if he had asked. She kept thinking about all those who knew things but said nothing, the ones who silently accompanied others, believing they had no choice. The Jews had walked with fellow Jews along Sobibór's 'Path to Heaven', to the end of a forest road that was dewy and green, bursting with bird-song. She thought of Kalina, and what might lie ahead. How she seemed to have brushed aside her partner's bruising blows, and how readily she embraced a future with him, staking her entire life on the path he was offering. And Lauren's grievance grew in the dark like an unpleasant forest fungus, not at herself, but towards Kalina, who failed to recognise that although help sometimes comes, it comes but once.

Then she slept deeply, like a traveller who had found rest without having reached the long-sought destination, but for whom everything was clearer. Her dreams still puffed and swelled as she slept, as the great starry skies orbited above the roof of the house, above the still, night garden with its secret nocturnal foxes and badgers. In her childlike resting position, legs tucked up, fingers curled, her mouth made a small map of saliva on the pillow.

Annemarie Neary

Annemarie Neary was born in Newry, Co. Down, and educated at Trinity College Dublin, King's Inns, and the Courtauld Institute, London. Her awards for short fiction include the Bryan MacMahon and Michael McLaverty short story competitions, the Columbia Journal Fiction Prize, a WOW! award, and the Posara Prize for stories about Italy. She has also been a prizewinner in the Bridport, Fish, UPP Short Fiction, Séan Ó Faoláin and KWS Hilary Mantel short story competitions. Her stories have been published in various places in Ireland, the UK and the US, and broadcast on RTÉ radio. Her novels are *Siren* and *A Parachute in the Lime Tree*. Her third novel, *The Orphans*, is forthcoming from Hutchinson in 2017. Annemarie lives in London with her husband and sons. www.annemarieneary.com

The Negotiators

They had landed in good time for the meeting. Moving through scuffed white doors into the clamour of the Arrivals Hall, the first thing Helen saw was a headless Uncle Sam. Back in London, it was still possible to escape the coming war, but not here. The wall beyond the exit was plastered with posters and flyers, some hand-daubed, others printed. Bush had taken a corona of daggers to the heart. There were bloodied eagles, a flaming White House, while Blair was just a poodle on a leash.

'Welcome to Algiers,' said Bill.

Beyond the barrier, their driver was holding up a hand-written sign: *Daunt Petroleum*. He shunted Helen's case into the boot and ushered her towards the passenger seat. The two men sat together in the back like schoolchildren. Bill the lawyer, Justin the geologist. As the car moved off, passing beneath the rows of date palms that lined the airport road, she realised with a dart of clarity that she was responsible for them. She had been the one to insist they come here.

The glass doors at the offices of the state oil company were clouded with fingerprints. Last time, Dr Lellouche had been there to greet her. He had ushered her into the top floor conference suite with its view of the bay and served her gritty coffee from an ornate copper pot. Today, they were assigned a windowless room with a ceiling fan and a wall clock that made an arthritic click with each jump of the minute hand. Justin was on his feet, pacing back and forth, while Bill listed points in his A4 Black n' Red. Neither had wanted to travel to Algiers, not now, but she had convinced them that a drilling permit here would be a game-changer, that this was the time to steal a march. And they were on board now, she saw; the desire to win bred into them.

It was twenty minutes before a tiny brisk woman swept in and took her seat at the head of the table. There was a prim superiority about Maryam, her midnight blue headscarf and Ferragamo shoes, her pale pinched face. While her two male colleagues shook hands methodically with everyone in the room, she alone remained seated, settling a beige cushion at the base of her spine, arranging her papers into a neat pile. She glanced at Helen, then took off her small steel wristwatch and laid it out on the table in front of her.

'What happened to Dr Lellouche?' said Justin.

The click of the minute hand appeared to remind Maryam that it was up to her to answer. 'It was his time,' she said.

From the start, Maryam seemed to decide that Helen was someone who could safely be ignored. She addressed all her remarks to Bill. Helen resolved to let things run, for a while at least, but by the time they reached the more contentious clauses, the ceiling fan had stopped working and the pace began to slow. The rotors kept moving for a while in loose, lazy circles before the negotiations themselves became deprived of air. Meanwhile, Maryam made straight for the rapids. Clause 10. Social Fund.

'You can call it whatever you like,' Bill was saying, 'but we both know it's just a slush fund.'

'We'd be taking on a hefty work programme,' Justin added. 'And don't forget we know that reservoir inside out.'

'Your technical competence is not the only factor here,' Maryam said, tapping the document in front of her with a slim propelling pencil.

Things had a habit of kicking off when Bill got going. 'Let's park that one for now,' Helen said.

A trickle of sweat was making its slow descent down her back when a rattling trolley announced a break for sweet, lukewarm tea.

In the Ladies', she was standing by the open window, letting the warm air play across her face, when Maryam emerged from the end cubicle. She rinsed her hands and, reaching for a small jar on the shelf beneath the mirror, began smoothing rose-scented cream into her pale fingers. The silence built up around them.

'Maybe we should just agree the deal between us,' Helen smiled at the mirror.

Maryam gazed out the window towards the hill where the hotel was situated. 'Have you travelled much?' she said.

Helen spoke back to the mirror and said she had actually, though mainly for work. She liked to go to France on holiday. 'Do you know France?' she said.

Maryam was flexing her small, pale hands, examining each nail in turn. 'I was born there,' she said. 'In Lyon.'

'Oh, I've been to Lyon,' Helen said, relieved to find a chink of commonality. 'It was during the festival. The lights, you know? I was with a friend.' She hadn't got used to referring to Steve in the abstract, and was surprised how despondent it made her feel. She heard her own voice tail off.

Maryam waved a hand. 'There is always the obvious version,' she said. 'Top ten things to do, et cetera.' When she spoke next, it was almost to herself. 'If you travel, you should discover something real. If you remain always on the hill, you will learn nothing.'

Helen tried to break in, but Maryam raised a hand. 'You want something from us. And so, you need to open your eyes and your ears.'

This woman was lecturing her; she couldn't believe it.

'This afternoon, for example, there will be a demonstration.'

'Yes,' she said. 'I know about—.'

'Many people will be on the streets to show solidarity with Saddam. We call him Fahl. It means male beast. Stallion, lion. You find that amusing? I think you do. But if you wish to understand us, you must travel down from your hill.' She replaced the hand cream on the shelf with a clink.

Back at the hotel, in a rush of gin and tonics, Helen and the others sat on the terrace and looked out beyond the orange groves at the stacked white city, the wide scoop of bay. From a distance, Algiers looked serene, unspecific; it was all white cities by all blue seas.

'By the way,' Justin said. 'Slush fund, Bill? That was a bit harsh.'

Bill raised his hand for the waiter. 'You think they'll build a single school? We're talking Mercs and Perks here.'

The terrace was moving into shadow, and the sprinklers had begun spitting out across the scorched grass and the clumps of spiky, nameless flowers. Helen had had enough of Bill and his willingness to crater the deal for the sake of a one-liner. She tugged at the strap of her bag, caught around the leg of his chair. By the time she got to her feet, she had made up her mind to be better than expected.

'Let's reconvene at six,' she said. 'You can check the structure of that fund we agreed in Namibia, Bill.'

As she left, she imagined what they would say about her. That she was hungry for promotion, desperate to succeed, that the job was everything to her now. And it was true that being on her own had fostered a determination that wasn't there before.

Inside, the hotel smelt of burnt paprika and a kind of manufactured sweetness. She felt a headache coming on. Last time, she had met the commercial attaché at the embassy for a lunch of lamb and flatbread under the steady gaze of the Queen. His advice had been twofold: expect no largesse from the state oil company, and never leave the hotel unaccompanied. So much for that.

The lift door pinged open on the third floor, where pierced metal sconces cast shadows onto the dark red walls. Beyond the identical doorways, the fringed damask curtain was grand enough for a sultan. Although she already knew the curtain was a tease, it was still a disappointment to find nothing much behind it, just a cleaning cupboard crammed with metal buckets and a pastel-coloured regiment of plastic bottles.

Helen sat on the indecently large bed and switched on the TV. The news shuttled from the Pentagon to the Al-Rashid hotel and back again. Nothing had begun. Not yet. She downed a glass of water, then another and another. Peeling off her tights, the long-sleeved shirt, she stepped into the shower.

From her case, she selected the kaftan she'd bought on the advice of the Human Resources manual, in case of official receptions. It looked like something her mother might have worn to Civil Rights marches in the sixties, and didn't quite reach her shocking white ankles. Combining two long scarves, she contrived something that would cover her head and neck, then took a look at herself in the full-length mirror. The result was a million miles from Maryam, but somehow it calmed her, as though the effort she had made conferred the right to be an interloper. She remembered some water and her passport. This time, she had taken the one with the harp on the cover. On the flight out, she had joked about that to the others – not implicated in airstrikes, do not kidnap. But she had sounded glib, and the joke had fallen flat. Before each trip, she had developed the habit of laying out both her passports – the back-to-front harp and the party-hatted lion and unicorn. Whichever one she chose, she was left feeling incomplete.

She made for the fire escape, crossing from carpet onto a blank concrete stairwell where clots of flies had invaded the cracked corners of the landings. She exited by a row of industrial-looking bins and was momentarily disorientated to have found herself at the back of the building. Two men in chef's whites and checked trousers, smoking on a broken bench, glanced up and away as she walked along the gravelled drive towards the gate. She looked back at the hotel with its blossom trees, its carefully whitewashed walls, and relished the escape.

She was almost at the gate when she realised that a member of staff had followed her out from reception. She noticed him appraising the kaftan, and wondered just how wrong she could have got it. She made a gesture towards the city. 'Explore,' she said, as if imperfect English came with the outfit.

'Most guests take a driver,' he said.

'It's OK,' she said. 'I can walk.'

On the other side of the gate, the road swept around the hill in ever-widening curves. The footpath soon deteriorated, and her shoes became coated in a reddish dust. She was forced onto a narrow kerb, teetering precariously beside the blaring traffic. The closer she got to the city, the more specific it became, until it materialised around her in a mass of greyish cubes and oblongs punctuated by the occasional concrete minaret. When finally the road reeled out at sea level, Helen found herself in a large deserted square.

There were traces of a crowd in the tide of plastic bottles round the fountain, in the cigarette butts scattered amongst the detritus of a flowering tree. Although the people had moved on, the air still shimmered. At one end of the square, stacked trestles and cardboard boxes, and crescents of half-eaten watermelon were all that remained of a market. A woman crossed in front of her, the small triangular veil on her face like a white lace handkerchief. She was pulling along two small children, each carrying a green balloon. For a moment, she looked as if she might be about to say something. But then she hurried on.

At the far end of the square, young men sat silently under houses fretted with ancient scaffolding. She could hear faraway chanting, like the echo of her own blood in her ears. And then she realised the demonstrators were penned in behind the military vehicles barricading the end of every street. The bark of a loudhailer, a helicopter's rattle; those sounds conjured up a small space she kept cordoned off, a place that had been home once, where marches were volatile things and it was all too easy to find yourself in the wrong place at the wrong time. She had worked hard at developing the persona she displayed to colleagues and adversaries alike, until it had become her default mode. Speed, industry, these things worked. And so, she hurried on. She noticed a group of men watching her from outside a metal-shuttered café whose torn umbrella read Orangina. Her instinct was to move away, but she forced herself to acknowledge them. She nodded, but no one nodded back. And who could blame them? She was in fancy dress after all, and had come to take their oil. It felt shameful to crave the reassuring artifice of the hotel, but she knew she shouldn't be here.

As she moved back the way she'd come, she realised the crowd had broken through. High on disobedience, they were spreading across the square. She recognised the tight coil of tension in the air, the hard snap of its release. She lowered her head, quickened her pace, but she was too freckled to belong here, too screamingly redheaded beneath the makeshift veil. When she saw the two men approach, she let out a cry that came from long ago. Now, as then, it was swallowed by drums and chants. And then they were onto her, one on either side, taunting and jeering, pulling on the fringes of her improvised hijab. She felt alien, exposed. And so, she ran. She ran until her lungs were raw, until the balls of her feet burned. She ran herself back in time, to a state of fearfulness she scarcely recognised. She ran all the way to the main road. When she slumped against a doorway to catch her breath, she struggled to understand why she had bolted when she had built a career on standing her ground. The water in her bottle was warm now. It made her queasy, but she drank it down anyway in hoarse little gulps as if it might restore the professional Helen, the one who had cared so fervently about a petroleum licence that no one else thought worth the chase.

She was just about to tackle the hill when she heard a car moving slowly behind her. The driver pipped at the horn. As he came alongside, she recognised the hotel livery. She didn't think he was the man she'd spoken to at the gate, but she couldn't be sure. At first she hadn't noticed the figure in the back. Now that she realised who it was, she felt caught in the act, wrong-footed.

Maryam patted the seat, 'Come now,' she said. A flash of something, amusement or disdain, passed across her face as she scanned Helen's limp kaftan, her filthy shoes. Once Helen was inside, Maryam spoke to the driver in Arabic, gesturing in the direction of the hotel. The leather creaked as she settled back into the seat.

'I tried to telephone,' she said. 'But the receptionist said you had already left.' She affected surprise, as if this had been someone else's idea.

Helen pulled the thin cotton of the kaftan tightly around her calves. 'I came down from the hill,' she said, as if that alone merited a prize. She cast a sideways glance at Maryam, who was sitting there impassively, her hands folded in her lap. But if she recognised the words as her own, she gave no indication.

Helen visualised the intricately braided strands of favour and compromise, risk and reward, stretching out between them. She ought not to have put herself in Maryam's debt.

She should have stayed where she was, on the other side of the table.

She watched the city lose its particularity again as they climbed back up through the orange groves. In the car, the distance between the city and the high ground of the hotel seemed nothing at all. As they turned in through the gates, she tried to find a way to acknowledge the rescue, and yet accord it little weight.

'I appreciate the lift,' she said. It was so inadequate a word as to be insulting, but it was as far as she felt able to go right now. 'We'll move things on tomorrow.'

'Tomorrow?' Maryam allowed herself the full measure of contempt. 'Can't you see that everything has changed?'

In the hotel, the bellboys were kept busy. Their gilt and purple luggage carts were permanently full, and every lift was stuck on 5. But there was still the same strange music in the bar. There was still gin. Helen sat on the hotel terrace with the others as they drank, watching small fires bloom and fade across the darkening city.

The waiter explained that there had been rioting. 'But they are only burning what needs to be burned.'

Bill drained his drink. 'Well that's good, isn't it?' he said, raising his empty glass.

Helen felt a keen sense of having fallen short. She wondered where in the sprawling city Maryam lived, whether she had even managed to get home. Her face flared as she considered the rescue, and her own lack of grace.

'Nightcap, Helen?' said Justin. 'One for the road?'

But she felt the need for CNN, for certitude and safely packaged news. Making her way back to her room, she passed through the urgent seethe of night insects, along the blind arcade that shaded off the pool area from the rest of the hotel. On the other side, she could hear a lone swimmer surging on, then flipping back again, moving in the dark.

Martina Devlin

Martina Devlin is an Omagh-born novelist and journalist. She has had nine books published, including *About Sisterland*, set in the near future in a world ruled by women; *The House Where It Happened*, a ghost story inspired by Ireland's only mass witchcraft trial; and *Ship of Dreams*, about the *Titanic* disaster. Prizes include the Royal Society of Literature's V. S. Pritchett Prize and a Hennessy Literary Award, while she has also been shortlisted three times for the Irish Book Awards. A current affairs commentator for the *Irish Independent*, she has been named columnist of the year by the National Newspapers of Ireland. Martina is vice-chairperson of the Irish Writers Centre. www.martinadevlin.com

No Other Place

'White roses for this year's bouquet, with ivy for remembrance. What do you say, Willie?'

Alice bends to sniff a rosebud, while a tabby cat weaves figures-of-eight between her ankles. She is slight – a breath of sudden wind could whirl her high above this overgrown garden.

'I know, Willie, I know. You want your milk. Just let me get these flowers gathered up.'

As she straightens, pain catches at her, and she gasps, pressing the heels of both hands into her lower back. With an effort of will, she heaves her mind back to the flowers.

White roses for hope, she thinks. His hope, and hers too. She must hold tight to hope. This roof over her head might be lost. The flow of words reduced to a trickle from her pen might vanish. Even Willie might disappear – tempted by a household with more titbits. But hope she can carry on her back, like a tortoise with its shell. So long as she stays true to hope, it stays true to her.

She looks away from the garden, with its jungle of foliage, towards the house – a Church of Ireland rectory without a rector. It's a substantial building, impressive enough, in its time. But the shabbiness of neglect undermines its claims.

So many addresses over the years. Always on the move. Yet here she is, back where she started, near enough. She was born a handful of miles away, and grew up in a house that sat fair and square beside a crossroads. How she wishes she was rooted by a crossroads again. A world of possibilities beckoned at them. Out here, the world keeps its distance: holding her at arm's length.

Alice turns back to the rosebush, one hand cupping a bloom. The penetrating blue eyes examine it for imperfections before she takes a pair of kitchen scissors from her cardigan pocket and guillotines the stem. With the whisper of promise, the rose lands on a spill of ivy in the basket at her feet, followed by eight of its sisters.

'Morning, Miss Milligan.' A police constable advances, his moustache as stately as the bicycle he is wheeling.

She hasn't heard him approach, and is irritated by this proof of her deafness. However, she doesn't let it show. 'Good morning, Norman. Isn't it a glorious summer's day?'

'Aye, glorious is the word for it. It's set fair to be a scorcher the-day.' He looks for somewhere to prop the bike, finds nowhere suitable, and lays it flat on the laneway. 'I have somethin' for you, Ma'am.' One pocket after another in the dark green tunic is patted until paper crinkles in the fourth and a letter is withdrawn. 'You forgot this yesterday when you called tae the barracks tae sign for your post. I'm just headed out on me rounds, an' thought I'd save you the trouble. You took the Free State one wi' you. But you left the one from England behind.'

Heavy-hearted, she accepts the brown envelope and sees her name and address typed on the front. It must be another bill. No matter how she economises, or how hard she works to reduce the backlog, she can't keep pace with them. She hasn't bought a new hat since – when? It must be the green felt one when Mr de Valera took office more than seven years ago. Really, it's beyond her pen's power to earn enough to hold these bills at bay. The half-year's rent is always a particular worry.

She had to borrow the most recent instalment from one of her brothers. The shame of it – her independence undermined.

She turns the envelope over. At least it hasn't been opened, like yesterday's letter from Dublin. Whoever has oversight of her post is scrupulous about leaving bills unread. Perhaps he regards it as ungentlemanly to cast an eye over her unpaid accounts, whereas scanning her private correspondence is a question of duty. With an expulsion of air halfway beneath a snort and a giggle, she tucks the offending letter into the waistband of her skirt – bad news can keep.

'You look warm, Norman. Would you like a cup of tea?'

'A drop o' tae wud be just the ticket, Ma'am, but on'y if you're makin' it anyway. I'm parched, so I am.'

'The kettle's on the boil for my breakfast. Usually today's a day I spend quietly, reading and praying. But there's time enough for that. Come in.'

Alice makes her way through grass that hisses underfoot, towards the front door lying ajar. He follows her into a porch with rust-coloured tiles, and on into a wood-panelled hallway from which a staircase ascends.

'Shall we be informal and use the kitchen? Everything's to hand there.'

Her quick step leads the way past a drawing room on the left, and a dining room and then a study on the right. His boots sound a tattoo on the floorboards, their racket embarrassing him.

In the kitchen at the back of the house, she lays the basket of roses on a deal table. The kettle is bubbling on the range kept lit, winter and summer, for cooking. She lifts the kettle and splashes water into a metal teapot, swooshes it twice clockwise with a twist of the wrist, and empties the contents into the sink. 'Why, you're still standing, Norman. Sit down, please.'

He removes his peaked cap and sets it on the chair alongside his seat. That range is too close for comfort. Should he offer to open the back door? But she's as old as his granny, she probably feels the cold. Taking out a clean, ironed handkerchief, he mops his forehead and neck. He fingers one of the silver buttons along the middle of his tunic, each disc stamped with a harp topped by a crown. If only he could undo them. But he ought to leave them fastened up – he is on duty, after all.

Alice, who misses nothing, observes his dilemma. Her invitation to shed the jacket withers on her lips. Let him swelter, him and his buttons! The crown has no business with the harp, to her way of thinking.

Tealeaves added, she returns the teapot now brimming with boiling water to the range. 'I'll just put these roses in water while the tea draws.' She opens a press and stretches on tiptoe for a Belleek china vase. Are the shelves getting higher or is she shrinking?

Too late, Norman realises he ought to have offered to hand it down to her. Not that she'd accept help from him or anyone else in a hurry – a headstrong one and no mistake. He watches her arrange the flowers, puzzled by the close attention she devotes to the job – placing them stem by stem, moving some an inch one way or another. 'You've green fingers, Miss Milligan. Them's fine roses.' On a surge of emotion, he adds, 'Like queens, they are, the way they hould up their wee heads.' Mortified, he halts. It's only a jug of flowers, when all's said and done.

She nods. '*And these I gathered at the dawn/Remembering you/Wet in the gleam of morning…* The garden is gone horribly to seed. I haven't the time to see about it, with the house to keep straight too. But I've always loved flowers. When I was just starting out, and felt a pen name was more appropriate, I chose a flower. Iris. Iris Olkyrn.'

'The brother is married tae a woman be the name of Iris. He used tae be a corporal in the Inniskillings. On'y left last year, when he got married. Thon Iris, she's powerful afeard o' war comin' an' he havin' tae enlist again. Experienced men wud be expected tae offer theirselves. But the brother says to her, says he, "Iris, you shud know better nar tae go lookin' for troubles – they come lookin' for you soon enough".'

'He's right, Norman. I hope Mr Chamberlain is right as well, and war can be avoided. Too much blood has been spilled already this century.' Her eyes fasten on the roses, a shadow settling on her face.

'I doubt war's on the way, so it is. An' it grieves me I won't be let join up. The sergeant says the police is a reserved occupation. So if it's tae be war, I'll spend it in uniform, but not a sodger's. If you don't mind me askin', why did you choose Iris, Ma'am? For tae be a poetess, an' that?'

'She was the Greek goddess of the rainbow. I can never see one without stopping to admire it.'

'I can never see one wi'hout wishin' for a pot o' gold!'

Her smile is polite. Wealth has never interested her, although freedom from this perpetual anxiety about paying bills would be a relief. 'Iris was a messenger of the gods. She rode on a rainbow between heaven and earth. I saw it as a metaphor for my work, trying my poor best to reach out to others. To help them understand what we could achieve, acting together. Like Iris, I used to travel about a fair bit myself, back in the day. I thought nothing of flitting from Belfast to Dublin or Cork. The railways were my chariot – I had the timetable memorised. My father was the same, he knew the times upside down and inside out. Happy days! Now, I hardly ever leave Mountfield. I count myself lucky if I get the length of Omagh.'

'I'm a bike man meself. I love mine. God bless the Royal Ulster Constabulary and His Majesty the King for supplyin' it.'

'Hush, Norman, today's no day for blessing kings. If you only knew—' Repenting her sharp words, she stops abruptly.

Shock has immobilised his face.

Alice covers her mouth with the back of her hand, almost laughing aloud. The young are so prudish.

He clatters to his feet, intending to leave. She's a Fenian to the core – just as the Sergeant said. The silver hair could fool a man if he didn't keep his wits about him. But she's betrayed her true colours.

'Don't go. Forgive me, I know you have your line of business to consider. You're Constable Gibson, as well as Norman, all grown-up now. Do, please, sit. Let's have that tea. Truly, I meant no offence. I spoke out of turn. Today's a sad day for me, you see. An anniversary.'

Half against his will, he resumes his seat, although tempted to replace his cap in a show of authority. However, Norman's granny, who lives with the family, has impressed on him that only yahoos keep their heads covered indoors. She was in service, and remains an authority on etiquette.

From the same press which housed the vase, china is produced, decorated with peacocks in a cacophony of shimmering greens and blues.

The young policeman finds its near-transparent fragility as alarming as his hostess's anti-monarchy sentiments. 'A beaker's good enough for me, Ma'am. I wud'n want tae break one o' them delicate wee boys.'

'They're sturdier than they look, Norman. I'm afraid there's only bread and butter to go with your tea. No jam.'

'Ach, a cup in the hand is all I want, Miss Milligan.'

She pours the strong tea and sets it in front of him, along with a jug of milk and a bowl of sugar. He serves himself only one spoon of sugar, although his preference is for three. Everybody in Mountfield and beyond knows how she's fixed. Poor as a church mouse, for all her highfalutin ways. Meanwhile, she cuts the loaf and lays overlapping slices on a plate, devoting as much attention to their arrangement as to her floral display.

'I've noticed ladies is powerful fond o' flowers,' he offers, between mouthfuls. 'Me ma grows away at them. Though me da says there's no eatin' in a dahlia. A head o' cabbage wud be more tae the good.'

Alice sits opposite, her tea untouched. 'Flowers serve many purposes, Norman. I like to cut them as an act of remembrance, to keep faith with those who've gone ahead. I make what you might call a ceremony of it.'

'Oh aye, you mentioned an anniversary earlier. I'm sorry for your loss. A relative, I take it?'

'The bond was comradeship, not family ties. But a loss, undeniably. This bouquet' – she indicates the roses and ivy – 'marks the death of a fine man. An honourable man. I was privileged to know him.'

Norman relaxes, at ease now. A spinster mourning a lost love – sure they're ten-a-penny since the war twenty-odd years back.

She realises how he is interpreting the flowers but doesn't correct him. People prefer to elevate romantic love above loyalty, fellowship and a common cause. Let the boy make his assumptions.

'Is he long dead?'

She frowns at the freckled hands on her lap. Involuntarily, their fingers reach out and interlace, one hand seeking comfort from the other. But her voice is steady. 'They killed him twenty-three years ago today. It happened in London. I was there. On the pavement outside. Waiting. With other women from our circle who believed in him. When the bell tolled that morning, to say it was done, the crowd bellowed its approval. Not words – just a thunderous roar. Of victory, I suppose. The power of might. I can hear it echoing still.' She shudders. 'I felt as if the human heart was beyond all understanding, that day. To cheer at another person's death – it left me hardly able to put one foot in front of the other to leave that place. I tried telling myself his ordeal was over: he was at peace, finally. But it took me a long, long time to find any peace, myself. Those were wild times. Frightening. They ran out of control.' A clock ticks, and she gives her head a quick shake. 'Yet I never felt more alive than I did back then. They were exciting times too, you see. Dense with dreams. Overflowing with possibilities.' Unexpectedly, she smiles. 'I always gather flowers on the third of August. In honour of him. And the dreams and possibilities we shared.'

Norman scrapes a tealeaf off his lower lip. He supposes the old lady must be talking about one of her rebels. Hanged or shot for disloyalty, and good riddance to bad rubbish. Which one of those traitors she's commemorating, he doesn't know and doesn't want to know. They were a nest of vipers, trying to murder away the link with Britain. Isn't the British Empire the last word in magnificence? Envied by other countries with piddling wee empires? It's a privilege to be born British. Those renegades were rotten to the core – they're better off dead. He's not prepared to listen to any more of this rebel nonsense. His granny always says he should make allowances for her, and his ma backs her up. But he's had enough of Alice Milligan. There's no excuse for it – and her from good Protestant stock, not even a papist who knows no better.

Seizing his cap, he pushes back his chair from the table. 'Thankin' you for the hot drop, Ma'am. I'd best be on me way.'

She pays no attention, engrossed in her own train of thought. '"Sure he's dead now, Alice, for better or for worse." That's what my brother used to say about my shrines, as he called them. "Is he?" I'd answer him back. "I wouldn't be so certain". There's an alchemy that sparks between memory, belief and imagination – in that space, he's alive. He always will be.'

Just then, the cat noses in round the door jamb and assesses the lie of the land. Tail aloft, he parades towards his saucer. His disgruntled mewls at its emptiness penetrate her reverie.

'Poor Willie, you must be starving.' She lifts the milk jug from the table and empties it into the chipped saucer.

Norman hovers by the door, cap under his arm. Despite being vexed, he is naturally courteous and reluctant to leave without a pleasantry. 'The size of him! You could harness thon cat to a cart and get a day's work out of him.'

'Handsome, isn't he? There's great companionship in a puss.'

'I dare say you call him Willie for your brother, the captain, God rest him.'

'No, in fact, it's for Mr Yeats. He visited our house in Belfast, and sat opposite me in the library for hours on end, discussing poetry. We always had cats about the place. Mama was partial to them. The day he came, one of the pups was teasing a couple of the cats, and Mr Yeats decided enough was enough. He lifted the two cats onto his lap – both black, I remember – and petted away at them as we talked rhyme and reason, and everything in-between. He's another one gone, just a matter of months ago. But I can see his long fingers, as clear, as clear, stroking the cats, and that dark wing of hair flopping into his eyes. Mr Yeats, it was, who advised me to write plays. He never thought much of my poetry. Didn't come right out and say it, of course, but I knew. You can always tell with another writer. My work was too effusive, I suppose you might call it, for his taste.' She slants a glance at him. 'Goodbye, Norman. Be sure and give my regards to your grandmother. She worked for us, donkey's years ago. Back when we lived in Omagh, in a house with fir trees in the garden. The games I played in that garden, with my sisters and brothers! And your grandmother, not much older than us, busy in the kitchen. We could hear her singing while she worked – Maud had a voice to shame a thrush. Does she still sing?'

'Ach, not for a brave while now. Her breathing's not the best. I'm sure she'd wish tae be kindly remembered tae you, Miss Milligan. I'll tell her you were askin' for her. Well, I'll bid you good day.' He catches at the door handle, intending to pull it shut behind him.

'Leave it open. There'll be nobody coming or going, apart from the bould Willie here. Still, I would not wish to have barriers of any kind erected this day. Amid the free flow of air, of thoughts, of memories – that's how today should spend itself.'

She doesn't live in the real world, thinks Norman, as he slips away.

As though the ghost of that judgement filters through, she lets fly a peal of laughter, clapping her hands together. 'No world is totally real,' she cries.

Cheerful again, she carries the flowers into a drawing room impregnated with accumulated years' worth of turf smoke. A framed pencil sketch of a bearded man stands on the mantelpiece of a handsome marble fireplace, once white but somewhat yellowed by age, and she places the vase next to him.

'God bless you, "verray, parfit, gentil knight". You waved me into a seat beside you in the Ulster Hall, the day the news broke about your knighthood. I was late for the meeting, delayed by a thunderstorm. You wouldn't go up onto the platform, for fear they'd announce it. I thought you altered looking – strained, weakened. And no wonder. You were just back from the Putomayo. Even so, you insisted on putting yourself out for people. Always first on your feet to offer your chair if a lady needed one. And you'd take no end of trouble checking train times for delegates to our conferences. I could never get permission to visit you in prison. Another Alice had that privilege. But you waved at me in the courtroom, and sent your counsel over with a message. "Write a poem about this, Alice," you said. I suppose you meant it as a joke. But I took you at your word.'

Head bowed, she leans against the mantelpiece. Through the years she wrote, and wrote, and wrote. Verse, stories, drama, journalism. Did any of it make a jot of difference? His words lit a flame. But hers? Did anyone hear her? Or was she just talking to herself? Perhaps it's irrelevant if they listen or not – maybe what matters is the act of writing.

Returning to the kitchen, she pours her cold tea down the sink and refills the cup from the pot. The cat's had the last of the milk. She'll have to take it black. A sip to brace herself, and from her waistband she retrieves the dreaded envelope delivered by Norman Gibson. Two stamps on the top right-hand corner, one for a penny and the other a ha-penny. She looks at George VI's profile. The bicycle-provider, she thinks. Among other roles. A figurehead, of course. Kings reign, they don't rule. Bicycles are supplied only in their name.

He's her fifth monarch, imagine! None of whose rule she accepts. But whether she assents to them or not, each one has been a reality. Victoria, then Edward VII, followed by George V, succeeded by the short reign of Edward VIII, who abdicated for the love of Mrs Simpson. Such a burden for Mrs Simpson. And now this George, his brother, reigns in his place. Which tells her that kings and queens endure.

As she must.

Fancy! She has something in common with those British kings and queens. They persevere, and so does she.

To give up is not in her nature. Here she was born and here she'll stay in this territory they say is theirs. And, after all, they have the crowns on postboxes and policemen's uniforms to support their case. But by living here, she's planting a counter-claim. Planting. She half-smiles at that. A word with more than one meaning in this northern pocket of Ireland.

Her amusement pinches to a pucker at the envelope in her hand. Whose bill is this George-with-his-crown conveying? More to the point, how will she find the wherewithal to pay it? Breadknife to hand, she slits the flap.

The Lost Property Office at Paddington Station regrets to inform her that a handbag she wrote inquiring about, left behind on a train from Bath to London, has not turned up.

Thank goodness it's not a demand for money. As for the handbag, it was on its last legs. Besides, all her life she has mislaid possessions. Memories she can retain, and friendships, even minute details about events. But not objects. When she went to hear Mr Parnell speak in Dublin, back in the last century – she couldn't have been more than twenty-four – she lost her purse. Fortunately, it contained nothing more than a stamp and a pen nib. She used to have a flower from a wreath left on Mr Parnell's grave. For years, she kept it carefully, but she can't lay her hands on it now. That's what comes of all her gipsying about. A life spent on the move.

She only tried to trace the handbag because of some poems left inside it. One of them showed promise, although it could use some reworking. She ought to have polished more – she lacked the patience for it, preferring to tumble words out of herself in the exhilaration of inspiration. Letting them fall where they may.

'There's no call to go hoking in handbags for your poems, Alice,' she tells herself. 'You have them inside you.' She opens a drawer in the table, finds a pencil, and turns the communication from Lost Property face-down on the table.

Willie, who has been stalking imaginary prey between the table legs, springs onto her lap. Round and round he circles, flexing his claws, and she waits until he settles – listening for the noise, midway between purring and humming, to rise up. Only then does she place the pencil point on the back of the letter. The hand holding it is knobbed with rheumatism. Yet still it works for her. A prickle along the back of her neck. A rushing in her ears. Letters form into words and words shape into phrases.

Alice writes.

For Alice Milligan (1865–1953)
She loved no other place but Ireland

Rosemary Jenkinson

Rosemary Jenkinson was born in Belfast in 1967. She studied Medieval Literature at Durham University and since then has had a variety of jobs, including teaching English in Greece, France, Poland and the Czech Republic. A first collection of short stories, *Contemporary Problems Nos. 53 & 54*, was published by Lagan Press in 2004, and a second, *Aphrodite's Kiss*, by Whittrick Press in 2016. Other stories have appeared in the *Sunday Tribune*, *The Stinging Fly*, the *Fish* anthology and *Verbal Magazine*. She is also a playwright and among her plays are *The Bonefire*, *The Winners*, *Johnny Meister and the Stitch*, *The Lemon Tree*, *Meeting Miss Ireland*, *Basra Boy*, *Come to Where I'm From*, *Planet Belfast*, *Bruised*, *Wonderwall*, *Ghosts of Drumglass*, *1 in 5*, *Stitched Up*, *Love or Money*, *White Star of the North* and *Here Comes the Night*. Her writing for radio includes *Castlereagh to Kandahar* (BBC Radio 3) and *The Blackthorn Tree* (BBC Radio 4). She was writer-on-attachment at the National Theatre Studio in London 2010. *The Bonefire* was winner of the Stewart Parker BBC Radio Award 2006.

The Mural Painter

It was on 2 November that Davey Black first saw the woman appear on the other side of Carlingford Street, look up at the mural and make the sign of the cross. She was about thirty, pale, and had hair that curled down in spirals. The moment Davey saw her, he felt the scaffolding sway. Before he could steady himself, she was gone.

He clattered down the ladder onto the street and walked over to Johnny Weir who was standing outside the Cosy Bar, having a fag.

'Did you see that woman?'

'What woman?'

'The woman who crossed herself?'

'Some doll crossed herself round here? Sure she wouldn't dare,' said

Johnny, his small eyes slanting at the thought.

'But I saw her. Just there.'

'Huh, have ye been sniffing them paint fumes, Blackie, or wha'?'

Johnny Weir laughed loudly, but he sucked at his cigarette viciously, the implication being if any woman did dare to cross herself in this street, she'd be up in smoke quicker than Joan of Arc.

A taxi wheeled round the corner and the driver shouted out good-humouredly, 'Blackie, every time I see you, you're on the skive. No wonder you're never finished yet!'

The taxi sped off with a cheeky rip of the horn. Davey went back to his perch and picked up the spray can. He shook it, enjoying its maraca rattle, and went back to the green fades round the poppy wreath, all thoughts of the woman gone. An hour later when he next turned round, he saw the cloud lying over the mountains like lagging. He estimated it was another half an hour at most before the rain would come. With the mountains there, you never needed a barometer. He put the covers back on the paint tins.

'Are you offski?' someone shouted from the door of the Cosy.

'Aye, sure Michelangelo never had to deal with these temperatures,' he grinned.

It was no wonder he was behind schedule. Johnny Weir had commissioned him for this mural of the Somme and it had to be ready for Armistice Day. He'd be hard-pushed to finish it in time, but he'd make it. The outline was there, all it needed was the stencils and the colours.

'So, how'd it go today, Davey?' asked Elaine Black.

She set two big plates of pork chops and champ down on the table.

Davey dried his hands and sat down with her.

'Chilly, but I got a good run on it,' he answered.

It was on his tongue to say about the woman, but he decided against it. His mother only liked to hear tales of the boys. She'd brought up three sons and her natural bias against girls had been strengthened by her husband having left her for another woman.

'The paper was full of complaints today,' said Elaine, vigorously cutting her chop. 'Sure, what do they want, murals of hearts and flowers? What does that mean to the people? We want to commemorate our dead, don't we?'

'Course we do, only…' Davey was hesitant. 'Johnny Weir told me today I would have to put up the names of their volunteers.'

'But I thought it was just for the Somme.'

'I know, but they want a wee roll call of their dead too.'

'Well, I suppose they're paying for it,' said Elaine, closing down the conversation. She wasn't a UVF supporter but accepted that they were calling the shots.

After dinner, Davey went up to his room. He lay down on the bed, clenching and unclenching his fingers, hoping a bit of exercise would keep the arthritis at bay. He was thirty-eight now, and there was a little white in the blond flecks of his stubble. Working outdoors was hard but, sure, didn't he still look young next to the drinkers? Johnny Weir was tucked up in the Cosy most of the day, but had skin that looked like it had been scoured by a Brillo pad.

His mind went back again to the strange woman that afternoon with her curled hair and lean, pale features. She'd looked foreign, perhaps Eastern European, though he didn't know why. She'd just seemed 'other' to him. He played the vision over and over in his head, searching for meaning in why she'd crossed herself in front of his mural. Maybe she had done it out of respect for the war dead in her own country. Or out of fear of the paramilitaries.

He recalled how she'd met his eyes, and he thought that perhaps she'd liked him. He looked down the bed to his thickening middle. At times he thought his mother had tried to spoil him for other women. Giving food was to her almost a lover's act, a substitute for kisses, as though she was swelling him up with her love. He made his mind up that if he ever saw the woman again, he would go to her.

Two weeks later, Armistice Day dawned dark and dismal. The wind was fluting through the chimney pots in a mournful parody of a marching song.

In the morning, Davey and his mother made their way towards the mural, he in his black funeral suit, which was the only suit he had, and his mother in a bright dress muffled by her dark coat.

A large crowd had gathered in front of the mural. A few hardy souls were standing to the left of it, forming a windbreak from the gusting north-easterly.

'Here's the man himself,' a couple of the boys from the Cosy said and shook Davey's hand hard while Elaine beamed with a graduation-day smile.

At eleven on the dot, Johnny Weir walked up. He was sober but, as Davey noted, he must have had a big Friday night on the lash as his face was as bright as the poppies behind him.

'Right, folks,' Johnny Weir shouted. 'We're not going to have you hang around on a day like this, so let me introduce Mr Hughie McKee, who's going to dedicate this glorious new mural to the proud men of 1916.'

The crowd applauded. Stinging rain began to whip in and Hughie McKee glanced up at the sky and said, 'It looks like the rain is baptising our wee mural itself,' and everyone laughed.

It was at that precise moment that Davey happened to look round and see her. She was standing at the back of the mural, crossing herself, unseen. He moved past Elaine, weaving and pushing through the crowd. The woman was already walking away.

'Hey,' he called at her softly, but she didn't seem to hear.

He quickened up and tried to catch her elbow round the side of the Cosy, but his hands were so frozen he wasn't even sure if he'd touched her.

A few moments later, she stopped and turned. He looked into her face, observing her glinting eyes and the dinges of hunger in her cheeks.

'I saw you once before,' he said, the words stumbling out of him. 'Where do you come from?'

Her curls were beaded with pearls of rain. He stood awestruck as her skin suddenly became paler, illuminated by a rift in the clouds above. He'd never seen anyone more delicate or beautiful.

She reached out and touched his cheek with her fingers.

'You know you can do better,' she said in broken English. 'You'll be brave when the right time comes.'

She paused, then walked on down the wet road.

He could hear the words read by Hughie McKee fluted on the wind: 'I am not an Ulsterman, but yesterday, the first of July, as I followed their amazing attack, I felt that I would rather be an Ulsterman than anything else in the world...' and the sentiments coupled with the sight of the departing woman moved him to his core.

'Finally, and most importantly,' concluded Johnny Weir, 'we have to thank the artist himself, and a pure, God-given talent he has: Mr David Black!'

Elaine looked around the crowd, panicking, but he was nowhere to be seen.

'Mr David Black!' persisted Johnny Weir. 'Where is he? He was here a minute ago.'

'He must be very modest,' added Hughie McKee waggishly.

'Well, we'll end it here with a big thank you to the community for sharing the day with us,' said Johnny Weir unconvincingly.

There was a mild clapping, but it couldn't mask the overriding feeling that with the artist going AWOL, the whole dedication had petered out.

It was an hour later when Davey drifted home. After the woman had spoken to him, he'd gathered his senses and followed her along the street, but no matter how quickly he'd moved, she'd stayed ahead. At one point, a leaf had fluttered off a tree and delivered itself into his hands like a message, and by the time he'd looked up again she had disappeared. He'd searched the streets feverishly, longing to see her, but she was gone.

As soon as he came through the door, he could see that Elaine had worked herself up into a state.

'Where in hell's name have you been?'

'I saw this woman,' he replied. He felt tired and dreamy.

'A woman? You were off gallivanting with a woman?'

'I wanted to speak to her.'

'Oh, God, the embarrassment you put me through. "Mr David Black", they kept calling. And you off with a woman. Who do you think you are, Picasso?'

It seemed odd to him that his mother was so angry.

'And who is this woman? Would I know her?'

'She's from Eastern Europe.'

'Eastern Europe! Some bloody Polish slut, I'll bet. Have you been drinking, David Black?'

'Oh, Mum.'

He smiled to himself and went up to change. Through his window, he could see a pigeon sitting motionless on a chimney top like a frozen statue on a plinth, staring down at him. He felt so far away from the world; he didn't hear his mother's calls for lunch.

In the following days, Davey was often seen hanging round Carlingford Street even though there was no more work to be done on the mural.

'He told me about this Eastern European woman he's after. Prob'ly knocking off some Roma fucking beggar right now. I'd burn the bitch out if I found her. Great artist, but loop-the-loop when it comes to women, if you ask me,' said Johnny Weir, tapping his head to his pals in the Cosy.

Davey, aware of people's stares, took the decision to stay away for a while. The more he mused about the woman, the more he wondered if he'd imagined her. All he understood was that she'd come to him to help change his life. But surely she had to be a ghost, for hadn't she first appeared to him on 2 November, All Souls' Day in the Catholic calendar? And yet, and *yet*, how was it that she made him yearn and burn in bed at night? Ghosts weren't meant to do that. Even above the hollows in her cheek, there had been a small round of pink, stippled by the stinging rain. An artist knew this, he would *know* when flesh lived and breathed. At night he rocked in his bed with the fleshly vision of her and hoped his mother didn't hear the creaks and turns of his passion.

In the following weeks he began to draw the woman. When he drew her, she was sometimes naked, sometimes wearing clothes. Overall, he decided he preferred her spiritual and clothed. He wasn't sure what he would paint next, but he knew he was on the edge of finding a new way. From now on, he wanted his art to reflect the numinous.

He was drawing her one afternoon about three months after the dedication when the phone rang and Elaine called him down. It was Johnny Weir.

'Blackie boy, the Cosy's just had a meeting, and it's been decided we'd like you to do another mural for us.'

Davey's heart dropped. 'What's the subject?'

'Just a wee commemoration for the boys. I'll fill you in later.'

Davey was torn. He knew it was good money but, still, he'd sworn to the woman's image that he would never work for the paramilitaries again.

'I don't think I can, Johnny,' he said regretfully.

'What's wrong with you? It's nothing you haven't done before.'

Davey saw that Elaine was hovering, nervous-eyed, at the door, so he told Johnny Weir he would have a wee think and call him back later.

'Was that a job off Johnny Weir?' asked Elaine.

'Aye.'

'Well, why in hell didn't you say yes?'

He retreated up the stairs.

'Skulking up in your room. Get out there and earn some money!' she fired at him, following him half-way up. 'The community are talking about you, you know. They think you're mad, pining after some woman!'

An hour later, she knocked on Davey's door. She pleaded with him to take the job. Davey couldn't bear to see her cry and in no time he had agreed to phone Johnny. He watched her dry her tears and gave her a kiss. When his mother had gone downstairs, he said sorry to the drawing of the woman.

He lowered his face to her image and, closing his eyes, he pressed a kiss on her. The kiss had a million times more feeling and reverence than the one he had applied to Elaine's dry, papery cheek. He wondered how the community seemed to know everything about him. Did they absorb it all by osmosis? He lay on the bed next to his drawing listening to the rain that crackled on the roof like static, a sound that made him think he was no longer properly tuned-in to the world.

For the first few weeks, preparations for the new mural went well. Davey met with Johnny Weir, received his brief for a new 'men with guns' commemoration and quickly mocked up his outline. Davey's proposal was to have a backdrop of Cave Hill behind the gunmen, and at first Johnny Weir wasn't sure about it, suspecting that Blackie was trying to dilute the image of the volunteers in some sort of sappy romanticism.

'But it's beautiful,' persisted Davey and then, when that didn't work, he tried a new tack. 'And your men are as strong as the rock. They've risen up from the land to fight for it; they're on the edge like that cliff.'

Suddenly Johnny Weir burst into a smile. 'You know, Blackie, you're right. You're as odd as the divil, but you're a fucking genius, you know that?'

They shook hands and it was agreed that Davey would start the next week. Spring was approaching. There was a stretch in the days and a new mildness.

On the morning of 10 March, Davey opened his paints at the wall opposite his Somme mural. The weather was breezy and full of the energy of early spring. The Union and Ulster flags billowed like sails, and it was as if he was up on a crow's nest looking out over the city. It had rained overnight, and the wet Blue Bangor slates on the roofs were almost neon as they reflected the blue of the sky. He'd replaced his old combat jacket, which looked like it had been paint-balled, with one that looked fresher, wanting to be smart when the woman came back to him, as he knew she would. He realised she wouldn't be happy that he was working on a mural of gunmen again, but he'd speak to her about it and explain that his particular gunmen wouldn't strike fear into the community.

'Good to have you back, Blackie,' called Johnny Weir, steadying himself with the first medicinal pint.

Davey worked hard all day, blocking out the outline. At one point he felt the woman behind him, but when he turned there was no one there, except for a bird sitting grooming itself with its tail up all dapper, as if preparing to go on a date. He took the bird as a sign that he was about to meet her.

The weather stayed fair but on the third day Davey finally made the decision that he needed to see the woman. If she wouldn't come to him freely, he would bring her to him.

A cold wind had kept Johnny Weir and the lads penned in inside the Cosy for most of the morning. When Johnny Weir finally came out, he noticed that not only was Davey nowhere to be seen, but a few people from the street had come out 'for a wee nosey' and were exchanging opinions on the mural. He walked half-way across the road and took a look. 'What the fuck…?' he muttered to himself.

Davey had been busy that morning. Overlooking the gunmen was the image of a woman with a beatific smile, her hands closed votively.

Johnny Weir felt a prickle of rage and his face quickly went the colour of a red peach. He called the lads out, and there was angry talk of who this skinny scallion of a woman was with the smile on her gub and the curly-wurly hair. 'Making the mocks of us,' they fumed. What maddened them was that the woman looked decidedly like some saint who belonged to the Catholic Church, but what maddened them more was when they heard one of the women say, 'I like her. It's about time we had a woman on the walls instead of just fellas all the time.'

'How would the Volunteers have got out the door in the morning if it wasn't for their mummies?' the girl next to her agreed.

When Davey was sighted coming back down the road, Johnny Weir said to the small crowd, 'Go you on home.' They saw the bristles in his hair go taut and his piggish eyes narrow. They scattered silently.

Davey dreamed as he turned into Carlingford Street that the woman would be standing there. Of course he was worried that Johnny Weir might be up in arms about the mural, but if the Cosy truly objected, the woman could easily be removed. But what he wasn't ready for was all the boys standing there, waiting for him. When he saw their faces trigger at the sight of him, his heart jumped.

He turned and rocketed away, his boots scudding, the boys belting behind him. In Ardenlee Street, Minford caught him by the hood and it nearly choked him as he was pulled back into the midst of an engulfing violence. He could hear the crack of a hand against his cheekbone. He tried to spin away, but they grabbed him by the arms and held him up like a canvas. He closed his eyes tight and could hear Johnny Weir breathing like a pitbull as he fired punches into his face. They let him fall, and he could hear a fusillade of kicks, feeling their boots raise him up and down on the tarmac like bombs detonating beneath him.

He thought he could hear a woman's voice shouting above the men, and he said to himself, 'She has come, she has come to me,' and he could feel her above, as though she had floated down from heaven.

The men walked away and the woman sank to her knees and touched his shoulder.

'Oh, my wee darling, my wee darling,' sobbed Elaine, who'd been heading down to the mural to bring him his lunch.

Above him, Davey could hear the woman recite the words, 'At the going down of the sun, and in the morning, We will remember them…' but slowly her voice faded into his own, and the last thing he knew before his mind drifted away was that the only woman there was his mother.

Bernie McGill

Bernie McGill is the author of *Sleepwalkers*, a collection of stories shortlisted in 2014 for the Edge Hill Short Story Prize, and of *The Butterfly Cabinet* (named in 2012 by *Downton Abbey* creator Julian Fellowes as his novel of the year). Her work has been placed in the Seán Ó Faoláin, the Bridport, and the Michael McLaverty Short Story Prizes, and she won the Zoetrope: All-Story Award in the US in 2008. Her story 'A Fuss' appeared in *The Long Gaze Back* in 2015. She is the recipient of a number of Arts Council of Northern Ireland awards and was granted a research bursary in 2013 from the Society of Authors. Her second novel will be published by Tinder Press in 2017. She lives in Portstewart in Northern Ireland with her family. www.berniemcgill.com

The Cure for
Too Much Feeling

With Rita it had begun gently, a slight quiver in the hand, acid in her stomach, a tight sense of weariness in the afternoons when she had finished an early shift at work. She made an appointment to see the doctor and described the symptoms to him. He tested her heart, her blood pressure, cholesterol levels, good and bad, made enquiries as to the efficiency of her digestive system, suggested that, maybe, she should consider taking a break. He mentioned a food diary. 'You may have developed an allergy,' he said. 'It sometimes happens in later life.' So she took time off her job at the mini-mart and booked a coach trip to Connemara where it rained non-stop for three days and her symptoms grew worse. The people on the bus were full of grief. Every time one of them sat down beside her to tell of the loss of a spouse or a dog or of a winning Lottery ticket, she experienced a twinge of pain in her chest, a sensation like a growing knot at the back of her throat. At the Twelve Pins, where a widow confessed that she had never liked her husband of more than forty years, Rita felt the sweat gather between her shoulder blades, the skin on her upper arms begin to rise and tingle, and had to ask to be let out of the coach for a breath of air. Bit by bit, she began to believe that her growing trouble was not related to the consumption of dairy or gluten or (God forbid) potatoes, but was a newly developed susceptibility to other people's misery. She had never experienced any bother like this before. She suspected there was no antidote. She ate a cooked breakfast in the hotel every morning and returned to Belfast several pounds heavier. From then on, she resolved to avoid people and their stories of woe as much as she was able.

There was no husband to trouble the surface of Rita's life. She'd had a child once, a girl, but she'd given her up almost immediately. She was very small and wrinkled with startling black hair that stuck out from the side of her head like a crow's wing, and she cried, Rita remembered, for no reason at all. The child was the consequence of a rainy evening in the back of a white Mark 111 Ford Cortina in 1976 when her after-school shift at the chippy had ended and the owner (Mr Percy, red-bearded, married with three young boys) had eyed the laddered knee of her black uniform tights and said it was a shocking bad night to be walking home. He had a four-door saloon with synchromesh gearbox and double wishbone suspension, four more inches of extra interior width on the earlier model, the Mark 11. She remembered very clearly the walnut-trimmed dashboard, the bucket seats, his freckled fingers on her leg, working the threads of her laddered tights apart into a hole big enough to slide his hand and then his arm through, round the back of her thigh, up inside her underwear. She didn't remember agreeing to anything, but she hadn't wanted to appear ungrateful. It was raining very hard by then. She got beard rash all the way down her neck and had had to stuff her ruined tights and knickers in the Doric, for fear her mother would see them, but her mother figured it out herself when the waistband on Rita's school skirt had had to be let out a second time. She was sent away to an aunt in Belfast where such matters were more easily explained. After they took the baby away, she got a job in the ciggie factory where her aunt worked, with a good bonus and free packs of fags and what if she did stink of tobacco most of the time? The money smelled only of money. She stayed away from men because the episode in the Cortina had been surprising, messy and, to be honest, a little painful, and she didn't want any more babies to trouble her. Her aunt had been glad of the company; her uncle was away at sea. They had to move house when work started on the motorway; the whole street was being demolished, but she doesn't know if her aunt ever gave her uncle their new address because Rita never laid eyes on him and then the aunt smoked herself into an early grave and there was Rita with a job and a house and what more could you want? She got a good payout when the factory closed, took a few shifts in the mini-mart to get her out of the house.

She couldn't work out what had caused the change. Up until the age of fifty-six she'd been as immune to other people's troubles as was everyone else around her. It was a kind of creeping sickness. She was too embarrassed to go back to the doctor and tell him what she now knew, so she adopted strategies for survival. In the days and weeks after the Connemara trip, Rita learned how to carry herself careful. Open fires were to be avoided, she found; they drew stories out of people, and pubs were bad too, of course, for alcohol is a known tongue-loosener, and as for a pub with an open fire, forget about it, her stomach would never stick it. Rita had an open fire in her little yellow-bricked terraced house, but she put a pillow up the chimney and had an electric bar fitted. It was much cleaner without the soot. She didn't have to miss out on a drink: the mini-mart had started doing gin and tonic, ready-mixed in those handy cans that you could keep in the fridge and pop open when the mood took you and the tonic never went flat and the can was always cold.

Still, it was a loss to find that she was no longer able to nibble at tragedy the way that she had done before, couldn't say, 'Isn't it shocking about that poor woman the other morning, black ice on the road early?' and then set it aside and get on. She couldn't hear, 'They're sitting up with Dan Reilly,' and nod and go about her business. She was laid low by other people's misery, it sapped her energy, brought her out in a rash. She couldn't sit down to enjoy the news. Even a second onscreen of Syria or Gaza or a Greek island beach would have her clutching at her stomach with cramps. She was near-crippled by the look in the children's dark eyes, the sorrow of it seeping into her. She began to avoid local radio in the mornings when it was all phone-ins and shouting to outdo each other's hurt, and if she listened sometimes in the afternoons to the anniversary and birthday requests, she was always careful to switch off at five minutes to the hour, before the bulletins came on. She tuned in to Classical FM, though she had to be careful around a violin solo. Once she found herself a few bars in to Beethoven's *Funeral March* before she realised what it was. She just made it to the dial in time. A-flat was not a good chord for her. She didn't read newspapers or true-life magazines. She was untroubled by the vagaries of the Internet. She would occasionally flick through the mail-order catalogues and imagine the lives of the cardigan-ed, white-toothed people there. She averted her eyes from the head-scarfed woman who sold the homeless magazine outside the bank in town. She stopped her ears at bus stops, scissored through every charity appeal that dropped through her door, but despite her careful efforts, every once in a while something would seep through. A chance remark overheard, a hand on her arm at the till in the mini-mart, a glance in the window of the TV shop where the largest screens were tuned to twenty-four-hour news, and then it could take several episodes of stock-piled Val Doonican shows to restore her to herself. She had been managing fairly well until the day there came a knock on the door and Rita's chest began to tighten even before she opened it.

It was the girl, of course, although she was no longer a girl: forty years old she would have been by then. Rita had always known it was a possibility that she might turn up. That same lick of black hair; something in her thin lips of the set of her own mother's mouth; she knew her straight away. She asked her in and gave her tea and told her she didn't know who the father was, which was only half a lie, since she had never heard Mr Percy's first name. It showed her in a bad light, she knew, but it seemed kinder that way. Supposing that he was still alive, supposing that the girl managed to locate him, Rita didn't reckon that Mr or Mrs Percy or their by-now middle-aged sons would want anything to do with either one of them. So the girl – the woman – whose name was Anna (a neat name, easily remembered, only two letters, back-to-back) went away again.

On Sundays Rita took a bus to the south side of the city, where she was unlikely to meet anyone she knew or anyone who knew her, and where she could walk in peace in the green areas without anyone passing remarks. She was coming through Botanic Gardens one day in January, the cold biting at her cheeks, when a sudden shower of sleety rain drove her up the incline to shelter under the grey bulk of the Museum. She'd never been inside, but it was draughty under the concrete canopy that hung like a lip over the entrance, and the rain bouncing off the steps and down through the dripping trees and off the head of the statue of Kelvin by the park gates was lowering her mood. And, she remembered, it was free to go in.

She found herself in a large open space, the ceiling more than fifty feet up, concrete and glass and steel on all sides. She decided to take a ride in the lift, to act like someone who'd intended to make the visit. On the fourth floor, she stood for a while at the glass balustrade, looking down through the dizzying atrium to the ground floor below, at the purple shirts of the museum staff, at a woman seated in a lime green anorak, leaflets fanned like palm fronds on the glass-topped table beside her. She watched as people crossed the foyer, shaking umbrellas, checking signs for floor descriptions, finding their way. The walls and ceiling were a blinding white. Moments later, the lift pinged to a halt to her left, and a group emerged: three women, half a dozen small children. One of them, a boy of two or three, fell back, dragging his mother by the hand, shouting to her that he wanted to go back in the lift, but she walked on and as he dropped to the floor, his cries began to echo and bounce off the walls until the space was filled with a hundred children crying. Rita gripped the balustrade, its bevelled edge marked with dozens of small fingerprints, and forced herself to stand there, with the light bouncing off the glass, and the cries ringing round her. Then the mother picked the child up and balanced him on her hip and carried him through the heavy wooden door to the adjoining gallery that closed solidly behind them.

A sign beyond the lift indicated an exhibition of portraits in the direction opposite to the one in which the crying child had been taken. Rita liked to look at pictures of people; there weren't many places where you could study faces safely. Even in a café or at the bus stop, people sometimes caught you staring, took it as an invitation to speak.

She made her way to the gallery, but the portraits were not at all what she had been expecting. They were modern for a start. She had imagined pearls and ruffs and silks but these were all hoodies and scowls and tattoos and, God preserve us, an entirely naked woman, straight browed, navel-pierced, gazing out, the delta of her shorn pubic hair precisely at Rita's eye-level. What were they thinking, hanging that up on a Sunday for anyone to see? Rita coloured and turned her eyes away, walked quickly past, putting safe distance between her and the unabashed woman, stopped to slow her heart in front of a painting of a man in a red V-neck sweater in a blue wall-papered room.

They were so lifelike, some of them; you couldn't tell they were paintings at all, even up close they looked like enlarged photographs, there was hardly any sign of marks, but 'oil on canvas' it read on the wall panel, or 'oil on linen' or 'on gesso' or 'on board', so they were paintings, all of them, she checked every one as she passed. She felt a little hoodwinked by this. She thought it was a bit of a cheat. Where were the brush strokes, the thickened slabs of paint, the pencilled marks, the rubbings out? She wanted, she realised, honest artifice, evidence of work. It was only in the blades of grass in the background, or in the leaves or the petals or occasionally, in the eyes, in the way the white oil of reflected light hit the liquid black of the iris that you could tell that this was a worked thing. 'Because the eye is a giveaway,' she said to herself, and then realised she'd spoken aloud. When she looked around, the museum attendant showed no sign of having heard her.

She had completed a circuit of the room and was nearing the exit when she noticed a painting she had missed on her way in, in her hurry past the naked gazing woman. This one, entitled *Washing Mother's Hair*, presented two figures, both side-on, inclined towards each other, their faces in profile, oblivious to the onlooker. The scene was viewed as if through the frame of an open bathroom door, an elderly woman seated on the edge of the bath, her head bowed over the sink; another woman, younger but not young, facing her, pouring water from a white plastic mixing jug over the other woman's head. The hair was plastered to the old lady's scalp, the bones of her neck and of her small skull showing through under pink skin. A yellow towel lay over her shoulders, over the white of the full slip she was wearing, the skin on her upper arms crinkled as tissue paper, the veins on her legs and on her slippered feet, raised and wormed and blue. With one hand, she had gathered the corners of the towel under her chin like a shawl; the other hand gripped the wash hand basin, like she feared she was in danger of falling. Her daughter's dark hair was tied in a low knot at the nape of her neck from where it sprang, curly, down her back. The girl looked weary, her back bent in an uncomfortable position, stretching to reach over her mother's bowed head to rinse the water from her hair. There was something about the composition that held Rita, something ritual in the scene, in the triangulation of the two figures over the bathroom sink, their physical closeness in the cramped room, the daughter's right hand, pouring water, her left hand outstretched, like a benediction, something easy between the two of them that said, 'We know who we are to one another and this is what we do.' It seemed to Rita that if she could stand there for long enough, if they would let her stay, if the purple-shirted attendant would put out the lights and lock up the gallery and go home and leave her there, that she might witness a quiet miracle. The girl might squeeze the last drop of water out of her mother's damp hair and set the jug down on the deep-tiled window sill, beside the toothbrush and the shampoo bottle and the aloe vera plant that was growing there out of a used margarine tub; she might lift the yellow towel and twist it round her mother's head, and slide an arm under the old woman's elbow to ease her up and steady her, might turn her round to face the bathroom door, and walk her straight out of the picture frame, past Rita, and up a darkened hallway to a cushioned chair by a crackling fire where the old woman's hair would dry and settle into soft white curls. And it seemed to Rita that she would then be privy to the sort of act of casual intimacy that passes unannounced in homes everywhere where people are tired or hurting or weak and still going about the everyday business of caring for one another and of being loved. But Rita didn't stay. She turned on her heel away from the painting and walked out the gallery door, down the four flights of stairs to the ground floor, past the milling people with their spattered raincoats and their dripping umbrellas, and out of the museum into her careful life and the still falling rain.

Tara West

Called a 'true original' by Glenn Patterson, Tara West had already established a career as an advertising copywriter in Belfast when she wrote her first novel, *Fodder*. The book was published by Blackstaff Press to widespread critical acclaim and established her reputation as a talented new Irish voice. Her second novel, *Poets Are Eaten as a Delicacy in Japan*, was published by Liberties Press in 2013 and was described by Ian Sansom as 'The funniest book written by a Northern Irish author this century'. Liberties will publish her memoir about depression and recovery, *Happy Dark,* in 2016. Tara has appeared at numerous festivals including the West Belfast Festival, the Belfast Book Festival, and the John Hewitt International Summer School. She has an MA in Creative Writing from Queen's University, Belfast, is a member of the Society of Authors, and has received a number of Arts Council Northern Ireland Awards for her writing. She lives in Co. Antrim with her husband and daughter.

The Speaking and
the Dead

There are always suicides at these things, Elaine thinks, pressing gold hoops into her long lobes. She steps up to the mirror above the empty grate and slashes peachy lipstick across her mouth, ignoring the rest of her face and hair. She has been to see Jolene the Psychic Medium before; suicides always come through at Jolene's shows. Depressed people seem much more dependable in death than they were in life. Or maybe they are just like Jolene. Maybe they're attracted by her friendly aura, or blue aura, or whatever it is.

Elaine checks her bag: purse, phone, keys, Lambert & Butler, vodka in a Sprite bottle, then pulls down a slat in the blinds to check the street for her lift. Behind her, Paul snorts and snuffles on the settee, tattooed elbow over his eyes. Her husband spends every Saturday afternoon drinking at the club and every Saturday night snoring on the settee. They speak more to the dog than to each other these days. She tries to imagine what it would be like if he choked on one of those snores. Lighting a cigarette and sighing out smoke, she turns back to the window.

Suicides seem happy to explain things to Jolene, things they couldn't explain to the ones left behind, as Jolene calls them, as though the dead are just calling in from Benidorm, and not, as Elaine suspects, from emptiness. If they've gone anywhere at all.

Or maybe they know Jolene will protect them, because the ones left behind can't be trusted to speak to them directly. They get emotional, and maybe the ones who've passed to the other side don't want that. Elaine doesn't want that either. She doesn't want to cry in front of everyone. Elaine doesn't even cry at the backstories on *X Factor*, when her friend Jacqui can hardly swallow vodka for the lump in her throat. The bottle always ends up drained though.

A small red car pulls up outside, thumping with Jacqui's music: Neil Shite Diamond. The car toots urgently, as though Elaine is the one who's late. She yanks the blinds closed, stubs out her cigarette and leaves the room without looking back. In the hall, she fondles their dog's white muzzle and straggly ears. Poor old Pepper and his swampy clouds of stink. He lifts his milky eyes to her and farts airily.

Elaine ushers the dog into the living room. It's warmer in there. And Pepper will give Paul something to really choke on.

Jacqui and her daughter Lauren fill the front seats of the car like inflatables after a day at the beach. Neil Shite Diamond sings in place of a greeting and the car creaks and dings as Elaine heaves herself in. She silently compares her own substantial frame to the women in front. She nudges ahead in the slimming stakes, but Jacqui wins on points for being a martyr to her thyroid.

Over the years their friendship has grown into an unspoken competition, fought in the arenas of weight, food, poverty, victimhood and whatever else could be construed. Jolene offers them more chances to get ahead. Who, if either of them, would be contacted? Who would come through from the other side? Would it be yet another of Jacqui's attention-seeking distant relatives, the ones with mysterious new qualities of love and forgiveness? Or would it be Elaine's son Matt, who killed himself when he was eighteen?

Elaine delves into her bag and pushes the contents around. She has seen every kind of medium: amateurs in living rooms, stars in big hotels, Romany in fairground tents and squinty oddballs over Skype. All sorts have come through to talk: a neighbour's violent ex-husband, an Indian-sounding stranger, her mother's childhood friend, an old teacher, but never Matt. Maybe tonight he'll come through. Jolene is said to be the best psychic medium around.

'So where's Fuckface?' Jacqui asks Elaine, as Lauren mashes the car into gear. They drive quickly through the estate, Lauren's lumpy gear changes rocking them in their seats. Elaine hands across two cigarettes and Jacqui inserts one in her daughter's mouth.

'Asleep on the settee,' Elaine says. 'Where's Ballbag?'

'Round his ma's,' Jacqui says, lighting up. 'Complaining because I never give him liver. I says the only liver I'll ever fry will be his. Didn't I, Lauren?'

Hooting at her own joke, Jacqui swaps the unlit cigarette in Lauren's mouth for her lit one. She's wearing her blingy earrings and sparkly top, the one she reserves for 'do's'. She reminds Elaine of a Christmas bauble.

Swaddled in a hoodie and jogging bottoms that reveal her cellulite, Lauren doesn't speak. She was born into a sulk and never shook it off. Jacqui natters and laughs at her own jokes on the way to the hotel. That's one of the things Elaine likes about her. There's no pressure for her to talk when she's with Jacqui. Jacqui fills the gaps.

They wait in a queue of cars at the hotel and Jacqui folds her arms and complains about the disabled, the old, the people who park over two spaces and the people who aren't long-time fans like her and Elaine. She demands that her daughter drops them right outside the door, and Lauren brakes with belligerence when they reach the glass entrance. A horn blasts behind them and they swing round to see a white limo, the driver making shooing movements with his fingers.

'Oh my God, it's Jolene!' Jacqui squawks, her thin hair swinging. 'We can't keep Jolene back. Move the car, Lauren! Move!'

Jacqui twinkles her fingers at the limo as Lauren shunts the car forward, braking with added sarcasm.

Pushing the door open with a foot, Jacqui uses the doorframe to haul her sparkles out. Elaine follows, holding her handbag close. She has only ever seen Jolene onstage before, where she seemed to glow. She has never seen her 'in real life'.

A chauffeur opens the limo door and Jolene emerges, followed by her manager, a small man in a dark suit with short white hair. Jolene wears white jeans, a white leather belt with a silver buckle; her loose black curls fall over a white, floaty blouse. She looks serene; professional make-up has softened her hard features. The manager accompanies her into the packed and noisy hotel lobby, and Elaine and Jacqui join the rest of the audience filing into a huge conference room, gawking and rubbernecking at Jolene.

She looks a lot smaller when she's not on stage. If it wasn't for all the white, Elaine would lose her in the crowd.

Elaine and Jacqui have four glasses of Diet Coke each, topped up with handbag vodka stored on the floor below their chairs. Curled into her seat, Lauren eats Maltesers and thumbs sourly at her phone. She hasn't looked up since they sat down, eight rows back from the temporary stage. Around them, the audience chats and cackles. It's overwhelmingly female and faces are flushed and bright. Two men test the sound system, the quickest one-twos Elaine has ever heard. She wouldn't like to face so many women, hope hanging in the air like static.

The audience 'oohs' as the lights dim and Elaine grips her ticket, feeling her heart thump-start in her chest. The ticket says Jolene is 'One of Ireland's Most Gifted Psychic Mediums'. Elaine's ticket number is 289. It cost £18. She glances up as Jacqui joins the audience in enthusiastic applause. Jolene is walking on stage, her clothes bright under the spotlight. Elaine twists her ticket to the light. At the bottom it says in small silver letters: 'A fun-filled night of astonishing entertainment!'

She never noticed that before. It must have been Jolene's manager put that on, maybe to attract more people or something. Jolene wouldn't put that on. Jolene's hardly having a giggle up there. She wouldn't think this was fun or entertainment. Rubbish singers on *X Factor*, that's fun. Old episodes of *Porridge* and Peter Kay and children disco dancing, that's entertainment. You wouldn't call this fun or entertainment, all these women in the dark, desperate to know.

Jolene adjusts the small mic that is clipped to her floaty blouse and the sound system pops and squeals as she welcomes everyone. The crowd settles into a rustling quiet. Jacqui sits very straight, although she still looks like a ball. She leans this way and that, neck straining.

'I'm behind a pair of Hattie fucken Jacques here,' she whispers. 'Can't see a thing.'

Onstage, Jolene closes her eyes, presses her forefingers to her temples and splays her hands. The audience is silent. Elaine pinions her palm with her thumbnail.

'Yes,' Jolene says in her sharp Belfast accent. 'OK, now. I'm getting something.'

There is no sound, apart from the crunch of Maltesers. Elaine lifts her drink and hits her teeth on the glass.

'Does anyone ... can anyone...' Jolene's eyes spring open and she scans the room. 'Yes. There is someone here with us.' She presses her fingers to her temples and closes her eyes again.

'Someone is coming through. I … I can see the letters. B. And E. An older woman. B and E … Betty? Beth?'

There is muttering in the audience. Elaine sets her drink down and pushes her palms into her armpits.

'It's an older lady,' Jolene says, eyes still closed. 'And she's looking for someone. A younger woman. A daughter, is it? Is there a woman here whose mother was called Betty? Beth?'

No one responds beyond murmuring.

'It's very important. I have a mother here. I think she's a mother. Who is she looking for? Her name is Beth or Betty.'

Silence – then a voice chirrups from the back of the room. The soundman jogs across and hands the mic to a small, brittle, blonde woman.

'HELLO,' the woman booms, almost eating the mic. The audience ducks at the squealing mic and the soundman moves it away from her mouth. 'Sorry,' she says, the mic squealing again. 'My mother was Bella. She passed away last year.'

'What's your name, love?' Jolene asks.

'Angela.'

'Of course. A beautiful name.' Jolene smiles beatifically. 'Your mummy was really into her cleaning, wasn't she, Angela?'

Angela nods, placing a hand over her eyes.

'She was a real neat freak, wasn't she, Angela?' Jolene gives a soft laugh. 'The type who scrubbed the front step?'

Angela can be heard to sob. 'Yes.'

'Well, she's come through for you tonight, Angela.' Jolene presses a finger against a temple. 'And she left you … she left you … a piece of jewellery. Would that be right, Angela?'

Angela nods, sobs held tight in her shoulders.

'It was gold, right, Angela?'

Angela nods.

'Beth is glad you have it now—'

'Bella,' Angela says.

'Yes. She gives you that with love, Angela.'

Jacqui leans forward to the floor, and Elaine holds out her glass to have it topped up with handbag vodka.

'I swear that woman came through last time,' Jacqui throws back to Elaine.

'Hogging broadband,' Lauren mumbles, without looking up from her phone.

'Wait,' Jolene says brightly. 'There's someone with her, Angela. Someone else who has passed to the other side. A man. Is that her husband? A brother? Maybe a neighbour? Does that make sense?'

Angela breathes shakily into the mic. 'That could be my daddy. He passed away fifteen years ago.'

'Well, they're together now, Angela.' Jolene gives her warmest smile. 'Your mummy isn't on her own. And she's smiling, Angela. She's not suffering. She's watching over you. She'll always be watching over you.'

Angela holds a crumpled tissue to her mouth.

'She has to go now, Angela,' Jolene says softly. 'But she's still smiling. She has a lovely smile.'

The mic fizzles as Angela takes her seat, a tissue pressed to her mouth. Elaine takes a good few gulps of vodka as the soundman moves away and the audience applauds.

'Thank you so much, Angela,' Jolene says, pacing the stage. 'We understand your pain. We've all been there. Thank you for sharing with us tonight.'

Jacqui is getting fidgety. She's going to have a relative coming through soon. Elaine rolls her eyes.

Jolene walks the stage, fingers to temples. 'They're coming through thick and fast tonight. Yes, I have a woman. She's had a very hard time. I can see the letter L. L or I. Who knows a woman who had difficulties? An L or I in her name. L and I? Who knows this woman?'

The room rustles and heads turn, looking for the owner of L and/or I. Elaine notices her glass steaming up as she drinks.

'It could have been a recent death,' Jolene says. 'Or it could have been years ago. Who knows her? Someone must know her, that's why she's here tonight. She needs to speak. L or I in her name.'

No one responds.

'She has grey-brown hair. Blue eyes? Yes, blue eyes. And she's worried about something. Something that was left unsaid. Who knows someone with an L or I in her name?'

Jolene shades her eyes, as though the spotlight stops her from seeing the audience. There are no raised hands. The silence goes on.

Jacqui bounces to her feet, her head barely reaching above the Hattie Jacques in front. She gives her twinkly wave. 'Me! I know her!'

'Ah,' Jolene says, walking back across the stage. 'I knew it would be this side of the room. She was guiding me over this way. What was her name, was it Elaine maybe?'

Elaine starts in her seat, but hasn't time to think as the soundman pushes along the row and steps on her toes as he holds the mic up to Jacqui's mouth. She takes it like a pro.

'Her name was Lorraine,' Jacqui says.

Jolene smiles approvingly. 'Yes, that's it. Lorraine. Lorraine's here with us tonight. And what's your name?'

Elaine retracts from the soundman's Lynx-smelling body. Jolene must know Jacqui's name by now. Jacqui has claimed more dead people over the years than a morgue.

'My name's Jacqui,' Jacqui trills. 'Lorraine was my second cousin.'

By the time the interval comes, Jacqui has claimed Lorraine, a painter and decorator named Phil and a pipe-smoking man known as Lorenzo.

Elaine clasps her bag under her arm as she, Jacqui, Lauren and a chatty, perfumed mob cram in cigarettes outside the entrance. Jacqui is complaining about her alcoholic neighbours as Elaine nods along.

There was only one suicide in the first half. Someone who had 'died by his own hand'. Elaine had felt sweat spring onto her top lip. She was ready to stand, take the mic, tell Jolene everything. She just needed to know for sure. But his name began with G and his sister was in the audience and she claimed the suicide as Gavin.

Why? Why Gavin and not Matt? Where was Matt? She knew where his body was, but where was *he*? Was he nothing now? She needed him to come through. She needed to speak to him, to know why he hadn't talked to her, why he hadn't asked her for help – she was his mother; she was there to help. She could have done something, why didn't he speak to her? Maybe she should have tried harder to talk to him? What happened, Matt? Where did you go?

Back in their row, they settle more drinks below their seats and Jacqui shoves Elaine with a sparkly arm, offering a tube of Pringles.

Elaine takes a few of the crisps. Jacqui and her dead relatives. Jacqui and Lorraine and the never-heard-of-before Phil and Lorenzo and God knows how many others. You win, Jacqui.

'Fancy a KFC after?' Jacqui asks.

'Alright,' Elaine says.

An hour into the second half, after Cal (drowning), Ruth (alcoholism), Jean (cancer) and Aodheen (complications), another young man comes through. There is some confusion; Jolene knows there was a deep sadness surrounding the end of his life, but she isn't sure what happened. He was a wild one, he loved a laugh. A woman near the front stands up: it was her nephew. He died of an accidental drug overdose.

Elaine checks her watch. She could've been this drunk at home and enjoying some Dr Hook while she was at it. She might give Jolene a miss next time.

With warmth, sympathy and efficiency, Jolene dispenses with Stevo the druggie and his auntie Cathy, and walks around the stage rubbing her neck, as if to loosen tired muscles. The show will end soon.

Jacqui drains the last of her drink and sighs. 'Aye-aye-aye.'

Jolene plants a hand on her forehead. 'I'm sorry. I feel the spirits moving on now. This is how it goes. They come to speak to the ones left behind and then they move on. But remember, if your loved one hasn't come through tonight, it doesn't mean they won't ever. There is always next time. I'm also available for private consultations. Lift a flyer on the way out and I'll be there for you.'

Jolene stops talking and presses a finger to a temple.

'Wait,' she says. 'I have someone else here, it's a man, he's quite young. I see the letter A. He seems happy, which is strange, because he didn't get to live out his life as he hoped. Does anyone know a young man with an A in his name?'

There is a general murmur, but fewer faces turn to look – they've had enough. Elaine pushes her thumbnail into her hand. Could this be him? Matt wasn't happy, he hadn't been for a long time. He was silent and angry, although as a boy he had been sunshine and smiles, always making her laugh. Maybe that's what Jolene's manager meant by entertainment? That the people you love can make you laugh? No, that can't be right. Could it be him?

'Does anyone know him? An A and I think, yes, there's a T in his name. He's looking for a woman, but I can't tell what the relationship is. He's smiling; he seems like a happy soul. Who knows him?'

Elaine perches on the edge of her chair. Could he be happy now he's dead? Is it a relief for him to be dead? When he wasn't surly and silent, he was in a rage; he screamed at Elaine and Paul, always stayed in his room. The school complained and he stopped going. Paul said it was his age, said he was worse when he was a teenager, giving back cheek, lighting fires, making trouble. Elaine would have been relieved if Matt had lit fires, been brought home by the police, got drunk and vomited in the linen basket, that would have been normal. But maybe Paul was right. Maybe it was his age.

Matt had tied an extension cord to the door knob and fed it through the banister so there would be enough of a drop to break his neck.

They got Pepper that year, a collie-looking mongrel. Elaine gripped his fur every night till she slept. She and Paul were breathless with pain. Soundless. How they loved that dog.

'There must be someone here who knows this young man,' Jolene says, shielding her eyes with her hand. 'An A and a T in his name?'

Elaine isn't sure. She's never been sure.

The audience stirs, but in a way that suggests their backsides are sore, they have kids to get back to, TV shows to watch.

No matter how many letters almost form his name, Elaine has always held back. And then someone stands up before her and claims him for their own. But maybe that's why he never comes through. Maybe you have to be willing to meet them halfway? Maybe this time…

Jacqui bounces up. 'I know him.'

Elaine kicks over her glass.

Eyebrows rise as the soundman makes his way over and hands Jacqui the mic. The Hattie Jacques protest.

'His name's Anthony,' Jacqui says.

'Oh,' says Jolene, frowning a little. 'So, how well did you know Anthony?'

'He was my cousin's stepson.'

'I can see a football top…'

'He was buried in it.'

'Well, all he says is … Anthony's a bit of a joker…'

'That's our Anthony, alright.'

'He says, well, he says, see you soon?' Jolene shrugs. 'He's waving and smiling and he says see you soon.'

Titters ripple through the audience.

Jacqui hands the mic back to the soundman and sits down, unperturbed.

Elaine lifts her handbag from the floor and sweeps off drips of Diet Coke. What was she thinking, meeting Matt halfway? She was stupid. Drunk. All these people were here to be entertained. This is for fun, this is a game – even Jacqui knows that. Matt has gone to emptiness, is emptiness, and her desperation would serve as amusement for everybody else. She always hesitated because she never really believed he would come. She just can't let go of the hope.

The audience claps and whoops as Jolene smiles and thanks everyone for coming. She takes several bows and reminds them all to look out for her next tour, then the spotlight goes out and clunks are heard as mics are switched off. Jolene becomes a shadow retreating across the stage as the audience rises to leave.

Someone taps Jacqui on the shoulder, and she turns to face a hard-faced woman in the row behind. 'This isn't a competition, you know,' the woman says.

Jacqui pulls her sparkly top down over her middle and folds her arms. 'Well, imagine coming through and nobody wanting you,' she says. 'If nobody else claims them, I'll take them. I wouldn't have them going back to wherever they came from feeling like nobody wanted them.'

The hard-faced woman harrumphs down her nose and stalks away.

The stage is dark, and no one else seems to notice that Jolene has reappeared. Elaine draws her eyes away from Jacqui and leans to the side, straining to see. Jolene is speaking, but the audience is dispersing and shuffling towards the exit.

'Come on,' Jacqui says, orientating her roundness towards the door. 'KFC time. Let's go.'

'Wait,' Elaine says, twisting her way along the row.

'Where you going?' Jacqui calls after her. 'The door's this way. I'm starving.'

Elaine joins several other women at the front as Jolene shakes her head on the dim stage.

'He has grey hair,' Jolene says, her voice thin and small. 'I can't see him very well, but I know he has tattoos. Who knows a man with tattoos?'

'Ah, like, everybody?' comes a voice from behind Elaine.

'He wants to talk to a woman,' Jolene says, almost pleading. 'Does anyone know him? There are tattoos on his elbow. And sadness. That's all I see.'

Elaine feels a presence closing in.

'There you are,' Jacqui announces, linking her arm through Elaine's. 'You don't get your money back if nobody comes through for you, you know. Come on. Lauren's away to get the car.'

When Elaine looks back at the stage, Jolene is being escorted away by her manager.

Elaine doesn't feel like a KFC now, and Jacqui tuts and folds her sparkly arms. They drop her home, and Neil Shite Diamond thumps down the street and round the corner. Elaine waves, but Jacqui doesn't. Dieting is still a competition.

In the hall, Elaine drops her Coke-soaked handbag and opens the living room door. It smells like booze breath and dog farts, and Pepper's tail thumps happily against the floor. He tries to heave himself up, but arthritis makes him slow. Elaine squeezes her behind onto the settee beside the still-sleeping Paul and the dog collapses on her feet.

Paul's snoring has stopped and his stomach rises and falls; a slow, familiar rhythm. One arm is by his side and the other is over his middle, so she can't see his tattoos. She tucks her fingers around his.

Jan Carson

Jan Carson is a writer and community arts officer based in Belfast, Northern Ireland. Her first novel, *Malcolm Orange Disappears*, was published by Liberties Press in June 2014, followed by a short story collection, *Children's Children*, in February 2016. A pamphlet of flash fiction is forthcoming from The Emma Press in 2017. Jan's stories have appeared in journals such as *Storm Cellar*, *Banshee*, *Southword*, *Harper's Bazaar* and *The Honest Ulsterman*. In 2014 she was a recipient of the Arts Council Northern Ireland Artist's Career Enhancement Bursary. She was longlisted for the Sean O'Faolain Short Story Prize in 2015 and won the Harper's Bazaar short story competition in 2016. She was shortlisted for a Sabotage Award for Best Short Story Collection 2015/16. Jan has had two plays performed by local theatre companies. She has read widely in Ireland, the UK and America, including appearances at Cork, Dublin, Belfast and Edinburgh Book Festival.

Settling

Matt is in the kitchen deciding which cupboard will be saucepans and which is tall enough to hold the cereal boxes.

I am in the bedroom unpacking our clothes. Our bedroom is the emptiest it will ever be. We haven't built the bed yet. It's in pieces, leaning against the walls so it looks like there are ladders leading from our apartment to the one above. Last night we slept on bath towels with rolled-up jumpers instead of pillows. When we woke Matt had cable knit patterns pressed into his cheek. I closed my eyes, ran my fingers over his face and read him like Braille. 'This is the beginning,' I read and he said, 'Amen to that,' turning the other cheek, which was similarly indented. It would have been the perfect moment to make love, but we hadn't the curtains up yet and the neighbours could see right into our room from their kitchen.

This afternoon our furniture arrived. My father loaned a van off Uncle Graham and drove it over on the Larne-Cairnryan ferry. All the way down in one go and straight back up for the last boat home. We didn't ask him to do this. He insisted. My father likes to play the martyr.

'It's a wild, long run by yourself,' I said. 'Would you not like Matt for the company?'

'I'll be grand myself,' he replied. 'I'll take half an hour in the Gretna Services.' This was his way of saying, 'I wouldn't stop you leaving, but I'll be misery itself if you do.'

For weeks he'd been running a kind of sales pitch every time we mentioned moving. He wanted us to stay put. He couldn't bear the thought of grandchildren he would hardly ever see. He'd read in the paper that Belfast was one of the best cities in Europe now, maybe even the world.

'For what exactly?' Matt asked every time he said this, and Dad couldn't remember but he thought it was either young people or restaurants.

'No offence, Mr Campbell,' said Matt, 'but Belfast's shite. We'll never get anywhere here. If you're at all serious about your career, you've to move to London.'

'There's nothing for us in Belfast,' I added. This was not entirely true. It was also cruel. But Matt demanded solidarity on the important issues such as politics and moving to the Mainland, and the way he'd taken to wearing a suit jacket, casually, with jeans.

'Right,' said Dad, 'on your own heads be it.' This was the thing he always said when a line had been drawn and there was no talking round it. Round he came with heavy-duty bin-liners and packing boxes, booked the van to Scotland and loaded it up himself. He'd have carted our sofas to Russia if it meant getting shot of us quicker.

I wanted to say, 'It's not you I'm done with, Dad. It's this place.' But I knew he couldn't tell the difference.

Early this afternoon, he pulled up outside our apartment and sat on the horn till we came down. 'Mweeeeep, mweeeeep, mweeeep' it went, like a labouring cow. People in other apartments peaked their blinds to glare. It was a muggy day. My father had stripped down to his vest: lardy winter skin lining his sunburn just above the elbow like the two halves of a Drumstick lolly. He'd been in the van for hours – windows up, blowers stirring stale heat – and smelt ripe. We did not touch. His arms were full of bedside cabinet, then bookcase, bed and dining room table. When empty they were already reaching for the next load. They had no interest in holding me.

Though he's a man of almost seventy, my father sweated everything out of the van himself, piling our furniture up on the pavement so passers-by could see all our belongings, even our toilet brush and the box marked 'underwear'.

'Did you get a good eyeful?' he called after anyone who slowed to stare. His voice was vinegar sharp on the vowels, butter on the consonants. I'd already begun to tune the old tongue out and balked at the sound of him, as if catching my own voice on the answering machine. How odd he looked here in London with the joggers slamming by and the possibility of Japanese food just half a block away. More real and also less than he was in Belfast. Older. He would not stop for dinner. He took a cup of tea standing up, a round of toast with jam, and was back on the road before three.

'Text me when you get in,' I said. But he never did.

I told the caretaker that my father was the removals man. I said, 'That's what all the old folk are like back home: genuine characters.' I said this sort of laughing, but in a low-down voice so Dad wouldn't hear. Afterwards, I felt ashamed. I had a hot shower. The dirt came off in layers but the guilt persisted. I almost told Matt what a bitch I was, what a heartless cow. But then we got a Chinese in and I forgot to be ashamed because I was hungry and there were so many things to put away, so much to be getting on with.

'Where are the saucepans?' Matt shouts from the kitchen. I pretend not to hear. I have purposefully left our saucepans in Belfast. The non-stick was peeling off, leaving coal flakes in the rice. I have also abandoned the chopping boards, mugs and everyday glasses, which had gone hoar-white from the dishwasher. I want nothing broken, chipped or peeling here, only shiny new belongings. This is not Belfast. It is ok to want good things here. Tomorrow, I will say, 'It looks as if we've left a couple of boxes behind. We'll have to make an emergency run to Ikea.' I might even blame my father for our lost kitchenware. It is easy to imagine him finding our chipped juice glasses and keeping them. 'They're grand, so they are,' he'd say, training himself to drink from the unchipped edge.

Matt has moved on to the crockery. At the far end of the hall I can hear the distant chink of side plates stacking. Meanwhile, in the bedroom, I am making a mountain of our clothes. I have upended all our boxes and suitcases, forming one rainbow heap. Socks swim through sweaters; pants and dresses tangle themselves around black work tights; bra hooks sink their teeth into cardigans, leaving long, looped plucks in the wool. I stand knee deep in the muddle of it, shoeless because I haven't unpacked my slippers yet. It is like Primark on a Saturday afternoon. I could easily lie down and sleep.

'Do you want the left or the right side of the wardrobe?' I shout into the kitchen.

'Right,' replies Matt. 'Just for handiness sake.'

This makes sense. He always sleeps on the right side of our bed. He prefers the right side of everything: sofa, pavement, car (which he insists upon driving though I'm the one with the no-accidents license). I decide to hang his clothes on the left. Nothing should be the same in London. London is meant to be a beginning rather than a next chapter. Everything should be different here. I wish we could afford a new bed and big city haircuts, a sofa which isn't puckered around the shape of us sitting down. I'd like a whole wardrobe full of someone else's clothes.

I go rooting through the jumble and pull out Matt's blue sweater. It still smells of our old flat in Belfast. This can be fixed with washing. I slip it on a hanger and hold it up to the window so the last, frail fingers of sunlight go prickling through the fabric. In this moment it is more beautiful than a sweater should be. One-handed, I carry it across the bedroom and slide the wardrobe door open. My grandmother is in the wardrobe, sitting on a deckchair. I think she is reading the *Belfast Telegraph*. It is hard to tell in the dark.

I am very surprised to find my grandmother in our wardrobe. I had been expecting emptiness, maybe some coat hangers left by the previous occupants. I am particularly surprised because my grandmother is dead. Even if she wasn't she would not be in London on account of her pains and an ill-defined fear of the other sort which, in her latter days, covered everyone who didn't live on the Beersbridge Road.

I am so surprised I make a noise like a stood-upon dog and close the door immediately. My own face comes howling out of the wardrobe's mirror. Here is my mouth, hung open like a trout's. Here are my eyes, bruise-stained from too much first-night champagne. Here is my white face, hanging like a ghost. I haunt myself, and the shock of this makes me step back sharply, clawing my heel on a suitcase. For a moment there is no pain off it. Then my whole foot begins to scream. I don't look down. I'm afraid there may be blood. Matt will be furious if I've got it on our clothes. We don't have a washing machine yet, and he has a horror of launderettes. He doesn't want anyone seeing the stains we make.

Matt is a very private person. He still locks the bathroom door against me, even when brushing his teeth. London will be a deep breath for him. He has been craving anonymity since his first day in school. Anonymity is something that doesn't exist in East Belfast. The houses are simply too close together, the walls too thin. Matt is determined that we won't get to know our London neighbours. He doesn't want to make new friends or host dinner parties using our Jamie Oliver recipe book. He hopes to order all our groceries online so we don't even have to encounter shopping people. There will be less people in our life now; three or four would be ample, Matt says. There is no room in this plan for a dead grandmother, even if she stays inside the wardrobe.

I open the door, slower this time, hoping Nana will be gone. But she is still inside, the newspaper spread across her lap like a well-pressed tablecloth. She is holding her glasses in front of her face, humming 'Onward Christian Soldiers' as she moves the lenses slowly across the page.

'Nana,' I say very quietly so Matt won't hear and come into the bedroom. 'What are you doing here?'

'Just reading the paper, Pet,' she says. 'Seeing who's died this week. Your man that used to do my decorating is gone. Cancer. Only forty-two, with three wee ones left behind.' She holds the obituary page up for me. I pretend to read, drifting my eyes quickly from left to right, but in the thin light of the wardrobe the print is nothing more than dots and indistinguishable scratches.

'Oh, dear,' I say. 'The same fella done our living room.'

Now the shock of her has settled, I'm not sure how I should be different around my grandmother. Surely we can't be the same since one of us is dead? But it's too late for hysterics. The time to scream is when you first see a ghost, not five minutes later when the pair of you are already passing the chat back and forth like winter flu. I can picture us going on like this for hours; setting the East to right over tea and thick slices of toasted Veda. Give my grandmother a good meaty subject and she can go for hours, like Paisley himself, no pulpit required. Not that I'd mind. There are things I had been meaning to ask before she died. Generic old-folk questions like, 'Do you remember the Blitz?' and, 'How did you meet Granda?' and other things I'm actually interested in, such as 'Uncle Stevie: proper gay or just a wee bit affected?' If given the chance I'd definitely ask what Nana said to my ma the night before she ran off with the bread man.

'I know you thought I was sleeping,' I would say. 'But I could hear the noise of youse laying into her all the way through the ceiling. My dad swearing and my ma guldering back. The dog going ballistic in the kitchen and you screaming like a bloody banshee. Mostly you, Nana. You've a voice on you that would lift paint when you're angry. What did you say to make her leave?'

Then I'd wait a few seconds, folding my arms defensively across my chest, letting my grandmother think I was pissed at her, before I said, 'Sure, weren't we all better off without my ma? She was a right headcase.'

Then we would laugh like donkeys. My grandmother throwing her head back, allowing the laugh to come out of her nose and her mouth, her eyes and belly, as if her whole body was farting laughter and she couldn't hold it in.

Nana's dead, I remind myself; she might not be up for the banter anymore. I bring all the funeral details back: the up-from-the-country cousins in their interview suits, the salad cream sandwiches and fruit loaf spread with Flora margarine, the white lilies that sat on her coffin and left powdery orange stains like little flames licking across the living room wallpaper. Matt in the corner, his face so straight that it looked like he'd ironed it along with his shirt. Me, crying – bawling my eyes out – though we're not the sort of family who do tears at funerals. Particularly old folk's funerals, which are not as sad as children's, or sudden deaths such as car accidents and stabbings. I couldn't help crying. I was ruined with the grief. There had always been a closeness between my grandmother and me, something like coming across your own face, reflected in a window. Then she'd died and it was gone overnight. Now, here it is back – the feeling of being on-your-own-easy with another person – and I can't bear the thought of losing it again.

I lean into the wardrobe and place a hand on Nana's shoulder. I brace myself, expecting to slip right through her, but she is surprisingly solid: warm and spongey beneath several layers of knitwear.

'Funeral's on Tuesday, to Roselawn,' she reads, making a noise with her tongue that is both shock and sympathy. 'Tchup, Tchup. Tchup. Would you credit that? I'd have put good money on him being Protestant. He did such a nice job with my tiles.'

Later, I will wonder why I am not, in the moment, afraid. I am only surprised and full of the sort of gladness associated with finding a long-lost item beneath your bed or in a coat pocket. I will decide that ghosts of your own family are too familiar to be frightening. I've heard people say they are capable of cleaning up their own child's shit while other children's turns them. I wouldn't know. We don't have any children, and Matt says there's no room for them in this apartment. But the principles are similar. I'd be hysterical if I found anyone else's dead grandmother in my wardrobe. But I know this version of Nana too well to be afraid. She is wearing the red cardigan I bought her for Christmas last year, habitual white Kleenex clouding out of the cuff. It is impossible to be afraid of a thing that came from BHS in the 20% off sale. My dead grandmother is just a collection of similarly familiar details: furry carpet slippers, moley eyes and my grandfather's watch circling her wrist like an over-sized bangle.

'I thought I'd never see you again, Nana,' I say, hunkering down beside her so our faces are almost touching. I can smell the stale end of a recently-sucked Polo mint souring on her breath. 'I never got the chance to tell you how much I love you.'

'Catch yourself on,' she snaps.

My family does not do sentimentality.

'No, honestly, Nana. You've no idea how glad I am to have you back.'

'Well, I've no plans for leaving any time soon. You'll be plagued with me.'

My grandmother doesn't seem to realise that she's dead or that she's currently sitting in a wardrobe in Hackney. I won't be telling her. How would I? I can't think of any words beyond 'sorry', and afterwards she might leave. I climb into the wardrobe beside her. It's a big one and could easily fit four people, maybe even a table. I kiss her twice on each cheek. Her skin is like leaves or petals pressed inside a book. She pats me on the back, as if comforting a child. The smell of loose tea and gingernut biscuits is thick on her. I have not, until now, missed home or thought I ever would. The bridge of my nose smarts, as if it has been struck. This is the feeling of tears beginning to form. This is the moment I start to split in two.

'Put the kettle on, love,' my grandmother says. 'I'm parched.'

She has always known when to turn a conversation round. All of a sudden I have the driest thirst for tea.

'I'll be back in a wee minute,' I say. 'You stay where you are, Nana. Finish the obituaries.'

'I'm not going anywhere,' she says and winks. Or perhaps I just imagine this in the dark.

I close the door behind me, lean my ear against the wardrobe and try to hear her breathing or shuffling the newspaper. I can hear nothing but London louding outside the window. Everything is louder here. Everything is quick and straight and sure of its own skin. It is not a place for grandmothers or any other truths unseen. With the door closed and the sound of her silent I can't even recall her face, but my arms remember the exact shape of her absence and how heavy it is to hold.

In the kitchen, Matt has quit stacking plates. He is now lining the cutlery drawer with knives and forks. His back is turned against me, but I can tell he is smiling. He is happy here in our open-plan kitchen. He is not missing Belfast at all. He is imagining the rest of his life in London, only going home for Christmas, eventually whittling this down to every other Christmas and the bigger family weddings. I can tell this from the cut of his shoulders and the way he is handling the teaspoons: quickly, smoothly, confidently, like a person who knows exactly what he will do next.

'Where's the teapot?' I ask.

'I left it in Belfast,' Matt says, turning so I can see how he has already developed a new, London smile. Teeth. Gums. Tight lines like a ventriloquist's dummy, descending from either corner of his mouth.

'What? Why did you do that?'

'We don't need a teapot. You're the only one who drinks that kind of tea. Just dunk a bag in the mug.'

'It doesn't taste the same.'

'Bullshit. It tastes exactly the same if you leave it in for a few minutes.'

'I want a teapot,' I say.

Then I am crying all over our yet-to-be sorted Tupperware because I don't just want a teapot. I also want to see people I recognise in Tesco's, and I want iced fingers for a Friday treat and my sister, three streets over, with her badly behaved children. I want drizzle in the summer and shops that don't open till lunch on the Sabbath, old men who say 'mornin'' when you pass them with their dogs, dry humour, proper drinking pubs and bloody James Nesbitt, every single time you turn the television on. I want home. But I also want to be here in London, where the future is.

'You're just tired,' says Matt, setting the teaspoons down so he can hold me. 'It's a big change, but you're going to love London. Everything will be easier here. Just give it a chance.'

He lifts my hand to his face, traces my finger across his cheek and says, 'This is the beginning', like we are two people in a romantic movie.

'Amen to that,' I say, because he expects me to.

Inside I am thinking, the cableknit marks have faded away, the moment has passed, yet here we are playing it out like last night's reheated leftovers.

I use my mobile to go on the Easyjet website, looking up flights back to Belfast two weekends from now, and then two weekends after this, all the way through to Christmas. I do this in the wardrobe with the door closed because Matt will not understand. He is not like me. He is already rooting here, planning his Monday morning commute. I am not like him. I can't be only looking forwards. This is a form of weakness and I am ashamed.

My grandmother watches me from the corner of the wardrobe. 'Are you doing the computer on your mobile?' she asks.

'Aye, Nana,' I say. 'I'm just looking up something here. I'll make you another cup of tea in a minute.'

'Them things'll give you finger cancer,' she says. 'There was a programme on the telly about it last week, and microwaves are just as bad, only it's cancer in your stomach you'll get off them. I wouldn't have either in my house for fear they'd kill me.'

'You're probably right, Nana,' I say, and, sitting in the wardrobe with the door closed, I honestly believe that she is.

Later in the evening, I am leaning against our kitchen island watching Matt nuke last night's noodles in the microwave, and I find myself saying, 'Nana, used to say microwaves could give you stomach cancer.'

'Your nana was hilarious,' Matt replies. 'Remember the way she used to lift the disposable cutlery in Marksy's to save on washing up.'

'And the day she forced those poor Mormons to come in for a fry.'

We laugh at my grandmother like she is the elderly character on a television sitcom. We laugh and drink one whole bottle of wine. Half-cut, I can pretend that she isn't here with us, dozing in the wardrobe. I can laugh like I don't even know her. We open a second bottle of wine and laugh about home. Cruelly. Fondly. With an enormous sense of relief. The place lends itself to mockery. So we mock. It is easy to do this in London. Belfast is three hundred miles behind us now. For all we know, it might be gone.

Tonight we will sleep on the sofas: Matt on one, and I on the other, because our bed is still in bits against the wall. Matt will fall asleep first, exhausted from carting our furniture up six flights of stairs. I will struggle to sleep through the sirens screaming below our balcony and the people next door who play Fifa all night with the volume turned up. Round about 2pm I will hear the sound of my grandmother's hearing aid singing like struck glass as it dies. I will get up from my sofa and go to her in the wardrobe. She will be reading the *People's Friend* or knitting. She will be on the phone with her sister in Lisburn or possibly even praying with words learnt years ago in Sunday School. She will be just as I remember her, even the wet click of her dentures slipping in and out when she laughs. I will curl myself around her gnarly ankles and use her slippers for a pillow, angling my cheek against the fluffy parts. I will make an anchor of my grandmother and hold on.

In the morning she may be gone or we may drink tea together and say it does not taste the same without a teapot.

Either way, I will be splitting in two.

Lucy Caldwell

Lucy Caldwell was born in Belfast in 1981. She is the author of three novels, several stage plays and numerous radio dramas. Her most recent novel, *All the Beggars Riding*, was shortlisted for the Kerry Group Irish Novel of the Year and chosen for Belfast's One City, One Book campaign. Other awards include the Rooney Prize for Irish Literature, the Dylan Thomas Prize, the George Devine Award for Most Promising Playwright, the Imison Award, a Fiction Uncovered Award and a Major Individual Artist Award from the Arts Council of Northern Ireland. Her short stories have been broadcast on BBC Radio 3 and 4 and published most recently in *Granta: New Irish Writing*, *The Long Gaze Back: An Anthology of Irish Women Writers*, *Belfast Noir* and *All Over Ireland: New Irish Short Stories*. She was shortlisted for the 2012 BBC International Short Story Award and won the Commonwealth Writers' Award in 2014. Her debut collection of short stories, *Multitudes*, was published by Faber & Faber in 2016.

Mayday

Ten days later, the package finally comes. It is a small, brown, padded envelope, her name and address typed on a white label. The postmark is the Netherlands. Inside is a blister pack of tablets, one round and four ovals. No instructions, no warnings, and nothing to identify the sender. She pops out the round tablet there and then, in the hallway, and tries to swallow it down, but her mouth is too dry. She feels it stuck at the back of her throat. She makes it into the kitchen and pours a pint glass of water, drinks the whole thing down. The glass has a dried scum of lace at its neck and the water tastes stale. She can still feel the sensation of the tablet, lodged. There was a fresher, a Geography student, who died after taking diet pills that he bought online. Boiled alive: that's what the newspapers said. There was a photo of him in his hospital bed, face swollen so much he appeared to have no eyes, the skin on his torso and arms peeling off in raw red patches the size of sycamore leaves. His parents had released it as a warning, a deterrent to others.

It is the last day of April and she has, by repeated calculations, less than one week remaining.

A memory: aged eleven, a Junior Strings weekend away in Carnlough. On Sunday morning the Catholic children go to Mass in the big church on the Bay Road; the handful of

Protestants were supposed to stay in Drumalla House and sing hymns with the cello teacher. She goes with the Catholics: the walk along the rocky shore, the sweetshop in the village afterwards. The sense of something forbidden. Her friends line up to receive Holy Communion and she copies them, kneels and opens her mouth and lets the priest place the dry disc of wafer on her tongue. She chews, swallows. Afterwards they tell her she's going to Hell. They are falling over themselves to tell her. She's committed a Mortal sin, and because she can't go to Confession she can't be forgiven. And she *chewed*. They are beside themselves with glee. She cries. The cello teacher tells her it's nonsense, tells the others they're being silly. Tells them that, incidentally, the word used in John Chapter 6 to describe the consumption of the Eucharist can be understood as 'to gnaw' or 'to munch', so there they go, and now enough of all that. They say they were only joking.

She hasn't thought of it for years, but it surfaces now. The dusty room they practised in, the bars of sunlight. The pebbles on that little rocky shore. The gules of light in the stained glass windows of the Catholic church.

She doesn't know what to do with herself now, with the hours remaining. She checks her phone. 11:11 is the time. Tomorrow, at this time exactly, the other pills, all four of them at once. There is still time today, if she hurries, to make the midday seminar. But she hasn't been to lectures all week, hasn't done the seminar prep. She likes the module, likes the tutor, wants to do well. Last term, her supervisor said her idea had PhD potential, and she replayed the words in her head for weeks. So she goes up to her room now and sits at her desk and flips through the handout and reading lists. *Gender, Family, Faith: Norms and Controversies*. Paradise Lost *in Context*. *Civil Wars of Ideas: Politics vs Religion*. You can't get away from religion, in the seventeenth century. She reaches for the Norton anthology, opens it at random. A ballad. She skims the first couple of stanzas:

Farewell, rewards and fairies,
Good housewives now may say,
For now sluts in the dairies
Do fare as well as they.

Lament, lament, old abbeys
The fairies lost command;
They did but change priests' babies,
But some have changed your land.

And all your children stolen from thence
Who live as changelings ever since.

She stops, heart pounding. Sluts. Illegitimate children. Changelings, and fairies to blame them upon. Nothing feels neutral any more, she thinks. It never will again.

And then: wise up, she tells herself, and then she says it aloud. Wise up. Wise yer bap: that's what they used to say in school. Wise yer bap. She forces herself to tap her laptop awake and type out a few lines of the ballad. It's going to be fine. It's all going to be fine.

She closes her laptop and lies down on her bed, scans her body for any signs that it's starting to feel different. What if nothing happens? What if it is too late? The thing is you find out and you think, OK, nine weeks, that's ages. But then you do the online calculator and realise with a horrible rush that it's already more than six weeks, coming up to seven. It doesn't feel fair, the way they count it. Nine weeks is nothing. Nine weeks gives you little more than a fortnight. She found the website that night, Sunday, and by the Tuesday had made up her mind and placed the order. But it still might be too late. If she hadn't found out until a few days later. Or if it had happened while she still lived at home, or before she had a credit card or a PayPal account. It doesn't bear thinking about, but the thoughts keep marching back, a fortnight's well-worn grooves. If you were in England, the GP would have prescribed it to you, the exact same thing. You'd have taken it already, under medical supervision. It would already be over. If this doesn't work, she still has options. London, or Manchester: she's researched the clinics online. She wonders will she tell her mum, if it comes to that. Her mum would make the appointments, book the flights, pay for the hotel. Hold her hand in the waiting room and hug her afterwards. Her mum wouldn't rage at her, or weep like mothers do in films. Her mum would be pragmatic, calm: her mum would handle it all. Why hasn't she told her mum? Her mum has raised the three of them to believe that they can do whatever they want, that they're as good as men, that it's a woman's right to choose. Her mum would help her. Her mum would be here, now.

She aches for her.

Another memory: the Junior Debating Club, fourth year, or maybe fifth. Kerry Ferguson passing round A4 pictures of babies smiling in the womb, sucking their thumbs. The women should just have them, Kerry Ferguson said. They should have them and give them to people who want them. Almost nobody voted For. Afterwards, when her mum asked how her day had been, she was too ashamed to mention it.

The day passes slowly, seeps into evening. The sky through her Velux window is high and pale. The sounds of her housemates coming in, the clatter of pans, the smells of cooking. Someone smoking in the yard; the smell of it turning her stomach. Is anything happening yet? Eat and drink as normal, the website says, avoiding alcohol in case it skews your judgement. She hasn't felt hungry all day, has eaten just granola bars, handfuls of Crunchy Nut Cornflakes. One of her housemates taps on her door. Is she OK? Yeah, fine, she says, period cramps. Oh God, poor you, I've Nurofen if you want? Nah, thanks a million, but I've got some here. Fair do's. Here, we're going for a pint in a bit if you feel any better. Thanks, I reckon I'll just stay here though, watch something. OK, cool, give us a shout sure if you need anything. Cool, seeya. Bye.

The sky is streaked with pink now. Her phone beeps with a text from her mum: her grandma has been taken to the Ulster again, another chest infection. Every time it happens they think it's going to be it this time, but it somehow never is, and after a five-day course of antibiotics Grandma's discharged back to the nursing home to lie corroding in her rubber-sheeted bed. She can't think what to text back. Does her mum mean she should visit? She can't set foot in a hospital: what if it started happening there, in front of all the nurses and doctors? (If there are complications and you have to go to hospital, don't tell them. They can't tell, and they don't have to know. The treatment in any case will be the same. No tests can prove what you've taken, what you've done.) She starts to reply, deletes it. Her phone beeps again. *Don't mean to alarm you*, her mum says, *it's the same sad old story, just thought you'd want to know.* A string of x's and o's. Then a third message: *Are you back for Sunday lunch?*

She blinks. Sunday. Sunday lunch. *Hope so*, she replies, then, *Sorry, in middle of essay crisis. Sorry to hear about Grandma.*

Dad's with her now, her mum says. *It's just so very sad, isn't it. Poor Dad.*

I'll text him, she says.

A few minutes later her mum sends another text: *Good luck with essay!* followed by a fountain pen emoji, some books, a cup of coffee and a hamster head. Then another text: *Sorry! That was meant to be a lucky cat. Need my glasses!*

An evening from her childhood: this time of year, these lingering days and pale, light skies. Their dad has asked their mum to call in on their grandma the odd time during the week, and one night after swimming they do. They scramble out of the car and race across the green then stop, for reasons they can't put into words, and wait. A chill wind is coming from the lough, cutting straight through their uniforms: green pinafores and blue summer blouses. Their hair scorched dry on top but still damp at the nape of their necks, the sharp, clean smell of chlorine on their skin. Their mum reaches them, takes her youngest daughter's hand. The pebble-dashed terrace of houses, each with its dolls'-house gate, impeccable roses or trimmed box-hedge borders. Beyond them the garages, beyond that the forest. It's not really a forest, though they call it that; just a close-growing cluster of larch trees at the back of the estate. The fallen needles make the ground feel soft and springy and not like ground at all. They absorb all sound, too, the road on one side, the estate on the other, so that as soon as you're through the first row of trees you could be miles or years from anywhere. But now their grandma's face is looming pinkly in the bubbled glass beside the door, and the door opens inwards, not enough to let them in. Their grandma touching her hair: What's this, now, is something the matter?

Her minister is there; he's stopped by after the Mother's Union. There are slices of buttered fruit-loaf on the table-nest as well as a plate of oatmeal biscuits. The electric heater is pulled out to the centre of the room, its face aglow with all three bars. The minister stands, greets their mum, then all of them by name. The Reverend knows you from the photographs, their grandma says, and touches her hair again, straightens her blouse. Her youngest sister steps forward, pirouettes. Do you like our new hair? They've all had it cut for the summer term, from almost waist-length to bobs, because of nits – but he doesn't need to know that, they see the warning in their mum's eye. They all shake their heads to show how it swishes. The Reverend says, Vanity, vanity, and their grandma laughs, but his face is serious. Vanity, vanity! he says again. Vanity in young ladies is a terrible thing to behold, for it takes deep root, and what grows crooked cannot be straightened. Their grandma looks at him and stops smiling, and after that she won't admire their haircuts or even meet their eyes, and they are confused and afterwards their mum is furious.

His face was red and his hair was white and his eyes were bright blue. He's dead, now, and soon Grandma will be, whether or not it happens this time. The larch trees are gone too, lopped down to stumps.

She makes herself remember, instead, those Tuesday swimming lessons at Olympia. Imagines watching afterwards, through the observation window in the second floor cafeteria, the lane-ropes being dragged into place and the club swimmers powering up and down in their powder-blue caps, flipping into easy tumbleturns, length, after length, after length.

Her housemates go out. She texted him twice, then a third time. He didn't reply. Her phone said the messages had been delivered, and once she even saw the *dot, dot, dot* of him composing a reply, but then the dots went away and the reply never came. She saw him a week later in the Clements in Botanic and he was obviously scundered, said he'd lost his phone and only just got a new one. Give us your number, sure, he said, and she did, but she knew he wouldn't contact her, and he didn't. After that she could hardly tell him – could she? – why she'd been trying to get in touch. It should be his problem too, but it just isn't, the world doesn't work like that. So he'll never know any of this. He'll never even suspect. For a strange moment, she feels almost sorry for him. Something about that makes a sort of sense in the middle of the night. But when she wakes, the feeling is gone.

She can't be in the house. She walks into town, but it's too early for the shops to be open, and then it starts to rain, heavy and dull. Yesterday's high, light skies have closed right down, thick cloud and raw, damp air. It is the first of May. Mayday, she thinks. She remembers from Guides that you have to say it three times in a row. Mayday, mayday. She goes back to her student house. Two of her housemates are up, both hungover, smoking in the kitchen. She makes a cup of tea, sits with them a bit. Talks; hears herself talk. Laughs. Tells them about the Sunday in Carnlough, the Holy Communion. They all laugh about it. She goes up to her room. At 11:11 she takes the second lot of pills: all four of them. They're chalky and bitter under her tongue. At 11:41 they've hardly dissolved at all. Her jaw aches with the effort of holding her mouth and tongue still. She gives it until 11:45, watching the minutes pass on her phone. Then 11:50. That has to be enough. She gulps some water from her bottle. She can't go out again now. The pills are likely to start working within two hours, but may take up to five, or in some cases even longer. She opens her laptop and goes to the website, checks to see if there's anything she's missed. Then deletes her browsing history again: clear history, reset top sites, remove all website data.

She waits for the guilt to start, the regret, but it doesn't. What does she feel? She tests out emotions. Scared, yes. Definitely scared. She's deleted her browsing history seventeen, eighteen times. But they have ways of finding these things out: and somewhere, etched onto the internet, is her name, her address, her PayPal account, what she did. When, where and how. She, or anyone who helps her, could be jailed for life. So, scared.

What else does she feel? Sadness. She wants to have babies one day. She wants to see the blue line and feel giddy with excitement, check its weekly growth. She wants to want it. But not like this. The other thing she feels, to her surprise, is relief. An overwhelming, incredible sense of relief: that she is doing the right thing.

When the bleeding comes, the first dull smear on toilet paper, and then the first, warm drops, she will be so relieved (and sad, and scared) all over again that she will cry. She's bought maxi-pads instead of her usual Lil-Lets, and the trickling feeling between her thighs will make her think of her first ever period, of climbing into her mother's lap and feeling too big to be there, sobbing. Everything that is irrevocable now: all that has been lost. You mustn't think like that. She will remind herself: the bleeding and cramps are likely to be worse than a normal period, and there may be clots. Light bleeding may continue for up to three weeks. In most cases, four to six weeks after the bleeding stops, your period will resume. She will recite it to herself, over and over again, like a litany, a prayer. She will be one of the lucky ones. She will. She will.

Roisín O'Donnell

Roisín O'Donnell grew up in Sheffield, with family roots in Derry. Her short stories have been published internationally and appear in the acclaimed anthologies *Young Irelanders* and *The Long Gaze Back*. In 2014, she was a finalist in the Bath Short Story Award and received an Honorary Mention in the Fish Flash Fiction Prize. Nominated for a Pushcart Prize and the Forward Prize, she has been shortlisted for many international writing awards, including the Wasafiri New Writing Prize, the Cúirt International Short Story Award, and the Hennessy New Irish Writing Award 2016. Her fiction appears or is forthcoming in *Structo*, *Popshot*, *Unthology*, *The Stinging Fly* and elsewhere. The current recipient of a Literature Bursary from the Arts Council of Ireland, her first collection of short stories, *Wild Quiet*, was published in 2016. She lives in Dublin. www.roisinodonnell.com

The Seventh Man

Ebb-tide has come to me, as to the sea. I am no longer immortal.

Here in this place, autumn light falls through the hospital window and outlines everything golden. It picks out my husband's fleece-lined lumber jacket on the back of the door, slung there casually as if on a passing visit. It glints on the yew-red prickles in his stubble, and burnishes the shadows that cup his sleeping eyes. It illuminates the tubes through which they feed him his enchantment. It gilds the brass clipboard at the end of the bed, on which our consultant Doctor Furlong has written the painfully legible words 'no change'. And as I look on the new narrowness of my husband's blanket-outlined shape, I feel it in my pores; the crinkling of my humanity. With the six others, it was never like this.

I seduced each of them from the rocks of Beara, starting with the Spaniard I dragged up from the deep. Spluttering brine, he let me haul him from his sinking Milesian galleon. His fingers locked in the ropes of my hair. My lips blew life into his.

I could have saved hundreds of others, but I only needed one. I kept this skinny skipper from A Coruña in my cottage on the cliff, strengthening him with hearty broth, honeyed words and home-brewed poteen. He saw me as the Madonna; a black-haired seraph, crackleware skinned. *Santa Maria!* he'd yell, when he stumbled from bed in the small hours, sending the storm lantern swinging. For the waves that had swept him to Ireland had stayed inside his skull, leaving him forever listing; the world a tilting deck.

'Would you ever look,' the locals clucked. 'The kindness of that girleen.'

'The way she looks after that man of hers.'

'It'd put the heart across ye.'

Bewitched, those locals were. During that time, my magic was strong. My slate eyes were the grey of the Beara cliffs. My voice was fierce as the wind that rummaged through the peninsula. My lips were the red of the storm-battered trawlers below on Bearhaven Bay. The spirit of one young man would allow me to survive another few hundred years. I'd never needed this type of tonic when I was younger, but it was a solution when I began to get old. Around crackling fires, the Irish wove yarns about 'The Hag of Beara, the oldest woman in Ireland', but they never suspected it was I, the sweetest girl from Sneem to Ballybunion.

As for the young Spaniard, his spirit was rich and plentiful, though his soul was wandering. Each Samhain, I magicked his speech so he couldn't tell anyone my secret. When he begged a local Spanish-speaking captain, '*Señor, por favor ayúdame. Estoy bajo el control de esta mujer loca.*' All the captain heard was a dolphin's clickering, while I grew fat and gorgeous on the young man's energy. Yes, that one served me well. He was my first husband.

'Cara?' The night-nurse whose name pin says *Blessing* touches my arm. 'Will you sleep in the Relatives Room, dear? You'll get a crick in your neck.'

I shake my head. Her black eyes pitch their stubbornness against my own, knowing they will lose. You cannot win against insanity.

'I'll tell Doctor Furlong on you,' she pouts in mock offence.

'Doctor F. can eff off,' I reply.

'What are you like?' She shakes her head and leaves the room. Through the glass panel on the door, I watch her amble down the corridor towards the nurses' station. Her blue scrubs look like the comfiest and cleanest garment on Earth.

The silence seems louder after Blessing has gone. Orange streetlight falls through the metal binds, laddering my husband's bed with barcode shadows. I rearrange my legs in the bedside chair, and the creak of the springs could be that of my aching limbs.

For twelve nights, I've slept upright with my leather jacket wrapped around my shoulders like wings. Each morning, I've binned the dead chrysanthemums in the plastic Ikea jug on the bedside locker, and I've bought new ones from Nancy's Blooms on the corner. They never last more than a day. My nervousness kills them off. The flowers don't so much wilt as internally combust, scattering petal-debris across the sill.

During the day, I sit on the radiator by the dust-opaqued window, sipping cups of plastic-y coffee from the hospital vending machines. Searching for something safe to look at, I've counted the number of lampposts on the street below and the number of silver shamrocks on each one. I've counted the number of beeps from the traffic lights each time a pedestrian crosses the street, and the number of times my husband's heartbeat peaks per minute. I'm not sure what else to do. His chest rises and falls slowly, like a stingray's wings. This feeling is unchartered. My husband is dying, and for the first time in history, this has nothing to do with me.

I snatched my second husband from the Skelligs while he was kneeling, trying to find words with which to adore his God. His brown cassock grazed my thighs, and his rosary beads clinked cool as pebbles from a mountain river bed. He'd come from the island of Iona, and he believed in me as if I were a deity. In his eyes my hair was hay-blonde, and my features were soft. This kind man saw me as a quiet redemption. In a stonework beehive, I sated my thirst on his soul.

How many times have I re-cloaked myself over the centuries? Sometimes I've been feral and sharp-witted; other times, tame and homely. I have metamorphosed so often to suit each husband's fantasy, I no longer know which version of myself is real.

Magicking myself was easy, and I magicked the locals too. In Castletown, and as far away as Ballinskelligs, people believed my family were fishing folk who lived in Bearhaven Bay. For nuptials, I'd magick some bewildered ole fella into walking me up the aisle. There'd be a veil, a kiss on the cheek and a button-hole stuffed with a white carnation. It was smokescreen rather than sorcery. I didn't deceive them. I just created a spell that prevented them from questioning. They believed what they wanted to.

Third and fourth blur into a tangle of straw, whitethorn and sex. One was invading, the other defending. One was hiding from something, the other from something else. All I can recall is that I could have guzzled the serum of their youth indefinitely, and that a legend gathered around one of them once he was gone. They said that he'd been put under a spell and was sleeping under Lough Derg, and that he would ride forth on a silver-shod steed. These mortals are fools, for I'd slung his bones into the ocean and forgotten him immediately.

My fifth husband was fleeing, lusty with treason, when I seduced him on the sound off Bere Island. His Ulster aristocracy were so brimming with plots and scheming, they didn't notice the man weakening a little each time he lay with me. 'Kathleen,' the man said one morning, shirtless and frowning at the new hollows below his ribcage, 'Do ye not see how pale I've become? How thin?'

'Hush, *mo grá*,' I told him. ''Tis probably but a touch of the *féar gortach* – the hungry grass. Those cursed patches are common round here. Did you keep a loaf handy, as I told you?'

'Probably not. That could be it, I suppose.'

These husbands were gullible as rain-yellowed sheep. They didn't know what to believe. By the time the Ulster aristocrats set sail from the shore of Lough Swilly, my second husband was already dwindling, and I was bored and gorgeous again. Leaning over the bow of the ship, I watched Atlantic dolphins race the stern. It was unlike me, to wander so far from Beara, among people whose trickful sing-song accents befuddled my charms. As we sailed the Cork coast, I dived overboard and swam homewards. I'd gorged myself on enough of my second husband's energy to last another century. The man fled across oceans, trailing his relics.

When my husband is awake, he talks about his body as if he's already outside it. 'PSA levels have dropped a little, and the liver is doing well. That's grand news, isn't it?'

'Bloody brilliant,' I say. 'When will we get to go home?'

'Cara, don't be like that.'

He clasps at good news and rattles it like a toy. He sits up in bed and kills me with his fake smiles, his fever-bright eyes, his effort to look well. But I know better. My life stretches back to the last glacial maximum: Ireland covered in ice sheets. Through volcanic winters, past Mesolithic hunter-gatherers and the Viking raids, I've seen it all. I know when a man is about to depart this life.

Doctor Furlong pauses at the foot of the bed. 'Well,' he says, 'things seem to be fairly stable.' His nasal voice sounds as if something is trapped inside it. He carries his usual air of mild annoyance, perhaps at the strip-lighting polishing his bald head, or at the patients themselves. 'Yes,' he adjusts his small round glasses. 'All things considered.'

I glare at him, and he becomes fascinated by something beside his left shoe. This man will always tell me if the news is good, but he'll never say it's bad. He'll say it's *not so good* or *not as good as we'd hoped*. It's as if this precious body were a weather forecast or an election promise. *Not quite as good as we'd expected.*

Today, Doctor Furlong clears his throat, 'Mrs Connolly? If I might have a word?' And he takes me into the Relatives Room and shuts the door behind us.

'How the chestnut horses shone,' my sixth husband said, 'and how our bayonets gleamed when we marched out from the Royal Barracks in Dublin in 1914. Along the quays, factory girls, dockhands and toffee-nosed clerks alike all stopped to lift their caps and wave their kerchiefs at us. The streets were a flutter with well-wishes.'

I stroked his head. 'Shh, *a stor*, the past is done.'

His first horse was shot from under him, somewhere at the front near Armentiéres. Three years later, he returned to a different country. Stepping off the gangplank, a crowd jeered from the docks; the Irish Sea, the River Liffey and the sky over Dublin were an angry kelpie spitting in his face. Raw egg slimed his cheek. Egg shell littered the upturned collar of his great coat. Old friends turned, lowered their eyes and shuffled away, as if he were a bad omen. He lingered in his hometown for as long as he could bear it, and then he stepped out into the howling night.

Many men were on the run in those days, caught on the wrong side of history. Shapes darted between dry stone walls. Ireland was an anthill teaming with men trying to outrun their own shadows. That was a good time for finding husbands. My sixth knocked on the door of my cottage one growling December night, 'Sorry, Miss, if you'd happen to have some shelter? An outhouse? Anything?'

I kept him with me.

Between six and seven, a long time passed. Men no longer came praying or invading or fleeing or hiding on the coast of Beara. Sometimes I'd see a fine-looking young man in a bright rain-proof coat, but he would normally be accompanied by a woman in a matching coat who shouted, 'Look, Babe, let's take a photo over here!' Those rare young men who ventured out here alone had hand-held GPS devices and were so hell-bent on hiking the three peninsulas of Kerry that they were oblivious to my enchantments. Meanwhile, I grew weaker, with only the wind for company, and in the bubbled mirror with the crazed and flaking edges, my reflection aged. I spat into the merciless salt-spray of the Atlantic gales. 'How are you meant to seduce a husband these days?'

I liked the sound of *Tinder*. It sounded like *timber*: things being chopped and tossed onto the fire. Smouldering, sparking, cracking. An excellent start to a marriage. When the man onscreen asked where I'd like to meet up, I replied, 'the Beara Penninsula,' and he replied, 'A woman after my own heart. A hiking date it is then so.'

After that, what happened was a navy jeep with a bumper sticker that said GONE FISHING, a checked shirt and a rough-bearded smile. 'Now I know what you're thinking,' the tall man said. 'I'm a little older than in my profile shot, but so are you if you don't mind my saying so, and besides, you can't judge a person from a thumbnail.' He inhaled a sigh, exhausted by this rehearsed sentence, and took off his cap to scratch his head. 'If it's not too forward of me, how old are *you* anyway?'

'Nine thousand and twelve,' I answered truthfully.

The man laughed. 'I knew you'd be good fun.'

And so we set out to sea, on a gin-clear day, as the fishermen call them, two weeks before Bealtaine. A shift in clouds, a shaft of light, and the landscape appeared in a zenith of green and teal. As we walked round Cahermore and sailed his boat, the *Branwyn Morrigan*, out to Lambshead and Dursey Island, Ireland drenched herself in blinking sunlight and garlanded herself with rainbows. I tried to keep things normal, to follow my usual seduction routine. But the afternoon became scalded onto my retinas, like the aftermath of staring too long into a furnace. After that, I always kept my phone by my bed, waiting for some words from him, and that blue light got into my head, until I could think of little else.

The second time we met, he took me home to his bungalow outside Bantry, and I giddily noted the upturned currach by the front door, the sigh of nets on the lawn, and the lobster pots strung from his windows on slate-blue ropes, as if they had absorbed the sea's colours. I remember the sincerity with which he went about preparing dinner for me, while I sat on the corner of the kitchen worktop, swinging my heels against the cupboards. We talked while he chopped fistfuls of parsley and diced spuds and threw smoked haddock into the sizzling pan.

Conversation was as easy as breathing. He told me of seastorms and doldrums, of opportunities missed or seized. He laughed and mourned for his mistakes. And he drew my past from me like venom from a wound, leaving me feeling *young* for the first time in history.

Am I afraid of his death or my own?

His hair is fine as fish wire; strong auburn in a certain light, other times light-softened to a mousy grey. In those early weeks after we met, I panicked myself into multiple kidney infections. Venusian dimples aching. Inner tract burning with an acid excess of love. I was soothed only by his hands; the timbre of his voice. 'He's just another husband,' I codded myself. 'Just another source of youth I'll guzzle until I am full.' But then, one bright morning before he boarded the *Branwyn Morrigan*, he bounded up to give me a bristly kiss, and as the boat pulled away, he shouted something into the wind; three small words which changed everything.

White lights and sliding doors. A stuffy heat that dries out your eyeballs. The aspidistra in one corner of the Relative's Room has been dying for a long time. GIVE BLOOD, say the tiered leaflets on the magnolia walls, GIVE THE GIFT OF LIFE. Doctor Furlong looks at his hands, 'Cara. You know we're doing everything we can. But it's only a matter of time.'

Time is all I've had. From one era to the next. Endless, infinite, boundless time since before the mountains had settled. A banquet of minutes has left me on the edge of narcosis, as after an obnoxious feast. I'm tired of time, nauseated by it. After tasting the moments with my seventh husband, I want nothing else. On our wedding night, the clocks went back and neither of us noticed. Insomniac with happiness, for one night we were an hour ahead of the rest of Ireland. Living a future with only us in it.

'Cara, are you listening?' the doctor says. 'As I said, putting your husband's affairs in order might not be a bad idea. Cara?'

I stand and leave the Relatives' Room, shutting the doctor's voice behind me. My trainers squeal down the warren of magnolia corridors. As I walk, it occurs to me that perhaps I'll never find my way back to this ward again. I imagine the hospital as a cream-coloured Rubix cube with my husband locked inside it, and me standing outside, frozen.

Night is coming. The cold autumn air needles my skin as I step out of the hospital. A few smokers huddle around a bin at the main entrance. Rush hour traffic is building; the motorway beyond the hospital entrance is a red river of taillights. Lining the carpark, fingerlings of leafless branches try to grasp the dying light. And on unkempt summer beds, the black heads of sunflowers nod their bright petals onto the tawny earth. I stop and close my eyes, running my hands through my hair. I could return to Beara and start over with number eight... But I can't leave this place any more than the wind can pick itself up and walk away.

Whenever I had ancestors, I don't remember grieving. Or walking across a hospital carpark towards the copper haze of autumn trees feeling as if I'd left my spleen behind me.

The most dangerous thing you can do on this earth is fall in love.

I have survived everything but this.

It's only ever occurred to me to use my gifts to steal time from my husbands. But what if I could give time back? What if I could summon the lifeblood of a captured Spaniard, the breath of an Ulster aristocrat, the pulse of a soldier caught between wars? The moment the thought occurs to me, I'm swivelling and flying a crow-straight route back into the hospital. The sliding doors gasp open. I swoop along the corridors without touching the ground, sending nurses squealing and scattering, causing metal blinds to chatter like teeth. Double-doors bang open.

Dr Furlong is standing near my husband's room, but with one blast, I pinion him against the wall, and he hugs his clipboard. On his glasses, my ghastly reflection swells. He sees me now as I truly am: a skeletal apparition with white streaming hair, surrounded by a black confetti of bats and plumes of noxious Beara sea fret. My marmoreal bones have been polished to the patina of ivory. And inside my ribcage, my heart is pickled to the texture of roast beef. The doctor's eyelids twitch at the approach of the inevitable. At this exact moment, he admits to himself that he always knew I was weird. My arboreal arms seem to reach and stem and branch towards him. His lips part in the process of framing a scream that never emerges. Hospital lights palpitate, fizzing as my reflection flies along black curtainless windows.

My husband is awake but not afraid when I enter the room. Tomorrow he'll wake up hungry and he'll wonder why the warmth has returned to his fingers, why his heartbeat has steadied, why his IV drip has been disconnected, and why there's a pile of bones under the radiator. He'll flex his fingers in disbelief, feeling the vitality surge through them, and he'll touch his side, where the pain will have vanished. And he won't remember sitting in a Mexican restaurant on a Cork side street, a hot city breeze drifting through the open shutters, and a comfortable quiet swishing between us like a secret. He won't remember the first night we lay together and how we stumbled into the shower afterwards, weak-kneed, drenched, leaving steamed-up love notes in the bathroom mirror. Or that weekend in Mayo, how the Fiesta gave up the ghost somewhere outside Mallaranny, or how racing each other across the beach at Achill, I got to the sea first.

I shut the door behind me and glide towards the bed.

Acknowledgements

Many people offered suggestions and advice in terms of writers and locating specific work. I'm particularly grateful to Professor Susan Cahill, Carlo Gebler, Dr Caroline Magennis, Hugh Odling-Smee, Glenn Patterson, Dr Sheila McWade, Thomas Morris and Ian Sansom.

Special thanks to Professor Margaret Kelleher of UCD, who is a font of knowledge and an indefatigable supporter of Irish literature and of writing by women.

I owe a debt of gratitude to the very helpful staff of the National Library in Dublin, Susan Kirkpatrick in the McClay Library at Queen's University Belfast, and to the National Folklore Collection in UCD.

I knew that this book was long overdue, but Lucy Caldwell urged me on from the start, and consistently reminded me so much that these stories needed to be in the world.

Patricia Craig kindly agreed to write an introduction for the book, which is knowledgeable, articulate, and more than I could have asked for.

The book-as-object is significantly enhanced by Martin Gleeson's wonderful cover design.

A heartfelt thank you is due to all the writers who contributed stories and reinforced the diversity of talent and the strength of the narrative voice in Northern Irish writing.

And finally, thank you, New Island – Edwin Higel, Dan Bolger, Hannah Shorten, Mariel Deegan and Shauna Daly – for the many ways they helped me and this collection. They were as enthusiastic about this book as *The Long Gaze Back*. Thank you for your commitment to Irish writing, to the short story, and to championing writing by women, new and forgotten.

The Long Gaze Back
An Anthology of Irish Women Writers
Edited by Sinéad Gleeson

978-1-84840-420-5; €19.99; C Format Hardback; 300pp

The Long Gaze Back, edited by Sinéad Gleeson, is an exhilarating anthology of thirty short stories by some of the most gifted women writers this island has ever produced. Taken together, the collected works of these writers reveal an enrapturing, unnerving, and piercingly beautiful mosaic of a lively literary landscape. Spanning four centuries, *The Long Gaze Back* features eight rare stories from deceased luminaries and forerunners, and twenty-two new unpublished stories by some of the most talented Irish women writers working today. The anthology presents an inclusive and celebratory portrait of the high calibre of contemporary literature in Ireland.

Featuring stories by: Niamh Boyce, Elizabeth Bowen, Maeve Brennan, Mary Costello, June Caldwell, Lucy Caldwell, Evelyn Conlon, Anne Devlin, Maria Edgeworth, Anne Enright, Christine Dwyer Hickey, Norah Hoult, Mary Lavin, Eimear McBride, Molly McCloskey, Bernie McGill, Lisa McInerney, Belinda McKeon, Siobhán Mannion, Lia Mills, Nuala Ní Chonchúir, Éilís Ní Dhuibhne, Kate O'Brien, Roisín O'Donnell, E.M. Reapy, Charlotte Riddell, Eimear Ryan, Anakana Schofield, Somerville & Ross and Susan Stairs.

Silver Threads of Hope
An Anthology
Edited by Sinéad Gleeson

978-1-84840-181-5; €14.99; C Format Hardback; 320pp

Collected and edited by Sinéad Gleeson and with an introduction by Anne Enright, *Silver Threads of Hope* is a remarkable anthology of short stories written by some of Ireland's leading writers.

From the parodied etiquette of Celtic Tiger dinner parties to the first tentative signs of new-found love in a coastal tattoo parlour, the collection features stories that evoke feelings of sadness, happiness and humour.

Silver Threads of Hope showcases some of the finest Irish writing in one of the country's most celebrated forms.

Featuring stories by: Kevin Barry, Greg Baxter, Dermot Bolger, John Boyne, Declan Burke, John Butler, Trevor Byrne, Emma Donoghue, Roddy Doyle, Dermot Healy, Christine Dwyer Hickey, Declan Hughes, Arlene Hunt, Colm Keegan, John Kelly, Claire Kilroy, Pat McCabe, Colum McCann, John McKenna, Belinda McKeon, Mike McCormack, Siobhan Mannion, Peter Murphy, Nuala Ní Chonchúir, Phillip Ó Ceallaigh, Keith Ridgway, William Wall and Mary Costello.